Leslie Kelly

She's No Angel

HQN™

ISBN-13: 978-0-373-77215-5
ISBN-10:   0-373-77215-7

SHE'S NO ANGEL

Dear Reader,

It's time for more Trouble!

If you've read my earlier books set in the town of Trouble, Pennsylvania, you're already aware that it's an odd, quirky little place. Dark and dour, not very friendly and not very quaint. It's definitely not the type of setting for a sweet sitcom...more the type of place you'd find in an episode of *The X-Files*.

Probably the oddest, quirkiest thing about Trouble is Mortimer Potts—town patriarch and grandfather of the three superhot Taylor brothers. Max Taylor's story was told in my August 2006 HQN Books release *Here Comes Trouble*. Now it's Mike's turn.

Mike Taylor is the strong, serious, protective youngest brother. A no-nonsense cop who likes things orderly. So the last woman he'd want to get tangled up with is one like Jen Feeney, a funny, feisty, tough-talking temptress who's landed on the bestseller list by writing about why a dead husband is better than an ex-one!

To make things worse, Jen's related to the two nutty old ladies who kidnapped Mike's grandfather the previous year...and who may be tangled up in an old murder. All his instincts say to stay away from her. But that's the one thing Mike simply cannot do.

Honestly, Jen Feeney is my favorite heroine *ever* and I really fell in love with Mike while writing this story. I hope you love them every bit as much, and that you enjoy every minute you spend in Trouble.

Happy reading!

Leslie Kelly

To Bruce. Just Bruce.
I'm so glad you like that I'm no angel.

She's No Angel

PROLOGUE

OF ALL THE PLEASURES in the life of Mortimer Potts, he'd have to call being the patriarch of a small Pennsylvania town among the finest. In the single year that he'd been living in Trouble, having purchased the bulk of it to save it from bankruptcy, he'd watched the place emerge from its cloak of depression the way a pretty flower might pop out amid a field of weeds and scrub. Not fully in bloom yet, it merely offered a hint at the color curled within its tightly wound petals. Observing it blossom had become his favorite pastime.

But the town wasn't his *greatest* pleasure. It couldn't compare, say, to spending time with his family—his grandsons and new granddaughter-in-law. Or having an eighty-one year-old body that could perform all its necessary functions without benefit of odious amounts of fiber or Viagra. At least, *most* of the time. There had been that one occasion with the Feeney sisters when he'd discovered what the hoopla over that little blue pill was all about. It was a wonder his heart had survived the unexpected adventure. Still, watching the town emerge from its sleep was infinitely better than needing the obituaries to see who he'd outlived.

"I heard that sigh," a disapproving voice said, the clipped

British accent unaltered by decades of life in the U.S. "You're thinking of those wretched sisters again, aren't you? Either that or the time we rescued the harem in forty-six."

Mortimer smiled in reminiscence. "A noble adventure."

Roderick, his manservant—and best friend—sniffed, the same supercilious sound of disapproval he'd made since the day they'd met. "I doubt the sheikh would have been so quick with his golden reward if he knew how many of his wives *thanked* you personally."

Ahh, yes. He did enjoy being thanked.

His fond memories quickly faded, Roderick's words suddenly making him feel very old. Gone were his journeys to other continents, where he and his majordomo had been freewheeling adventurers. Or even, in his later years, where they'd been freewheeling parents, the two of them raising Mortimer's grandsons.

Having lived life as a citizen of the world, he'd seen no reason to bring the boys up any other way. So while other youngsters their age studied faraway places by reading about them in textbooks in stuffy schoolrooms, *his* grandsons were visiting those spots. South America. Africa. From sampans in Shanghai to digs of ruins in Greece, Mortimer and Roderick had taught the boys not merely how to think, but how to *live*.

Now, however, there were no more adventures. No more trips to other continents. If he were foolish enough to get on a horse today, he'd be more likely to break a hip than to win a race across the desert.

"Is everything prepared for Michael's arrival?"

Roderick nodded. "Right down to his favorite dish." His brow scrunching in disgust, he added, "Chili. How very—"

"Don't tell me, let me guess," Mortimer replied, his tone dry. "Pedestrian?" It was one of Roderick's favorite words.

"I was going to say *uninspiring.*"

"No, you weren't."

"You can't read my mind, Mortimer."

Chuckling, Mortimer said, "I know you well enough to know how it must have pained you to shop for canned kidney beans."

Rod laid one hand on Mortimer's broad, oak desk and leaned over, as if exhausted. "You've *no* idea. It is impossible to purchase fresh chili peppers, or even cumin, in this town. I had to settle for a few of those dried-up, yellow envelopes full of mystery spice." He sounded as disgruntled as if he'd been forced to substitute Chicken of the Sea for beluga.

"How very pedestrian," Mortimer murmured, purposely gazing at his paper, though he saw Roderick puff up like a porcupine out of the corner of his eye.

What a funny, prickly man. And the truest friend anyone could ever ask for. They'd been together since the Second World War, crossing the globe in search of adventure. Mortimer's family money and high spirits had led the way while Roderick's common sense had kept them out of trouble. Well, it hadn't kept them *out* of trouble, but it certainly had extricated them from a few…tricky…situations.

Even when the occasional marriage had divided them, they'd remained close, and Rod had been the first person a widowed Mortimer had called when he'd experienced the second great loss of his life—the death of his daughter. As always, the stoic Englishman had come to his side, stepping forward with Mortimer to parent three orphaned little boys, who'd lost their father less than a year before in the first Gulf War.

"The point is," Rod said, as usual changing the subject

when he was losing an argument, "Michael has developed horrifyingly middle-class tastes."

Mortimer smiled, lifting his drink to his lips, eyeing the amber-colored whiskey and suddenly wishing he'd helped himself to one of the beers he'd put on ice for his grandson. "Yes, he has, but considering he is a New York City police officer, I'd say that's probably appropriate."

"A police officer." Roddy couldn't have sounded more disdainful if Michael had decided to become one of those male go-go dancers. "If he *had* to go into law enforcement, couldn't he at least have gone into the MI5?"

Grunting, Mortimer lowered his drink, still wanting that beer. "Aside from the fact that he's an American, not a Brit, and would therefore have been more likely to choose the CIA, my grandson could never be a *spy*. He's far too noble."

Roderick's eyebrows rose until they almost blended in with his gray hair. "The boy's the toughest fighter I've ever seen."

Well, yes, he was that. The youngest of Mortimer's three grandsons had reacted differently to the loss of his parents than his brothers had. Morgan, the oldest, had become an adventurer, much like his grandfather. Max, before settling down with his new wife last year, had been a playboy, with women dogging his every step.

Michael, though… He'd grown hard. Tough. Self-protective. And the boy did have a bit of a temper. Mortimer suppressed a chuckle, remembering the time he'd bailed his teenage grandson out of jail. He'd been arrested for brawling with three boys who'd made the mistake of harassing a young lady Michael liked. A born protector, that one. "He needs a good woman, that's all."

"Surely you've learned your lesson about matchmaking."

Roderick managed to sound both scandalized and interested by the idea. "Hasn't the woeful expression on the face of your secretary been enough to cure you of such impulses?"

Hmm…true. His latest effort had backfired. When Allie, his assistant, had left here an hour ago, she'd seemed very blue over her botched summer romance. "Perhaps Allie and Michael…"

"No. He'd chew her up and pick his teeth with her bones."

Roderick was probably right.

"Michael needs someone much tougher." Slowly pouring himself a drink and sitting in the leather chair opposite Mortimer's, Roderick pursed his mouth in concentration. "Someone smart. Independent. A woman who won't let him dominate her. Who will stand up for herself. Someone…"

"Tricky."

"I was going to say *strong*. Self-confident."

"Yes, yes," Mortimer said, waving an airy hand, "but sly. One who'll humor Michael's need to protect her, never letting on that she doesn't *really* need protecting. You do know how much he likes taking care of people."

"Taking care of *women*," Roderick said with a sigh.

Yes, Michael did do a lot of that, especially since he'd become a police officer. But something had happened to the boy a few years ago, involving two women. His grandson had gone from a smiling good guy with a mildly quick temper to a brooding good guy with a lightning-fast one.

A good man in a fight. While Maxwell was the grandson Mortimer would have loved to have with him when he'd entertained a half-dozen ladies of the evening in a dingy, shadowy Bangkok bar, Michael was the one he'd have loved to have at his back in the alley *behind* that bar later that night. When the ladies' protectors had tried to relieve him of his belongings.

They hadn't succeeded. But they had left Mortimer with an interesting, half moon-shaped scar on his shoulder. One of many.

As for Morgan… He'd have liked to have had him along when he'd been forced to claw his way out of an ancient tomb in Oman, where he'd been walled up for smiling at the wrong sultan's wife.

"I suppose I cannot talk you out of this?"

Mortimer stared at his friend. "Were you trying to?"

The other man flushed slightly, then shrugged, giving up all pretense. "No. I don't like to see him so hardened…. He needs to find something more for his life."

"So we're agreed." Like Roderick, Mortimer wanted to see that smile return to Michael's face. No, he would never become a prankster like his brother Max. But there was no reason for Michael to go through life with his guard always up. "He needs someone who will make him stop taking himself so seriously."

"But he won't go into that willingly," Roderick said. "We'll have to make him *think* things are very serious indeed."

Lifting his glass again, Mortimer tried not to laugh. "Are you saying we're *partners* in this sly, matchmaking venture?"

Shaking his head so hard a strand of graying hair fell over one eye, Roddy stood. "That is *your* purview." He headed to the door, but before leaving, looked over his shoulder. "Though I suppose I can be counted upon to…supervise."

Mortimer hid his triumphant smile.

Roderick continued, "Now, where do you think we'll find this completely contradictory strong/weak, intelligent/dim, exciting/calming, tough/loving woman?"

When put that way, it did sound impossible. Then the image of a face swam into Mortimer's mind. He was surprised he hadn't thought of it sooner, since he'd been quite enjoying reading the young lady's sarcastic advice-to-the-lovelorn book this morning. She was feisty and brash, yet pretty and soft. Just the ticket for Michael, who needed to play protector but could never be with a woman who'd let him ride roughshod over her. "You know, it so happens I recently met a young lady who would be perfect."

Roderick waited expectantly.

"Her name," Mortimer said, drawing out the suspense, sure of his friend's reaction, "is *Feeney.*"

He wasn't disappointed. Roderick began to sputter, then turn bright red. "No. Not those two…"

"Their niece. A lovely young woman."

"Is she a murderer, too?"

Mortimer knew what Roderick was referring to. There had certainly been gossip about the Feeney sisters, Ida Mae and Ivy. He wasn't *sure* it was true, however. "That's never been proven."

Roderick marched back into the room, picked up his halfempty tumbler and tossed the remnants of his whiskey back in two gulps. Finishing, he breathed deeply and said, "You're willing to risk Michael's well-being by involving him with a Feeney woman. I say, Mortimer, have you quite gone off your nut?"

Perhaps. Some people certainly thought he had, at many times in his life. Including, most recently, when he'd purchased this weary town and taken up residence in a ramshackle old mansion. "Who better to liven up Michael's life than a woman he can never be sure of? Is she good…is she bad? Is she trustworthy…or dangerous?" He smiled and chuckled, liking the idea more and more. "Oh, yes, I think young Miss Feeney could be the answer to our prayers."

"Do people pray for devil-women?"

With a frown, Mortimer snapped back, "She's a nice girl."

"Must not take after her relatives." Obviously seeing Mortimer was not to be swayed, Roderick let out a long-suffering sigh. "I do hope you know what you're doing. Do you truly want to find yourself tied to the Feeney sisters?" As if he knew the moment he'd said the words that he'd given Mortimer a risqué opening to reminisce about his adventures with Ida Mae and Ivy, Roderick immediately threw his hand up, palm out. "Don't answer that. There are some things I just don't want to know."

Still chuckling as Roddy left the room, Mortimer settled back in his chair. Sipping his whiskey. Thinking of Borneo. Of his wives. Of Carla, his daughter. He also thought of three little tearstained faces watching him from across a flower-laden casket and remembered the vow he'd made on that day, to see to it that his grandsons lived very happy lives.

Maxwell certainly was. His happiness with his new wife rang clearly in his voice every time he called from California, so there was one taken care of. While Mortimer had not set out to "set up" his middle grandson, judging by how things had worked out, finding the right woman had been the key to Max's happiness. So perhaps it would be the same for the other two. But since neither seemed interested in following their brother down the path of wedded bliss, they might need a nudge.

His oldest grandson Morgan was currently in China, photographing the great terra-cotta army near Mount Lishan for *National Geographic* magazine. Oh, what Mortimer wouldn't give to be with him; though, of course, his knees could barely manage the stairs of his house these days.

Anyway, with Morgan out of the country, beyond Mortimer's reach, there was only one single grandson near enough to work on. That was the youngest. The one who probably most needed a soothing, loving relationship in his life to counter the violence he dealt with on a daily basis.

Yes, it was most definitely time for Michael to fall in love. And if he needed a little assistance in that direction?

Well, Mortimer Potts was more than happy to oblige.

CHAPTER ONE

> Every man dreams of having a supportive little woman
> standing behind him. He just doesn't realize that even-
> tually she's going to be holding a cast-iron skillet aimed
> directly at his skull.
> —*Why Arsenic Is Better Than Divorce* by Jennifer Feeney

THE SIGHT OF A TALL BRUNETTE with a great ass trudging down
the side of the road would have been enough to make Mike
Taylor slow down for a better look, even if the woman hadn't
been barefoot. And swinging a tire iron. And, judging by her
tight shoulders and clenched fists, mad as hell.

But she was all of those. Which made her more interesting.

He quickly ran through the possible explanations. "No
broken-down car," he muttered as he pulled his foot off the
gas pedal of his Jeep, slowing to a crawl a few yards behind
her. "No houses around." Since leaving the highway, he hadn't
seen a single building or gas station. Just a few road signs
counting down the miles to hell…make that Trouble, PA.

So maybe she'd been mugged and had fought off her
attacker. Or maybe *she'd* been the attacker and was still
clinging to her weapon. His eyes shifted to the tire iron,
looking for any telltale signs that it had been used to beat

someone recently. Dripping blood, hair, any of that stuff. He saw nothing.

The woman trudged on, impervious to the dig of gravel into her feet as she stuck to the shoulder of the two-lane road. Her soft, filmy dress swirled around her thighs, the afternoon breeze kicking it up a bit higher with each step. High enough to let him know her backside wasn't her only terrific feature. The woman had some legs to go along with her obviously leather-skinned feet.

He suddenly suspected she was talking out loud. Something was making it impossible for her to hear the six cylinders pistoning a few yards behind her. Judging by the bounce of her brown hair across her shoulders, he suspected her one-sided conversation was a heated one.

"Interesting." He wondered why he wasn't tense, as he'd normally be if he spied a person armed with a dangerous object.

Not that this woman emanated danger. Everything about her screamed frustration, not rage. Which he would have understood if he'd seen a disabled car, a broken cell phone nearby and a pair of woman's shoes…what, stuck in the mud? Carried off by an animal? "Uh-uh." Didn't add up.

She was becoming more and more intriguing by the moment. He hadn't expected to stumble across *anything* intriguing this weekend. Not here, anyway, in the lousy little town his grandfather had been holed up in for the past year. His whole reason for coming here to visit was to try to convince Mortimer to bail out of Trouble. But pissed-off brunettes swinging tire irons did intrigue him, and would have even if he wasn't a cop.

He had no choice but to stop. No, he wasn't exactly in his jurisdiction. And, since transferring to NYC Police's cold case and apprehension squad a few months ago, rarely had cause to interact with current victims of crime. Or, considering the tire iron and her visible anger, potential suspects.

When he interacted with the living at all in his more recent cases, he generally spoke to former neighbors or family members. Or even descendents, given the age of some of the case files. Frankly, he didn't mind that as much as he thought he would when he'd been ordered to accept the transfer a few months ago. At that point, being forced "for his own good" to leave the twentieth-precinct vice squad had had him ready to tell the city to take their badge and shove it. It had felt like a kick in the gut.

An undercover investigation into a high-end club drug ring run by a slime named Ricky Stahl had ended in a number of indictments…and a few embarrassed public officials with druggie kids they'd rather nobody knew about. It had also meant a transfer for Mike. His bosses claimed the area had gotten too hot for him. Mike thought the transfer was more likely payback from embarrassed politicians.

Whatever the true motivation, he'd been shoved straight into 1PP, aka headquarters. He now spent most of his days pouring through musty, yellowed logs and evidence files that smelled as if they belonged in some grandmother's basement. When not there, he was on the streets, tracking down hesitant witnesses with failing eyesight and dim memories. Every one of whom wanted to serve him coffee cake while they relived the worst experience of their lives…the murder of a loved one.

Somehow, though, despite his initial insistence to anyone who would listen that he was being wasted, he'd grudgingly found himself getting interested in what he was doing. Maybe it wasn't *that* surprising. He'd read his grandfather's ancient

Ellery Queen and Mickey Spillane mysteries by the gross as a kid. Solving puzzles, sifting through clues, he'd gotten a real charge out of that stuff once. Who knew he'd get a charge out of doing it for real as an adult?

It challenged him, exercised his brain in a way that posing as a buyer or a john certainly never had. His first successful cold-case closing—solving the 1998 murder of a shopkeeper who'd been gunned down in his own storage room—had given him more satisfaction than he'd ever experienced in Vice. Not just because of how grateful the family had been, but because he'd felt triumphant at having solved an unsolvable mystery.

He'd been a cold-case junkie ever since. Fascinated by the past, putting together one piece at a time of each intricate puzzle. So maybe that was why he couldn't drive past the stranger…because she was a puzzle. Alone on the road five miles from town. Furious. Armed. And hot.

"Yeah. Time to stop," he muttered, not knowing whether the puzzle or the *hot* interested him more.

Behind him, on the back seat, the closest thing Mike had to a commitment—a scruffy dog—lifted his head off his paw and yawned audibly. "We're not there yet, go back to sleep," Mike said, not even watching to see if the animal obeyed. He knew he would. *Lie down* was the only command the lazy mutt ever heard.

Tapping his horn in warning, Mike pulled onto the shoulder behind the brunette. She swung around immediately, but, thankfully, the tire iron stayed down by her side.

Remaining where she was, she watched warily as he stepped out. He shaded his eyes from the late afternoon sun setting over the town of Trouble ahead, squinting through his dark glasses to make out the woman's features. He still couldn't determine much, beyond the suspicion that her shape from the front was as good as it had been from behind. Maybe better, judging by the plunging neckline of her halter dress.

Damn, the woman had more curves than a Spirograph.

She'd stopped right beyond a battered road sign, which read Trouble Ahead. Somehow, he already knew the sign was right.

"Afternoon," he said with a nod.

The woman wasn't dressed for changing a tire. Or walking barefoot down a country road, for that matter. No, she looked more like one of the rich princesses who strolled down Park Avenue shopping for glittery purses with their tiny Chihuahuas.

"Having trouble?" he asked as he approached her, the sun continuing to interfere with his vision. "Do you need help?"

"Do you happen to have a gun handy?" was her shocking reply.

Actually, he did. Not that he was going to reveal that to someone eager to arm herself. "Sorry. Not today."

He slowed his steps. Though he still didn't sense she was dangerous to *him,* she felt bloodlust toward someone else. Maybe the person who'd stranded her out here sans car and shoes.

"Then I don't need your help," she said, her words jagged, choppy, as if now that she'd stopped walking she could finally suck in a few breaths of air. The harsh way she punctuated each word underscored his first impression—she was mad as hell.

And, he suspected, even *more* hot from the front than she'd been from behind. That dress was cut lower than he'd thought, and the filmy fabric outlined some generous hips. "Are you lost?"

She frowned. "Do I look lost?"

"No. You look stranded."

"Score one for the big guy. Now, if you'll excuse me, I have another five miles to walk into town."

As he moved to within two feet of her, the woman's own form blocked most of the sun until just a few rays spiked out from behind her head, like a huge halo. The effect was dazzling—blinding—but he still pushed his sunglasses up onto his head.

No one had ever accused him of being sentimental or sappy. But the way the light caught her hair, reflecting on individual strands of brown, gold and red and turning it into a veil of color, he couldn't help staring.

When he forced himself to focus on the stranger's face, he suddenly had to suck in a quick, surprised breath of his own. Because that face was good. *Very* good, with the high cheekbones and hollowed-out cheeks that women begged plastic surgeons for.

She also had a small, straight nose and dark eyes that were a swirling mix of blue and stormy gray. They were framed by heavily lashed lids. The strong jaw, and a slight jut to her chin said she was determined. Despite being tightly clenched, her mouth was obviously designed with sin in mind. Her naturally full lips would never need that crap women used to make themselves look like injected-to-death movie stars.

She wasn't too young—probably right around his age, or maybe even older. There was a maturity in the strength of her profile, in the confident way she carried herself.

He liked what he saw. A lot. This was the first time in ages that he'd liked the looks of a woman so much he'd actually begun to wonder whether he owned any unexpired condoms.

And she was staring at him with pure malice.

"Bad day, huh?"

"You could say that."

"So, uh, why do you need a gun?"

"To shoot someone," she snapped, looking at him as if he were stupid. "Two someones, actually."

He quickly scanned the woman's features, looking for her true intent. He'd met a lot of criminals in his seven years on the force, and he knew angry, frustrated threats from legitimate ones. This one, judging by the resigned irritation in her tone—rather than rage—was all bark and no bite. At least, he hoped. But he still thought about his service weapon, and wondered if he was going to have to use it to stop her from following through on her threats.

Wouldn't be the first time he'd stepped between a murderous woman and her intended target. Just the thought of *that* incident made the scar in his right shoulder ache...and the one around his heart grow a little harder.

"Dumb question." Glancing at the object in her hand, he tried again. "Why are you carrying a tire iron?"

She frowned, appearing puzzled by the ridiculousness of the query. Tilting her head to the side until her long hair brushed her arm, she explained, "Because I don't have a gun, of course."

Well, color him stupid for not knowing that. "Is there someone in particular you plan to kill or would anybody do?"

"Don't worry. You're quite safe," she said, that jaw still tense but some of the stiffness easing out of her shoulders. "However, two little old ladies from hell better have gone into the witness protection program before I get back into town."

"Killing little old ladies." He tsked and shook his head, growing even less alarmed. But he didn't let his guard down completely. "That's not very polite."

"You don't know these particular old ladies."

Something that felt like a smile began to tug at his mouth. "I know it's against the law to kill them."

He quickly squashed the smile. Mike wasn't used to smiling…. He didn't have a lot to be happy about on the job, and his personal life was almost nonexistent. Having lived for his work for the past few years, he hadn't developed more than a nodding relationship with anyone outside the force. With his brothers living busy lives, he seldom got together with them these days. He hadn't laid eyes on Max or Morgan since Max's wedding in December. And now that his grandfather, Mortimer, had taken up residence in a shoddy town that looked like the setting of a Stephen King story, he never saw him, either. Other than the drooly dog in his Jeep, he was about as unencumbered, serious and solitary as a twenty-seven-year-old New Yorker could be.

"Believe me, it'd be justifiable homicide."

"You a lawyer?" He tensed, as any cop did at the thought of a defense attorney…almost always an enemy in the courtroom.

"No. I just play one on TV."

At first he thought she meant she was an actress—because she *could* be. Not only because she was so attractive, but because she had definite character. Then she rolled her eyes and huffed out an annoyed breath that he hadn't immediately caught her sarcasm. "I watch *Law and Order*, the original and all ninety of its spin-offs, okay? Now, unless you have a spare pair of women's size eight Nikes in your car, I really need to say goodbye."

As if assessing the chances, her eyes dropped to his feet, and for the first time, Mike realized, she really looked at him. She was finally *seeing* him. She'd been too ticked off, too frustrated to even spare him a real glance until now.

Now she glanced. Oh, she definitely glanced.

Her unusual eyes darkened to almost charcoal-gray and her lips parted as she drew in a few more deep breaths. He could see the way her pulse fluttered in her neck as she cast a leisurely stare from his boot-clad feet, up his faded jeans, his Yankees T-shirt, then his face. She stopped there, a flick of her tongue to moisten her lips indicating she'd seen the guy women spent a lot of time coming on to until they realized he was interested in nothing more than the few hours he could kill with them.

"Sorry, no spare footwear," he finally said. He waited for a flirtatious comment, a come-on, a request for a lift.

He got none of those. Just a shrug, a sigh and a frown. Without warning, she swung around and started striding away, saying over her shoulder, "Okay. Have a nice—"

"Wait," he said, jogging to catch up to her. He put a hand on her shoulder, stopping her in her tracks. But the moment his hand landed on her warm skin he realized his mistake. Looking at her had affected him. Touching her nearly stopped his heart.

Her skin was smooth. Silky. Warm and supple under the sun's strong summer rays. And though she probably should have smacked his hand away, given that he was a complete stranger, she didn't. She simply watched him, her eyes leaning more toward blue now, slowly shifting colors like one of those old-fashioned mood rings girls had been so crazy about when he was a kid.

"Yes?" she asked, her voice sounding thick, more throaty than it had before, which was when he knew what mood her blue eyes indicated: Awareness. Interest. Heat.

Definite heat. It was instantaneous. It was mutual. And it

was also entirely unexpected considering the woman was a complete stranger…a stranger in need.

Finally, after a long, thick moment, Mike pulled his hand away, noting the whiteness his touch had left against her sun-pinkened skin. Her pale, creamy complexion wouldn't do well for much longer in this heat. He cleared his throat, wondering why his mouth had gone so dry. "Can I give you a ride somewhere?"

She hesitated, as if still affected by his touch, before replying, "Thanks, but I'm not that desperate. I don't get into cars with total strangers."

Smart. He didn't blame her at all, especially considering some of the stuff he'd seen on the job. Still, he didn't want the woman to keep stubbornly walking down the road until her feet blistered and her soft skin turned apple-red. "Do you want to use my cell phone to call for help?"

She paused, pursing her lips as she thought about it. Then, with a sigh, admitted, "There's nobody to call. AAA wouldn't come out unless my car was actually *here*. And the only family I have in town are the ones who stranded me."

"The old ladies."

"My aunts." Still frowning, she added, "I don't think I'd want the police to come help me out considering I am planning to kill those two when I get back to town."

That startled a one-syllable laugh out of him, which he immediately halted. He also made a mental note not to tell her he was a cop. "Don't you know anybody else in Trouble?"

"Nobody I could call, except maybe just an elderly friend of my aunts', who we ran into at the store yesterday. I can't even remember his whole name. It's Ports, Potter…something like that."

"Potts. Mortimer Potts."

"You know him?" she asked, sounding surprised—and hopeful.

"I'm on my way to his house."

A relieved smile finally appeared on her pretty face. "Are you, by any chance, one of his grandsons?"

"Yeah." He put out his hand. "Mike Taylor."

She reached out and put her hand in his, and again he couldn't help noticing how damned soft the woman was. As if she regularly bathed in some milky lotion that made her skin constantly feel like silk.

"I'm Jennifer Feeney. Jen. Your grandfather mentioned you were coming into town today. He seems like a...*nice* old man."

Mike noted the hesitation. No doubt, Mortimer was a nice old man. But that obviously hadn't been the first word that had come to the woman's mind. No. People usually described Mortimer as many things other than nice—eccentric, wild, dashing.

Nutty.

Not that Mike or his brothers much cared what other people thought of their grandfather. They knew him; they'd lived with him, traveling around the world on one adventure after another. There wasn't a single thing any of his grandsons wouldn't do for the man. Including taking down anyone who ever hurt him.

Though now eighty-one years old, Mortimer was remarkably healthy, except for some arthritis that had limited his physical activities. Anyone who saw him would think he was a sturdy seventy-year-old, with his shoulder-length white hair, tall and lanky frame, and blazing blue eyes. Of course, if he was in one of his *moods,* and happened to be wearing a

1940s military uniform, an Arabic thobe or chaps and a holster, they might go right back to that nutty part.

"You're the one who lives in New York?"

He nodded.

"Me, too. I'm just visiting."

"Small world." Only, not. Because New York was one big city and he was constantly amazed when traveling by how many people he ran into from there. "So does this mean we're not strangers, and you'll let me give you a ride into town?"

She hesitated, then glanced down at her bare feet. She didn't have much choice—if she stayed on the gravel shoulder, her feet would be torn to shreds. If she moved to the hot blacktop, they'd be fried.

Turning her head to look over her shoulder at the long road winding toward Trouble, she finally nodded. "Okay." Then she narrowed her eyes and stared at him, hard. "But be warned, I'm keeping the tire iron. I *can* defend myself."

The fierce expression was such a contradiction to the soft, silky rest of her that Mike had that unfamiliar impulse to smile again. Instead, he merely murmured, "Consider me warned."

JENNIFER FEENEY HAD NEVER liked the town of Trouble. Not since the first time she'd laid eyes on it as a little girl. Her parents had brought her here twenty years ago, to visit her father's reclusive sisters. She'd heard stories about the town of Trouble, and her elderly aunts Ida Mae and Ivy, since she was small. They had come to visit once or twice, but nothing had prepared Jen to visit them in Trouble.

Even as a child, she'd felt the strangeness of the place. From the wary watchfulness of the residents to the tangled bramble where parks had once stood, the town laid out an *Un-*

welcome mat that urged visitors to leave. It was hard to imagine her cheerful, teddy bear of a father had grown up here.

Worst of all had been the two shadowy buildings where the aunts resided. The old Victorian homes hovered over the north end of town, side by side, two dark birds of prey on vigilant watch for fresh meat. Though she'd only been eight during that visit, Jen had already had a good imagination. When she'd seen the two houses, with their sagging facades, shuttered windows and worn siding, she'd immediately thought of *them* as the sisters.

Ida Mae's house was dour and forbidding, what was left of its paint the color of a stormy sky, angry and wet. Its jagged railings and the spiky bars over the windows had given it the appearance of a prison. The black front door seemed like an open mouth waiting to swallow anyone who ventured onto the crumbling porch. Unadorned, ghostly against the clouds, the place had perfectly matched its owner, the dark and stern Ida Mae.

Ivy's was even worse.

It had apparently once been a gentle yellow, but any cheery gentility had long been eradicated. Tangled vines crawled like garden snakes up toward the roof. Cracks in the water-stained walls revealed odd shapes that had looked too much like spiders and monsters to her eight-year-old eyes. And the whole foundation had appeared slightly sunken on the right, as if the house were a stroke victim whose face hadn't quite recovered.

Where Ida Mae's house was merely dark and unwelcoming, Ivy's was a freakish combination of lightness and rabid death. Garish and frightening. Much like the old lady herself.

Of the two of them, Ivy had scared her the most, because she was so terribly unpredictable. At times a charming hostess, then a raging shrew, she was the one Jen *should* have tried to avoid. But she'd also been the most interesting, so often talking to herself, or to invisible, long-dead friends.

The one-sided conversations and stories the woman told had fascinated Jen. She'd often sat unnoticed, listening, until Ivy snapped out of one of her trances long enough to shoo her away. Sometimes with a threat to sell her to the child catcher who, in Jen's dreams, looked just like Ivy. Rail-thin, bony and menacing.

She supposed she ought to thank the aunts for one thing: they'd made finding out she was adopted a bit more bearable. She'd taken the news from her parents shortly after her twentieth birthday with surprising good grace. Surprising to *them*, she supposed. Considering she'd long wished she didn't share the blood of the aunts, the news hadn't been all that unwelcome.

Over the years, though she and her parents had lived in Connecticut—not *too* far away—the visits to Trouble had been few. Until a little over a year ago when her father, after having a massive heart attack, had elicited a promise from her to take over the care of his elderly sisters. She'd promised, of course. She would have promised him anything at that point.

Her father had, thankfully, survived and he and her mother had retired to North Carolina last fall. But because he'd been so weakened by the experience, Jen had insisted on keeping her promise. She loved him too much to allow him to deal with the old witches on a regular basis. That was exactly the kind of stress his doctor said could end up killing him.

Taking over the aunts' mangled finances, she'd made sure their electricity remained on and their account at the grocery store was paid. Ida Mae and Ivy supposedly had money, each having been widowed by wealthy men—Ivy under suspicious circumstances.

But they were miserly and kept whatever they had well hidden. So it was a good thing Jen's first two satirical advice books had exploded in popularity: she was supporting the pair.

She sensed her father wouldn't be happy about that, but she didn't want to bother him with it. Besides, what else did she have to spend her money on? It wasn't as if she had a husband and kids. And though she liked nice clothes, she couldn't see paying a fortune for them. She hadn't wanted to give up the same rent-controlled apartment she'd been living in since she'd gotten her start as the "Single in the City" advice columnist at *Her Life* magazine fresh out of grad school. So her living expenses hadn't gone up after her unexpected success.

And, the aunts lived in Trouble, Pennsylvania, which wasn't exactly on the top-ten list of towns with a high cost of living. She wasn't sure it would even hit the bottom ten, since it was a *town* only by the loosest definition of the word.

Still, she *was* paying the bills, which was why she'd come on this most recent trip. The aunts were both in their seventies, Ivy so frail she looked as if a falling leaf could knock her down. Jen wanted them to move out of their dangerous, death-trap old houses and into an assisted-living facility where they could torment professionals, rather than each other.

Preferably one far away from New York City.

The minute she'd mentioned the possibility, however, they'd made their position clear. They'd tricked her out of her shoes, out of her car, and stranded her in the middle of nowhere.

"Guess they didn't like the idea," she mumbled as she followed the dark, sexy stranger who'd come to her rescue.

"What?" asked the dark, sexy stranger in question as he came to an abrupt halt in front of her.

She almost walked right into him. Except she somehow

didn't, mainly by sticking her hand out so it landed hard on his back, sending him stumbling a step forward. "Sorry."

"At least you didn't knock into me with the hand holding the deadly weapon," he said as he turned around to face her.

Though from some men the comment would have sounded teasing, he sounded very serious. As if he'd wondered if he'd been exposing himself to danger by walking in front of her… As if she might have cracked him over the head and stolen his car.

"I'm really not dangerous, you don't have to be nervous about giving me a ride," she said, trying to ease his worries.

Finally, a twinkle appeared in those dark, dreamy brown eyes of his, which indicated the man might actually know how to express good humor beyond that half cough, half laugh he'd let out earlier. "I'm so relieved."

"I was mumbling about my aunts," she said, wondering why she suddenly felt flustered.

"Talking to yourself, then?"

Again that twinkle appeared, and she wondered if he was laughing at her. But before she could decide, he swung around and started walking again, leaving her flustered. It was an unaccustomed feeling. And an unwelcome one.

Then she gave herself a break…. How could she *not* be feeling a little flustered when, for the first time in months, she'd met a very hot guy who didn't want to throw her in front of a train because of the books she'd written?

A hot guy. Oh, yes, indeed.

Her aunts had consumed her thoughts, but nothing could stop the genuine, feminine response to a man like this one for long. Walking behind him, she couldn't help noticing the way the man filled out his jeans. *Perfectly.*

A great male tush was probably the only thing that could distract her from the dark emotions she'd been having about her aunts, and she enjoyed the view during the last few steps to his Jeep. He was, quite simply, magnificent, from the tips of his jet-black hair to the bottoms of his feet.

She didn't see a lot of sexy, rugged males these days, not since she'd left her columnist job at *Her Life* to focus on her books. The last two new men she'd met had moved into her apartment building in recent weeks. One, old Mr. Jones, looked like Frankenstein's sidekick, Igor, and had already been over to borrow everything from the phone book to toilet paper.

Fortunately for anyone he might call, he hadn't seemed to need them both at the same time.

But at least he wasn't downright slimy. Unlike Frank, the new super hired by her landlord. At their first meeting, he'd made some pretty revolting come-on suggestions involving his tool belt, some chocolate syrup and a tube of lubricating jelly.

When he'd found out she was a published writer, Frank had started scheming. Claiming his grandfather had been somebody famous once, he swore he had tons of stories he could tell her. She, he proposed, could write the stories and they'd split the money fifty-fifty, getting rich together.

Uh…like she hadn't heard *that* before.

But things hadn't gotten really bad with Frank until he'd recognized her from the picture on the back of her latest book. All pickup attempts had ceased as he'd proceeded to blast her for making his last girlfriend dump him. It seemed the woman had grown a spine. Or some good taste. Or just a *dis*taste for chocolate syrup and lubricating jelly.

Despite having a romantic track record that made Bridget Jones's look stellar, Jen didn't long to be standard bearer for hard-ass women. But if her books helped one woman decide to ditch a pot-bellied, greasy-haired guy with onion breath and jeans that hugged the crack of his butt, she figured her job had been well done.

Of course, she'd had to live with leaky pipes, stuck windows and a broken ice maker for the past few months. Not to mention hate mail and, recently, some disturbing phone calls that had forced her to have her phone number changed. Twice.

Despite what some men thought, Jen's sarcastic books were meant more as black-comedy satires than advice-for-women pieces. Erma Bombeck with snark. Dave Barry with cattiness. That was what the reviewers said, anyway. Even with a master's in psychology, she'd never set herself up as some kind of marriage counselor. The books were the result of letters she'd received from readers of *Her Life,* battle stories from friends and coworkers.

And her own experiences with men she'd dated, including four straight Manhattan losers interested only in money until 6:00 p.m. and only in sex until 6:00 a.m.

Women's romantic misery was, after all, a universal, timeless theme. She'd even included some of her crazy old relatives' tales. Aunt Ivy was a font of information regarding the battle of the sexes…and if some of the stories were true, she'd been a lethal weapon during that battle for many years.

But some men just had no sense of humor and didn't get the joke. Probably, despite that tiny twinkle, like this one. The one whose jeans rode his hard body perfectly, hugging lean hips and enfolding some strong male thighs in their faded blue fabric. Those flinty brownish-black eyes might have shown a tiny hint of humor, but his short, barked laugh really hadn't. It had sounded creaky, as if it didn't get much use.

Nope, not much of a sense of humor here. Just as well. A jolly disposition wouldn't go with that rock-hard jaw, wide, tightly controlled mouth and his thick, dark hair cut short and spiky. He looked like the type who should be dressed in army fatigues, holding an AK-47, blowing up buildings on a big screen at a movie theater. Tough enough to be dangerous… Sexy enough to be the next box-office action hero.

With about as much personality as a two-dimensional character. He was so sure of her he didn't even wait to see if she was coming. Nor was he courteous enough to offer her any help. Her feet could be bloody stumps for all he knew.

This guy obviously hadn't learned charm from his very eccentric grandfather, who'd been so gentlemanly he'd make a young Cary Grant seem like a bum. And to hear her aunts talk, he was just about as sexy, too.

Don't go there, a voice in her head screamed as she remembered some of the innuendo the women had dropped after their meeting with Mr. Potts. She did *not* want to know what went on in the Feeney sisters' bedrooms, especially since seeing the *Kama Sutra* sheets in Ida Mae's washing machine.

Jen didn't know which bothered her more—the idea of Ida Mae and Ivy *sharing* a man. Or the thought that her seventy-something-year-old relatives were getting it—wildly—while she hadn't had even the most basic, boring, twist-push-thrust missionary sex in so long her diaphragm probably no longer fit.

"Buckle up," her reluctant rescuer said as she got in the Jeep, casting a quick glance at the mixed-breed dog sprawled on the back seat. The animal barely lifted his head in greeting.

Man's best friend was just as polite as the man in this case.

"Don't worry, he's friendly."

Right. Just like his owner.

"The worst he might do is drool on you."

Her pretty new Saks sundress was already windblown, grass-stained, and dinged with the gravel and road dirt her car's tires had flung at her as she'd tried to chase down her aunts. A little dog drool probably wouldn't hurt much.

"What's his name?" she asked, mainly to fill the vehicle with conversation as they started to drive toward town.

"Mutt."

"Mutt," she repeated. "That's all?"

The driver shrugged. "I tried other names. It's the only one he even remotely answered to. So it stuck."

Wonderful. A guy so cryptic and self-contained he couldn't even be bothered to name his dog. Good thing he wasn't in the running for Mr. Personality. And good thing she wasn't in the running for a man. Uh-uh, no way.

It wasn't that she didn't like men—despite her books, she *did* like them. She especially liked having sex with them. Not that she'd had any recently—like, since her first book had been published and her then-lover had read it. He'd been out the door before she'd done her first book signing. Which had also been one of her *last* book signings considering the number of men who'd shown up to yell at her for ruining their formerly docile girlfriends and wives. Or shown up to make her see the error of her ways by using smarmy charm to try to pick her up. Ick.

That had been two years ago, and since then, the former Single in the City girl hadn't had as much as a date. But she sure had made friends with the UPS delivery woman who regularly brought the plain brown wrapped packages Jen ordered from sites like havesexalone.com.

Not that it mattered. Her life was too full to deal with any more complications…male ones in particular. Especially moody, six-foot-two piles of hotness like the one sitting beside her. Whether sex with another person was involved or not.

She just couldn't afford any distractions, not today when she was involved in World War III. Because they might have won the first skirmish by leaving her out here in the middle of nowhere and stealing her car. But when she found Ida Mae and Ivy, the war was really going to begin.

CHAPTER TWO

Widows get to wear black…which is so much more slimming than divorcée red.
—*Why Arsenic Is Better Than Divorce* by Jennifer Feeney

THOUGH HER SISTER WAS ENTIRELY convinced they'd taken care of their "little problem," Ivy Feeney Cantone Helmsley—now just Feeney again—was still hiding.

Ida Mae might think they'd put a stop to the schemes of *that girl,* but Ivy wasn't so sure. Despite not being a true Feeney—not one by blood, anyhow—the girl had shown some surprising resilience and spunk over the years. Ivy should know…she'd tried to break the child more than once. But the stubborn chit had kept coming around.

So Ivy wasn't taking any chances. Which was why she was skulking, alone, in her basement. This was her regular hiding place, her security zone. She felt safe here, with Daddy clutched in her arms. Well, half of him, anyway.

"Force us out of our house," she whispered, keeping her voice nearly inaudible. "She thinks she can make us leave our home? Well, she'll have to find us first, won't she, Daddy?"

That wouldn't be easy. The one place the girl had always been frightened of was this cellar. Ivy couldn't see why. Personally, she found the dankness of the musty, cavernous room completely comforting.

She supposed the girl's fear could have something to do with the fact that she'd been locked down here for a few hours when she was ten or eleven. Ivy didn't regret shutting her in. The little sneak had needed a lesson, and no real harm had been done, even if Jennifer's father, Ivan, had read Ivy the riot act over it.

Funny…the girl had later stepped forward, telling her father she might have twisted the lock on her own, by mistake. Ivy had almost liked her that day, as much as she *could* like any nosy intruder. That was saying a lot since Ivy didn't like many females, her sister included most times. Plus, her young niece had always been much too pretty for Ivy's liking.

Ivy was the pretty one in the family. She always had been.

But she didn't like the girl today—or trust her. Which was why she remained hidden.

Here in the dark, oblivious to the dampness of the rough stone walls, Ivy was free to look at her treasures without fear of interruption. Not from the girl, not from the girl's parents, not even from Ida Mae.

If Ida Mae suspected what was hidden beneath the stairs, she might force her way down them. Which was why Ivy never let on that this was where she kept her most prized possessions. Let Ida Mae think they'd all been burned up in the fire that had killed Ivy's husband and destroyed their home up in New York City back in sixty-six. Ida Mae didn't have to know *all* her secrets.

To this day, Ivy remained frightened over just how close Ida Mae had come to finding out the most important one. Over a year ago, her sister had stumbled upon Ivy's most *precious* container. When Ida Mae had seen Mama's old knitting box in Ivy's room, she'd demanded to know how Ivy could still possess it when it should have long since ceased to exist.

Ivy had had to protect the box and the secrets it contained, fighting Ida Mae with all her strength in order to do it. Then, though it had nearly killed her, she'd sent the knitting box away, far from Ida Mae's prying eyes. Because her sister, too, knew the secret of the box, and she would easily find that which Ivy had for so many years concealed. And might try to force Ivy to destroy it, to protect that secret.

How ironic that she'd given her greatest treasure to the safe-keeping of the very girl she now wanted to murder. Jennifer.

Ivy had actually entrusted the case and its precious cargo to Jennifer last year when her niece had been working on one of her books. The combination of her desire to hide the case from Ida Mae and her own vanity—since Ivy had been thrilled to think of her story immortalized in print—had made her entrust the container to Jennifer's young hands.

Right now, she was angry enough with the girl that she wished she'd never given it to her. "No, no, not safe," she reminded herself.

She didn't fear Ida Mae. Ivy had felt a strange presence lately, as if someone had been in her house, touching her things. She'd been hearing whispers of people who couldn't be there, seeing odd shadows on the floor. Finding things moved or missing. Getting calls from hateful-sounding strangers. So though she didn't like to admit it, her most important possession was *still* safer with Jennifer.

Unless, of course, she and Ida Mae decided to kill the girl, in which case Ivy would still get her box back, since she, alone, knew where Jen had it hidden in her apartment.

"There's still the rest," she whispered, sitting in her usual spot and gazing across the basement as she so often did.

Every day, while her sister was next door taking her nap, Ivy would visit her past in the cellar. She'd lovingly open the sealed plastic bins and unwrap her treasures, one at a time. Like her photo albums. Her autographed LP's from her favorite stars like Buddy Holly, the Big Bopper and Ritchie Valens.

What an almighty crime that they'd all three gone down in a blaze of glory at the same moment. If any of them had been clients of her first husband's, she'd have suspected him of tampering with the small plane they'd been traveling in. Such things weren't, as she knew, beyond producer Leo Cantone, whose soul had been darker than Ritchie Valens's thick, black hair.

Ivy thrust off the thoughts of Leo, whom she'd once loved, then grown to hate, and stroked the urn holding her father's ashes. Well, half his ashes. Since the dust-up over Ida Mae's hiding him in a sugar canister last summer, filling his real urn with ashes from her charcoal grill, Ivy had insisted they split him rather than passing him back and forth. She liked to think her half included Daddy's big, strong arms and hearty belly laugh, but not his black, cheating heart, which had been the reason Mama'd probably killed him.

The women in her family could never abide cheaters. Or abusers. But especially not cheaters.

"My lovely things," she whispered. Ivy longed to creep over there and open them, to lose herself in the images of her youth. Like the framed, autographed photo of her standing on a stage, flanked by Frankie Avalon and Bill Haley after one of Alan Freed's rock-and-roll revues at the Paramount. Or the newspaper clipping showing a laughing, soaking-wet Ivy in a slinky gown rising out of a fountain after a party at the Ritz.

A snapshot of her doing the twist with Leo at the Peppermint Lounge, him only as tall as her forehead, though seeming bigger because of his money and his presence.

But she couldn't risk it, couldn't make any noise at all in case the girl returned and heard.

She made do by mentally going over all her other treasures, also contained in the bins. Like the fork Ricky Nelson had used when they'd dined with him in Chicago. And the silk scarf she'd stolen from Cass Elliott's dressing room. All lovingly preserved in plastic, kept in waterproof containers, and hidden beneath stacks of old newspaper and dusty sheets.

None, though, were as good as the knitting case, which held a secret *within* a secret. A hidden pocket that even the girl didn't know about held the most treasured remnants of *him.*

Eddie James.

Ivy had to close her eyes for a moment, letting only a few of the memories—good and bad—creep into her head. Much more and she'd go crazy, she surely would.

Some would say she already had…on *that* day, the last time she'd seen Eddie. Or Leo. It had been a violent, bloody day on which she'd also lost her beautiful home to fire. Lost everything, everyone…maybe even her mind.

"Enough now," she whispered, still clutching the urn, immediately clearing her thoughts of her old life, of which Daddy would never have approved.

Shifting on her rickety lawn chair, she sighed, wishing she'd thought to bring a nice, quiet magazine down with her. One of those ones with pictures of today's movie stars, all bawds and cads, but entertaining just the same.

She also wished she'd brought one of her fancy hats. The damp air was no good for her thinning hair. "Drat Ida Mae and her thick hair," she muttered sourly, before clapping a hand over her mouth. She'd forgotten to whisper, so she kept her hand there, listening intently for any sign of life from above.

Silence. Thank goodness.

She'd wait another hour or two, then creep upstairs and see what she could see, not sure which she hoped for more: the girl to be gone, or Ida Mae to be wrong about something for once.

Ida Mae had felt sure *her* plan would work, instead of Ivy's. As usual, she had bullied Ivy into going along. So they'd thrown the girl's clothes in her suitcases and dumped them outside next to her fancy car. The keys were in the ignition and the message couldn't be clearer. So maybe she *had* returned to town, seen the car, gotten in it and driven away, having received the answer to her ridiculous suggestion that they move from this place.

Or maybe she hadn't—maybe Ida Mae had been *wrong,* and the girl was right now preparing to drag them from their homes.

Ivy stroked the urn harder, pursing her lips, wishing her sister had just gone along with one of *her* ideas for a change. It certainly would have been more assured of success.

After all, the girl couldn't be plotting against them if they'd waited for her to get back, tied her up, thrown her in the trunk of her car, then pushed it off a cliff.

"You know, you really don't have to keep clutching that thing. It's not like I can leap over and attack you while I'm trying to drive. Especially not on these windy roads."

Mike watched out of the corner of his eye as his reluctant passenger jerked to attention. Her fingers immediately clenched, then released, relaxing against the iron bar she'd been holding tightly since the moment he'd met her.

The iron bar she'd thought he was afraid of a while ago.

It *almost* made him laugh, her thinking she could frighten him. All hundred and twenty pounds of her, with her slim arms and slender shoulders. Mike really had nearly chuckled about it back there when she'd sought to assure him she wasn't dangerous…to him, at least. As if he'd really had something to worry about.

He couldn't remember the last time a woman had made him laugh. And wasn't sure he liked the idea that this quirky, ballsy one had already nicked a tiny chink in the armor he generally kept in place around himself with everyone but his family.

"Sorry," she mumbled. "I'm not usually this bloodthirsty."

Her self-deprecation and weariness reaffirmed that she was frustrated…not deadly. Not that he didn't think a woman *could* be—he knew better. But he'd already ruled out a genuine danger factor with this one. If she had a gun, he might have been worried. But a tire iron? He could have that out of her hand almost as fast as he could slap a pair of cuffs on her wrist.

"I guess I'm just still steaming and irritated."

"At the old ladies?"

"They stranded me out there. Tricked me out of my own car and took off."

"How'd they get you out of your shoes?"

"Long story."

"You don't want to tell because you're embarrassed that you were outwitted by a couple of old ladies, admit it," he said, knowing, somehow, that it was true.

She didn't try to deny it. Instead she laughed, a thick, throaty chuckle that came from somewhere deep inside her. Add it to the list of things he already liked about the stranger. A list growing longer by the second. Which was really out of left field since on the rare occasions Mike had gone out with a woman lately, she'd always been more quiet…soft-spoken and sweet.

Unchallenging, his brothers would say. And Mike wouldn't argue it. He had enough strife in his day job; he didn't want it after hours. Particularly not after his last serious relationship, which had blown up in his face. Violently. With him on the receiving end of a bullet meant for his girlfriend, courtesy of her own psycho friend who'd been coming on to him for months and had decided she wanted Mike for herself.

Crazy shit that. Especially when his girlfriend had then dumped him, determined to be loyal to her "friend in need" and certain he'd led the woman on.

"Okay. I admit it, I'm humiliated."

She leaned down to drop the iron bar to the floor, and as she did so, that thick, amazing hair of hers swung across and brushed the bare skin of his arm. He immediately tensed, every sense he owned heightened by that soft touch and the sweet fragrance of her shampoo. Not to mention the even sweeter fragrance of her body, so close to his.

His hands curled tighter on the wheel, as if by their own will, and he suddenly had a mental image of sinking his fingers into those soft curls. He liked dark hair. Liked seeing it sprawled across his chest. Liked wrapping his hands in it while looking up at a woman riding him into sexual oblivion.

Not that he'd been ridden lately. His last sexual encounter had happened sometime before he'd started working cold cases. Hell, if he was honest with himself, it had probably been sometime before the last election. Dealing with women was his brother Max's strong point. Mike wasn't the charming one; he didn't have the time or the patience to play the games most females liked to play before they'd unzip their skirts.

"Oh, boy," she said, interrupting his mental pictures of what she'd look like wearing nothing but her long brown curls.

"What?"

The woman winced, then lifted one foot up over her knee, causing that flimsy, nothing-of-a-dress to slide dangerously high on her thighs. Mike shifted in his seat, the intensity building inside him again at the sight of all that creamy skin.

Just a pair of legs, he reminded himself, tightening his jaw against his own reactions. That was all they were.

But good legs. Definitely good.

Though the summer breeze had pressed the dress against her body in delightful ways earlier, he hadn't realized how incredible her legs were. Nor had he pictured the lacy pink edge of fabric at the top of them that said she was wearing those sexy, silky shorts women sometimes used as underwear. Tap pants? Something like that, he was pretty sure.

Now he didn't merely shift, he stretched and arched, the tightness of his jeans signaling her effect on him. He might be single by choice these days, but that sure didn't mean he couldn't appreciate a great pair of legs, or imagine what they'd feel like wrapped around his hips. Or his neck.

And those shorts... Did she *have* to be wearing sexy lingerie, too? What was it with women, anyway, the slinky dresses, the silk undies. What was wrong with jeans and plain cotton underwear?

Other than the fact that they would be much too rough against the silky perfection of her skin. Would mar it, redden it, and never do it justice.

Hell. He was in trouble here. Big trouble. Part of him wanted to grab the hem of her dress and yank it back down to her knees. Another part wanted to ask her if she'd like to pull over to the nearest secluded spot and have wild, crazy sex.

He'd seen a movie once where a woman claimed she wanted total honesty, for a man to say he didn't want to trade lines or play games. She swore she longed for no pretense, just for a guy to say, "I want you, let's cut to the chase and go for it."

It was tempting. It was also bullshit. Though it sounded good, it was a total lie. They *all* wanted the strings, even if they swore they didn't. And Mike wasn't into strings. He hadn't been, not since the last time he'd almost gotten hanged by tying himself up with them. Well, not hanged exactly. Just shot.

So he didn't think telling this woman he wanted her was a good idea, particularly after a ten-minute acquaintance.

It was only when he heard her hiss in pain that he was able to stop casting quick glances at those thighs and the pink fabric caught between them and pay attention to her foot…the one with blood on it. "Jeez, lady, what'd you do to yourself?"

"The road wasn't exactly paved in cotton."

"So why didn't you stay put and wait for help?" he growled, hearing the annoyance in his voice but unable to hide it. Did the woman have no common sense?

"Waiting around for help's not my thing," she muttered.

Yeah. He was getting that. *Stubborn woman.*

She poked and prodded at her foot, still oblivious to the peep show she was providing. If he was any kind of gentleman, he'd tell her. Then again, Mortimer was the gentleman of the family. Mike had never even pretended to be one.

"Ouch," she said with a wince, touching the tip of her index finger to a particularly raw spot.

He rolled his eyes. "Why didn't you say something sooner? I would have helped you to the Jeep." Or some other nearby flat surface where she could get off her feet. Preferably landing on her back.

"I guess I didn't feel anything. I was too busy walking on a cloud of righteous anger," she said, still never glancing at him. Instead, without asking permission, she opened the glove compartment and dug out a few wrinkled-up napkins. Wetting one with her tongue, she put it on the ball of her foot, which was bleeding in two or three spots.

"Perfect, add infection to your pain," he said with a disgusted sigh. Reaching into the back seat, he flipped the lid on a small cooler there and grabbed a bottle of water. As he lifted it out, he shook it off, then tossed it to her. "Here. Clean it with that. The spit-on-a-cut thing only works if it's your mother's spit."

"Thanks."

She opened the bottle, wet the napkin and cleaned off the sores on one foot, then the other, apparently not minding when specks of blood—and the water—flicked onto her dress. A few drops also plopped onto the high arch of her foot and slid down her heel, onto her leg, landing just above her other knee. They glided up her bent limb, riding a long, soft line of flesh, weaving an intricate trail across the ridges of her skin. His hands tightened on the wheel. His jaw and jeans tightened, too.

When the droplets reached the lacy fabric of those panties of hers and rode on underneath, she finally noticed. Sucking in a surprised breath, she glanced down, realized that her dress was hiked up almost to her crotch, and immediately looked over at him. Mike managed to keep his eyes forward, as if he hadn't been stealing glances at her like some horny fourteen-year-old peeking into the girls' locker room. He still saw out the corner of his eye as she grabbed the hem of her dress and yanked it down. And wasn't sure whether to give thanks or curse his luck.

"You could have said something."

Playing dumb seemed the safest course of action. "About what?"

She frowned in disbelief. "I thought boys outgrew their fascination with girls underpants by the time they hit twelve."

That immediately sparked a genuine laugh, and Mike had no control over it. It spilled out of his mouth, as warm as it was unfamiliar, tasting strange. But feeling…good. When was the last time he had really been amused by something? Before his transfer, perhaps. Before the drug case that had brought about that transfer, even.

The ridiculousness of her claim echoed in the car and within two seconds, she was chuckling with him. Laughing at herself. "Okay. That didn't come out right."

"No, it didn't."

"I meant…"

"I know what you meant. You were talking about that boys' elementary-school urge to catch a glimpse of some fellow third grader's Strawberry Shortcake panties."

"Well, it so happens that I don't wear Strawberry Shortcake panties," she retorted.

"Yeah. I know," he murmured, unable to get rid of the tiny smile still tugging at his lips.

"You *were* looking."

"All the male angels in heaven would have looked." Never glancing over at her, he continued, "We might not want to see the pink cotton under your school uniform anymore, but we are instinctively bred to zone in on anything made of silk and lace. Especially when it's resting between a pair of soft thighs."

Where in the hell all that had come from, Mike honestly didn't know. He couldn't remember stringing together such a thought in a long time, much less actually saying it to someone. A woman. A stranger.

A stranger who was watching him from the other seat, her jaw hanging open and her cheeks a little pink.

"Don't go grabbing for the tire iron, I'm still not going to leap on you," he said, his tone dry. "I was just making a point." Returning his attention to the road, he noted the few small scattered buildings that made up the outlying area of the town of Trouble. And another one of those Trouble Ahead signs. "Who named this place, anyway?" he muttered.

She cleared her throat, glad for the subject change. As was he. Talking about a woman's silky panties and her silkier thighs was a bad idea less than an hour into a relationship.

Not that they were in a relationship! No way. Their *acquaintance* was going to last approximately twenty minutes…the length of time it took to get her to her car.

"Probably the same person who named the towns of Paradise and Intercourse, Pennsylvania," she said.

He wondered if he ought to point out that some considered paradise and intercourse connected but figured he shouldn't. They'd managed to skate off thin ice and he definitely didn't want to glide back out onto it. He just needed to get this woman to her destination, push her out of the Jeep and keep on going to his grandfather's house. Where his world was normal. Not involving kooky women who got pissed off and walked until their feet bled. Ones who made him laugh. And leer.

"The name Trouble definitely suits some of its residents. My relatives included."

"You going to tell me how they ditched you?" he finally asked.

She sighed, then shook her head in resignation. "We went for a drive, then pulled up at a rest stop outside town. I, uh…made a suggestion they weren't happy about and they demanded to leave. When we got to the car, one of them started screeching about her handkerchief blowing away and demanded that I chase after it."

"Let me guess. You kicked off your shoes to run?"

"Uh-huh."

"And they got in the car and left without you?"

"Yep."

"Where does the tire iron fit in?"

She made a sound of frustration. He glanced over, seeing a look on her face that matched it.

"Aunt Ivy waved it out the window as they drove away, yelling that she'd hit me over the head with it if I tried to force her to move out of her house. I picked it up along the way and was fantasizing about shoving it up the old witch's nose."

Bloodthirstiness obviously ran in the family. But he figured it wasn't the time to point that out, particularly since she'd finally let go of the tire iron.

"She better not have scratched my car when she dropped it," Jen muttered, sounding more disgruntled than genuinely angry.

Hmm. Tire iron flying out the window of a moving car. He somehow suspected she wasn't going to get her wish for no scratches. She'd be lucky if there were no dents. But that was for her to work out with her aunt—and her insurance agent— so he kept his opinion to himself.

"Why would you try to force her out of her house?"

"I'm not trying to force them. But I suggested that they move somewhere more appropriate."

Like a mental institution, from the sound of them. But he figured he'd better not say that, either. He'd been doing a lot of keeping his mouth shut since he'd met her, which really wasn't surprising considering he genuinely liked to mind his own business and let other people mind theirs. However, they still had a few minutes to kill, and he was curious, so he asked, "Why do you think they should move?"

"Because they each live in ancient monstrosities that are held together by the beehives and termite nests hidden in their foundations, and the congealed dust and mildew on the walls."

"Pleasant."

Grunting, she rolled her eyes and crossed her arms over her chest. Her nicely curved chest, which curved up even higher with the pressure from her arms. Not quite into stop-your-heart territory, but definitely beyond the wonder-if-they're-real zone.

Real. Oh, yeah.

He cleared his throat and glanced away.

"They're in their mid-seventies, one's already had a hip replacement. Yet they insist on living in these two old mausoleums that could fall down under a strong spring breeze. Neither can drive—"

"They took your car," he pointed out.

"Neither can drive *legally*," she clarified. "Ida Mae had her license, but it was taken away because of her vision. Or the road-rage charges. I can't remember which."

Again, she startled a small chuckle out of him. Must be some kind of record. Or maybe it was simply because it was a bright, sunny day, he was far away from the city and he had a long weekend off. He'd probably be laughing at Mutt right about now if he hadn't stopped to pick up his unexpected passenger…. It didn't necessarily have to do with the woman herself.

"When they're not refusing to let workmen in their house to fix things—unless they're young and good-looking, of course—they're calling me to bitch about each other."

"Not exactly a pair of Red Riding Hood's grannies, huh?"

"Only if Red Riding Hood's granny owned a shotgun and wanted a wolfskin coat for the winter."

He heard a note of something in her voice—maybe, though she'd probably hate to admit it, a tiny hint of admiration. As though she couldn't help liking the ballsiness of the old ladies, even if they drove her crazy. This one didn't like being thwarted, and her relatives were a big old thorn in her side, but something told him she admired them just the same.

"So, you tried to make them leave their homes?"

She sat up straighter. "I *suggested* that they move into an assisted-living facility where they could have each other for company and have medical help at the push of a button."

Sounded reasonable. And while he would never expect such a thing of his grandfather, who had enough money to surround himself with staff and live anywhere he damn well chose, he certainly understood the concept of wanting an elderly relative taken care of. Especially taken care of somewhere *other* than in the crappy town they were entering. "They disliked the idea so much one of them threatened to kill you?"

"She threatens to kill everybody, including cookie-peddling little girls if they ring her doorbell during *The Jerry Springer Show,*" Jen muttered, waving an unconcerned hand. Then she glanced at her mangled feet. "I just didn't expect they'd hate the idea enough to maim me over it."

That soft, wistful tone in her voice told him a lot, hammering home the fact that despite her groaning about them, she cared about these aunts of hers. Cared about them a lot. And was hurt by what they'd done. "Are you giving up?"

Not answering for a moment, she leaned back in her seat, her chin tilting up and her eyes narrowing. From the other side of the Jeep, Mike could feel the temperature go up a degree or two as she got all hot under the collar, every bit of softness and hurt disappearing. Her muscles went tense, which merely emphasized the smoothness of the skin over those muscles, and the slenderness of her body.

"I never give up when there's something I want, Mr. Taylor." Her jaw stiff, she stared out the window. "Never."

ALTHOUGH SHE HAD NEVER BEEN married, Emily Baker liked to think of herself as an expert at love. After all, every expert had to start somewhere, most times by studying rather than doing. And though she'd never *done* it, heaven knew she'd *studied* it. Being in love, that is.

She'd been a student of love for years. Ever since she'd been a teenager growing up in the town of Trouble, longing to go see the big wide world but knowing she'd be *here* until the day she died.

That hadn't stopped her from dreaming, of course, or from learning all there was to know about love. She'd been a bridesmaid to all her friends, watching their courtships with genuine happiness…and only a little bit of envy. She'd read all the romantic novels she could find and gone to the movie shows whenever a juicy love story was set to appear.

Studying. Never doing.

Fantasizing. Never living.

Longing. Never loving.

It had been a given that she'd never leave this place, not with her being the only daughter of an aging set of parents who'd always needed her. Her younger brother had moved away and built a life of his own, but Emily had stayed, month after month, year after year. Eventually, as she'd known she would, she had ended up alone. Her father had died in the late nineties, her mother following him two years ago. And she'd finally been free of all her responsibilities. Free to finally start to live her own life.

Free. In her seventies...when it was too late.

Somehow, through all the years of watching over others, her own life had slipped by. She'd grown old with the town until now she barely remembered the girl she'd been. The girl who'd daydreamed of winning the heart of Cary Grant. Or the young lady who'd longed to find a big-hearted man who'd want to settle down and share a normal, middle-class life with her. Or even the middle-aged woman who sometimes thought there might be a widower out there who needed someone to help him raise his children.

She was none of those anymore. Her dreams had sparkled like faraway stars in a night sky at different times in her life. And each had eventually flickered out, smothered by the reality of time and age. Those thoughts had long since been put away.

But it didn't matter so much anymore. Because she didn't need dreams of her own romance...not when she had so many others to enjoy. When she lost herself in the movies that had become her secret life, she lived every blissful moment, experienced all of the anguish and the joy of falling in love.

Whoever had invented those VCR machines had to be the greatest person on earth. Because ever since her brother had bought their parents one as a Christmas present way back in the eighties, she'd found a world of love and romance that were the closest thing to heaven she'd ever known.

She knew every line from *Casablanca,* every word to the songs in *The Sound of Music.* Could ask Rhett Butler where she would go and what she would do if he left her in a perfect Vivien Leigh accent. She had held her breath endless times through the ending of *Titanic,* praying that this time it would turn out differently.

Romance. Love. Fantasy. All at the flick of a switch.

She used to watch the daytime stories, in addition to her cherished movies, but these days they seemed comprised mostly of intrigue. Or just sex and cheating. Not the "you're the only one for me, I can't live without you" tales her soul craved.

Right now, her video collection took up an entire spare bedroom in the house she'd inherited from her mother. Alphabetized and organized by her very own cataloging system, the films were her special secret, always there, behind a closed door. Her private haven from the world.

It was only recently that she'd found reasons to come *out* of that haven. And the two main ones were, right at this moment, lying on the floor of her living room, sharing one of the most tender, lovely scenes she'd ever personally witnessed.

"He likes you," said a young woman's voice, so filled with happiness it made Emily's heart ache to hear it.

"I like him, too," was the laughing response as a dark-haired man bounced a sweet baby on his stomach. "He's perfect, Allie."

The three of them—man, woman and baby—were sprawled out on the carpet, the strange man having won little Hank over immediately with his warm voice and gentle tickling. They were laughing, touching, loving. Forming the new family Emily had prayed her young friend—and tenant—Allie Cavanaugh would find.

And now she'd found it. The handsome young drifter Allie had fallen so madly in love with earlier this summer had come back for her. He'd been waiting here for her when Allie had gotten home from working at Mr. Potts's house this afternoon.

Emily had seen him outside, in his car, and had known immediately who he was. She'd been worried at first, knowing how hurt the girl had been by his rejection last month. But when Allie had brought him inside to meet both her and the baby, the gleam of love shining in the man's startlingly violet eyes had been completely undeniable, especially to an expert like Emily.

Which both thrilled her…and broke her heart. Because it meant one thing: she was going to be alone again. The single mother and her one-year-old son, who'd become Emily's family since moving into the small upstairs apartment last fall, were now going to be part of someone *else's* family. This man's.

"As it should be," she murmured, watching from the dining room as she laid out plates for supper.

Before calling them in, she wiped her cheeks with the sleeve of her dress. She wouldn't want the blissfully happy young woman to think for a moment that Emily wasn't thrilled that, once again, true love had conquered all.

If only it had, just once, done so for Emily.

CHAPTER THREE

"My husband died" is so much simpler to say than "My husband screwed our eighteen-year-old babysitter in the back seat of our Lexus and is now shacking up with her in Laguna Beach while I try to bleed the bastard dry for child support."
—*Why Arsenic Is Better Than Divorce* by Jennifer Feeney

THROUGHOUT THE REST of their brief drive into town, Jen's reluctant rescuer kept the conversation to a bare minimum. Keeping his hands tight on the steering wheel, his jaw remained rock hard, his lips firmly set, making her wonder if she'd imagined the smile she'd seen once or twice since they'd met. He sat up straight, military-like, and with the single exception of the line about her panties, he hadn't made any effort to flirt with her. Or pick her up. Or even ask for her phone number.

From some men, she'd think the behavior was just gentlemanly. But she sensed that Mike Taylor, though he'd certainly been good to come to her aid, didn't much care about things like being a gentleman.

She knew his type. She'd *written* about his type in her books. He was the dark, sexy, intense brooder who could have a woman on her back with her legs over his strong shoulders within five minutes of meeting her.

Then he'd be gone. On to his next challenge, his next woman in need. The lonesome cowboy or hardened soldier, having satisfied his basic urges and taken care of his little woman, would head back to battle, leaving her behind to clean up whatever messes he'd caused along the way. Typical story…he saves the world, she pays the electric bill.

How many women had written to her about this type of man during her days as the Single in the City columnist at *Her Life?* How many more had she talked to when writing her books?

Tons. And they all had the same story. The classic Mr. Hot and Deadly might be wickedly good in the bedroom, but he failed in nearly every other aspect of a relationship.

So just have sex with him.

Though the idea came out of nowhere, it certainly did have merit. It wouldn't be the first time she'd had no-strings sex. Being the Single in the City girl, it had almost seemed like her sacred duty to be out there participating in the bar hookup scene on the occasional Saturday night. Of course, that had been many years ago, when she'd been twenty-three, stupid and horny.

Now she was twenty-nine, wise…and still horny.

Being honest, she had to admit the idea of having sex with him had *not* come out of nowhere. Her body had been intensely aware of him from the moment he'd stopped to pick her up. She'd just been too angry at being ditched to really consider it until now. But how could she not have noticed his hot, masculine smell and the coiled strength of his body? Especially once they were enclosed in the small confines of his Jeep.

He was just about the hottest thing she'd ever seen and Jen had gone past amber straight to red alert right around the time he'd oh-so-casually mumbled that line about silky panties and soft thighs. Even now, minutes later, she had to shift in her seat as his words rolled around in her brain again, the memory of that gruff voice driving all other sound away. The rumble of the engine, the hiss of the air conditioner, the whoosh of the world passing by as they drove through it…

Ceased. To. Exist.

There was just the echo and his low, nearly inaudible breaths. And maybe the thudding of her own heart. Having opened the floodgates in her mind, she was now nearly drowning from the erotic possibilities playing out there.

"You cool enough?" he asked, glancing over at her, as if he could feel the temperature rising with the heat of her thoughts.

Jen quickly nodded, crossing her arms in front of her, where goose bumps suddenly rose.

He noticed. Was there anything he didn't notice? "Sorry, turn the AC down if you're *too* cold."

"I'm fine," she muttered, wishing he'd just shut up, stop looking at her, stop noticing everything about her. She needed him to get out of her head so she could figure out what to do about her interest in him.

Because there were definitely some issues preventing her from *acting* on that interest.

First, she was staying with her crazy aunts who would probably drug Jennifer and steal the man for themselves if she ever did get him into her bed. Second, she was so out of practice with the let's-get-it-on game that she wasn't even sure how to tell him she was interested in no-strings sex. And third, he'd shown almost no sign that he was the least bit attracted to her.

That, more than anything, kept her from so much as making

a suggestive offer to pay him back for his help. If she'd felt certain her interest was returned, she might have given it a shot. But he hadn't, other than that one comment about her underwear, which almost seemed not to have happened at all given how reserved he'd been for the rest of the drive.

She was too weary, wary and on guard to risk rejection right now. Especially after having been so soundly rejected by her own relatives less than an hour ago.

Jen knew she was attractive, but men had as often spewed at her as flirted with her lately, especially after her appearance on a national morning show to promote her new book. She'd gotten both creepy propositions *and* hate mail from men afterward. Those she could usually ignore, but some nasty calls to her unlisted home number she could not. They'd concerned her, which was why this trip to Trouble had been so perfectly timed.

"So," she said, trying to fill the silence, "your grandfather said he just moved here last year?"

He nodded.

When he didn't say anything, she reached in and tried to pull a few more teeth…er, words…out of his mouth. "I thought most people chose to move *away* from Trouble. My father certainly did. He took off right after high school and never looked back."

"My grandfather's not most people."

"I noticed."

He glanced over, as if to see if she was being snarky. She wasn't. She *had* noticed what an intriguing man Mr. Potts was. And if she didn't want to drag her two aunts out of town so badly, she would probably have liked to get to know him better.

Apparently seeing the lack of criticism in her expression, he admitted, "He bought the town last year."

Jen's jaw dropped. *"Bought?"*

"Most of it," he clarified. "I guess due to some mismanagement and embezzlement, the place was on the verge of bankruptcy. Or extinction. So they advertised for an investor—" he sighed "—and Grandfather answered the call."

She didn't know people could buy entire towns, unless they made $20 million a movie or were dictators of small countries.

He shrugged. "The place is getting back on its feet."

Not that Jen would have noticed.

"He sold them back their municipal buildings—at a loss."

"Not much of a businessman?"

Mike laughed—for real this time—a low, lazy sound that sent shivers of awareness bursting through her. Seeing him genuinely amused, complete with the flash of a dimple in his cheek, nearly melted her into a puddle on the seat. Lord, the man was handsome.

He quickly stopped laughing, as if surprised by his own reaction. "He doesn't give a damn about business, but Grandfather inherited Midas's fingers because there's nothing he touches that doesn't turn to gold."

They were passing a dilapidated old shopping center, obviously abandoned for years, with weeds growing up through the cracks in the parking lot. The boards on the windows were either completely obscured by graffiti or else falling off altogether. Jen glanced at it, then back at him

"Don't say it," he said. "My brothers and I have been working on him to unload this place since the day he bought it."

Mr. Potts had mentioned grandsons—plural. She just hadn't been able to wrap her mind around the idea that there could be more than one man this sexy in Trouble. "Well, it seems we both have elderly relatives we'd like to get away from this place."

"I think your job is going to be tougher than mine. Grandfather will find something else to distract him. A gold mine for sale in Nevada…a desert island up for auction. Something."

"He sounds wonderful," she murmured, meaning it.

Mike looked over, flashed that devastating—but scarce—smile, and nodded. "He is."

Jen suddenly wanted to keep driving. To bypass the aunts' houses and keep riding around in this Jeep with the smelly dog in the back and the wind whistling by the closed windows. Where she could get this guy to smile at her, and maybe even laugh again. And make more comments about her soft thighs.

But suddenly, they reached their destination and she realized how right he'd been. His task definitely seemed easier than hers. Because her aunts obviously hadn't had a change of heart about moving.

Their feelings were underscored by what was awaiting Jen in Ida Mae's driveway. When they pulled up in front of the house, Jen spotted her car, pointed out toward the road, the driver's side door standing open. A big scratch marred the passenger one.

"Son of a bitch," she muttered under her breath.

A tic started in her temple. It quickly turned into a pounding when she noticed the rest of the things on the ground, beside the car. Her makeup case lay open in the dirt, a new bottle of foundation and a tube of toothpaste—without a cap—beside it. She suspected the shiny, glisteny liquid winding a snail-like trail from the case to the grass beyond it had been caused by the expensive shampoo she'd picked up at a Manhattan salon.

Her nice new Italian leather suitcase—one of the few things she'd upgraded after her recent financial upswing—lay half-open. A splotch of pink fabric, visible from the road, said her new silk dress had been yanked off a hanger and shoved inside. And if she wasn't mistaken, that was the strap of her new Cole Haan sling backs sticking out of the obviously broken zipper.

Okay. She'd upgraded her shoes, too.

"Think they want me to leave?" Sarcasm dripped from her words as Mike Taylor pulled into the driveway she'd directed him to.

He followed her stare and whistled. "Yeah. I think so." Then, getting a good look at the houses, added, "Good God, someone actually lives here? I thought these places were abandoned the first time I came to town."

Weary, and not wanting to get out and fight the battle lying ahead, Jen leaned back in the car seat and closed her eyes.

He obviously noticed, and sighed. "You want me to drive you around the block a couple of times before you get out?"

It was as if he'd read her thoughts and the offer tempted her. She'd listened for a note of sarcasm in that gruff voice, but instead heard only a quiet resignation. As if he'd accepted the possibility of being stuck with her for a few more minutes and, despite not liking the idea, was willing to help her out for a little while longer.

How *very* nice.

And how very strange that suddenly some unexpected moisture stung the corners of her eyes. Moisture. As in *tears*.

Jen never cried...*almost* never. Yeah, yeah, she'd cried when Sirius Black had died in the Harry Potter books, but she sure never cried at stupid, sappy movies like *Titanic* or *The Lake House*. So why, for heaven's sake, had tears appeared in her eyes just because a man was being grudgingly considerate?

It had to be because of the lousy day she'd had. On top of

the lousy week she'd had. On top of the lousy month of hate mail and nasty phone calls she'd had.

Bad timing and exhaustion, that was why she was being such a girl. During her visit with the aunts, she'd spent half her time shuffling them to their doctors appointments and their hair appointments. When not chauffeuring them, she'd been cleaning their carpets, washing their linens, scrubbing their dirty kitchens—all because they refused to let her pay a "stranger" to come in and do housework. Not to mention the fact that her feet were bloody and raw. Good Lord, it was a wonder she hadn't bawled like a baby when she'd seen her ruined Cole Haans.

Those were the real reasons for the tears. Definitely.

Not this guy. Not his gruff consideration. Not his reluctant niceness. *Not.*

"You okay?"

Squeezing her eyes tight one last time, to ensure no moisture escaped from them, she nodded. "Yeah," she said as she finally lifted her lids, blinking rapidly, making sure she'd gotten herself under control.

Moisture gone? Check. Crisis averted? Check. Battle about to begin?

Most definitely.

THOUGH HIS UNEXPECTED passenger insisted she would be all right and that he could leave, Mike just couldn't do it. Maybe it was the way she winced when she saw all her things littering the ground beside her car. Maybe it was because of her threats—and her visible anger that had returned in the past few moments. Maybe it was because of the rawness of her bloody feet, about which he still felt guilty as hell…. He'd known when he'd first spotted her that they had to be sore from walking on the gravel and he still hadn't offered to help her to the Jeep.

Whatever the reason, he couldn't watch her get out, then drive away. Not without making sure she was okay first. *And* making sure she didn't commit a murder.

So after she thanked him and then basically told him he could go, he muttered, "Hold on a minute." Without an explanation, he got out, walked around to the passenger side door and opened it. "Stay here."

She stared up at him, as if trying to figure out whether he'd just discovered he wanted to play gentleman, or if he had something else in mind. He *did* have something else in mind. Namely her blistered, bloody feet.

Striding over to her suitcase, he unzipped it, trying to avoid tearing the dress sticking out of it. When he felt its silkiness between his rough fingers, he half wished he hadn't bothered. Because it reminded him altogether too much of the silky fabric the woman was wearing underneath her dress.

"What do you think you're doing?" She started to get out.

"Wait, you need something on your feet," he said. He quickly examined the first pair of shoes he found, a pair of spike-heeled sandals with a torn strap that had been caught in the suitcase zipper. There was only one way to describe them; they were high-priced, first-class screw-me shoes. Perfect for driving a man crazy with lust, but not for soothing blistered heels. "Definitely not," he muttered from between clenched teeth.

"My feet?" she said. Her jaw dropped, those expressive eyes growing wide and round. "You're…"

"I'm getting your damn shoes, would you stay where you are?" he growled, tossing the sexy shoes aside, trying hard not to think about how they'd feel digging into the backs of his legs while he was between hers.

Her mouth snapped shut, but she continued to watch wide-eyed, as if not believing he was poking around in her stuff, trying to find something to protect her feet. The feet he hadn't given a damn about when he'd first picked her up.

Guilty conscience. That was the only reason he was reaching into the dangerous confines of her luggage, pushing aside all sorts of silky, sexy things that made a sweat break out on his brow. Did the woman not own anything but underwear? How many frigging bra and panty sets did one female require? Blue ones, pink ones… He was losing his mind here. And had she never heard of sneakers?

Finally, feeling the rubbery sole of a flip-flop, he tugged it out, then felt around for the other one. It wasn't there. "I guess your aunts weren't really worried about doing a good packing job," he said as he tossed her the shoe.

"Try that one," she said, pointing toward a smaller case.

He did as she suggested, unzipping the smaller case. She was right, the other shoe was inside. Thank God.

Tossing it over, he rose and stepped to the Jeep in time to watch her slip the flip-flop on her bare foot. "You're not taking that with you," he said, nodding toward the tire iron.

Tilting her head to one side, she stared up at him for a moment, then sighed. "You're right. I probably shouldn't."

"You still feeling violent?"

She stared hard at the screw-me sandals. "Do you know what I paid for those shoes?"

Whatever it was, it couldn't have been enough to cause the instantaneous reaction in *him*. "Give me the tire iron."

"What if I get a flat tire?"

"Call AAA. You'll have a car with you this time."

She handed the iron bar over grudgingly, then stepped out of the car, hissing as her weight shifted onto her feet.

"You all right?"

"I'll be fine." She was entirely focused on her belongings and her scratched car, staring at them, then at the two old houses. And suddenly her anger appeared to fade again. He could have sworn he saw a tiny, reluctant smile playing around on those full lips of hers. "They are tough old birds, aren't they?"

"Just don't wring their necks and stuff them."

She laughed, as though he'd been teasing her. He supposed he had been…. *Where did that come from?*

Jen bent over and began picking up her things, shoving them into her bags. Without asking if she wanted him to, Mike began to help her. He avoided anything silky, sticking only to toiletries. Even that was a little dangerous considering he wanted to lift a bottle of creamy lotion to his nose and smell it, to try to figure out whether it had provided the incredible scent wafting from Jennifer's soft skin.

"Do you want me to come in with you?" he asked, having no idea where the impulse had come from. He could honestly say it wasn't out of fear that she was going to do anyone harm—despite her anger, he knew she wasn't going to hurt her elderly relatives. No, he had made the offer because of that hint of vulnerability he'd seen earlier during their drive. And the touch of humor he was seeing now.

He liked this woman. He sensed he could like her a lot. Considering he already *wanted* her more than he'd wanted anyone in ages, it was probably a pretty dangerous combination. One that should have sent him running, considering his track record with relationships. As in: two typical losses at the end of long, drawn-out, nine-inning matches. And one total strikeout, complete with a hospital stay for a bullet wound.

"That's nice of you, but no thanks."

He still didn't go. Even with Mutt whining from the back seat, wanting either to get moving or get out, he just stood there, waiting to see if she needed him.

Women often needed him. His brothers thought he liked that. Hell, maybe they were right. Maybe he did have some basic urge to take care of people who couldn't take care of themselves, quite often attractive women. He had the feeling anybody who wanted to be a cop had the basic urge to protect. And, in his line of work—particularly when working vice—he met a lot of women who'd been abused or taken advantage of. By pimps, dealers, hustlers. There was always somebody in need.

Maybe this woman wasn't like any he'd met on the streets of New York. She was, however, still in need, whether she knew it or not. Even if all she needed was for someone to make sure she had a pair of shoes on her feet.

He wasn't abandoning her. Not yet.

"I'm going to be fine," she said with a resolute nod. "Obviously I have a lot to say to my aunts…."

"Are you sure you can say it without a weapon in hand?"

"My tongue has been registered as a lethal weapon in a couple of states."

There was a suitable comeback to that, he was quite sure. And it would have rolled out of his brother Max's mouth immediately. But Mike wasn't wired that way, to grab any opening a woman provided and charm his way through it. No. Instead, he kept his reactions deep inside, schooled in giving no one an advantage by revealing his thoughts. Especially like the ones flooding his mind right now…the heated images of what her tongue was capable of doing. Wicked things. Amazing things.

She glanced at the house. "I feel like I'm heading into the lion's den." Her face was a little pink. Probably from her stroll in the sunshine—not a subtle admission that she knew what had been going through his mind. And certainly not that her thoughts had echoed his.

"Have any idea what you're going to say?"

"Not exactly. They don't understand," she said, not looking very sure who she was trying to convince more, herself or him. "I need to make them see that I'm talking about *The Love Boat* on land for seniors. Not the nasty, run-down home for the indigent that they're picturing."

"Sounds reasonable." And it did. To *him*. A twenty-seven-year-old single male living in a small house in Queens. If *he* were the one being asked to leave his home and move into a sterile "retirement community"? Well…he wasn't so sure.

"Thank you, Mr. Taylor. I really do appreciate you stopping, but I can handle this on my own now."

He stared into her face, noting the blueness of her eyes, a contrast to the stormy gray they were when she was angry. She looked calm…resolute. Able to take on any challenge. He suspected her relatives would have more trouble on their hands with a determined Jennifer Feeney than with an enraged one. Because something told him this woman didn't give up when there was something she wanted. Ever.

Oh. Right. *She'd* told him exactly that, hadn't she?

"Goodbye," she said, putting out her hand to shake his. She didn't suggest they see one another again, didn't offer her phone number or ask for his. And since he already knew she didn't give up on anything she wanted, there was only one conclusion he could reach: she *didn't* want him. The attraction was purely one-sided.

That, it seemed, was the end of that. The interesting interlude was over and he'd never see Jennifer Feeney again. By her choice. He wondered why the thought bothered him so much, considering he'd known her all of an hour.

Left with no other option, he put out his hand. Ignoring the cool softness of her skin against his, he said, "Good luck. Don't kill anyone."

Without another word, he got in his Jeep, and drove away.

RIGHT AFTER SHE'D BEEN DROPPED off in the driveway by Mr. Hunky-but-aloof, Jen calmly finished picking up all her things. Well, pretty calmly, considering how painful it was to see the mangled shoes and broken luggage. If her parents had been around to hear the words coming out of her mouth, they would have regretted wasting their money on her parochial-school education.

Somehow, she put aside her anger and managed to repack. Though she suspected Ida Mae and Ivy were watching from their windows, no matter how many times she looked toward them, she never caught as much as a twitch of a curtain.

That didn't mean anything. The old structures were so dark inside—as forbidding and unwelcoming as a pair of caves—either of the aunts could have been standing behind an uncurtained window, studying her every move. Her gaze would never have been able to penetrate the murky recesses of the houses to see them. But she *could* see them in her mind. Arming themselves in case she came in. Or praying to the gods of mean old ladies for her to get in her car and drive away, never to bother them again.

Fat chance. *Not giving up, not giving up, not giving up.*

When, she wondered, had it become a crime to offer to pay a fortune to put up your relatives in a pricey, lovely retirement village where they could be waited on, kept fed and entertained, with lots of elderly single men to keep them occupied?

She simply had to explain—had to make them see.

Once she'd picked up all her things, she carried them to Ida Mae's porch and reached for the doorknob. It was, for the first time she could ever recall, locked.

Pounding on the door, she cupped her hands around her eyes and tried to peer through the dirty inset glass. About all she could make out were the tiny dead bugs stuck between the window and the door frame. "Aunt Ida Mae? Come on, open up, we need to talk about this," she yelled before pounding again.

A full minute went past. No Ida Mae. No Ivy. But from somewhere above, she heard the squeak of a window. Quickly backing off the porch, down the front steps, she looked up just in time to see a toothbrush come sailing through the air.

It was hers. And it landed in the dirt.

Jen gritted her teeth as the window slammed shut. "I'm not leaving," she shouted, glaring at the second story of the house.

The window slowly groaned open again.

"Aunt Ida Mae?"

This time, her hairbrush was sent flying. It landed in a patch of mud a few feet away from the toothbrush.

"This is war," she muttered, marching back up to the porch and trying the windows to the parlor. Though they didn't budge, she wasn't about to give up, and made her way around the entire perimeter of the house. Knowing the old woman wasn't too concerned about security in this small, quiet town, she tried every single window, certain Ida Mae wouldn't have locked them *all* since she'd ditched Jen in the middle of nowhere.

"Damn," she muttered, trying the last one, to no avail.

Still not giving up, she went next door to Ivy's monstrosity, only to discover the same thing. "They're pretty serious," she whispered, still not sure whether to scream and pound on the door or laugh at how darned determined they were.

The warped back porches of both houses nearly touched each other, and the two sisters went back and forth constantly, never trying to keep each other out. If Ida Mae had locked her door against Ivy, her sister would likely have taken offense and burned her house down.

Some would speculate that it wasn't the first time.

Despite being a Feeney, Jen was not an arsonist. "But I am capable of a little breaking and entering," she murmured. Especially because she paid the bills on these two houses.

Eyeing a small window into Ida Mae's laundry room, she gave it some serious thought. It was already dingy and cracked, and would be just big enough for her to squeeze through.

Well, *maybe.* Given her recent love affair with two guys named Ben and Jerry, who'd substituted for any real man in Jen's life, she had some serious hip action going on and she suspected some in the hood would say she had *back.* But she still suspected she could push herself through and pop out the other side like a cork emerging from a bottle.

Only to land on her head on the washing machine and bleed to death because, given her mood, Aunt Ida Mae wouldn't lift a hand to call 9-1-1, if they even had such a thing in this town.

Okay. No breaking and entering.

She couldn't force her way in, and she knew the best thing to do when dealing with the Feeney sisters was to outwit them. Or outwait them. So, deciding to make them think they'd succeeded, and, hopefully, let down their guard, she went around front, got her stuff and threw it into the trunk of her car.

"Put away your weapons, start celebrating," she whispered as she started the car. "Just *unlock a door.*"

As she drove off, watching the houses in her rearview mirror, she waited for one of the women to come out on her porch and do an end-zone happy dance. Jen couldn't watch for long, however, because she hadn't gone a single mile when the car's engine started to sputter. Quickly glancing at the gas gauge and seeing it firmly below the *E,* she groaned. "Oh, no, you did *not!*"

But they had. The two maniacal old women had gone on a joy ride and emptied her tank. And for the second time that day, Jen found herself stranded, thanks to the wicked Feeney sisters.

CHAPTER FOUR

When Napoleon dumped Josephine, don't you think
she was dying to run around saying, "That thing about
a man's height and his length…it's true, it's true!"
—*I Want You, I Love You, Get Out* by Jennifer Feeney

AFTER MIKE HAD DROPPED JEN OFF at her aunts' houses, he'd
made the short drive to his grandfather's place. With every
second, he'd tried to force all thoughts of the strange interlude he'd just shared with her out of his head. In the future,
he'd probably look back and grin, thinking about the sexy,
crazy woman with the tire iron. But for now, he was still too
focused on the *sexy* part of the equation. Which wasn't good.
He didn't need to be thinking that way about anyone right
now, especially not a woman who had a violent streak. A
woman he'd never see again.

He got as far as his grandfather's driveway before he remembered the one thing he had neglected to pack. The dog
snuffling against the back of his neck reminded him of the dog
food still sitting on his kitchen counter at home. He had
nothing for Mutt.

"Sorry, boy," he said as he drove up toward the house.

He knew better than to just get out and leave a trip to the

store until later. Mortimer would insist on giving Mutt an entire grilled sirloin, which would make Roderick sniff and mumble stuff about cooking for dogs. They'd snipe at each other like an old married couple—Roderick would get his feelings hurt, Mortimer would be completely oblivious and Mike would sit in silence all evening.

Uh-uh. No thanks.

The crotchety and affectionate, love-hate relationship between the two men might make people who didn't know them wonder *how* close they were. Looking at them under today's standards, their relationship might be questionable. But Mike knew better. In *their* day, Mortimer and Roderick had forged a completely unbreakable brotherhood, fired in battle, cemented during years of adventure and treasure-hunting. They'd been the modern-day equivalent of pirates, with women on every continent. Even stuffy Roderick had, per Mortimer, "cut a dashing figure" in his day.

Which made it strange that they were both now alone, and had been for many years. He didn't doubt his grandfather would have liked to fall in love one more time, and he suspected Roderick would have, as well. They'd spent so long raising Mike and his brothers, though, they seemed to have let those dreams slip away. Now that the two old bachelors had taken up residence in Trouble, Pennsylvania, the odds of them meeting the kind of women they'd met in the capitals of Europe were slim to none. So they were apparently stuck with each other for life.

"I know Grandpa would welcome you right up at the table, pal, but old Roddy's pretty particular." Reaching over his shoulder, he scratched the animal's scruffy head. "He won't like cooking for a dog, not even one as superior as you."

Besides, even if he did, Mutt didn't handle table food well and Mike would spend the night cleaning up after a sick pet.

That cinched it.

So, doing a quick turnaround, he headed back to Trouble, hoping the small grocery store carried the right brand. For a mutt, Mutt was pretty finicky.

For some reason, his foot lifted off the gas pedal and he slowed down when he passed the old house where he'd dropped Jennifer off a few minutes before. He'd seen no sign of her.

That was good. Great. Perfect. So why, he wondered, had he been holding his breath, half hoping to see her yelling curses up at the window? Alone. Stranded.

In need of rescue again?

The idea was stupid and he kicked himself over it as he ran his errand. Why one hour in the company of a woman would have him wishing he'd *have* to come to her aid again, he honestly didn't know. Talk about selfish.

Hell, maybe his brothers were right and he did have some kind of protector fixation. One more reason to stay away from women right now. All women. Especially the brunette who'd been filling his head since the moment he'd laid eyes on her.

Arriving at the store, he parked out front, then tied Mutt up to a pole by the door. Fortunately, the store was tiny and he could see him from inside. Even more fortunately, they carried the right brand, if not the same flavor of food.

He was heading back to Mortimer's Folly, as his brother Morgan liked to call the ugly old white elephant their grandfather lived in, when he saw something that made him wonder if he was some kind of jinx. Or just the luckiest son of a bitch on the planet. Because ahead of him, parked on the opposite shoulder of the two-lane road, was a car. And standing beside it was a very frustrated-looking woman.

It was all he could do not to let Jennifer see his amusement when he did a quick U-turn and pulled in behind her. Getting out, he called, "Problem?"

She glared at him through her bangs, which had fallen into her eyes. "I ran out of gas."

"Good. I was afraid the old ladies had ditched you again."

Shifting her gaze away as he reached her side, she admitted, "They used up all my gas and I didn't even notice it."

"You know, I have to admit, someday I'd like to see those two aunts of yours for myself."

"You can come to their funerals. They'll be next week. Ivy would definitely want an open casket."

"Still feeling murderous?"

"You have no idea."

Oh, he felt pretty sure he had *some*. Dangerous or not, the woman was cute as hell when she was mad. "I think you need to be a little more on guard with those two."

That full, sexy mouth of hers pulled tight. "No kidding." She gazed longingly at his Jeep. "I don't suppose you have a spare gallon or two?"

"No," he admitted, "but there's a gas station a quarter mile away. Let's go."

She hesitated for a moment, staring at him with those big, incredible eyes. She looked tired and annoyed still, but also wore that hint of vulnerability he'd seen before. She'd obviously had a very long day and looked about at the end of her rope.

Mike reached out and took her arm, giving her some physical support. And maybe some of the emotional kind, too. Not even realizing he owned such a gentle tone, he murmured,

"On second thought, you've been through enough today. Why don't you wait in your car, I'll be back in five minutes."

She nodded slowly, not pulling away. A tremulous smile curved her mouth up. Not her usual smile of snarkiness or mischief, but one of relief, of gratitude. "You know, it's not going to do my reputation any good if people find out a nice, considerate guy came to my rescue not once but twice today."

Ha. As if anyone would recognize him as a nice, considerate guy. Seemed they were both suddenly acting out of character. "I won't tell if you won't."

Opening her car door, she got in. "Fair enough. Thank you."

She didn't say anything else as he walked away, nor much when he came back ten minutes later with a small gas can. Though he offered to follow her to the station after he'd put some gas in the tank, she insisted she'd be fine.

He didn't press it. Whatever moment of weakness she'd allowed him to see earlier, it was under control now. She was staunch and resolute, appreciative, but also once again very self-confident. So accepting her final thank you and knowing there was nothing more for him to do, Mike got in his Jeep and drove away from her for the second time that day.

JENNIFER DIDN'T LIKE THE END of anything. Whether it was one of her books that she was having a great time writing or a visit from her parents or simply the joy of the holiday season, she hated reaching The End.

She especially hated watching people leave. Particularly people she'd just met—sexy people—who she'd like to get to know better. Like *him*.

But it obviously wasn't to be. Like before, he'd played the hero and ridden away on his Jeep Wrangler steed. Big, strong, silent. As she watched Mike Taylor's taillights disappear into her history *again,* she felt like a saloon girl watching the handsome lawman ride away in some cheesy western.

Pathetic. She was thinking like one of the women who wrote to her talking about how wonderful her own handsome hero had been before he'd turned into a cheating toad.

This latest incident was simply the crap-flavored icing on her mud pie of a day. One for the to-forget books.

After filling up her tank at Trouble's one and only gas station—paying prices that would make an oil baron blush—she headed downtown. Her mood had slipped from mostly gray and cloudy to nearly black and stormy. A big part of her wanted to just keep driving, straight back to New York. She had a book to finish—her third—with a hefty check waiting at the end of it.

But she had a feeling that if she left, she would never be able to make herself return to Trouble and see her aunts again.

While that appealed to her on one level, on another, she knew that, as twisted as they were, she'd miss them. Miss their stubbornness and their independence, their caustic natures and the aura of mystery that had always surrounded them.

No. She wasn't going anywhere. Not until they'd hashed things out, face-to-face.

But first things first. She steered the car toward the local store. Once inside, Jen ignored the shelves full of expired canned goods for a nickel to scout the first-aid area for bandages and antiseptic to clean her blisters. She managed to find a tube of stuff that didn't look as if it had been produced during the Carter administration. Adding a toothbrush to her cart, she paid for her things just as the store closed at six.

Six o'clock on a Friday night and the town was closing up

shop. Rolling up its sidewalks. The one stoplight in the main square had already stopped changing from red to green and turned into a flat, blinking yellow beacon that screamed, "You're in the middle of nowhere! Get out while you still can!"

"Unbelievable," she muttered, glancing across the street at the one business that still appeared to be open. But it took a few minutes for her to muster the courage to actually go over and enter Tootie's Tavern. Because if the Travel Channel ever stopped doing shows on the ten scariest places in the world, and started naming the ten scariest places to *eat*, this would probably make the cut. She'd bet it was on an FDA watch list somewhere.

Finally, though, she forced herself inside. Knowing Aunt Ida Mae and Aunt Ivy were very untrusting, she suspected they hadn't even crawled out of their hiding places yet, much less unlocked any doors.

"Hey there, missy, thought you was gonna spend your whole week here without comin' in to see me!"

This comment came from the owner, Tootie herself, who was shaped like a box—as wide as she was tall—with hair the color of congealing sausage gravy. But she had always been nice to Jen as a kid. Even if Jen's mother had always made her throw away any cookie or treat Tootie had slipped to her during a family visit.

"Hi," she said. "I, uh, need to use the ladies' room."

Jen immediately wished she hadn't put it like that. She knew she'd been overheard when a meaty guy at a nearby table, wearing a Bud T-shirt and a backward baseball cap, snickered like a third grader who'd spotted a little girl's underwear.

That, of course, instantly made her think about the conversation she and Mike had had earlier…and his wickedly erotic comment about the soft fabric between a woman's soft thighs.

The soft fabric between *her* soft thighs had gotten a mite damp after the remark, that was for sure. And just thinking about Mike now could probably make it more so.

Forget it. He'd driven away—*twice*—without mentioning the possibility of seeing her again. Besides, she didn't like the big, strong, drop-dead gorgeous, dangerous, silent type.

Hmm. Maybe… *No.* Not her type, even though her friends all thought she should be happy with any guy who was *breathing.* But she wasn't that desperate. Yet.

"Sorry, sweetie, facilities are for paying customers only," the proprietress said with an apologetic shrug, her loud reply ensuring they were being overheard now.

Then the words sank in. Perfect. She was actually going to have to *eat* here? "Oh, uh…"

"Meat loaf's on special."

She was tempted to ask what type of meat was in it— armadillo, mastodon—but wasn't sure she wanted to know.

Unfortunately, every other place in town was probably already closed. This might be the only bite she'd have until she could get her aunts to let her in. That could take a week.

"Could you just get me a plain salad and an iced tea?"

Tootie nodded. "I'll have Scoot put in the order, but you'll have to sit at the counter. There's no tables."

She glanced at the counter, seeing a sea of men wearing red plaid and wife-beater T-shirts. All packed shoulder-to-shoulder, heads down, like horses at a trough. All probably having heard her ladies' room comment and right now thinking about her walking into the next room and pulling down her panties.

Eww.

"Can I get it to go?"

"Didn't she already *say* she had to go?" a phlegmy voice asked. The question was accompanied by a lascivious chuckle. Both had emanated from a guy at the closest table who, judging by his comma-shaped posture, was between one hundred and death.

Tootie leaned close. "I don't blame you, sugar. Some of these fellas act like mongrels over a bone when a pretty woman comes around. Me 'n' Scoot have taken to giving each other signals when we need help extricating ourselves from one when he gets over-amorous."

Scoot. That was the waitress. Tootie's assistant. Practically Tootie's twin. The hottest single ladies in Trouble?

"Ooo-kay," she murmured, keeping her eyes forward, focusing on the door to the ladies' room. "I'll be back."

Once inside the bathroom, however, she realized she'd made a tactical error. "This place is dirtier than the ground," she muttered, staring in dismay at the mildew climbing up the backs of the sinks and the peeling, puke-green linoleum on the floor. She'd be better off cleaning her cuts in a truck stop men's room.

If there had been a hotel anywhere in the vicinity, she would have given up for the night, blowing off Ida Mae and Ivy's houses for clean sheets, hot water that wasn't the color of dirt and free HBO. But, if she recalled correctly, Trouble had only ever boasted two inns and both were now closed. One—Seaton House, where she had once stayed with her parents as a child—due to the death of its former owner. And the other, the Dew Drop Inn—where she had *never* stayed with her parents as a child because the owner was a nudist—also closed. From what the aunts said, the owner, Mr. Fitzweather, had had a bit of a run-in with a dog during his nudist days and had since retired.

"This is ridiculous," she told her reflection, continuing to shift her toes to keep them protected by the flip-flops, so they wouldn't come into contact with the dirty floor. "There has to be *something* I can do."

Then she remembered something. And started to smile.

During Jen's last visit, Ivy had nastily told her that Ida Mae was a loose woman, praying for a burglar to come along and ravish her. In order to make it easier for said burglar, Ida Mae always kept a spare key under the rusty iron bench sitting on her front porch. Knowing Ivy, she'd probably forgotten she'd spilled the secret five minutes after the words had left her lips, just as Jen had forgotten the comment. Which meant Ida Mae probably *hadn't* removed the key.

A half hour later, when she returned to Ida Mae's, holding a plastic container full of salad, she checked. And hit pay dirt. The key was there.

"Oh, Luuuucy, I'm home," she called as she let herself into the house, hoping Aunt Ida Mae had calmed down and could be reasonable. She didn't dare hope for such a thing from Aunt Ivy.

"How did you get in here?" a stern-sounding voice said, emerging from the dark, cluttered parlor.

Jen immediately swung toward it and strode into the room, carefully picking her way through the maze of furniture. Good thing she'd become familiar with it during her week's stay because it was nearly dark outside and not a single light was on within. The heavy oak and crushed-velvet pieces stood in odd positions around the room, competing for every inch of floor space. It was like being inside a child's antique dollhouse which had too much toy furniture. Jen had never left this house without a bruise or two from having banged into something.

She'd already been bruised, battered and cut enough at her aunts' hands today, thank you very much, and didn't need any more war wounds. "I used your spare key," she said, plopping onto the sofa and opening her bag of food. She'd ditched the drink right after leaving Tootie's because, after sucking in a big mouthful through the straw, she'd had tea leaves coating her tongue.

"Who said you could come into my house?"

"Technically, Aunt Ida Mae, since I cover your mortgage, paid for the new roof and am responsible for all the utilities, I think it's partly my house."

That got the old woman out of the darkness. She came out of the corner and expertly wove her way across the room, flipping on a single lamp as she went by it. The whiteness of her round face, emphasized by dark circles under her brown eyes, said she'd been tense, waiting for this confrontation.

Ida Mae had probably never been considered pretty— though Ivy had. Judging by the pictures Jen had seen, the younger Feeney sister had been more than pretty; she'd been a knockout. But the older one would have to be described as handsome rather than pretty, even today at seventy-eight. Ida Mae carried herself well and was proud of her thick, snow-white hair. Usually up in a bun, it now hung loose, halfway down her back, stark against her pink housecoat. Thick and lovely, it was definitely her best feature.

Way nicer than her smile. Which almost never got any use. Kind of like Mike Taylor's.

"You can *have* your roof and your utilities."

Jen opened her salad, tore open the packet of Italian dressing that had come with it and squirted it onto the wilted lettuce. Ignoring the obvious impossibility of removing the new roof, she murmured, "So you want to sit here in the dark and get rained on?" she asked before taking a bite.

"That's just what you'd like, isn't it? To make me so sick and miserable I'll let you put me in an almost-dead-folks home?"

Jennifer couldn't contain a small laugh. Ida Mae was nothing if not blunt. "Look, can we please call a truce? I have absolutely no intention of forcing you to do anything."

"As if you *could*," the woman mumbled, eyeing Jen's salad.

Without saying a word, Jen pushed the container across the coffee table, watching Ida Mae grab an olive and pop it into her mouth. With Ivy, only liquor, ice cream or an oldies CD for the stereo Jen had bought her last Christmas could have done the trick. Ida Mae was much less picky when it came to bribes.

The ploy worked. The older woman slowly lowered herself onto the opposite chair, but kept griping. "Shocking lack of respect for your elders. Your dear, sweet father will be horrified to hear this."

"You're *not* going to bother my father," Jen said, her tone steely. "You know as well as I do that he can't handle the stress. Mom said he's just now strong enough to walk to the mailbox without coming back winded. None of us are going to do or say a thing to worry him."

Ida Mae sucked in her bottom lip. The only thing Jen could ever do to get the old woman to back off anything was say it wasn't good for Ivan Feeney. Ida Mae and Ivy did have a soft spot in their brittle hearts for their much younger brother.

"Sweet baby boy," Ida Mae said, sounding about as gentle as Jen had ever heard her. "I do wish your mother would have let us stay longer to take care of him."

Ha. *Smother* him was the better term. Jen's mother had almost shot herself when her two elderly sisters-in-law had come down to North Carolina to "help" her parents get settled in their new home. If they went back, Mom was likely to have a heart attack and end up right beside Dad.

Which was why Jen intended to take care of the aunts whether they liked it or not. "I'm very sorry my *suggestion* came across as an order."

Getting better. Ida's posture eased a tiny bit, but she wasn't finished grumbling. "Think I buried one husband and divorced another just so I could let somebody else order me around?" She didn't wait for an answer, instead grabbing a cherry tomato and a slice of green pepper. The aunts usually lived on canned tuna, so fresh veggies had to be a real treat. Even if they had come out of Tootie's greasy kitchen.

"I would like…I would *hope,* that you and Ivy would at least consider moving into someplace a little nicer."

Oh boy. Tactical error. She knew it the minute the words left her mouth.

Ida Mae's spine stiffened as if somebody had sent a bolt of electricity through her. She launched herself up on her sturdy legs and glared down, a bit of pepper flying out of her mouth as she snapped, "Nicer? You're saying my house is not nice? Well, young lady, you may feel free to stay somewhere else then."

"Aunt Ida…"

"Out."

She shrugged. "I'm not going anywhere."

The shrug, and reasonable tone, seemed to get Ida Mae's attention more than anything Jen had said. She appeared a bit nonplussed that her niece hadn't launched to her feet and started arguing back—as Ivy probably would have done. Ida Mae could handle anger. But she wasn't so good at holding up against calm, rational conversation.

Maybe that was one reason she never battled with her brother. Jen's father was the absolute epitome of a laid-back, kindly man. Which had made his massive heart attack at fifty-nine that much more frightening.

As if knowing she'd lost the skirmish—though, she'd never concede the battle—Ida Mae glared. "Fine. Stay then. Just be gone tomorrow."

Without another word, she bent down, grabbed Jen's salad and stalked out of the room.

THE LAST TIME MIKE HAD VISITED his grandfather in Trouble had been during the winter, at Christmastime, to be exact. So it hadn't quite hit him just how hot this part of Pennsylvania could be in August. Particularly in a monstrous old house with no central air-conditioning. Even his *hair* was sweating.

He hadn't noticed it as much when he'd first arrived the previous evening, since Roderick had served up a great dinner on the back patio. With newly installed ceiling fans spinning lazily overhead, an icy cold beer in his hand and his grandfather's fine company, he hadn't even felt the temperature.

Until he'd gone to bed.

Then he'd turned into Mr. Heat Miser from that old Christmas show.

His grandfather had said he'd looked into installing a system when doing renovations on the old monstrosity over the last year. But supposedly the lines of the oddly constructed building—which, in Mike's opinion, looked like a bunch of kid's card houses on top of one another—would be affected by installing central air. So Mortimer hadn't done it. He'd merely brought in a few window units, though none for the third floor.

Hence the sweating. Even Mutt had known better than to sleep up here. He'd come in with Mike the night before, then turned right back around and gone downstairs where it was cooler. Man's best friend. Huh.

Mike had to concede it: the steaminess of his first night in the house might also be attributed to the dream he'd had. He couldn't remember all the details. But he definitely remembered it had involved Jennifer Feeney, a bottle of massage oil and a pair of his handcuffs.

It had also caused him to wake up as hard as a tree trunk.

"Get out of my head, lady," he muttered as he got up, knowing there was no point trying to sleep any longer. When his feet hit the floor, he groaned. Even the scratched old wooden floors of the attic room were hot, and it was only 9:00 a.m.

His brother Max, who'd spent a few weeks here last summer, had sworn this third-floor room got the best cross breezes from the two turret windows. Supposedly, its greatest benefit was that it was out of earshot of Mortimer's snoring, which had been known to knock pictures off walls.

Mike was apparently a lighter sleeper than his brother. He'd heard his grandfather sawing away from one story below until at least 3:00 a.m. And if a breeze had come through the front window last night, it had tiptoed around him sprawled naked on the bed and gone right out the other side. Now that some rainy weather had rolled in, the humidity was thick enough to drink from a cup and his whole body felt sticky.

He didn't know how Max had managed to stay here last summer. Then he thought about his new sister-in-law. And he knew how.

His brother had fallen hard and fast for Sabrina, and more power to him. Maybe with one grandson settled, Mortimer would get some great-grandchildren who'd distract him from this mess of a town he'd purchased a little over a year ago.

The man was never as happy as when he had someone to scheme and fuss over, and a new baby would definitely fit the bill. The way Grandpa talked about Hank, his secretary Allie's kid, he sounded as if he'd already bought stock in Pampers. He adored the boy who was, to be technical, a relative, since he was Sabrina's nephew. Mike couldn't even imagine what Mortimer would do with his own great-grandchild…beyond loving him more than life.

Just as he had his grandsons, who'd never forgotten what he'd done for them when their parents had died. He hadn't shuffled them off to private schools or dumped them on paid servants. Hadn't treated them as if they were a nuisance. Hadn't allowed them to wallow in their own unhappiness. No. Instead, he'd become a true parent all over again, in every sense of the word.

Mike had only been a kid when his dad had been blown out of the sky during the first Gulf War. But he remembered full well how terrified he'd been of losing anyone else he cared about. So the death of his mother from cancer less than a year later had brought his entire world to a crashing halt.

Mortimer had made it start spinning again. Eventually. And as it had spun, he'd dragged his three grandsons across it, giving them the kinds of lives most kids only dreamed of having.

"Michael?" A tap on the door gave him about ten seconds' notice before it was pushed in by his grandfather. Which was just enough time for Mike to grab his shorts and yank them on.

It wouldn't have been the first time his grandfather had walked in and seen him sporting some morning wood. But that hadn't happened since he was fourteen. The memory of the sex talk Mortimer had insisted they have afterward still gave him chills.

He would do anything for his grandfather. But he didn't want to think about the man's wild sex life, which had, he said, served him well through a few marriages and many love affairs.

"Good, you're up. I was hoping you could do me a favor and go down to the market for a newspaper."

He certainly didn't mind, but was curious about the request. "I can't believe you don't have the *Times,* the *Journal* and the *Post* delivered to your doorstep every morning anymore."

"The town doesn't carry 'em. Besides, the only paper carrier around here dropped dead of a heart attack when Mrs. Sneed's pit bull came through her screen door at him."

The comment rolled out of Grandfather's mouth as if he'd been living in this Podunk town all his life. Obviously Mortimer was playing a new role: small-town old-timer. He even had a completely phony twang in his voice.

"Okay," Mike said. "I'll run down there right after I shower."

Grandfather frowned. "I could *really* use that paper."

A newspaper emergency? One reason leaped to mind. "Stock issues? Do you want me to check the market on the Internet?"

Mortimer shrugged. "Roddy does that computer thing for me every day. No, there's, er, some town business I need to find out about and it should be in today's paper. So, a bit of a hurry-up would be most appreciated."

The old man was nervous. His smile was too wide, his eyes too bright and he was bouncing on his arthritic legs. Whatever this town business was, it appeared to be important. If Mike didn't go for the paper, he felt sure his grandfather would. And Mortimer Potts and automobiles didn't go so well together anymore, as several wrecking companies around the globe could testify.

"Sure. You bet," he said, grabbing a pair of jeans.

"Take the back way, left at the bottom of the hill. It's quicker. Brings you right in behind the market."

"You live a mile from downtown either way," Mike replied, making no effort to keep the dryness from his tone.

Mortimer didn't answer, he merely kept his smile in place, then turned and hurried out of the room. Leaving Mike to wonder what, exactly, was going on with him.

He *really* began to wonder twenty minutes later. Because after he'd grabbed the paper and a box fan from the ancient drugstore and was heading back to the house, hoping he'd make it before the skies really opened up and dropped the moisture barely contained in the pregnant clouds, his cell phone rang.

"Michael? I've just remembered, that article isn't going to appear today. There's really no rush for you to get back."

His head began to pound. All he'd wanted this morning was a cold shower to get the sweat off his body and bring his skin temperature back down below a hundred degrees. But he'd been sent out on an emergency errand…which now wasn't an emergency?

"So, feel free to, uh, go see the sights or something."

See the sights. Right. The Holland Tunnel was the sight he most wanted to see today, but he'd promised to stay through Tuesday. He hadn't even had a real conversation with his grandfather yet—like the one he'd come here to have, which started with "Why don't you come back to New York with me?" and ended with Mortimer waving, "Bye-bye, Trouble!"

"I'll be back in a few minutes," he finally said with a sigh. Then, something up ahead caught his attention.

A brunette. Wearing a sexy jean skirt and bright pink top. Walking down the side of the road. "I'll be damned," he said, unable to believe what he was seeing. He began to smile, simply unable to fathom how this could be happening. *Again.*

"What?" his grandfather said over the phone.

"Nothing," he said. "Just, uh, maybe I will see the sights, Grandpa. I'll be back later."

"Good, good. Enjoy yourself. Have fun."

Fun? Well, he didn't know if he'd call rescuing Jennifer Feeney fun. But it sure was entertaining.

At least this time, she was wearing shoes. And she wasn't carrying any lethal weapons. Probably only because he still had her tire iron on the floor of his Jeep.

Dropping his phone back in his pocket, he pulled up beside her. He couldn't hide his rueful amusement as he lowered the passenger side window. "Good morning," he called.

She stopped and swung around, a glare on her face. It quickly faded when she saw and recognized him. Then those pretty cheeks pinkened and she nibbled a hole through her bottom lip.

Yeah. He supposed it would be a bit embarrassing to be outwitted by a pair of sneaky old ladies two days in a row.

"Hi," she said.

"Nice day for a walk." It was *so* not a nice day for a walk.

She didn't even blink. "Yeah. Great."

"I see you're wearing shoes today, at least."

She glanced down at her strappy, low-heeled sandals. They might be better than bare feet, but they sure didn't look as if they'd been made for walking.

They were very nice, however, for showing off those incredible legs, especially given the short jean skirt that hugged her hips and ass as if it was sewn on.

"You bet," she said, quickly looking in both directions, obviously hoping another car would pull up to her rescue, so she could avoid admitting what had happened. As if there was *any* doubt.

"So, where you headed?"

She lifted a hand and waved it in a generally forward direction.

"Where are you coming from?"

The hand came up again, waving just as generally the other way.

He felt laughter bubbling up inside him, and again wondered how this woman was getting around his stiff defenses so easily. No other woman had in a long time. Then again, seeing Jennifer Feeney try to get herself out of trouble was more amusing than just about anything else he could imagine.

He liked this side of her, this embarrassed side. It was cute, and showed there was a chink in that hard-ass armor she usually wore.

Yesterday she'd been spitting nails, revealing only a tiny bit of vulnerability when she'd run out of gas. Today she was obviously just as furious…but a whole lot more humiliated. What was that old saying? *Fool me once, shame on you…. Abandon me in the middle of nowhere twice—now who's the idiot?*

"I take it you did make it to the gas station and haven't been walking the streets since last evening?"

"I did."

"Did the aunts let you in?"

She so obviously didn't want to talk about this. "Uh-huh."

"Did they have you arrested for breaking and entering?"

"I found a spare key."

"Good." Still idling on the road, not worrying about

blocking traffic since there was none, he pushed harder. "If you didn't sleep on the street, I guess that means you got things worked out with your aunts and they let you stay?"

"Mmm, hmm." Her eyes went down and her feet scuffed in the gravel. She looked like a kid trying not to admit she'd failed a test at school.

Mike couldn't take it anymore. "They got you again, huh?"

Sighing heavily, she nodded. "Yeah. The biddies got me again." Having admitted it, she suddenly shook off any embarrassment and he saw the fire sparking in her eyes.

This was the Jen Feeney he'd met yesterday. And damn, didn't she look fine. "Want a ride?"

This time, she didn't even hesitate. Striding to the Jeep, she opened the door and hopped up into the passenger seat, frustration and humiliation rolling off the woman in great almost tangible waves. "Get me out of here."

"Where we goin'?"

"Anywhere," she snapped. "Just drive."

CHAPTER FIVE

They say the world's best diet is the divorce diet. Every newly single woman, fantasizing about making her ex regret what he lost, drops weight faster than ever before. Personally, I think she ought to be satisfied with the two hundred pounds of useless fat she got rid of the day she lost the ex.

—*I Want You, I Love You, Get Out* by Jennifer Feeney

"GOOD MORNING."

Startled by the sound of Allie Cavanaugh's voice, Emily turned around from the sink where she'd been peeling peaches for a pie. It was late Saturday morning and she hadn't expected to see Allie at all today. She'd thought she would be joined at the hip to her young man, Damon Cole, who had come back last night.

Emily wasn't a bra-burning modern woman—she'd been living in her strict parents' home throughout the sexual revolution. And the closest she'd ever come to free love in her youth had been when there was a romance double-feature at the old Trouble Movie Palace. But she also wasn't a prude. So when Allie had asked her for permission to invite Damon to stay a while, until they could find a bigger place to live,

Emily had immediately agreed. Not only to make Allie happy, but because she longed for the girl's company a bit longer. When Allie and her baby moved out, Emily didn't know how she'd stand the silence.

She'd have to pay a visit to the Wal-Mart in the next town and see what was in the $5.50 video bin.

"Having a nice weekend so far?" she asked, laughter in her voice. She imagined her young friend had been having a *very* nice weekend, considering she and her young man had disappeared upstairs at seven o'clock last night and hadn't been out since.

"Hank's cutting a new tooth," Allie said with a small sigh. "He was up every two hours."

"I would have taken him."

Allie came up and put her arm around Emily's waist, giving her a squeeze and a kiss on the cheek. She was a demonstrative child, bright and funny, her gamine face and curly hair perfect for her sunny disposition. "You're a darling, but if Damon wants me, he gets Hank, too. He might as well know what he's in for."

"How did he do?"

Allie helped herself to a slice of peach. "Beautifully. I think Hank kept waking up just so Damon would sing to him."

A good man. A very good man. She'd known that as soon as she'd met him. And not at all surprising that he was good with the boy, considering what he *really* did for a living. He'd been traveling with his family-owned circus, performing as a "Gypsy King" this summer. In truth, he was a child psychologist. He'd just been taking some time off to deal with a personal tragedy.

"Now, I didn't come down here to steal your peaches." Allie snagged another slice. "We've been invited to a party."

Emily immediately put the knife down, her eyes wide. "A…party?" She didn't attend many parties, not in Trouble. Once in a while she took the bus up to visit her brother and his family in Pittsburgh, but as for local socializing, the Saturday night bingo game was about all the excitement she got.

"Mortimer called a few minutes ago."

Emily's heart picked up its pace. Her hand immediately went to her hair as she wondered how long it had been since she'd had the color touched up or a decent cut.

"His grandson is home for the weekend and Mortimer has decided he wants to invite a few people over for an impromptu dinner party tomorrow night."

A dinner party. At Mortimer Potts's house. *My, oh my.*

She knew Mr. Potts, of course, through Allie. She'd even gone on a trip with all of them to the shore over Fourth of July weekend, to look after Hank while Allie worked. That had been quite a nice holiday. Particularly on one morning when she'd been feeding Hank on the terrace of the suite overlooking the ocean…and someone had joined them for a lovely meal.

A bit of heat rose in her cheeks just at the memory of it.

"He said he and Roderick are planning something spectacular and want everyone there by six. There's room for all of us and the car seat in Damon's car, so we'll leave around 5:45, okay?"

Something suddenly dawned on her and she lowered her eyes. "Yes, of course. But, you know, I don't mind babysitting Hank here, where he has his own things."

Allie frowned, appearing confused, then her jaw dropped. "You think I'm inviting you to come along to *babysit?*"

She hadn't, at first. But it made more sense than the alternative...that she'd be wanted as a guest. After all, what did she have in common with such dashing, world-traveling, noble gentlemen like Mr. Potts and his handsome friend Roderick Ward? She was a small-town down-to-earth woman who'd never lived more than ten miles from where she lived right this very minute and had never spent more than a week away from Trouble at a time. Why on earth would they want anything to do with *her?* No matter how lovely that summer breakfast on the terrace had been.

"I can't believe you thought that."

"Well, it makes sense, dear."

"Now, get this, you are invited as a *guest.* I have tons of stuff for Hank at the house. Mr. Potts set up a whole nursery for him when I was living there last fall, remember? He'll be adorable and everyone will fuss over him, then I'll put him to bed at seven and we'll have a lovely evening. Together. Got it?"

She got it. And had to laugh at Allie's bossiness. She was playing the part of mother today, the role Emily usually played.

"Now, do you have something fabulous to wear?"

"Fabulous? No. Not fabulous." Though she did have a pretty lilac dress she'd worn to a friend's grandson's wedding last spring. It might do. "But perhaps I have something nice."

"I'm sure you do." Allie smacked her peach juice-smeared lips together. "God, you *must* bring this pie."

"If there's any filling left," Emily replied tartly.

Allie ignored that. "Everyone will be so impressed with your baking. And I know you'll be gorgeous."

"Now, that's silly." Flustered, she turned back to her

peaches, peeling another one. But her hands were shaking, and she made a mess of it, taking away more flesh than peel.

"Emily, is there something wrong?"

"No, no, nothing. But being invited to dine with hi…*them*. It's unexpected, that's all."

Allie's grin turned decidedly cheeky. *"Oh."*

"What?"

"You're blushing."

"I'm not."

"Yeah. You are." Allie pressed another kiss on Emily's cheek. "Don't worry, I'll never let Mortimer know you have a crush on him." Then she strolled out before Emily could protest.

And protest she would have, because Allie was wrong. Quite wrong. It wasn't Mortimer Potts who'd earned a little piece of Emily's heart last month.

It was his handsome British friend, Roderick Ward.

JEN DIDN'T KNOW WHICH WAS worse—being tricked and stranded by her aunts for the second day in a row, or having this intense, sexy man witness her humiliation. Again.

Not that she was so humiliated she'd turn down his offer of a ride. She wasn't *that* embarrassed. She'd jumped right in, though she was a lot closer to the houses—and, hopefully, her car—than she had been the previous day. Even with her bandaged feet she could have walked it easily.

But she didn't want to. She was still too frustrated—too angry and wound up—to even think about going back there yet. Ida Mae had surely not put her secret key back under the bench and the way Jen was feeling now, she might not be able to restrain herself from pitching a brick through a window.

Besides, after the crappy time she'd been having lately, she deserved to have a bit of pleasure. And oh, this man could provide some pleasure, of that she had no doubt.

If he wanted to. If she wanted to let him.

Who was she kidding? She *already* wanted to let him. Her panties had grown damp the moment she'd turned around and seen him behind her on the road. And she strongly suspected, judging by the way he'd stared at her bare legs when she'd climbed in beside him that he was interested, too.

It was too soon. She was twenty-nine years old, well beyond the age when she would even consider having crazy, reckless, no-strings sex. But that didn't mean she couldn't fantasize about it…or that she hadn't dreamed about it the night before. Her tangled sheets in Ida Mae's musty, stiflingly hot guest room had been proof of that.

"How'd they get you this time?" he asked after they'd driven for a few minutes, heading out of town toward the trio of mountains encircling it. Stark, rocky mountains that didn't look any more welcoming than Trouble itself.

"We went out to breakfast to talk."

"All three of you?"

Surprisingly, yes, even Ivy had come along, though only after Ida Mae had talked her out of the basement where she'd apparently been hiding out since last night. "Uh-huh. There was a pancake breakfast at the firehouse that they've been talking about all week and I knew they wouldn't be able to resist." She sighed, still unable to believe the way they'd duped her. "So I lured them with pancakes and the promise that the firemen would be serving them shirtless."

He glanced over, surprise obvious in his eyes. "Aren't they elderly?"

They were. But their advancing years hadn't seemed to

affect their libidos. That was one thing Jen sort of regretted about not being a blood relative to the two. "Yeah."

He seemed to know she didn't want to elaborate and obviously didn't want to know any more, either. "Were the firefighters really shirtless?"

"No. That part I made up. Which started our breakfast off on a bad note. But it quickly got better when they started eating, especially because Ivy was having a great time pinching the butt of any fireman who walked past her."

He smiled. Maybe. A little. "Going fine *until*..."

"Until I took out a brochure for the assisted-living center and asked them to just look at it."

"Bad move," he said, shaking his head. "First rule of engagement—don't let your enemy see your battle plan too soon."

How funny that he already knew she considered this a battle. A war. He'd apparently gotten to know her pretty well in their short acquaintance.

She wished she could say the same. She knew his name and that he lived in New York. Knew he was here visiting his grandfather. Knew that he had a lazy dog. Beyond that, all she knew was that he was devastatingly attractive, grudgingly protective, and unpredictable. She didn't know when he was going to smile or maybe even laugh…or do something sweet like offer to drive her around the block so she wouldn't have to face her aunts. Or help her pick up her things off the muddy ground. Including her shoes.

An enigma.

"You should have left that for later. Like when you were in their houses, far from your car, with your keys in your hand and your cell phone set to speed dial 9-1-1 if they got violent."

"Do they have 9-1-1 in this town?"

"I think they have to. Of course, it'll probably ring eighty times while the town secretary runs over from the diner to answer it."

He obviously knew a bit about Trouble, too.

"I knew it was a bad move to pull out that brochure, but things seemed to be going pretty well. Anyway, Ivy was so upset, she spilled her juice all over herself. Ida glared me straight to hell before dragging her to the ladies' room to clean her up."

Not saying where he was headed, Mike turned off the main road onto a smaller, single-lane one. It was overgrown, with trees untrimmed in a decade hanging across it, nearly creating a tunnel of green. Seeing a sign for a state park, she nodded her agreement. Maybe spending some time with Mother Earth would prevent her from wanting to bury her aunts in it.

"Let me guess," he said after a moment, "they ducked out a back door?"

"How'd you know?"

"Stories like this always end with somebody ducking out the back door. You're lucky you weren't in a restaurant where they could stick you with the tab."

She scrunched her eyes shut and shook her head. "I hadn't even realized Ivy stole my wallet until they were gone. I had to write an I.O.U. to the firehouse for three pancake breakfasts before they'd let me leave."

Suddenly, he shocked her by bursting into laughter. Not that first rough bark he'd so grudgingly let escape his succulent lips yesterday, or the later ones he'd quickly controlled, but a genuine, heartfelt laugh that he made no effort to disguise.

That laugh changed everything. Every little thing.

She stared at him from the passenger seat, seeing the way

his dark eyes crinkled…and noticing the flash of a dimple in his right cheek. He looked younger—more approachable, less intense. And while her body had been wanting to have sex with the dark brooder since the first time she'd seen him, the rest of her now responded with warmth and appreciation to the laughing guy who sat beside her.

Now she didn't just want to have sex with him. She wanted to get to know him. Wanted to peel back that tough-guy exterior and see more of the inner man.

Though, of course, peeling off his clothes and seeing the outer man would still be good, too.

"Well, this is a good place to cool down and relax," he said as he pulled into a weed-choked parking lot, once flatly graveled, now strewn with dirt and downed tree limbs. "And at least it's not raining anymore."

The park had apparently been forgotten, because despite the huge, peaceful green lake and small sandy beach, the whole area told a tale of abandon. Every picnic bench was broken and warped, the paint gone, bird droppings littering the surfaces. No recent trash marred the ground, no beer bottles from teenagers who came up here to escape prying parental eyes. The vegetation was thick and overgrown, tumbling over the path leading to a dilapidated playground and the one down to the beach. Plus, the place was as quiet as a tomb.

"I wonder why nobody comes here," she said softly.

"How do you know nobody comes here?"

"Well…*look* at it."

"I have. I found it last winter when I was here visiting." He cut the ignition and leaned back in his seat, staring out the windshield. "I don't know if anybody even remembers that it's here. I came to be alone. To think."

To escape. She almost heard the words, though he didn't say them. She suddenly wondered what he had needed to escape from, suspecting it was his family. From the brief interaction she'd had with Mr. Potts, she suspected he was social, chatty and loved to entertain. Exactly the opposite of his taciturn grandson.

"It's a good place for that." Reaching for the door handle, she said, "I want to look around."

"Be careful, the ground's pretty uneven and wet from the rain." That stern, serious tone was back, all signs of his laughter evaporating like the raindrops were from the windshield. Mr. Dark and Intense was back. And instead of her heart feeling light and fluttery the way she so ridiculously had when she'd witnessed that devastating smile, she went back to the standard feeling she'd had around this guy since he'd picked her up yesterday: physical want.

"I just need some air," she said, stepping outside. She immediately regretted it because though the drizzle had stopped, the air itself seemed composed of pure H_2O. The humidity hung like a shroud, and she immediately felt damp. As if she'd been working out at the gym.

Okay, that was a stretch. She never worked out at the gym. She hated the freaking gym and all the plastic women and obnoxious guys who frequented it. Especially since every man in New York pretty much had a Wanted poster with her face on it. So lately her workouts had been confined to the treadmill in her apartment, and the pool on the roof of her building.

She'd never admit it out loud, but she'd also been sticking close to home lately because of the crap she'd been dealing with from her nasty phone caller/letter writer. If he kept tracking down her phone number, he might know where she lived. So she'd been staying in, a lot…. Another reason she'd been happy to make this trip to Trouble.

Ha. She'd have been better off with her creepy caller. At least she wouldn't have been left stranded two days in a row.

Idiot—sure you could be worse off—he could be a killer.

Jen didn't even allow herself to dwell on that possibility. The harassment was just the downside of fame. She'd pissed a guy off. He was getting even. It would all go away soon. Period. She refused to even consider anything else.

"A swim would be nice," she murmured, thinking longingly of gliding beneath the smooth surface of the lake. Now that she was standing outside, being smothered by a wet blanket of air, she wanted nothing more than to kick off her shoes, walk through the damp grass surrounding the sandy beach and dive in.

Tempting. Despite her lack of a bathing suit, it was *very* tempting.

Standing by Mike's Jeep, Jen saw puddles of light beginning to take shape on the uneven ground. The sun was trying to slough off the morning clouds and break through. It succeeded briefly, hot rays of it touching her cheeks and blinding her for a second.

Blinking a few times to adjust her eyes, she noticed the way the streaks of sunlight turned the green water into a crystallized playground. Beams sparkled and danced on the small, lapping waves, creating a million tiny diamonds on its surface.

"Wow," she murmured, hoping the still-heavy clouds wouldn't shift back across the sun too quickly, casting the day in dull, washed-out gray again. "It looks beautiful."

"It looks wet. And cold."

She wasn't surprised to see Mike had also left the Jeep and

now stood a few feet away. She *also* wasn't surprised to see him staring at the shoreline. It appeared she wasn't the only one longing to dive into the cool waters of the lake.

But in his stare, there wasn't mere interest, there was something that looked like raw desire. *Hunger.*

The thought made her legs grow weak. Oh, to be looked at by this man in such a way. The idea took her breath away, and Jen again acknowledged how long it had been since she'd been intimate with anyone. She didn't mean just sex.... She'd missed being *wanted.* Being watched by coveting eyes and reached for by desperate hands. Being touched by thorough fingers and kissed by a ravenous mouth.

Being stroked, being held, being pleasured.

Wrapping her arms around herself, she strove to control the shudders of want that threatened to roll through her. She had a good imagination—a writer's imagination—and her mind had filled with possibilities. Possibilities she couldn't possibly try to make come true, not with this virtual stranger. She couldn't. Definitely could *not.*

But she *could,* perhaps, get some of what she desired from the soothing water. It could touch her. Stroke her. Hold her. Cool her heated body.

"It's a lot more welcoming in the summer than it was last December," he murmured, still not focused on her. The lake seemed to be singing the same siren's song to him as it was to her. He was feeling the mugginess and the heat of the day as much as she was, judging by the sheen of sweat on his face. She could smell the hot earthiness of his body—musky and masculine—and felt herself break out in a sweat, too.

God, they both needed to cool off. Badly. Though for different reasons.

A big part of her wanted to strip out of her clothes and walk naked into all that liquid. A bigger part wondered what he'd do if she did.

Would he watch? Would he join her? And where would it lead?

"You know, all I wanted this morning when I got up was an icy shower after a long, miserable night in a sweatbox."

Sounded like the night she'd had. "You didn't get one?"

"My grandfather had a newspaper emergency."

She didn't ask for details on that strange statement. Instead she kicked off her shoes and walked into the grassy area beside the parking lot. Her bandages might not last long, but she couldn't bring herself to care. She suddenly wanted to soak her aching feet and hot legs more than anything. Even more than she wanted to get over the writer's block that was preventing her from finishing her next book, a situation, she was sure, that was caused by her unwanted phone calls.

"Can't resist, huh?" he asked, following her down the slope.

"I'm desperate."

"Ditto."

They reached the sand of the tiny beach, which was littered with old, dead leaves and broken tree branches. Above them, a few enormous oaks and maples shaded the whole area, keeping the little bit of sunlight out and holding in a moist coolness rising off the lake. Thick moss covered the sides of the tree trunks, soft and spongy, a shade of green so rich it almost hurt the eyes. The air smelled of wet earth and summertime and tasted heady—almost drugging. And the only sounds were the tiny waves lapping at the sand and the drip of raindrops falling off the leaves onto the ground.

It was an intimate place. A secluded, mysterious one that

delighted every one of her senses. And when the water touched her, she knew her sensual delight would be complete.

So she kept walking. Right to the water's edge…and into it. "Ohh," she moaned, tilting her head back and closing her eyes as liquid comfort surrounded her.

"Good?"

"*So* good. Silky smooth and deliciously cold." She wanted to arch and writhe in it, but settled for moving deeper until her calves were wet…then her knees.

God, what she wouldn't give to take off her clothes, toss them to the shore and dive in. She opened her eyes, seriously considering just diving under anyway, her clothes be damned, when she saw Mike's big, hard chest—his big, hard, *bare* chest—right next to her, a few inches from her shoulder.

"I couldn't resist," he said, his voice low and gravelly.

Oh. My. God.

He was naked. This dark and dangerous man she'd been fantasizing about since yesterday had stripped off his clothes and followed her into the lake at this secluded park where he could do anything to her and nobody would hear a thing. Not a yell, not a scream…of pleasure, she had no doubt.

Then she looked down. Damn. He was wearing jeans.

But she still felt like howling in pure joy at just the sight of him. She lifted her gaze, slowly, marveling at his amazing shape. His flat, rippled stomach and trim waist were emphasized by the low-riding, unbelted jeans. The weight of the water was tugging them down and she could easily make out the strip of lighter, untanned skin, below his hips. Where the sun usually didn't reach.

She gulped. Then kept looking.

Layers of muscle across his middle said the man worked

out, and his chest was broader than her kitchen table. The shoulders looked too wide to fit through a doorway, much less into any standard men's clothing.

He was all tan and hard and utterly, mouth-wateringly delicious. Jen clenched her fingers into fists, willing them to behave, not to lift of their own volition and tangle in the dark, curling thatch of hair on his chest.

Unable to resist, she followed that spiky, wiry hair with her gaze, going back down for another hungry examination. She breathed heavier, noting the way it traipsed down his body, over his stomach, and disappeared below his jeans in the middle of that same wickedly tempting line of pale skin just south of his hips.

A line that grew even wider as his wet jeans grew heavier.

There must have been an earthquake because she would lay money that she felt the bottom of the lake moving beneath her. Was she still standing? Was she even breathing? Was she drooling down her chin? She honestly didn't know, she just kept *looking*.

And she suddenly wondered if he'd kept his jeans on because he didn't have anything on underneath them.

Her heart did an outright cartwheel in her chest at that thought, and her thighs shook, almost causing her to fall right on her butt in the lake.

"You okay?" he asked, grabbing her elbow, as if realizing she'd suddenly gone all female and weak-kneed like one of the women she warned women not to be in her books.

"Fine," she said, then had to clear her throat and repeat herself. Because the word had had about as much sincerity as a politician's campaign promises.

He didn't let her go, keeping his grip tight as he stepped

in closer. Close enough that she could see the ridges of his skin, and the individual strands of dark hair swirling around his flat nipples. Even the pucker of an old scar on his shoulder.

"Jen? Are you sure you're all right?"

"Oh, God, no I'm not all right, you're killing me," she finally said, wondering if she sounded as helpless as she felt.

Before he could even ask what she was talking about, she gave up all efforts to be good. To be sane. Instead, she lifted a hand to his chest, stroking the tips of her fingers across that hot skin, following a long, thick ridge of muscle, sliding past the scar. She savored the touch as she lifted her other hand to his head to tangle her fingers in his hair and tug him down. "Taste me," she whispered. "Please."

His eyes flared a tiny bit, but he didn't resist her. His mouth came down on hers, open and hot and hungry. Jen licked at his tongue, needing to sample every bit of him. She arched and he shifted; she tilted her head and he lifted her up.

All without allowing as much as a breath of air to come between their starving lips.

Soon she was completely under his control, her hips in his big, strong hands, the V of her thighs pressed against a rock-hard erection straining against his jeans. At the feel of his response, she started to shake, suspecting she would have fallen if he hadn't been holding her.

They kissed as if they needed each other's mouths to keep their hearts beating: sucking, licking, giving and taking. He tasted sweet and hot and so delicious Jen wanted to cry at how good it felt. When he moved one hand up to cup the bottom of her breast, flicking his fingers over her taut, aching nipple, she didn't want to cry, she wanted to *yell* at the pleasure of it. Yell and howl and moan and beg.

She settled for arching harder into him, silently demanding that he intensify the touch. Swirling her tongue around his in a dance of hot desire, she moaned in satisfaction when he finally tugged her cotton shirt down to reveal her breast. Her lacy bra provided almost no coverage at all, and the feel of his fingertips scraping across her barely concealed nipple—tweaking it, plucking it—nearly sent her out of her mind.

She *wanted* to go out of her mind, to go crazy and wild, and pull him down until he covered her throbbing nipple with that hot mouth and sucked. Hard.

But in a moment, she lost the chance. Because without warning, without any indication that he didn't want to roar forward into sensual bliss, he ended it. He slowly let go of her hip and disentangled his hand from her shirt. Pulled his mouth away. Took a step back.

"No. That's enough." He said the words as if they were drawn out of him by barbed wire. But his stiff form told her he meant it.

He'd kissed her, tasted her, touched her...and *wanted* to stop. How damned pathetic was that?

Only one thing kept her from sinking into the bottom of the lake and drowning herself out of embarrassment. Despite having pulled away, he was feeling every bit as affected as she. She *knew* it.

Though his eyes said no, that they were finished, and he kept shifting away, he was obviously still reeling. Because without another word, he turned and dove completely into the water. He swam out several yards with long, even strokes, as if a big-toothed sea creature were after him.

She wasn't a big-toothed sea creature, but for a moment,

Jen was tempted to chase after him. But she wouldn't. He'd said enough. He'd meant it. They were done.

Done...but not finished. Not by a long shot. Even now she was so on fire, so exploding with hunger that she didn't know how she was going to stand it. She wanted to claw at her own skin to stop the burning and the maddening want. There seemed to be no way to end the frustration.

Suddenly his idea didn't seem so bad. *Get drenched and swim off the intensity.* So without another thought, Jen dove beneath the surface, still in all her clothes, and did exactly that.

IVY FRETTED ALL MORNING, wondering what the girl would do when she got back. Ida Mae had insisted that this time she'd have learned her lesson and would get out of town. But Ida Mae had been wrong yesterday, hadn't she? And she could be again.

Things had been going so well, too. They'd been having a nice breakfast and there'd been all those lovely boys. Then Jennifer had had to start carping on that ridiculous idea of hers that they should move, and Ida Mae had seen red.

Ivy wasn't so mad about it anymore. Oh, she'd never leave here, certainly, but she had taken a peek at those brochures Jennifer had forced on them. At least their niece wasn't trying to dump them in a rat-infested, pee-scented insane asylum. Judging by the dollar figure mentioned on it, the girl had some money to spend, too, and was willing to spend it on *them*.

That had made her feel better, though, not good enough to *want* to see Jennifer yet. She hadn't quite gotten over the desire to box the child's ears for thinking she could tell her elders what to do. But the price tag had, at least, dampened Ivy's urge to kill her. For the time being.

Whether she came back or not, Ivy's knees couldn't take

another day in the cellar, so she sat in her kitchen, sipping tea, peeking out the front window every so often to see if the girl had returned. Perhaps she was again prowling around the house, thinking about breaking a window, but slyly tricking them into believing she'd left just so she could sneak back and use a secret key, as she had yesterday evening.

"My, she does have spunk," Ivy whispered, talking only to herself. Her cat, Holly—who'd originally been named Buddy, until Ivy had found out she was a girl—meandered in, so Ivy turned her attention to her closest companion. "Right, dearie? Spunk and will and wit." Much like Ivy. Which was, perhaps, the reason Ivy had developed a reluctant fondness for the child when she'd been fond of very few other people throughout her life.

Despite how much Ivy had tried to shake her off, the stubborn little thing had stuck close over the years, until there were times when Ivy *almost* forgot she didn't like her. She'd found herself singing with the child, or dancing around the living room. Or even, on one occasion, baking cookies…at least until Ida Mae had come in, seen the jar of *special* powder in Ivy's hand and put a stop to it.

"The girl wouldn't have told anyone," Ivy muttered as she bent to stroke the cat. "Even if she'd known, she would have found a way to protect us, like a true Feeney woman."

Just as she had in her book, when she'd included some of Ivy's own history.

At first, when her niece had asked if she could include the story of Ivy's tumultuous marriage and Leo's murder, Ivy had been horrified. But once she'd thought about it, acknowledging that Jennifer could be discreet and was a talented writer, she'd cooperated. That cooperation had included one of the greatest acts of trust in Ivy's whole life: she'd given over her treasured knitting box full of secrets.

When she'd read the final product, before it was turned in to the publisher, Ivy had scoured for a single incriminating comment and found nothing. Her worries had faded and she'd honestly felt flattered. To think, Jennifer had immortalized *her* in an international bestseller, even if neither Ivy nor Leo had ever been mentioned by name.

The child had been careful to not only keep Ivy's identity secret, she'd made it clear that, despite the provocation of a wretched husband, the woman in the story hadn't actually *killed* anyone. It was an example story Jennifer had used to show why some men just deserved to be put down like the dogs they were. The book made it seem as if Leo's own villainy toward others—not his wife—had brought about his destruction.

"Well, maybe she doesn't know as much as she thinks she does," Ivy whispered in a singsong voice. "Still, she's a strong one, isn't she? Like *me*. We almost like her, don't we?"

Guts. Jennifer had guts—almost enough to deserve the Feeney name, even if she wasn't a true Feeney by blood. And though Ida Mae wouldn't admit it, Ivy knew one thing: Mama would have adored the child. Just as she'd adored Jen's father...Ivan.

They all had. And still did.

"Our darling baby boy," she crooned, watching Holly overcome her aging bones to jump up onto the table. The animal dipped her face into the teacup and lapped at the rapidly cooling liquid.

"Sweet little Ivan...do you ever suspect the truth?"

Even if he had sometimes wondered, surely no one else

had. They'd all played their parts. Ida Mae and Ivy had acted the typical teenagers, embarrassed that their parents had delivered a new baby at such an advanced age. When in truth, all they'd ever done behind closed doors and shuttered windows was rock him, fuss over him and kiss him to bits.

He'd been their source of joy, right up until Ivy had moved away to marry Leo. She knew now that it was for the best. But at the time it had felt as though her heart was being ripped out of her chest at leaving Mama, Ida Mae and that boy.

But there'd been no other choice. Papa had died; Mama had been under suspicion, the whole town knowing she'd threatened to kill him if he was bad again. If anybody had started looking too closely at the Feeney women—and the baby who'd entered their lives when Ida Mae and Ivy had been in high school—they might have learned too much. Such as how the child had been conceived. And what had happened to his father. How he'd *really* died, for instance. "Ida Mae, Ida Mae," she whispered.

A sharp pain stabbed through her brain, making her fingers clench in Holly's fur. "Leave me alone," she mumbled, talking to the pictures in her head that would never be still. She lifted her hands to her face, pressing her fingers against her skull, rubbing away the pressure. So much pressure. So many memories. So much... How could she stand it anymore?

Why couldn't she make all the dark thoughts go away? Could it be because of the ghostly voices she sometimes heard on the phone, calling to accuse her, either in heavy, prolonged silences or in a few spiteful words? Or the feeling she sometimes had that she was being watched by an invisible presence? "Leave me alone," she repeated.

"Are you all right?" a voice asked from behind her.

She looked up, certain she'd see Ida Mae, though the voice had sounded deeper. How her sister could have entered the house and gotten past without being seen, she didn't know…. Ida Mae was a tricky one, all right.

"Fine, fine," she insisted, peering across the room at the figure standing in the shadowy recesses of the hallway.

"You need to stop thinking about it, Ivy. Rest."

That voice…not Ida Mae's. A man's voice. "Leo? Daddy…"

"Take care, Ivy. Take care."

No. Not her horrid husband. Not Daddy. Her heart started fluttering as if it would burst through the finely veined skin of her chest as the truth dawned. *He'd* come again.

"Eddie?" she whispered.

But there was no response. No more words. No more shadow. Nothing. Maybe there never had been.

As usual when the ghosts of her past came to call, Ivy just couldn't be sure.

CHAPTER SIX

> Why is it that when a woman gets ready for a special
> date with her spouse, she buys a new dress, new teddy,
> sexy hose and does the thorough going-to-the-
> gynecologist shave…and he swaps one Mets jersey for
> the other and maybe puts on a clean baseball cap?
> —*I Love You, I Want You, Get Out*, by Jennifer Feeney

JEN DIDN'T KNOW WHICH FELT more uncomfortable during the
nearly silent ride home—her wet clothes or her bruised ego.

Her jean skirt clung to her thighs and grew a size smaller
as it dried, almost cutting off her circulation. Her panties had
climbed between her cheeks and stayed there. Plus her wet
shirt was dripping rivulets of pink-tinged water down her arms
as the dye let go. She imagined her chest and stomach looked
as if she'd fallen asleep in a tanning booth. Her formerly white
bra, every lacy bit of which was revealed under the clinging
cotton fabric of her shirt, would now have to be worn only
under dark colors unless she bleached the heck out of it.

But somehow, *none* of that was as uncomfortable as the realization that she'd just thrown herself into this man's arms,
and he'd thrown her back out.

Big. Strong. Bare arms.

He hadn't bothered putting his shirt on and it was all she could do to keep her eyes looking forward as he drove. She wasn't very successful. Sister Martha, her third-grade teacher, would have looked at the rippling, flexing muscles on this guy. How could the ex–Single in the City girl be expected not to?

"Here we are," he said, his voice low and gruff as he turned into Ida Mae's driveway. They were the first words either of them had spoken since they'd picked their way out of the water and, by silent agreement, immediately gotten into his Jeep. "Are you going to be able to get in?"

"Oh. Sure." Frankly, Jen had been so flustered by the kiss she and Mike had shared that she hadn't even remembered her predicament until now. Funny how an amazing kiss from an incredibly hot guy could drive matters like having her car and wallet stolen by a pair of conniving thieves out of her mind.

Get real. Being kissed by Mike Taylor could probably have driven an impending tsunami out of Jen's mind.

She somehow managed to avoid answering his question with a "Why, no, I have nowhere else to go, why don't you take me to the nearest hotel." He had silently turned her down a half hour ago; why would now be any different? Besides, if she ever tried again to get this man into bed, it would be when she was dressed to kill, not dressed like a rat that had fallen down a sewer drain. "I'm sure they've calmed down."

"Have you?"

"That I'm *not* so sure of. Although our drive certainly did…distract me."

He cleared his throat. "Yeah, me, too. Look, I don't want you to get the wrong idea…"

"What, that you suffered through a kiss from a woman you barely know so you could let her down easy?"

With a snort of disbelief, he shifted to face her. It was then she noticed the heat in his eyes. He raked a thorough look at her from the top of her wet head to the bottoms of her pinkish legs. "Don't think I didn't want to finish what you started."

Yeah. He had. His expression said it all. "Why didn't you?"

His eyes widened, as if he couldn't believe she was being so honest. Well, that was the way Jen had always been. She couldn't change who she was at this late date.

"Do you always say what you think like that?"

She nodded.

"Okay. Then I'll say what I think, too." He reached over and ran the pad of his thumb across her bottom lip, which didn't soften her up, but instead made her tense with hunger. She wanted to bite his finger, and keep on biting and nibbling at him, all the way up that arm. "I wanted to lift your skirt and take you right there in the water."

She almost whimpered.

"But the truth is, I don't know you and you don't know me. I didn't have any kind of protection on me, and even if I had, it would have been wet from the lake. And we're both too old to be that stupid."

Well. Maybe *he* was. She nearly pointed out that "protection" was made to withstand moisture, which she could *so* have provided without any lake water at all. But he wasn't done.

"Plus, I'm not a hundred-percent convinced you're not nuts and I've had enough of nutty women in my life."

Nuts? He thought she was *crazy?* Jen's eyes flew open and her jaw dropped as she thought about that one. Men had called her a bitch before, that was for certain. But insane? She didn't know whether to be insulted or amused.

You have *threatened murder at least a dozen times since you met this guy,* her conscience reminded her. But he had to know she didn't mean it, not any more than Ivy meant it when she threatened to kill the president for scheduling a press conference during *Desperate Housewives.*

Boy. Maybe she was more like her aunts than she'd ever realized. Now wasn't that a scary thought?

"I'm not a black widow spider," she retorted, trying to keep the emotion out of her voice, but judging by the slight tremor, she didn't succeed. "I don't mate and then kill."

He seemed to have realized he'd hurt her feelings. He moved his hand to cup her cheek, sliding his fingers through her wet hair, plucking out a leaf. God, she must look a mess.

"I'm not afraid you're dangerous, okay? That came out wrong. I just meant I don't do the one-night-stand thing with strangers. Not anymore. I don't trust immediately, and believe me when I say I have my reasons for that."

She wanted to know those reasons because the shadow that crossed his features told her they were legitimate ones. Which suddenly made her feel a little better. But before she could ask him about them, the front door of Ida Mae's house opened and the wicked woman herself appeared on the porch. "Jennifer honey? What are you doing? And who's that with you?"

Jen sat back in her seat and gaped. Aliens had invaded while she was gone, and a kindly pod creature had taken over her aunt's body. That was the only way Ida Mae could manage such a sweet tone and such a welcoming smile.

"Why, child, your hair is all wet," the woman said as she

made her way down the steps toward the Jeep. "Come in, come in, before you catch your death of cold."

In the ninety-five-degree heat, yeah, *that* was going to happen. And inside would be worse. Besides, not only did Ida Mae not have air-conditioning, she never opened her windows, either. Jen figured she must be preparing herself for her future in hell.

At least Ivy's house had ceiling fans…not that Jen would sleep under Ivy's roof. Not unless she had a padlock for her door to prevent the old woman from stealing all her jewelry…or smothering her in her sleep as she used to threaten to do when Jen was a child.

Some people aged into their craziness. Ivy had had it going on for as long as Jen had known her.

Which was one of the things that had always made the old woman so darned fascinating.

"That's one of the lunatic aunts?" Mike said, sounding doubtful. "She seems like any other sweet old lady."

Oh, great. Just perfect. Now he almost certainly thought she was nuts and had made up the lunacy that had left her stranded on the road for two days straight. If she didn't already want to strangle Ida Mae for dumping her, she'd definitely want to now for feeding Mike's suspicions that Jen was a little past the loony road sign on the highway of life.

"Remember the fable about the crocodile who played nice in order to eat the trusting frog? Well, believe me, you're looking at a dozen pair of crocodile boots waiting to happen."

"If you say so," he said with a shrug, a smile lurking on his lips, as if he might be teasing her.

She knew better. This man didn't tease, at least not verbally. Physically was another story. Because if a woman had kissed the breath out of a man and then launched away from him, she would definitely be called a tease.

"Who is your friend?" Ida Mae asked, still smiling. It was a wonder her face didn't crack from the effort.

"I'd better go. If I introduce you, she'll have you in for tea and cookies and you're better off never having my aunts' tea and cookies."

He glanced down. "I'm not dressed for visiting anyway."

Without another word, Jen hopped out of the Jeep. Somehow, she managed to avoid choking on her heart as she watched him drive away.

Okay. *Heart* was a stretch. Her libido was what went into overdrive whenever she thought about that kiss in the water. And she had a feeling it would be revved up for a long time....

WHEN MIKE GOT BACK to the house, he hoped he'd be able to slip right up to his room, grab a change of clothes, then hit the shower. He didn't want to answer any questions, such as why he was barefoot and shirtless. Why his hair was wet...not to mention his jeans.

But luck wasn't on his side. The minute he stepped into the house, carefully pushing the front door closed behind him, he was startled by the braying of a stupid cuckoo clock—one of the few remaining ones that had come with the house—right beside his head. He instinctively jerked, dropping his boots.

And obviously getting his grandfather's attention.

"There you are!" Mortimer called as he emerged from his office. "Did you have a nice time?" He looked Mike over, from head to toe. "Oh. Got caught in a bit of a rainstorm, did you?"

Yeah. Sure. Rain. He'd just stripped shirtless and done a

barefoot dance in the rain, which was the only way he should be as sopping wet as he was. His jeans were sticking to him, clinging as tightly as if they'd been shrink-wrapped. Worse, despite the lapse of ten minutes since he'd dropped Jen off at her aunt's house, his hard-on hadn't diminished one bit.

He honestly didn't know how he'd been able to get into a sitting position in the wet jeans considering his dick was practically bursting out of his pants. It had been that way since the moment he'd noticed that woman devouring him with her stare in the lake. Kissing her—it had been amazing. Intense. So damn good.

But ending it had been wise. Smart.

So damn painful.

He'd regret it, he knew that much. Hell, he *already* regretted it. But he knew he'd done the right thing. He wasn't here to hook up with a woman, no matter how much he wanted her. Not so soon—not until he'd at least decided whether he could trust her or not. After all, Jennifer Feeney had been threatening murder one day ago.

"Must have been a downpour, you're quite drenched, boy."

Thankfully, Mortimer wasn't wearing his glasses. And the wet fabric of his jeans should disguise any, uh, unusual bulges. So if he wanted to think Mike had been caught in a storm to rival Noah's, that was okay by him.

"You look like you've just climbed out of a well, much like I had to when I leapt into one to avoid some Nazi soldiers scouting the French countryside. That was right after D-day, when Rod and I first met, both of us having lost the rest of our platoons during our jumps."

He knew how the two men had met—both of them being paratroopers, Mortimer for the U.S. and Roderick for the

Brits. From what it had sounded like, they'd saved each other's lives that day…and many more days after.

"Roddy was so young, just a boy, really, having lied about his age to enlist. But his French helped us avoid getting shot."

Mortimer's expression grew wistful; he was winding up to tell a tale. Normally, Mike loved to hear them. If Grandpa wanted to relive his days with soldiers, bandits, harem girls and Bedouins, Mike had no problem with it…when he was dry.

And not totally turned on by the memory of a sexy brunette in a soaking-wet pink top. The one that had clung to her full breasts and outlined her hard nipples so much he couldn't keep his eyes off them. In fact, he'd barely been able to keep the Jeep on the road during the silent ten-minute drive back to her place after their impromptu swim.

"I must tell you all about it," Mortimer said, clapping his hands together in anticipation.

"Absolutely, Grandpa. Once I'm changed, all right?"

He truly couldn't think of a better way to spend an afternoon than listening to the old man's stories of his life. Well, perhaps with the exception of going for another swim with Jennifer Feeney. With no clothes at all, this time.

Uh-uh. No time for that. No time to get to know her enough to trust her. No time to trust her enough to have her.

Unless… Unless he looked her up back in the city. Which suddenly sounded like the best idea he'd had all year. He smiled at the thought, certain he'd be able to track her down. Sometimes being a cop came in very handy.

Until then, stories and a few beers with Mortimer would do pretty well. The man had more tales to tell than anyone else he'd ever known, and his adventures were legendary, even, as recently as last year, when he'd been briefly kidnapped by two… "Old ladies," he muttered, suddenly going still.

"What?"

Shit. *Old ladies.* How on earth hadn't he realized it sooner? "I can't believe this," he whispered, his mind spinning as he put everything together. Jen's crazy, horny old aunts. The terrifying two days his grandfather had gone missing last year. Connected?

"What was that?" Mortimer asked.

"What were the names of those two women who drugged you and kept you tied up last year?" *In their bedroom.*

Mortimer's bushy brows pulled down in a fierce glare. "I told you before, I'm not telling. I don't want you doing your police thing, it was a misunderstanding."

Sure. A misunderstanding.

His brother's frantic messages about Mortimer's disappearance last summer had scared Mike so much, he'd come running as soon as he could. As had Morgan—who'd come all the way from Cairo. Only to find Mortimer grinning like a high-school football player laid by the whole cheerleading squad.

"I wasn't an unwilling participant," Mortimer insisted.

Mike gritted his teeth, well used to the argument. He had tried everything from pleading to browbeating to get the old man—or even his brother, Max—to give him enough information to go after Mortimer's kidnappers legally. But Mortimer was stubborn. He'd refused to even name the women, and had threatened Max with a decade's worth of the silent treatment if he did. He'd also donated new office equipment to the local police just so Mike couldn't get any help there, either.

"I'm not asking in an official capacity," Mike said, trying to keep calm. "I simply want to know their last name."

Mortimer kept frowning, appearing suspicious.

"You know I'm working cold cases now, Grandpa, in another state. There's nothing I can do to them." As much as he'd like to. "I give you my word."

"Well, that's a different story, then. I know your word is good." The old man had the audacity to smile. "I shared a few exciting days with the always delightful Feeney sisters."

"*Feeney.*" He stared in shock at his grandfather.

It was true. Jen's aunts had been the ones who'd drugged and kidnapped his grandfather for a geriatric orgy.

"Those two lunatics are still on the loose?"

"Ida Mae and Ivy are a danger only to themselves."

"And their niece," he mumbled.

But Mortimer's hearing, like his vision, was sharper than he liked to let on. He immediately stepped closer. "Their niece? What do you know about her?"

"I know they stranded her out in the middle of nowhere and I had to drive her into town last night. Then they ditched her again this morning, so I had to give her another ride."

Mike didn't add that he'd given her a little more than that in the lake. And a *lot* more than that in his long, restless dreams the previous night.

It was probably a good thing he hadn't known the identity of her maniacal aunts. If he had, he might have taken Jen's death threats a whole lot more seriously—not only because he suspected they'd drive anyone to murder, but also because crime obviously ran in that family. As, it seemed, did insanity.

He suddenly rethought his idea of looking her up in the city. Mike had had quite enough of crazy, determined women who didn't let anything stand in the way of what they wanted. The way Jen had taken what she'd wanted today in the lake proved she was as determined as she said she was. And just about everything else she'd said or done since he'd met her told him she was a little crazy, too.

"Pretty, isn't she?"

"Very," he replied before thinking about it. Then he narrowed his eyes. "Don't even think about trying that matchmaking crap on me, Grandpa. Max put up with it. I won't."

Mortimer brought a hand to his chest, his mouth dropping open, as if shocked at the idea. Mike recognized it as complete acting. "I mean it."

"Oh don't be ridiculous. The girl's not your type at all."

Right.

"You wouldn't be interested."

Of course not.

"You have nothing in common."

Not a damn thing.

"And she's much too strong."

Mike flinched. "What's that supposed to mean?"

"Well, I thought you liked more…biddable girls."

He wasn't exactly sure what *biddable* meant, but it didn't sound good. "How do you know what kind of *women* I like?"

"There was the one you brought to Easter dinner a few years back." Mortimer crossed to the window and peered outside, not appearing terribly interested in their conversation. "I almost mistook her for a costumed rabbit who entertained children, she was so silent and colorless, with those pinkish eyes."

"She was a kindergarten teacher." A pale one.

Mortimer nodded, as if his point had been proved.

"I've dated other women. And I've got the scars to prove it," he added, his hand rising to his shoulder. Mike rubbed the scar there, still almost able to feel the bullet going in, remembering his complete disbelief at what was happening.

"But it wasn't your girlfriend who shot you, was it?" his grandfather asked. "She was a tiny little thing who you met after she'd witnessed a crime, if I'm not mistaken. Yes?"

Mike didn't like to think about that part of the whole mess. He'd been stupid to get involved with a witness in need of protection. Maybe he'd deserved what had happened later for breaking such a basic rule of law enforcement. "Yes."

"She baked cookies that were hard enough to break my dentures," Mortimer said, shaking his head in disapproval. "And she was so sweet she made my few remaining *real* teeth ache."

Mike couldn't help grinning. His grandfather had very specific tastes in women. From what he'd heard, his grandmother had been hell on wheels. As had the two other women Grandpa had married after his first wife had died giving birth to Mike's mother.

"Her strange *friend* was the one with the gun, wasn't she?"

Mike couldn't deny it. Mortimer knew the whole story—he'd been right there for Mike at the hospital.

Whenever Mike had ever envisioned himself taking a bullet, he'd figured it would be doing something important. Stopping a bank robber, a suspected killer. *Not* diving between a psycho slut and his girlfriend, whom she blamed for Mike's lack of interest in *her*. Hell hath no fury, and didn't he know it. The guys at work loved reminding him of it.

"Well? Am I right?" Mortimer prodded.

"You think I should have been dating the one with the gun?"

"Never underestimate the attraction of a dangerous woman."

Like Jennifer Feeney, who'd been armed and threatening murder when he'd met her. All the more reason to stay away from the woman. He'd had enough to do with unbalanced females to last his whole life. And judging by her aunts, there was a serious lack of balance in that family.

"But I know you do like your shrinking violets."

Mike snorted. "I don't like weak women."

"No," his grandfather conceded. "You just like the ones who *need* something from you. Like protection."

Grandpa watched closely as Mike thought about his words. He'd heard them before. "You've been talking to Max and Morgan."

"Enough to be quite sure young Miss Feeney isn't your type… She's no wilting flower." A concerned frown tugged at the old man's brow. Lifting a hand to his grizzled chin, he rubbed it and mumbled under his breath.

"What?"

"Oh, nothing. Just…something about the girl. Something her aunts mentioned."

That she's feisty and tough and hot with skin like silk and a mouth made for pleasure?

"She seems to have attracted some negative attention through her work. Not that it's any of *your* concern, of course."

Mike had a feeling he was being played. But he still wanted to know more. Because usually, even in Mortimer's wildest fabrications, there was some kernel of truth to be found. You simply had to dig for it. "What are you talking about?"

His grandfather walked away. "I shouldn't have said anything. Just threats, I'm sure, because of her fame. Or infamy."

That really got his attention and he followed, not caring that he dripped water across the foyer. "Would you stop pretending you don't want to tell me what it is you're talking about and spill it?"

Mortimer paused in the doorway to his office and turned around, his eyes widened in innocence. Mike believed that about as much as he believed his grandfather didn't occasionally sneak out to smoke cigars against the doctor's strict orders. "You mean you didn't recognize her?"

He'd asked her if she was an actress. She'd said no...but maybe she was trying to hide her identity. "No."

"She's a famous—notorious some would say—writer. She's had a couple of very funny, slightly racy advice-to-women books that poke fun at men."

Perfect. A man hater. That explained why she'd been so prickly at first. But she'd warmed up, he reminded himself. She'd been funny and sarcastic. Good-natured. Even a little emotional, if he hadn't been mistaken about the suspicious shine in her eyes yesterday.

Then she'd been charming and sassy this morning. And at the lake? Unbelievably—heart-stoppingly—sensual.

A complex woman, that one.

"A few fellows haven't gotten the joke," Mortimer said, though Mike had almost stopped listening. "She started getting threats after appearing on one of those national morning talk shows and being interviewed in the *Times* book section."

He tensed. "Threats?"

"Hate mail, that sort of thing," Mortimer said with an airy wave of his hand. But he soon frowned. Almost as if speaking to himself, he mumbled, "The phone calls on her unlisted number are worrisome because whoever it is must know where she lives."

That got his attention. He didn't know which shocked him more—that she was famous enough to appear on one of those gabby, coffee-and-goofy-weather-guy-laden talk shows. Or that someone had actually stalked and threatened her.

He definitely knew which *bothered* him more. Damned if he could stand the thought of anyone hurting her. The cop in him stiffened at the thought. The man who'd had her in his arms an hour ago absolutely seethed at it.

"But, no worries, I'm sure," Grandfather said, "I imagine it'll all blow over soon. Surely no one would follow her here to Trouble." Turning again, he walked through the open doorway, saying over his shoulder, "Now, why don't you go get cleaned up before Roderick yells at us both for dirtying the floor?"

Mike slowly did as his grandfather asked. He showered, got cleaned up and dressed. But throughout every minute his mind remained on Jen.

She was from a family that was entirely bad news. She was potentially dangerous…physically, when it came to her aunts. Even more, she posed a danger to him emotionally. Because he already wanted her way too much for his own peace of mind.

So he needed to stay away from her. Period. End of story.

Which wasn't going to be easy since he fully intended to make sure no stalking nut job laid a stinking hand on her.

FOR THE LIFE OF HER, JEN COULD not understand why Aunt Ida Mae was being so nice. After what had happened at the fire hall, she'd expected her to be anything but. Yet for some reason, the old woman had been ridiculously friendly, smiling enough to crack her face since Jen had gotten back to the house yesterday afternoon.

Taking an ice-cold shower in an effort to cool off both physically and mentally, Jen had kept an eye out for an electric hair dryer to come flying into the tub. She'd dried off carefully, too, wondering if Ida Mae had put a snake or a poisonous spider in the towel. After all, why else would her aunt be nice to her, except to get her to let her guard down so she could whammy her again? Even Ivy had come over, in one of her sunny phases, all soft and genteel as if she'd stepped out of a Tennessee Williams novel.

Jen had been watchful and jumpy all evening, wondering what they were up to. It was like being in a haunted house only the undead zombies were real. And their names were Ida Mae and Ivy.

The surreal quality of the evening had been complete when the two sisters had insisted on pulling out a photo album to coo over pictures of Jen's father, Ivan—their adored baby brother—when he was a boy. From the stories her father told, the two of them had left Trouble shortly after their own father had died and had seldom visited, so she didn't completely buy this beloved older sister crap. But they put on a good show.

That didn't mean Jen was letting down her guard. She'd gone to bed certain the ceiling was going to cave in because they'd placed a pile of cinder blocks over her bed. But somehow, she'd survived the night. Not that she'd slept. Everything had been so normal, it had scared the hell out of her, leaving her restless and anxious.

Or maybe that had just been her thoughts about Mike Taylor. What he'd looked like without his shirt. What he'd *felt* like without his shirt. The way he'd tasted. Lord have mercy.

She'd eventually drifted off, and when she'd woken up safe and sound this morning, she'd *almost* felt guilty. She half regretted her pessimism toward the aunts, because they truly seemed to have calmed down about things and wanted to make amends. Throughout the previous day, nobody had brought up the "misunderstandings" and Jen hadn't said the words *assisted-living center* once. Everybody had been so nice, they might almost have been a normal family having a normal visit.

Then, a few minutes ago, she'd figured it all out.

"You mean Mr. Potts called yesterday and invited us all over for a dinner party this evening?" Jen asked, in as innocent a voice as she could manage. Meanwhile, in her head, she was thinking, *You sly devils*.

"Why yes, that's right," Ida Mae said, her tone so offhand, anyone who didn't know her might think she didn't care a bit.

"A party, how charming," Ivy added.

Ida Mae and Ivy were sitting across from her at Ida Mae's kitchen table, sipping weak coffee and munching on burned toast. You'd think for two women raised in a small town by a mother who was, supposedly, fabulous in the kitchen, they'd have learned a little something about cooking. The only thing they made really well, though, were their special cookies and spiced tea. And Jen knew enough about the aunts to not even think about consuming those. One never knew what spices were in the tea…or what ingredients were in the cookies. When in one of her moods, Ivy had been known to reminisce about her knowledge of poison.

She was joking, right? She had to be joking.

Or…maybe not. The stories of Ivy's involvement in the early rock-and-roll scene indicated she'd been a wild woman of high passions once upon a time. With lovers and scandals and, possibly, murder in her past. The kind of woman who, despite her age, had fit right into Jen's books about how crazy a man could make a woman. Crazy enough to kill.

Ivy's wild life had even helped inspire Jen to write her most recent book, about how much better it was to be widowed than divorced. Her aunt's first husband had apparently been a real slimeball. Ivy's own diaries as well as articles, correspondence and photographs had proved that.

The research Jen had done when working on her book had turned up a lot on Leo Cantone and his socialite wife. Archived articles and interviews showed Ivy had once been quite famous. Her husband had been connected to everyone in the music business—some he'd represented, many he'd ripped off. The man had been almost universally hated before he'd been murdered.

Even by his wife, judging by Ivy's journals.

Speaking of which, she couldn't believe Ivy had so calmly accepted that Jen hadn't brought her knitting box back with her this trip.

Usually Ivy clung to that box as if someone was trying to cut off one of her limbs. All Jen could figure was that the elderly woman had *really* liked being included in the book, even though her identity had been shielded. Didn't matter— Ivy knew the truth, and in her mind, the rest of the world had probably spent the past few months trying to figure out who the glamorous music producer's wife had been.

Whatever the case, Jen didn't completely write off her concerns about Ivy. Just like a woman didn't write off the hair standing up on the back of her neck when she walked to her car alone at night. The chances that something would happen were slim…but you never knew.

The problem was, she constantly kept you off guard. Ivy could be charming. And even fun…as she'd sometimes been when she'd grabbed Jen's hands and danced her around the room. The old woman had taught Jen the twist when she was twelve...*then* she'd threatened to toss her in the garbage heap if she didn't go away.

Scary. The woman could turn on a dime. Hadn't something like that happened less than thirty minutes ago? Ivy had been humming a top-twenty pop tune from the eighties. Jen had joined right in, the two of them singing a duet as they'd made coffee, just like a normal family. Afterward, Ivy had giggled and smiled at her.

Then *wham.* A shadow had crossed the woman's face and she'd angrily demanded to know how Jen knew *her* special song. As if she were the only person in the world who could have known the words to a tune that probably played once a day on every oldies music station in the country.

She was strange. Unpredictable. And judging from the research Jen had done into her aunt's history, possibly dangerous.

But now she was merely excited. "Isn't that lovely?" Ivy said, clapping her hands together. "Imagine, a party at the home of the wealthiest man in town. And the handsomest."

Ida Mae stared her into silence. "He knows you're here, Jennifer, and he most especially wants you to come with us, to celebrate his grandson's visit."

Aha. That explained it. Mr. Potts was their Mr. Dreamy and McSteamy from *Grey's Anatomy,* all rolled into one, and he had invited them to his house. But he wanted Jen there, too.

For a brief moment, she allowed herself to think he'd extended the invitation at Mike's request, because of what had happened yesterday at the lake. However, she knew that couldn't be the case. Ida Mae had been nice to her from the minute she'd gotten back yesterday...before Mike could even have spoken to his grandfather. The call had to have come in earlier. Otherwise, she figured, her stuff would have been all over the driveway again.

"We-ell…" she said, drawing out the tone as if regretting her refusal, "I really had planned to leave this afternoon. It's a long drive to the city."

"Oh, don't be ridiculous, child," Ida Mae said.

Ivy was more direct. "You can't leave. Mr. Potts wants you there. You'll ruin *everything*."

She managed an innocent look. "What do you mean by that?"

Ida Mae glared at her sister and Ivy picked up a piece of toast and shoved it in her mouth. Her jaw and scrawny neck worked frantically as she chewed, stuffing more crumbly bread between her lips to prevent herself from saying another word.

"Now, dear," Ida Mae said, her tone mild, "we haven't had a moment to be social since you got here last week."

"Maybe because you keep dumping me in the middle of nowhere and stealing my car," Jen murmured as she lifted her coffee mug.

Ida Mae shrugged. "Oh, that."

Yeah. That.

"You know, I am afraid we might have overreacted. You did say you were merely making a suggestion, isn't that right?"

Jen put down her mug and met Ida Mae's hard stare. "Yes. That's exactly what I said, and I *meant* it. So you didn't have to physically abuse me."

"Abuse," Ivy muttered. "Such a strange child."

"Silly misunderstandings," Ida Mae insisted.

Jen wished she'd had somebody to place a bet with on that explanation. She'd known that was what they'd say. "Uh-huh. Right."

"And now that we understand one another, perhaps it would be best for you to remain in Trouble for a day or two, in case we have any questions regarding the brochures you gave us. We will give them our fullest consideration."

How someone could have so much bullshit in their mouth and not choke on it amazed Jen. It was all she could do not to laugh. Ida Mae behaved as if this whole conversation had *nothing* to do with the fact that they wanted something from her.

"So, what do you think? Will you stay and explain more to us about this 'luxury resort for seniors' as you call it?"

Luxury resort might be stretching it a bit. So maybe Ida Mae wasn't the only one capable of spitting out bullshit.

"And then we can all go to the nice party this evening?" Ivy piped in, almost bouncing in her chair with excitement. "I have the loveliest new hat I can wear and I'm sure Ida Mae can find something to hide those fat legs."

Ida Mae came up out of her chair and leaned over her sister. "Take that back, you bald-headed—"

"Ahem." Jen wiped her mouth with her napkin, not wanting to see these two go at each other, even if it meant they left *her* alone. "I suppose I could delay my return home for another day."

But a party at Mike's grandfather's house. Could she *really* do that? Even to keep the peace and get her way with the aunts? After what had happened... The way he'd pulled away, then dumped her in the driveway. Was she up to it?

"And we'll all go to the party?" Ivy asked, her soft tone completely contradicted by the sparkle of interest in her eyes.

She sounded like a little girl who wanted to wear her best dress and visit her favorite playmates. Innocent. Vulnerable. Childlike. The Ivy who'd sometimes twirl around her parlor, talking to invisible friends and the ghosts of long-dead lovers.

Who'd smile and flirt with imaginary beaux and had filled Jen's head with the images of her wild and exciting youth.

What a woman she must have been.

"Yes," Jen said, not even sure why she was agreeing. Was it just to placate her relatives so they'd consider her offer? To have the chance to see Mike one more time?

Or maybe, strange as the possibility seemed, simply to make an old woman happy?

Honestly, she didn't know. She only knew that for the rest of the day, while she helped her aunts wash and press their best dresses, loaning Ivy a pair of gold earrings she knew she'd never see again, she began to feel a fluttering in her stomach. And as she picked out something of her own to wear—torn between a sweet yellow silk number and a bitch-red dress cut down to there and up to here, she thought about what he'd said in the car.

She and Mike were going to spend an evening together. A nice get-to-know-you evening, which meant they really wouldn't be strangers. And her aunts were on their best behavior, so the three of them would appear like nice, normal, non-nutty women.

So, not strangers. Not nutty. What, from his list of no-no's, would Mike have left to worry about?

She began to hum the same tune she'd been singing with Ivy that morning, wondering how the woman came up with her strange notions. Such as that she'd been the inspiration for a love song more popular than the theme from *The Bodyguard*.

Oh, to live in a fantasy world of the past, if only in your mind. It wasn't such a bad way to spend the final years of a long and exciting life, now was it? Compared to the quiet sadness of the world in which Ivy lived now, Jen didn't blame her aunt one bit for retreating into dreamland now and again.

A fantasy world... Was that what *she* was living in when she thought about what might happen tonight? How crazy was it to think Mike would look at her across a crowded room at the dinner party, lose all doubt, stop second-guessing the intense attraction they were both feeling...and do something about it?

Crazy or not, it was worth a shot.

With that in mind, Jen got ready, knowing tonight she would do whatever she could to get Mike Taylor to stop seeing her as a woman to avoid. And instead acknowledge her as the woman he wanted to go to bed with. She could start with her dress.

So, decision made. Bitch-red it was.

CHAPTER SEVEN

You ever wonder why a boy is so close to his mother?
It's because she's the only woman in the world who will
wipe his face, kiss his ass, laugh at his penis jokes and
think he's the most handsome man on the face of the
earth. Well, until the day he gets married and his wife
feels that way.
That lasts about 18 hours.
—*I Love You, I Want You, Get Out* by Jennifer Feeney

SHE WAS DRESSED FOR SIN.

When Mike caught sight of Jen walking into the house with
her two elderly aunts, he nearly fell down the rest of the stairs.
He'd been coming from his room, having changed out of his
jeans and put on the only nice pair of slacks he'd brought with
him. Mortimer seemed so damned excited about this stupid
dinner party, Mike hadn't been able to refuse.

He'd been looking forward to it for one reason: so he'd
have the chance to put the fear of God into those two Feeney
women, making sure they never tried to kidnap his grandfather again.

Not because of their niece. Not a chance.

Then he saw Jen standing in the foyer. All his certainty fled faster than a drug dealer who spied a marked cop car.

She wore a glittering red number that was cut low in the front, lower in the back and was short enough to fall about five inches south of heaven.

He should have told his grandfather to forget the whole evening. It had been hard enough to think about not having her when he pictured her in that wet skirt and top yesterday. Seeing her tonight—dressed like a woman created straight out of a man's fantasy playbook? He might as well just call ahead to the torture chamber and have them light up the fires. Because having made the decision that he was only going to get involved with her enough to make sure she was physically safe, looking and not touching was going to be the worst kind of torture imaginable.

So touch!

It couldn't happen. For several reasons, beyond the fact that she wasn't his type. She was related to people who made the Osbournes look like an average family. There was also the fact that his grandfather already adored her. Mortimer was trying to set them up, no doubt about it. But Mortimer would *kill* him if Mike stuck to his get-to-know, do-and-go routine when it came to women.

Then again, he probably wouldn't need to kill him—this particular woman seemed perfectly capable of it all on her own. She sure had the balls for it. Especially judging by her book, which he'd started reading last night. His grandfather had given him a copy of it, cautioning him to read it in the humorous light in which it was intended and not take it seriously.

If anybody took the book seriously, Jennifer Feeney would probably be in jail. Because the whole thing was about why women wanted to murder their husbands…and how they got away with it. It was also very well written. And *very* funny.

The moment he'd realized he could be in big trouble was when he'd acknowledged that—despite their short relationship and what he'd said to her in the car about them being strangers—he already knew her well. Better than women he'd dated for months. He could hear her voice speaking every word she'd written, and could predict the tone she'd use and the expressions on her face.

After putting the book down at around 1:00 a.m., he'd thought only of her for another long, hot night.

That, he knew, was the biggest problem of all: he was falling for a woman he'd only known a few days and had only kissed once. *Falling.* Not just wanting.

If it had merely been desire, he'd have had another sex dream and woken up with a hard-on. Instead, he'd slept hardly at all. He'd lain awake, picturing her face, hearing her sassy voice, replaying every conversation they'd had. And remembering their kiss in the lake. That *had,* eventually, given him a hard-on he'd had to take care of in the shower at the crack of dawn.

So, proof. Jen Feeney was no good for his nights, no good for his days, no good for *him.* No matter how much he wanted her.

"Good evening," Mortimer said, not noticing Mike at the top of the stairs. He pressed a kiss on the cheeks of the two elderly women. His grandfather also kissed Jen. Taking her hands, he pulled back and gave her a thorough once-over. "Miss Feeney, you are as lovely as your aunts."

She smiled and murmured something in return, so she didn't see the frowns on the faces of her relatives. They obviously didn't like competing for his grandfather's attention.

The way the skinny one was glaring at Jen, he hoped she had a bulletproof vest on under that dress.

Honestly, though, there was absolutely no way on this earth it would have fit. Because the red fabric clung to every inch of Jennifer's body, revealing every line, every indentation, every incredible curve. Though he'd been about to walk down the stairs to join them, Mike remained where he was for a second, to get a grip on himself. He tried to keep his attention off the young Feeney female and focus only on the older two. The criminals.

The one who'd glared the hardest—Ivy he'd heard Mortimer call her—was also the more whimsical looking of the two. From the broad hat that looked like a florist had thrown up on it to the yellow dress that appeared made of a hundred silky handkerchiefs, she seemed to have stepped off the cover of a 1958 issue of *Life Magazine*.

What he could see of her hair, beneath the horrible hat, was a puffy light gray, curled in thin, wispy ringlets beside her face. She appeared to float on a cloud as she moved, her hands waving languidly in the air and her half smile probably meant to be mysterious. The adoring expression on her heavily made-up face, now that her attention had returned to his grandfather, matched the quivery lightness of her voice.

The second sister—the one he'd seen when dropping Jen off—was sturdy and dour. With a stern expression on her square-jawed face, and a solid body clad in a dark, severe dress, she was her sister's opposite. But at least she wasn't wearing a hat, and her brilliantly shiny white hair seemed to catch his grandfather's eye because he commented on it more than once.

Which obviously annoyed the other one. Ivy had secretly pinched Ida Mae twice since they'd arrived. She'd gotten two pokes in return. All the while, they kept up a running stream of chatter, so nobody would guess what was happening. But Mike had a great vantage point from above and he saw every wicked exchange.

How, he wondered, could these two be the dangerous pre-dators he'd been picturing for the past year? They were more like a set of squabbling fifth graders.

Sighing, Mike returned his attention to the third Feeney woman. She was positioned right below him, giving him a perfect visual shot right down the low neckline of her dress. He tried to rise above his baser instincts to peek.

Baser instincts won.

Lord almighty, did he need a drink. Or food. Something to fill his hands, which were clenched and hot with the need to tear her dress down the middle. He wanted nothing more than to savor that tight line of cleavage where her breasts met and hugged one another like a pair of long-lost twins.

He wanted them hugging his face.

"Now, ladies, shall we go in and have a nice drink?" Mortimer wagged a finger at Ida Mae. "A little birdie told me you're not the teetotaler you made yourself out to be last summer. I could have used a drink then, you know."

Ivy tittered as her sister pinkened. "Well, maybe a tiny one," Ida Mae said. "Bourbon. Neat. Make it a double."

"I'll have a rum punch," Ivy purred. And the two of them linked arms with Mortimer, who led them away from the front door. He pinched Ivy's cheek here and Ida Mae's backside there as he accompanied them into the living room.

Jen didn't follow. She'd caught sight of Mike standing on the stairs and remained by herself, waiting for him.

"Hello," she murmured as he slowly descended, left with no alternative now that he'd been spotted.

"Hi." Staring toward the living room where the giddy voices of the ladies could be heard above Mortimer's low chuckles, he shook his head. "Those are your aunts, huh?"

She nodded. "In all their glory. Ida Mae's crocodile smiles yesterday? All about tonight's invitation."

She seemed to be trying to make sure he hadn't bought the old woman's act. She needn't have bothered. Once he'd discovered who her aunts really were, he'd remembered every wicked thing his brother and grandfather had said about them.

He wondered if she knew about last year's episode. Probably not. She wouldn't have come here tonight if she knew they were being entertained by her aunts' former kidnapping victim. "How'd they get you to agree to come?"

"Quid pro quo, Clarice," she said in a throaty imitation of Hannibal Lecter.

Damn, she'd already started tugging that smile out of him and she'd only been here five minutes.

"Just, you know, reminding you that I'm certifiable."

"Sorry about that," he mumbled, meaning it.

She acknowledged his apology with a slight nod. "They wanted to come so badly they were willing to agree to at least look over the brochures I brought."

He raised a skeptical brow. "You do know they'll toss them in the incinerator thirty seconds after they get home tonight."

With a confident grin, she said, "Yep. Which is why I made them do it before we came. We actually had a fairly civil conversation about it and I convinced them I'm not going to lock them in a prison or sell them to a brothel."

Mumbling, "They'd probably like the brothel," under his breath, he cast a slow, leisurely look over Jen. She had her shiny brown hair up in a twist that looked complicated as hell.

But he knew it would be down around her face within two seconds if he slipped his hands into it.

The halter dress that had merely been sexy from above was downright wicked close up. Tight enough to stop his breath. Low enough to stop his heart. Short enough to *start* everything else. Especially the uniquely male everythings.

"You look beautiful," he muttered, unable to help it.

Her eyes widened in surprise. He understood the reaction…. Mike wasn't the type to throw compliments at women. Since he suspected Jen already knew him as well as he knew her, she had to have realized that.

"You look good, too," she admitted, staring at the open neck of his dress shirt, then dropping her gaze down his body. She didn't try to disguise her interest. Just as she hadn't tried to disguise it yesterday at the lake. "*Very* good. I like you in jeans, but you do some *fine* things for a pair of pricy trousers."

She was forthright and honest. Tough and funny. And so far out of his league they weren't even playing the same sport.

His grandfather and brothers were right. He liked his women easy…. Not easy in terms of how fast they'd spread their legs, but easy in personality. Someone who would destress him at the end of a tough day. Not someone challenging. Not threatening. And yeah, okay, maybe a little bit in need.

Jen was so obviously the opposite of those things, he had no idea why she'd gotten so far under his skin. He only knew he needed to pluck her out and forget about her.

But she's in danger.

Right. She might be. After reading some of her book, he understood why some guys with no confidence, no sense of humor and even less intelligence wouldn't get the joke. So despite knowing he should get away from her, he needed to stay close. To make sure she *let* him stay close.

That, he was certain, was the *only* reason he reached out to cup her beautiful face in his hand and brushed a soft kiss on her lips.

It was just his bad luck that she didn't want soft. She wanted hard and deep.

She immediately collapsed into him, her arms twining around his neck, one slim thigh sliding between his. Unable to resist, Mike parted his lips, taking the deeper kiss she was offering, giving it back to her ten times over. Her mouth was sweet and hot and she met every thrust of his tongue, tilting her head to mate their lips together more perfectly.

He should stop. He was going to stop. Soon. Any second now.

But instead, he blazed forward, forgetting every reason she was all wrong for him. At this moment, she was completely right.

Dropping his hands to her waist, he tugged her even tighter against him. The hard tips of her breasts scraped his chest, the fabric of their clothes only heightening the intensity of it.

Mike brushed his fingers over the base of her spine, revealed by the low-cut dress. Her satiny skin immediately cooled his hot hands, and he had to touch her even more, flattening a palm over the small of her back. As they continued making love with their mouths, all thought disappeared—the old folks in the next room disappeared, the house disappeared. There was only heat and softness, exchanged breaths and tiny gasps.

The initial frenzy slowly gave way to a more sensual, sultry pace. Still licking into her mouth, tasting the edges of her teeth, feeling the softness of her tongue, he lowered his hand. Letting his fingers dip below the hem of the dress, he toyed with the lacy edge of her panties, almost groaning when he realized a lacy edge was all there was to them. She was wearing a thong and he'd bet big money that it was a red one.

God, how he wanted to find out. He was dying to push her back, through the half-open door into Mortimer's shadowy office onto his big leather couch. Or the matching wingback chair. His cock was ready to rupture his zipper as he pictured her on that chair, her legs draped over each side, her dress hiked up to her waist. And him using his teeth to remove that tight, damp thong from the curly slit between her thighs.

"I hope this isn't how he says hello to all his female guests," an unfamiliar—but amused—male voice said, banishing the sinful images from his mind.

Mike immediately removed his hands from Jen's gorgeous backside, but as he did so, he got one finger tangled in the elastic of her thong, accidentally yanking it. "Oh, my God," she whispered as they pulled their mouths apart to see a trio of people standing in the open doorway.

One of them—a young woman holding a baby—he recognized as Sabrina's sister, Allie. On one side of her stood a pretty gray-haired lady, and on the other side a tall, lean, dark-haired guy. All four of them—including the kid—were watching the spectacle he and Jen were making of themselves. And all were grinning.

"I'm stuck," he whispered as Jen tried to wriggle away from him, her face now turning as red as her dress.

"Yeah, I figured that out since I'm the one getting my ass flossed," she hissed back. Her eyes wide, she began sucking big gulps of air in through her swollen, luscious lips.

Finally, with a toss of her curly hair, Allie broke the silence.

"So, Mike, do you need some help getting your hand out of your friend's underwear?"

THERE WAS MORE ROMANCE in this house tonight than in a whole case of her favorite Harlequin books. From the moment they'd arrived and had seen Mr. Potts's grandson in an embrace passionate enough to scorch the wood floors, Emily had looked around and seen nothing but love.

Well, perhaps not love, not as far as the Feeney sisters went. Lust? Yes. They did display that, and had for many years. Tonight they'd both apparently set their caps for Mr. Potts.

Emily and Ivy were close in age, with Ivy just a couple of years ahead of her in school. Even way back then, Ivy had been boy crazy. She'd been quite popular—pretty and vivacious, and even, as unbelievable as it seemed now, friendly. Her sister was the only one she'd tormented on a regular basis. But she and her sister had left school early, not even graduating, though they'd both remained in Trouble.

Ivy hadn't stayed in town for long. She'd turned into something of a celebrity, if a scandalous one, during the sixties. Marrying a wealthy record producer, she'd gone to live in a fancy place in New York City. Every so often the local paper would publish a picture of Ivy chatting with some famous person at a glamorous party, wearing furs and jewels. She'd lived a life that seemed beautiful and magical to Emily, even if her husband hadn't been terribly handsome.

Then her great tragedy had struck. Ivy's husband had been killed and her house destroyed in a fire. She'd come back to Pennsylvania a changed woman. Strange. Distracted. Definitely not as nice. And more than a little bit fey.

She must have loved that man very much. Because despite

landing another wealthy husband—whom she'd also outlived—Ivy had never seemed happy again.

"She does seem rather happy tonight, though," she murmured under her breath, talking only to herself.

Allie, who was standing nearby, waiting for Damon to return from putting Hank to bed, overheard. "What woman wouldn't be happy a gorgeous man got his hand stuck in her panties?"

Emily giggled. She hadn't meant *her*—the niece. Who had been prettily embarrassed over what had happened earlier in the evening. What a lovely girl she was, and how charming. It was hard to believe she was a Feeney. Of course, the girl's father, Ivan, had always been a wonderful young man.

It was just as hard to believe *he* was a Feeney.

But it wasn't hard to believe men would go crazy over Jennifer, as they had for her aunt once upon a time. Mr. Potts's grandson, Michael, hadn't taken his heated stare off her all evening. The romantic tension between those two was so thick Emily could make a pie out of it.

"I meant that one," Emily said as she brought her teacup to her lips and sipped from it, casting a pointed glance at Ivy.

"Oh, the loony bird?" Allie rolled her eyes. "I thought she and her sister were going to stab each other with their tooth-picks whenever Mortimer turned his back on them." She put a hand on Emily's shoulder and squeezed. "Thank goodness they haven't even noticed that they have some competition tonight."

Emily gaped. Competition? *Her?* "You silly thing."

"I mean it. You look beautiful. Classy. Just what a neat old guy would want."

"If I were interested in a 'neat old guy' I certainly would not display that interest in front of those two. They'd scratch my eyes out if they thought I wanted Mr. Potts for myself. Ivy told me as much when we arrived."

Allie sat on the arm of Emily's chair. "Do you?"

Emily didn't answer. She merely sipped her tea, looking over the room as she had all evening. Watching for Mr. Ward to return from the kitchen, where he'd gone to check on the cook who'd been hired for the evening.

"Okay, I'll stop teasing. I know it's not Mortimer you're interested in. And I say go for it. Roderick needs someone to unstuff that shirt of his."

Shocked that she'd been found out, Emily slowly lowered her cup onto its saucer. "I don't know what you mean."

"Oh, come off it. Mortimer and I both know you're interested, which is one reason he had this party tonight and insisted that Roderick remain *out* of the kitchen."

"How could you…?"

"You blush whenever he's in the room," Allie said with a simple shrug and a sweet smile. As if that explained everything.

Mortified at the thought of what Mr. Potts must think of her—a silly old woman with a crush on his butler—she decided to leave immediately. Starting to rise, she said, "I have to go. I don't feel very well."

Allie's hand remained on her shoulder and she forcibly kept Emily from standing up. "You leave, and I'll tell Roderick myself."

"You wouldn't!"

"Sit your butt down. So far, those two old witches have been too busy fighting over Mortimer, their latest juicy bone, to notice another hunky eligible bachelor is in the house." She wagged her eyebrows as she peeked at Mortimer's grandson—quite a handsome young man with his stormy black eyes and blacker hair—then added, "I mean, a bachelor their age. Not Mike." Her expression turned dreamy. Besotted. "Or Damon."

"Damon has eyes for nobody but you."

"I know," Allie said with an enormous grin. "But I have to say, I'm glad we walked in on Mike Taylor with his hands down Jennifer Feeney's dress so there was no question she was taken. What a stunner."

"I am quite sure," Emily said, her tone tart, "that Miss Feeney was thinking the same thing of you! You are lovely, so glowing with happiness, it almost blinds me to look at you."

Before Allie could respond, Emily felt a tingling and a warmth in her body that said someone was watching her. Glancing toward the open doorway, she saw Mr. Ward, tall and neat and dignified. Similar to Mr. Potts in his traveling and adventuring, but so different from him in personality.

Where Mr. Potts was a lightning storm, Mr. Ward was a gentle rain. It sounded silly—the romantic musings of a tired woman. But it was true. That was how she thought of them.

She'd always been terrified of thunderstorms, but she loved the soft, nurturing fall of gentle moisture from the sky.

Before Emily could stop her, Allie rose and stepped over to Mr. Ward. "You know, Roderick, I have been telling Emily all about your amazing collection of antique postcards. Why don't you take her to your office and show them to her?"

Oh, that girl. Emily was going to strangle her one of these days. But Allie seemed oblivious to her angry stare.

"Why, I'd be delighted, Miss Baker," Roderick said, that English accent of his so mysterious and intriguing.

"I don't want to put you to any trouble…."

"Nonsense," he said as he stepped over and extended his

hand to help her up. As if she were a duchess going to tea. "I'm afraid I can never interest Mortimer in perusing my collection as he's seen all the landmarks depicted in the cards."

"Have you also?" she asked, nearly breathless at the thought. Suddenly, she felt all fluttery, weak and light. "Have you truly seen those places, too?"

Roderick gave a brief, self-deprecating nod. "I have. Yet my interest has never waned."

Imagine. This man had been all over the world. He'd seen places like the Taj Mahal and the pyramids of Egypt…. Things Emily had only ever learned about by watching *Jeopardy!*

And he wanted to share them with her.

It was a miracle. A fantasy. A dream. One she didn't want to end—at least not yet. So although her heart felt ready to explode out of her chest, she nodded in agreement and let him tuck her arm around his. He even patted her hand as he led her out of the room. But she somehow managed to keep her shoes on the floor, rather than a foot in the air.

Tomorrow she'd go back to being plain, sweet Miss Emily, Trouble's loneliest and most well-liked spinster. But for now, she was going to play the part of a romance heroine, meekly enjoying the attention of this very attractive, fascinating gentleman. She'd let herself believe for a while that her fantasies might come true. That the night could end with a dashing gentleman pressing an impassioned yet restrained kiss on her lips.

Deep in her heart, though, she already knew how it would end. In a few hours, she'd be curled under the covers, alone, watching whatever black-and-white double feature she could find on the classic movie channel.

JENNIFER ENJOYED THE DINNER—a spread of Middle Eastern dishes Mr. Potts and his friend had developed a taste for during their travels. She also enjoyed the company. Ignoring her competitive aunts, she'd had a delightful conversation with Mortimer's secretary, Allie, who was the most vivacious, lively little thing she'd met in quite some time. Her son, Hank, was utterly adorable, and her boyfriend couldn't take his eyes off either of them. They were like a Hallmark-movie family, one only found in fiction.

She enjoyed the drinks. She laughed quite a lot at Mortimer's jokes. She noticed the way Miss Emily and Mr. Ward kept stealing glances at one another during dinner—after they'd disappeared together for a while during cocktails.

And yet, she *experienced* none of it. She could focus on none of it. She could appreciate none of it.

Because all she could think about was the man sitting beside her, or across from her, or ten stinking feet away from her. The one who'd had his tongue in her mouth and his hands on her butt earlier and his fingers tightly around her heart from the minute they'd met.

Why on earth did she have to meet a man who fascinated her, attracted her and aroused her now, here, in this backwoods place that she never wanted to see again? Maybe it was *because* she was in this backwoods place, where nobody had ever heard of her. Least of all him. He could flirt with her and kiss her and feel her up all because he wasn't thinking, like every other man in the country, that she was hiding a knife behind her back, preparing to stick it between his ribs.

Though he hadn't touched her again since they'd been caught by their dinner guests making out like a hooker and her john, Mike had definitely stuck close all evening. Sometimes they'd joined in the conversation going on around them. Sometimes they'd lowered their voices and dropped into more intimate ones of their own. Not about their jobs—because, though she was curious, she didn't want to tell him what she did. Instead they talked about little things…. The weather. The town. Their relatives. Their homes in New York.

Intimate as in private, personal. *Not* sexual.

Though, being honest, that was okay. They were moving past the "we're strangers" barrier he'd thrown up between them yesterday. Well past it. And she suspected he no longer doubted her mental stability. He obviously knew her well enough to know she simply had a rather black sense of humor.

He knew her. That was what it came down to. Just as she felt sure she knew him.

And that was a double-edged sword. While it might make him drop his objections to something happening between them, all she could think was that it would have been much better if they'd just had sex at the lake yesterday and never spoken to each other again. Because, darn it all, she *liked* him too much.

Though he seldom laughed and it seemed to pain him to smile, he had a wickedly quick sense of humor and had her chuckling more than once. Particularly when talking about her aunts. He'd told her they reminded him of a female variation of the two old geezers from *The Muppet Show,* Statler and Waldorf. Ever since she'd been mentally hearing them cackle, "It was short…I loved it!"

That wasn't as bad as what he *might* have called them. Especially after Miss Baker had made an unfortunate reference to the murder of Aunt Ivy's first husband. God, it was a wonder the man hadn't gone back to thinking Jen was psycho, given her family's history.

"Having a good time?" Mike asked as the two of them met by the patio door to join everyone else for what Mortimer called his "little surprise" after dinner. The others had gone ahead outside, but Mike had waited for her while she'd made a quick visit to the restroom. She was glad she'd taken the time to swipe a tube of lipstick across her lips and dab some perfume on her pulse points. Because he noticed. He noticed *everything* about her, that dark-eyed stare both assessing and appreciative. She'd have sworn he leaned in the tiniest bit and inhaled deeply, absorbing her scent. Though that could, she supposed, have been wishful thinking.

She wondered if he was an artist…. He seemed to have the quiet, intense personality of one, and he was constantly watching. Never taking his focus off the people around him. Especially her. If only he'd put his *hands* back on her sometime soon so she wouldn't have to do naughty things to herself under the covers at Aunt Ida Mae's house. Again.

But there was no way a man that powerful could be an artist. Maybe Allie's boyfriend—he was tall and lean, dreamy with those violet eyes and that intriguing voice. But Mike? He was like a brick wall in comparison. Not quite as tall but twice as powerful. A man who could break a person in half with his bare hands…and then use them to turn a woman into a puddle of liquid want.

"Jen? *Are* you enjoying yourself?"

She shook off her distracted musings. "Yes. I never imagined I'd enjoy such unusual foods."

"Be thankful you were spared the camel tongue. It was a staple when we were growing up."

She chuckled, assuming he was kidding, then realized he was not. She knew from her aunts that he had been raised by his grandfather. But she wanted to know more—more about what had created him, and what made him tick now. "Sounds like you had quite an upbringing."

"It was normal 8:00 p.m. sitcom stuff when I was young," he said with a shrug as he took her arm to lead her outside.

"And then you lost your parents," she murmured.

His fingers tightened a bit. "I didn't *lose* them. They were both killed. My father by a ground-to-air missile, my mother by a disease."

Oh, God. Her heart ached and she immediately regretted bringing up something so painful. "I'm sorry."

"Yeah. Me, too."

Wishing she'd kept her big stupid mouth shut, she tried to backpedal. "But you have a grandfather who adores you. And his friend who obviously loves you like a father as well. It sounds as though they shared quite a past together, even though they seem like exact opposites."

"Roderick is Bert to Mortimer's Ernie."

She chuckled.

"They work so well together because they balance each other out. Rod is all down-to-earth common sense. Grandpa is...not."

That, she definitely agreed with. "I don't think I've ever met someone so...colorful."

"I know you weren't going to say *eccentric*," he murmured as he steered her over to the railing of the patio, which overlooked the expansive lawn. Everyone else had gathered out on the grass, sitting in chairs or on blankets

Mortimer and Roderick had placed in advance. "Because I think *your* relatives have cornered the market on eccentricity. Does your aunt Ivy realize the twentieth century ended several years ago?"

"I haven't had the heart to tell her."

"I don't think she'd believe you, anyway."

"Probably not."

They fell silent, making no effort to speak, or to draw apart. He still had his hand on her arm, and they remained where they were, not joining the others. Jen couldn't help thinking about the intense embrace they'd shared earlier. What it had meant—whether he'd been affected by it as she had.

And when it was going to be repeated.

Judging by his *physical* response, she had no doubt he'd been every bit as affected. Even now, if she closed her eyes, she could still feel the long, hard ridge of his arousal pressed against her pelvis. The memory made her grow warm and wet all over again. "Mike, we haven't talked about, uh…"

"Your tire iron?"

"No, *your* tire iron," she countered, unable to help it. He'd known where she was headed, he'd just chosen to avoid the topic. Well, he couldn't very well avoid it now that she'd mentioned the iron in his trousers.

His chest started to shake and he tilted his head back to look up at the starry night sky. The humidity of yesterday had finally given up, providing the air with a hint of cool relief. A breeze even blew gently across her body, lifting her hair and pressing her dress tightly against her hips and thighs.

"How in the name of God you can make me laugh when I'm trying so hard not to, is something I'd really like to know."

She hadn't actually heard a laugh. But she felt pretty sure

his chest had moved. Of course, it was so big and muscular, it might have moved with his regular breaths. But she'd take what she could get. "That laugh of yours doesn't get much use, huh?"

"While yours is on constant standby."

She shrugged. "What can I say? If you can't laugh at life—and yourself—what on earth can you laugh at?"

"Your books," he said.

Oh. Her books. Damn. He knew about them. "How did you…"

"Mortimer lent me one of them. I had no idea who you were until he told me. Your writing is caustic and abrasive and outrageous. Just like you."

Frowning, she asked, "Was that a compliment?"

"Yes," he said, staring her in the eye as if to make sure she knew he meant it. "It was. I liked it a lot. Are you working on another one?"

"*Working* is a relative term. I *should* be, since my deadline is moving in like a storm cloud on the horizon. But I've been a little distracted with the aunts."

"I can see why," he said. "I'll look forward to reading it."

"I'm surprised you're not running in the opposite direction, or reaching for a weapon, like every other man in the country."

Though they weren't touching, they were separated only by a sliver of night air, so she felt it when his whole body went stiff. An aura of tension oozed out of him, his voice hardening as he asked, "Men have threatened you?"

"I live in New York City. I get threatened by cab drivers every day of the week."

"Who doesn't? But you know that's not what I meant. What's been going on?"

"Nothing."

He turned to face her, his hand gripping her elbow. "Is there someone you're scared of?"

"My dentist. That bastard has torture tools that would have made Oliver North talk."

His hand tightened as he let out a half laugh, half groan. "Will you be serious?"

"No. I won't," she murmured, looking up at him in the moonlight and falling so deep into those dark eyes of his that she wasn't sure she'd ever be able to swim her way to the surface. "There's only one thing I want to be serious about and that's the conversation we had yesterday."

He let go of her arm. "Oh?"

Swallowing, she pushed on. "Do you still think I'm a nut?"

He shrugged. "Yeah."

Great.

"But you're growing on me."

He was... Was he *teasing* her? Looking intently at his face, she saw his lips tugging up at the corners, and suddenly he gave it up altogether, flashing one of those brilliant smiles she'd only ever seen once or twice since she'd known him.

Out came the dimple.

Away went her very last doubt.

Reaching up to twine her fingers in his hair, she pulled him toward her. "We're not strangers anymore, either."

"We haven't been strangers since the minute we met," he admitted. "That doesn't mean..."

"Yeah, Mike. It does." Not giving him a chance to stop her, she pulled his mouth to hers for a warm, wet kiss.

Sighing as she tasted his warm tongue, she silently invited him deeper. Into her mouth. Into her body. It somehow didn't matter that their friends and family were a few yards away on the lawn. Especially not when Mike lifted those big, rough hands, cupped her face, then slid them into her hair. It almost immediately fell out of its twist to land softly on her shoulders. He twined his fingers in her curls, holding her head, tilting her so he could go deeper.

Suddenly, out of the corner of her eye, she was sure she saw stars. Purple ones. Red ones. Blue ones. Then she realized she was seeing Mortimer's "surprise." He had arranged for a fireworks display and right now, dozens of them were shooting skyward, bathing the whole yard in brilliant sparkles of color. With her lips still pressed to Mike's, she had to smile in pure joy at the sight, as she always had as a kid.

When he slowly pulled away, she murmured, "For a second there I thought I was seeing stars."

"For a second there, I think we both did."

That thick-throated admission was so unexpected coming from this man. It erased her lingering concerns that she was alone in wanting more. He wanted her. Oh, yes, he did, judging by the storminess in his eyes, which caught and reflected the bursting fireworks, giving them a devilish red glint.

"Take me home," she ordered.

"To New York?"

She immediately remembered she had no home to go to around here. And she wouldn't, not until tomorrow. Though she wondered how she'd stand it, she knew she had to wait. "There's a hotel right off the interstate," she said, almost desperate to have him hard and naked between her legs. Especially certain parts of him, like the massive erection that seemed to press from the V of her thighs all the way up to her middle. "I'll tell the aunts I have to leave earlier than I'd planned tomorrow and meet you there."

He hesitated for a second. But only a second. "Ten."

"Ten," she replied, almost giddy at the idea that in a little less than twelve hours she'd finally *have* him. It didn't matter that they had almost nothing in common, that he was all wrong for her and she all wrong for him. Because the excitement they brought out in each other was entirely, totally *right*.

THAT CERTAINTY and her excitement carried her through the next *thirteen* hours, until eleven o'clock the next morning. At that point, sitting in the room she'd rented at the seedy no-tell motel—trying to ignore the stained carpet and mildewed bathroom—she was no longer able to avoid the truth.

The son of a bitch had stood her up.

CHAPTER EIGHT

Men have no imagination. They use guns. Every woman knows it's much more satisfying to dig her cheating bastard husband's heart out with a rusty nail file.
—*Why Arsenic Is Better Than Divorce*, by Jennifer Feeney

BUSY DEALING WITH the emergency evidentiary hearing that had drawn him back to New York unexpectedly Monday morning, Mike didn't notice right away that he hadn't heard from Jennifer Feeney. Not one word.

He realized it Friday evening as he returned to his small house in Queens. It had been another grueling day on the witness stand, being grilled by a defense attorney on a mission to get a bunch of evidence thrown out. As if Mike was going to let anything happen to undermine the drug case on which he'd spent a year of his life, and had been *forced* into a transfer over.

Fat chance.

He'd been completely unshakable on the stand and fortunately the judge had seen the truth. The defense motion to suppress the results of a search had been denied, and Mike had breathed easily for the first time in days. Meanwhile the defense attorney and his rich club-owner client, Ricky Stahl, had looked ready to kill somebody. Probably him. Because Mike's testimony and that search were critical to the case.

Stahl's malice didn't bother him. Any thug hated being brought down by an undercover cop who'd worked his way into his organization. Ricky was just another pig, pushing his junk on the spoiled young kids who partied in his clubs every weekend. Kids with more money than common sense, who were too anxious to go along and be accepted by their rich, jaded peers.

The whole thing had been so dirty it still made him feel as if he needed a shower.

But for now, it was done, at least until the trial started in a month's time. He'd performed his job well on the stand and knew he'd do it again in front of a jury. In the meantime, he was anxious to get back to work on some of the cold cases he'd been looking at, including the 1995 double murder of a teenage brother and sister shot in their own basement. That one had been hard to work—the parents still hadn't gotten over the horrific loss.

He wanted to solve the case for their sake, and also because the inconsistencies in the witness statements had been driving him nuts since he'd first opened the file a month ago. He'd brought the thing home, planning to do some work over the weekend, glad he was getting back to some kind of normal routine after the trip to Trouble and the work week spent at the courthouse.

But he couldn't get *entirely* back to normal because he now wanted his routine to include Jennifer Feeney. Who hadn't called.

Heading into the kitchen, he checked his answering machine. No red flashing light indicated a message. Just as there'd been no messages from her on his cell phone.

"She did get the messages, right?" he asked Mutt, who'd been stuck to his legs like a pair of pants since the minute Mike had arrived home. Grabbing a beer from the fridge, he opened the back door, nudging the dog to go out and do his business. He nearly had to lift Mutt up to get him to go outside in the rain.

The dog made it to the edge of the grass, did his thing and came racing in like a pup. Rainy days and feeding time were the only two things that made that animal run.

"So what do we do now?" he asked the dog as he absently scratched him behind the ears.

Mutt woofed once and nosed his empty food bowl. He obviously didn't care what Mike did about his woman troubles, he just wanted to be fed. Immediately if not sooner. And none of that dry stuff, bud, canned food only.

"You're so spoiled," he muttered, getting the dog his favorite canned food.

Then he returned his attention to the issue at hand. Jen's silence. "So you call *her,* dope," he told himself.

If he had Jen's number, he would. Maybe she was just feeling a little funny—embarrassed about the way they'd left things Sunday night at the party.

But this was Jen he was talking about. Shyness wouldn't keep her from calling. No way.

Surprisingly, that lack of inhibition was one of the things he liked best about her. All these years of being sure he didn't want any drama in his private life, and he'd fallen headfirst into an ocean of lust for a woman who defined drama. One who was unafraid to go after what she wanted.

Which left him wondering…what if she hadn't gotten his messages? He'd left *three,* one with each of her aunts on the phone, plus a written one shoved against the door of Ida Mae's house. How could she have not received *any* of them?

When he'd gotten the call from his former lieutenant at eight o'clock Monday morning that he had to return to the city immediately, his sex date with Jen had been the first thing he'd thought about. Probably because he'd been thinking about it all the previous night.

It'd be nice to *not* wake up with a hard-on like a pubescent fourteen-year-old one of these days.

He couldn't believe he'd come so close to *having* her, to satisfying the sexual need that had been driving him crazy since they'd met, and then had to bail out. Talk about bad timing—his was worse than the guy who'd landed the last spot on the *Titanic*.

Cursing the luck, he'd gotten the phone numbers from his grandfather, then called and spoken to one aunt and then the other. It wasn't that he didn't trust them to give Jen the message—they'd all been getting along fine Sunday night at the party. Her great-aunts had been so busy fawning over his grandfather they hadn't had time to snipe at anybody—not Jen, not even each other. He didn't think things could have changed that drastically overnight.

But he wasn't sure they'd *remember,* and he'd wanted to cover all his bases. As triple insurance, he'd swung by Ida Mae's at nine, as he was leaving town, to try to tell Jen in person. Getting no answer to his knocks, he'd jotted a note and stuck it in the door. She had to have gotten at least one of the messages. Right?

And since he'd already decided she couldn't be too embarrassed to call him, the only explanation was that she'd changed her mind. She didn't want to go ahead with an impulsive affair. Now that she'd returned to the city—to her real life and the kind of people someone with her fame and finances usually hung out with—she no longer had a *need* for him.

The idea that she'd taken care of that *need* with somebody else was about to drive him up a wall.

No matter what, he had to know. Reaching for the phone, he called a guy he knew who worked for the phone company and had helped with a few cases in the past. Not exactly police business, but it was worth calling in a favor.

And within a few hours, he had Jennifer Feeney's home address and telephone number in hand.

"It's good to be a cop," he told Mutt as he reached for the phone. It was 10:00 p.m., but something told him she wasn't an early-to-bed kind of woman, especially on a Friday night. Not unless she had someone in that bed with her. He still hoped that someone would very soon be him.

Whatever doubts he'd had about starting something with her had lightened Sunday night at the party when she'd been so damn gorgeous, funny and charming. Sexy enough to stop his heart.

They'd dissipated completely over the past few days, when he realized how much he missed her. She might be all wrong for him in the long run, but for now, she was absolutely *right*.

She answered on the fourth ring, her voice sounding a little groggy. Damn…maybe he had woken her up.

"Jen?"

"Who is thish?"

Not asleep. Tipsy. He almost chuckled, wondering what the woman who had more guts than most men he knew was like when she was drinking. "It's Mike."

A long silence ensued. Then she mumbled, "Mike. Mike…the no-good, jackass Mike?"

Uh-oh. "I hope not."

In the background, he heard a female voice screech, "It's him?" Another one immediately added, "Hang up on the bastard."

Oh, terrific. She was having a bitch session with some let's-get-together-and-hate-men girlfriends. He despised those things, he really did. Which was funny considering how much he'd enjoyed what he had read of Jen's book—which was basically the same event in print. All except for the historic murder cases she'd written about, like that of a 1960s music producer.

It hadn't taken much brainpower to figure out she'd been talking about her Aunt Ivy's late husband. The subject had, after all, come up at Sunday night's party. Hearing the woman had a murder in her background hadn't surprised Mike, but it had definitely concerned him, given what she'd done to Mortimer. So he'd done a little digging when he'd gotten home, surprised to realize the case was still open right here in New York City.

A cold case. Seemed pretty damned convenient. Prophetic, almost. And though he suspected Jen wouldn't like it, he was going to glance through that file when he had the chance.

He didn't merely want to satisfy his curiosity. Or rehash what the old woman and her maniacal sister had done to his grandfather.

He was also concerned for Jen.

It was one thing to laugh off a murder threat from a loony old woman. It was another to laugh off one from one who might actually have killed before.

"Well, come on, are you Mike-the-tease Taylor or not?"

Had she just called him a *tease?*

"It is Mike Taylor," he said, knowing better than to pick a fight with an angry, tipsy woman. "Maybe I should call back another time." When she was sober, and without her posse.

"Maybe you should kiss my lily-white butt."

He couldn't help it, he immediately laughed—the first time he'd done so since Sunday night. The woman killed him, she really did. Not only because of how cute instead of furious she sounded, but also because her idea was so appealing. Was that supposed to be some kind of threat, or punishment? Ha. Stroking and kissing and holding that perfectly curved ass were among the many things he'd wanted to do to her from the minute he'd seen her swinging those hips, walking up the road toward Trouble.

"This isn't Mike Taylor. Mike Taylor doesn't laugh. He's a block of wood." She mumbled something else, something that sounded suspiciously like "Especially below the waist."

The woman was going to hate herself when she sobered up.

"I should let you go since you're busy. But call me tomorrow. We need to talk."

"I don't need anything," she mumbled, almost talking to herself, "especially not from you-oo. I don't even like you and I know you don't like me."

"Not true."

"Bull. But it doesn't matter. I have an industrial-size vibrator and my best friend brought me some porn and my other best friend bought me a bottle of wine and five gallons of ice cream. And we're gonna sit here enjoying everything, not needing men at all."

Oh, boy. She'd definitely had a few glasses of that wine. Otherwise, he didn't imagine she'd be implying she and two of her girlfriends were sharing wine, ice cream, porn and vi-brators. Sounded like a porn movie all on its own. At the very least, a man's fantasy.

"Jen, didn't you get my messages?"

"Oh, I got the message all right."

He tried again. "The messages that I got called back to the city and couldn't make it on Monday."

Silence. Then she asked, "What messages? You didn't leave me any messages."

Oh, hell. She didn't sound tipsy anymore, she sounded... hurt? "I left you three messages."

"I didn't get them."

No. This couldn't have happened. "Look, I swear to you, I called twice and came by once to explain why I couldn't make it Monday so you wouldn't think I just didn't show."

She didn't respond for a second, obviously thinking over his words. He heard a muffled sound of the phone being lowered, then her voice saying, "He says he left messages and didn't really stand me up."

"Bullshit," another voice said.

"Liar."

"All men are scum."

That did the trick. Jen came back on, speaking directly into the phone. "Right. All men are scum."

And then she hung up.

"Who was that on the phone?"

Ivy nearly fell over in a faint as an unexpected voice intruded in her kitchen early Saturday morning. "You nearly stopped my heart," she said as she swung around to see Ida Mae.

Her sister had obviously come in without being asked. Some people were just so rude. Not that Ivy would say anything, or else Ida Mae would lay into her for the many times Ivy had crept into the house next door to *borrow* things. As if her fat-legged sister really needed so many pairs of stockings.

In Ivy's opinion, Ida Mae shouldn't ever wear anything but pants, though she knew it wouldn't happen. Ida Mae hadn't ever let go of her Trouble upbringing, even though she had lived out of state for many years when she'd been married. Like their Mama, she wouldn't be seen in anything but a dress outside the house. Or perhaps one of her many housecoats on the front porch.

Ivy dressed much the same way nowadays, but *she* had the legs for it. And when she was younger, why, she wouldn't have been caught dead wearing a frumpy Pennsylvania house-wife dress.

Oh, hadn't she cut a figure! She'd worn little braided Chanel suits in the 1950s and miniskirts in the sixties. If she hadn't been middle-aged when hot pants had been introduced, she would have worn those, too, with patent-leather go-go boots to go with them.

Had she still been married to Leo at that time, living the New York scene, she probably would have done it anyway. But Leo had been busy dancing in Satan's hellfire long before then, and her second husband, Alfred, was a much more con-servative sort. A nice man. Boring. Very easily shocked.

So, no hot pants for a forty-year-old Ivy.

"Answer my question, who were you on the phone with?" Ida Mae said as she took a cup and saucer down from the cupboard, making herself some tea.

Ivy considered warning her about how tea might make her

retain water, which Ida Mae certainly didn't need with those legs, oh, no, indeed. But she kept her mouth shut, just in case they happened to see Mr. Potts later.

"Are you hard of hearing today? Who was it?"

"Nobody," Ivy whispered.

Ida Mae stuck her lips out and frowned in a way that still scared small children. "Don't lie to me, I heard you shouting and saw you slamming down the phone when I came in."

Shouting? Had she been shouting? Why would she shout when there was no one to hear?

"Well? Tell the truth, was it Mr. Potts?"

Ahh, that explained Ida Mae's attitude. The two of them had been having a regular horse race over that man for more'n a year, ever since he'd moved to Trouble. While he was gracious and friendly, even inviting them to his house or for a stroll now and again, neither of them had ever been able to get him to come back into their houses for tea and cookies.

Some men, it appeared, actually did learn.

"Now, why would I shout at Mr. Potts?"

"I have no idea…. Why do you do *any* of the things you do?"

Though she supposed Ida Mae's question had been rhetorical, Ivy immediately answered, anyway, not giving it a second thought. "For love and family."

Ida Mae finally stopped frowning. Without a word, without a smile, without any overt acknowledgment whatsoever, she reached over, took Ivy's hand and squeezed it. Just once. That was all.

That was enough.

"Now," Ida Mae said as she stirred her tea, "tell me who it was. You sounded angry." She sounded grudgingly concerned, which was about as much as her older sister was capable of.

No real wonder, of course, not with the things that had happened to her when they were young.

"I don't know who it was," Ivy admitted. "The phone rang and nobody was there."

Ida Mae nodded, her interest piqued. "Did he breathe heavy or make any nasty suggestions or say he wanted to tie you up?"

"Would I have shouted if he had?" Ivy snapped. "Don't you think I'd enjoy the occasional naughty caller? This one doesn't say anything."

She didn't *think* he had, anyway. Sometimes, she almost believed she heard the whispers of familiar voices, long gone. But that was impossible, which made her wonder if the phone had even rung at all. But it had this morning. *Hadn't it?*

Ida Mae put down her cup and looked her in the face. "*Doesn't* say anything? This wasn't the first call?"

Ivy slowly shook her head.

"How long has it been happening?"

"More than a month. Since before the girl came. Now, this past week, someone's been calling and asking about her, too."

Ida Mae huffed out a breath. "Strange. Perhaps it has something to do with those calls she's been getting in the city. I wish she'd have stayed a while longer."

Ivy didn't. She still hadn't quite forgiven Jennifer for running out on them Monday morning, ruining their plans for a lovely luncheon with Mr. Potts. Just when Ivy had almost begun to think she could like her. A little.

Ida Mae had more reason to be fond of the girl than Ivy did, however, given the truth about Ida Mae and Jen's father. So Ivy forgave her for being worried. "She can take care of herself," Ivy grudgingly said. Offering comfort wasn't her strong suit. "I just want the voices to stop bothering *me* on the phone."

Though she said nothing, her sister's expression revealed her thoughts. She was wondering the same thing Ivy had been wondering: if Ivy's imagination had perhaps been running away with her lately. Maybe there had been no call, no whispers. Nothing but silly Ivy retreating into her fantasy worlds.

But to her amazement, Ida Mae thought no such thing. "I don't like this, sister, it worries me," she said with a frown.

Ida Mae expressing worry for *her?* Imagine.

"I have that uneasy feeling in my bones—something funny is going on. I've felt it for weeks."

When Ida Mae had uneasy feelings, they usually meant something. Her sister had a bit of their mother's shine on her…. She'd proved that more than once. Especially when it counted, like the times when Ivy had been in the most trouble.

The night Leo had died, for instance.

Ida Mae had known, somehow, that Ivy was in trouble. She'd shown up in New York City before Ivy had even had the chance to contact the family. With her strong shoulders and her firm presence, she'd stepped between Ivy and the police…keeping Ivy upright when her grief and rage threatened to down her.

Helping her hide the truth.

Too bad Ida Mae's intuition hadn't helped her avoid her *own* struggles and terrors. Like that night when she'd been seventeen and Ivy fifteen…and they'd *both* ended up with blood on their hands. That had been the first big secret they'd shared, hadn't it? For a little while, anyway, until it had become painfully obvious they'd have to tell their mama. Then she'd joined in, closing the circle of secrecy around them all, taking the truth with her to her grave, along with all her own secrets she'd kept close in her woman's heart.

"We'll be careful, you hear?" Ida Mae said, all no-nonsense

as she was in times of crisis. "We've both got pasts to protect, Ivy Feeney, and we both have to be on our guard to keep them private. So watch what you say, who you talk to and tell me if anything else unusual happens."

Ivy nodded, though of course she knew that might be a trickier promise than Ida Mae thought.

Because Ivy's entire life had been anything but usual. And she certainly didn't expect that to change at this late date.

JEN FELT SURE SHE HADN'T BEEN drunk the night before. Perhaps a teensy bit tipsy, but not drunk. She should know, right? Which made her curious about something. "Why do I feel like there's a guy with a hammer running around in my brain?"

"Maybe because you're hung over," said Ashley, her best friend, who, along with Jen, was reaching for the aspirin first thing Saturday morning. They were alone, their other friend Beth having left before midnight. Beth had a retail job and had to work today. God help her poor soul.

Ashley, who lived upstairs and had been Jen's best friend since she'd moved to the city after grad school, had also left at some point last night. But she'd come back down this morning to check on her.

"I'm not hung over," Jen insisted. "I wasn't drunk."

"Oh? Why'd I find you on your bedroom floor when I came in?" Ashley asked as she plopped onto a kitchen chair.

Jeez, she'd forgotten that. "I fell."

"Right." Ashley snorted. The noise plunged into Jen's ears like a Q-tip wielded by Attila the Hun. "Sober people fall out of bed all the time."

As if Ashley's voice wasn't bad enough, she suddenly heard ear-splitting music pouring through the vents between her apartment and the one next door. Just as she had every day since she'd gotten back from Pennsylvania. She groaned. "Does that man have to listen to his radio at that volume *all the time?*"

Ashley grimaced. "Yeah, I think Mr. Jones is trying to pretend he's young and hip. Ick. He's so nasty. The old fart seems to be outside lurking in the hall just laying in wait for me every time I come home." Crossing her arms on the table and leaning over it, Ashley got right back on subject. "So…you still claiming you weren't drunk enough to fall out of bed and are not dying of an acute hangover right now?"

"I was a little tipsy," she insisted, wondering who she was trying harder to convince. "I was doing that trick where you put your foot out from under the covers and let it touch the floor." So, hopefully, the room would stop spinning like a Tilt-A-Whirl ride. "But my bed's too high."

"You scooted too far?"

"Uh-huh. And I couldn't manage to climb back up." She rubbed her head, glad there was no lump. "How in heaven's name could I have been drunk on two glasses of wine," she mumbled as she dipped a washcloth in a big pitcher of iced water, wrung it out and lifted it to her brow. The tap water just wasn't cold enough.

"Maybe because you haven't eaten a thing in the past few days? Ever since you got back from Misery?"

"It's Trouble. And I ate ice cream." Almost a whole quart of it by herself. Last night. And the night before. Every day. For four days.

"With tequila chasers."

Whoops. She'd forgotten about the shots Beth had insisted on doing. One for each man who'd broken their hearts. Between the three of them they'd killed off most of a bottle.

"One tequila, two tequila, three tequila, *floor,*" Ashley said, sounding cheerful. Which just made Jen want to pound her.

"Why aren't *you* hung over?" she asked.

"I'm hurting a little. But I outweigh you by thirty pounds, and I've only ever had my heart broken twice."

Jen lifted her head from the sink and looked at her blond friend, who was six feet tall, built like an Amazon and probably as tough as one. "Men would be scared to break your heart."

"Yours, too," Ashley retorted.

"I guess. So why was *I* drunk?"

"I thought you weren't."

"Well, maybe I sort of overdid it." Judging by the serious pain, she'd very much overdone it.

Jen hadn't been drunk in *years,* not since her college days. Now she remembered why. "But no guy's broken my heart in—" she looked at the clock "—five whole days."

Not that her heart had been broken, but she'd been hurt that Mike had stood her up. "Other than that, it's been ages since anybody's gotten close enough to me to do any lasting damage."

"Yeah," Ashley said, "but don't you remember? You drank for every man who's said a nasty word to you because of your books."

"Call the distributor. There's no alcohol left in the five boroughs."

Closing her eyes, Jen rubbed the corners of them. She told herself to relax, waiting for the aspirin to kick in so she wouldn't feel each and every one of her heartbeats send out a message that said, "Payback time, loser."

"So, are you going to call him?"

"Call who?"

"*The* guy."

The guy. Mike. Her stomach clenched at the very idea. "He stood me up, remember? He's not interested."

Ashley cleared her throat, saying nothing for a moment. Warily opening her eyes to peer at her nervous-looking friend, Jen asked, "What?"

"Don't you remember his call last night?"

Finally, she stopped feeling her pulse pounding because her heart stopped beating altogether. She just stood there, jaw falling open, Ashley's words reminding her of what she'd forgotten. "Oh, my God, he did call, didn't he?"

"Uh-huh."

"What'd he say?"

"I didn't talk to him."

"What'd *I* say?"

"You called him scum and hung up on him."

She scrunched her eyes closed again. "I think he told me he'd left me three messages saying he couldn't make it Monday."

"Right," Ashley said, suddenly sounding sheepish. "But, uh, I think we chose not to believe him."

The whole conversation flooded back into her mind. All of it. Complete with porn and vibrators. "Oh, my God."

She wished her kitchen window weren't stuck because she needed to stick her head out of it and scream her guts out. *A chair through the glass. That'll work.*

Before she could throw anything, however, a jackhammer started pounding on Jen's front door. Each bang shot through her head and blew out a chunk of her brain. "Get my gun."

"You don't have one. And besides, it would be really loud."

Actually, she did have a gun. A very illegal one, given where she lived. Her agent had bought her one and forced it on her after some of the nastier letters she'd gotten from unhappy readers. A few more of which had been waiting for her when she'd gotten back from Trouble.

Not that she'd ever fire a weapon, though she might be tempted when it came to bad guys. Especially since she'd had an odd feeling when she'd gotten back to her apartment—as if maybe someone had been inside it. Her first thought had been the slimy super, but she had him pegged as a perv, not a thief, and she honestly didn't notice any of her panties or lingerie missing.

She'd chalked the whole thing up to an overactive imagination. But she'd also checked to make sure the gun was still locked away where it had been since the day she'd gotten it. The last thing she wanted was to think somebody had broken in, stolen it and planned to use it in a crime.

She really needed to get rid of the thing. Soon. Well, after she used it on whoever was jackhammering on her door much too early on a hungover Saturday morning.

But Ashley was right. It *would* be loud. She didn't need loud. She needed whispers and feather softness and oh, Lord, did she need coffee. Of all days to be out.

"Let me die," she groaned.

"Only the good die young, babe," Ashley said, still so darned chipper Jen wanted to strangle her. "Which means *you* are going to live forever."

Judging by the other women in her family, that was a distinct possibility. Her grandmother—who, some said, had murdered her husband long before Jen was born—had reportedly lived well into her eighties, though Jen didn't remember her. And Aunt Ida Mae and Aunt Ivy showed absolutely no signs of slowing down. No rest for the wicked, they said. That was probably true in their case.

She hoped if she did live a long life, she got to be as cunning and ballsy as they were. Despite not quite having forgiven them for their shenanigans of the previous week, she almost missed them. Distance definitely improved her feelings toward those two, as it always had. When not being tormented by them on a daily basis, she always found herself liking their quirky ways and their strength.

They were family. *Her* family. Psychotic and malicious and outrageous. But hers.

The knocking picked up again. It was now accompanied by a muffled voice calling, "Anybody home?"

Her head still hanging over the sink, she tilted it to glance at the door, trying to scrape her stringy hair out of the way. "Go die a slow, painful death you mean-hearted bastard."

"I'll tell whoever it is to get lost on my way out," Ashley said as she rose and walked to the door of Jen's small apartment. "Call me later if you want to do lunch."

"That would require consuming food." Moving slowly, Jen took the seat Ashley had vacated. Moaning, she dropped her face in her hands. "I don't plan on eating again for a week."

"I guess that means you won't want this," a voice said. A male voice. A familiar male voice.

No. This could *not* be happening. Not today. Fate wouldn't be so cruel, right? Man, it wasn't as if she'd ever kicked a puppy or taken a Snickers bar from a little kid. She'd just written a few books about killing men, that was all. Could karma really be paying her back as if she were the reincarnation of Genghis Khan?

Jen opened her eyes just enough to peek through her fingers. A pair of booted feet and khaki-clad legs stood right beside her chair. She knew without a doubt they belonged to the one man she most wanted to see…and the one she never wanted to see again, given what she'd said to him on the phone last night.

"This can't be happening."

"It's happening."

Looking up, her whole insides went gooey at the sight of his familiar spiky black hair, his dark eyes, that incredible face. And *not* because she felt nauseous. "How did you…?"

"Your friend let me in."

Some friend. Ashley had let a gorgeous hunky man in to witness Jen looking like a used toilet brush.

"I guess there's no way you'll leave and come back tomorrow after I've at least had a chance to get my brain working again?" Not to mention taking a shower and putting a comb somewhere within five feet of her hair.

She should have known better. Mike wasn't the kind of guy to go away when a woman asked him to. She'd known that about him from the very first—this was no Mr. Sensitive.

He was big and he was tough and he did what he wanted. Which was usually incredibly sexy and exciting, but right now, it just frustrated the hell out of her.

He didn't even respond to her request. He merely blew out a resigned breath—as if he didn't even believe she'd asked it, then sat down across from her. Pushing the chair out from the table, he stretched his long legs and crossed his arms over his chest.

"Jen?"

"Yes?"

"I'm not going anywhere."

CHAPTER NINE

Somebody should invent a new type of Barbie doll that looks pretty and new right out of the box, but has a special button marked How her Stupid Husband Will Eventually Make her Feel that turns her frumpy, useless and fat.
—*I Love You, I Want You, Get Out*, by Jennifer Feeney

MIKE COULD HAVE TAKEN PITY on her and left when Jen asked him to. But he had the feeling they had some bridges to mend. He needed to make Jen believe he hadn't intentionally stood her up. The best way to win any battle, he knew from experience, was to launch an attack when the opponent was vulnerable.

Not that he wanted to attack her physically. He just wanted to attack her defenses—the ones she'd thrown into place the minute she'd started to think he was exactly like every other guy she'd known or written about.

As for being vulnerable? Well…she looked about as pathetic as a kitten that had fallen down a well.

Jen's face was red, as if she'd been pressing an ice pack on it, and strands of her hair clung to her head. She wore plain, washed-out sweatpants and a spandex sports top that clung to her full breasts. He liked the shirt. A lot. As she glared at him with bloodshot eyes, Mike tried hard to feel pity for the hellish hangover she must have, and not amusement at how cute she looked with all her defenses down. Nor aroused at how hot that tight little top was against her amazing body.

"Just kill me and get it over with."

"That bad, huh?"

Slowly nodding, she wrinkled her nose and sniffed, finally noticing the brown bag Mike had placed on the table. A warm, yeasty scent rose from it. He'd thought breakfast might be a good ice-breaker.

Apparently not. Jen's face went white. "What is that?"

"Bagels."

Visibly shuddering and launching back in her chair, she waved her hand at the bag. "Get them out of my sight unless you want to see what kind of ice cream I was eating last night."

He couldn't hold a smile in any longer. "You got it bad."

"Yes, I do. Now stop it."

"Stop what?"

"Stop smiling. Don't do that. I can't take you when you smile. Go back to being Mr. Moody."

"You bet." He killed the smile, though he didn't imagine she could miss the way his shoulders were shaking with laughter.

"Why are you here?"

"I wanted to make sure you're okay. You said last night you didn't get my messages."

Her succulent bottom lip disappeared into her mouth and she gnawed on it for a moment. "You really left me messages?"

He nodded, keeping his stare steady and completely open. "Yeah, I did. I talked to both Ivy and Ida Mae. Plus I left you a note on Ida Mae's door at nine o'clock Monday morning saying

I had to return to the city unexpectedly and wanted to see you here as soon as you got back. You didn't get *any* of them?"

Shaking her head, she groaned. "Ida Mae and Ivy got mad at me on the way home Sunday night because I told them I was leaving the next morning. I guess your grandfather had invited us for lunch and they were afraid if I wasn't there, he'd cancel."

"But they couldn't talk you out of it…so to pay you back they kept my messages from you."

"Right."

Frustration made him lift both hands to his head and run them through his hair. "How in the name of God did you end up related to those harpies?"

"Hey, you can pick your friends. Can't pick your family."

As if anyone would choose to be related to those two.

Clearing her throat nervously, she said, "Um, I have a feeling that wasn't *all* I said to you on the phone last night."

"No, it wasn't." The annoyed tension in the air eased the tiniest bit as he remembered all of their conversation on the phone. Every sweet, naughty bit of it. But he decided to make her sweat. "You told me you didn't like me."

She nibbled her lip. "I did?"

"Uh-huh. That hurt my feelings, Jen."

Her bloodshot eyes widened, her mouth forming an O of surprise. She reached across the table and covered his hand with hers. "I'm so sorry. I do like y—" Suddenly, she yanked her hand away, obviously remembering who she was talking to. "You're so full of it."

Shaking his head mournfully, he admitted, "The only thing that made me feel better after that remark was knowing you had had a few drinks and certainly didn't mean it." Then, looking down so she wouldn't see his smile, he added, "And picturing you over here with your friends filming *Girls Gone Wild Part Forty*."

Groaning, she leaned back and stared at the ceiling, shaking her head back and forth. "God, I need coffee."

"Want me to make it?"

"I'm out. Of all freaking days to be out of coffee."

"Come on. I'll take you out for one."

She shook her head. "I think I'll just stay right here, not having to look at you, waiting for the ceiling to crash down on top of me and put me out of my misery."

Standing, he stepped over to look directly down into her face. Her eyes were closed, as if she hoped he'd just disappear by the time she opened them.

"Come on, you know you need it," he cajoled. "And so do I. I haven't slept much lately." His voice low, he added, "I've been thinking too much about how I should have spent Monday afternoon." In her arms. In her bed. In her body. Taking her, filling her, possessing her. Then doing it all again.

Those moody eyes flew open and she flinched, almost falling out of her chair. "Huh?"

All the tension in the room changed, becoming thick, more sensual, more aware. For the past five days, Jen had apparently been thinking they were through, that what they'd talked about Sunday night would never happen. Now that she knew he hadn't intentionally stood her up, she had to be wondering if they might get together after all.

"You can't want me now."

He did. Oh, he definitely did. He'd like to start by leading her into the shower, gently soaping her body and easing away the aches. Lathering her hair and wrapping it around his hands as he washed it. Stroking her temples to ease her headache. Filling her body slowly with the water roaring down on both of them.

But she looked as if she could barely stand up, much less have hot shower sex. So he didn't say any of that. Instead, he merely murmured, "Yeah. I do. But only when you stop looking as though you'd scream like somebody getting a tooth extracted without Novocain if I so much as touch you."

"You *can't* want me," she mumbled. "I look like the bride of Frankenstein's half-witted brother."

Reaching down, he grabbed her hand and tugged her up. Cupping her chin in his hand, he held her steady so she couldn't look away. "I'm dying for you, Jennifer. I've dreamed about you every night this week, every hour of those nights. And fantasized about you during just about every waking one."

"Oh." She licked her lips in blatant invitation.

Unable to resist anymore, he swooped in and kissed her. He swirled his tongue into her mouth, plunging deep and hard, showing her what he wanted.

When he pulled away, she muttered, "Oh, thank God I brushed my teeth."

Dropping his head back and laughing, he let her go and swatted her curvy butt. "Get your shoes. Let's go for coffee."

She nodded, still looking a little dazed. "Give me five minutes to get myself presentable." Jen glanced away and caught a glimpse of her reflection in a mirror hanging in the hallway. Her gape of dismay said she hadn't realized quite how bad things were. "Never mind. It'd take five *hours*."

He put a hand on her shoulder, standing behind her, their eyes locking in the mirror. Slowly rubbing his cheek into her hair, he moved to sample the smooth softness of her neck. He pressed an open-mouthed kiss there, licking lightly at the vulnerable nape. "It'll take a whole lot more than five hours to do everything I want to do with you," he whispered, watching as her delicate skin flushed in immediate reaction.

She shook a little, leaning back against his chest. Her mouth fell open, her pulse fluttered in her throat. For a second, he wondered if she'd say to hell with it and drag him to her bed.

He'd been noble enough to say he'd wait until she felt better a few minutes ago. But it had taken everything he had to say it. He honestly didn't know if he could manage it again.

"Soon," she finally said, her eyes sparkling with both promise—and regret. "I'm not going to sleep with you until I can be sure I'll be an active participant."

"Fine," he said, his hopes for hot sex killed but his need for hot coffee renewed. "Then let's go."

MORTIMER DID NOT LIKE BEING out of the loop. In all his years, he'd thrived on being part of every expedition, project or adventure he had instigated. And many of those he had not. He'd been on the front lines, leading the charge, battling his way through countless enemies or charming his way through an innumerable number of ladies.

Now, however, he was helpless. Completely uninvolved. Unable to do anything but fret and wonder whether the plan he'd helped set in motion was proceeding to its desired conclusion.

Not knowing whether his grandson was falling under the spell of the delightful young Miss Feeney was sending him mad.

"Are you still sulking about not having Michael here to dance on your puppet strings?" Roderick asked as he entered the office Saturday morning, carrying a tray with a teapot and two cups.

Their spot of strong English tea was a holdover of home that Rod had never let go, not even when they'd lived in Borneo.

Mortimer would rather have had a brandy, but his friend was becoming more and more insistent about the doctor and his silly rules. As if Roddy truly believed an occasional tipple—even a morning one—would send Mortimer to his grave when half the German army had not been able to. "I merely wish I could find out what is going on."

"Your wicked spies haven't updated you?"

Frowning, Mortimer admitted, "I don't believe the Feeney sisters parted on friendly terms with their niece. Whatever assistance I gained from them last weekend, like when Ida Mae let me know Jennifer would be walking home from breakfast last Saturday morning, is finished. Perhaps I could call Jennifer directly, just to say hello."

"You are shameful."

Mortimer gave his friend a sour glare. "And you have room to talk *how,* my matchmaking partner in crime?"

That was the one positive about this situation—at least Roddy was along with him for the adventure. He might claim he was not a matchmaker, but, like Mortimer, he'd been entirely charmed by Jennifer Feeney and had agreed that she and Michael made a splendid match. The girl's aunts agreed. Allie agreed. Everyone agreed.

If only the two young people in question would realize it.

"Stop worrying, he's a smart young man. You laid the groundwork well. I am sure the boy has, what do they call it, 'hooked up' with her now that they're both back in the city."

"Is 'hooking up' having an affair?"

"Not always, sir. While I believe *tapping that* refers strictly to having sex, *hooking up,* unless I am mistaken, is the term the young ones use for everything from dating to heavy petting to sex without repercussions for either party."

"Don't call me *sir.*"

"Don't call *me* a *matchmaker.*"

"Agreed." *Matchmaker.* "How do you know such things when I don't?"

Roderick shifted his gaze and cleared his throat. That meant he had no intention of answering truthfully. Mortimer almost laughed. His friend had a secret addiction to TV shows such as *The O.C.* and *One Tree Hill,* which seemed to abound with people hooking, tapping and scoring with their "baby's" daddy. But he'd not let on, not wanting to embarrass the other man.

"I supposed I'm more culturally aware," Roderick said.

"Bah. Culture. What, I ask you, was wrong with the old-fashioned terms? Court a woman, sweep her off her feet and into your bed, make passionate love to her and be done with it."

Roderick poured the tea and sighed wistfully. "True, true. Much more sensible. And romantic. But those days are over for both of us, I am afraid."

"Rubbish! You're in your seventies, not in your grave."

Rod sighed, rubbing at his back, which had apparently been giving him some trouble. "Some days it feels as if I am. I just don't have the physical capacity for romantic adventures anymore."

Mortimer reached for his cup, not letting his friend see his smile. Because although Roddy might think his romantic days were behind him, Mortimer happened to think differently. In fact, judging by the way the tips of the man's ears had turned pink whenever he'd exchanged glances with Miss Emily

Baker last weekend, romance was definitely still blooming here in Trouble.

"Say," he remarked, trying to sound casual, "have you seen that lovely Miss Baker lately? I do worry about how lonely she must be now that Allie's young man has come back."

He didn't add a comment about his secretary's relationship having been yet another matchmaking success for Mortimer. He and Roderick had had that conversation this week. He'd had it with Allie, too, who was blissful when a little more than a week ago she'd been heartbroken. Proof his methods worked.

"I'm quite certain the lady has any number of activities with which to entertain herself."

There went the ears. Pink as a mouse's tail. "Why don't you call her up?"

Roderick gaped. "C-call her up? Whatever for?"

To think the man used to be so quick. "Well…to 'hook up.'" Personally Mortimer thought it would be a good thing for Roddy to "tap that" and figured Miss Emily, being a spinster, would probably enjoy it, too. But, in this situation, baby steps were required. Besides, not being entirely sure of the contemporary lingo, he didn't want to say the wrong thing or use the wrong terminology.

Goodness, how much simpler terms had been when a mistress was a mistress and a wife a wife and never the twain would meet. As long as you were very lucky.

"I wouldn't dare."

"You're saying you're afraid? Of a *woman?* This cannot be the man who rescued a stolen harem with me."

Roderick's expression grew wistful, then he slowly shook his head. "We're much too old for those sorts of adventures, Mortimer."

"Nonsense. Had myself an adventure recently, didn't I?"

Grunting, his majordomo reiterated his feelings on that score. "Please, don't mention *those* two, you'll turn my stomach."

"They're fine ladies."

"*Ladies* is not a word I'd associated with the older Feeney women. Miss Jennifer, I will grant you, does seem cut from an entirely different piece of cloth altogether. A good girl that one."

"As is Miss Baker," Mortimer mumbled, sitting back in his chair and crossing his long legs out in front of him. The knees were acting up a bit today…. Must have been the pacing he'd done all week once Michael had gone back to the city.

"Ridiculous. Impossible. I'm too old for romance."

"But you're not too old to make a new friend," Mortimer said, closing his eyes, reminding himself of those baby steps.

"A…friend?"

The tone held interest. Roddy was on the hook; Mortimer just needed to reel him in. *Carefully.* "Yes, indeed, the lonely lady could use one. With Allie soon leaving, taking the baby, that dear soul will be completely alone. At the mercy of anyone who might try to take advantage of her." If he opened his eyes, he'd see Rod puffing up in his porcupine pose. But he didn't dare.

"That would be dreadful. She's much too kindhearted."

"Yes, she is. I wish she had a friend to talk to. Someone upon whom she could depend. A hand reached out in friendship would be a beacon in her lonely life." That was laying it on a bit thick, so he shut up, not wanting to tip his hand.

His friend fell silent, but Mortimer could almost hear the wheels of thought churning in Roddy's brain. He would bet his antique Egyptian pipe that he knew what was about to happen. Roderick would refuse categorically, then go away and stew on it for a while. He'd hem and haw, come up with a hundred reasons to forget the whole thing. Afterward, of course, he would do what he always did: exactly what Mortimer had suggested.

"Absolutely not," Rod finally said, slapping his hand on his thigh and rising from his chair. "No, indeed. That is quite enough talk of that."

Then he left. To stew. Which meant in about twenty-four to forty-eight hours, he would be calling on Miss Emily Baker. Upon that little fact, Mortimer would bet not only his pipe but his store of illicit Egyptian tobacco that went in it.

His lungs couldn't handle the stuff these days, anyway.

"Eh, God, it's not easy always being right about everything," Mortimer mumbled as he crossed his arms over his chest. And while thinking about pairing off all the people closest to him— while he, himself, remained a determined bachelor—he drifted into a nice morning nap with a smile on his face.

IF IT HAD BEEN A SUNNY Saturday morning, Jen might have turned around and gone back to her apartment right after she and Mike stepped outside. Even good Cuban coffee wasn't worth being stabbed in the eyes by merciless sunlight. Fortunately, though, it was overcast and, with her sunglasses, almost manageable.

Good thing, too. Her new neighbor Mr. Jones apparently hadn't gotten his "how to be a courteous apartment dweller in New York" lesson because even from here, on the street, she could still hear his icky eighties pop music blaring away. Weren't old farts supposed to listen to Perry Como and Andy Williams?

Silent and still in head-in-vise agony, Jen led Mike out of the building, which had once been a school in Chelsea. It had been renovated sometime in the past two decades, but barely touched since. Not that Jen cared. She loved the area, being right around the corner from the Chelsea Market and an easy cab ride away from her publishers or her agent.

Best of all, there was a fabulous bodega on the block that served amazing coffee. Without asking, that was where she headed, eschewing the franchise shops in favor of good Cuban brew. She knew from experience it was strong enough to melt paint.

When she was greeted by name as they entered, Mike said, "I take it you like their coffee."

"Their muffins are to die for, too, but today if anybody tried to make me eat one, I'd punch his lights out."

"Glad I brought bagels instead of muffins," he replied evenly.

The man did make her smile. Even though he tried to sound serious and strictly business, he had a sense of humor. He just didn't let it come out to play very often.

"Want to sit outside?" he asked as they got their coffee—black with three sugars for Jen—and walked out the door. If it had been a typical stifling hot August day in New York, she would have immediately said no. But the moisture that had been hanging over the entire northeast for weeks had provided another gray, drizzly day. Which suited her mood.

That didn't mean she was taking off her sunglasses, however. Not only did she want to keep light out, she also didn't want to scare any small children walking by who might see her blood-red eyes and think she was a zombie.

"So how'd you find out where I live?" she asked.

He shrugged as he sat opposite her at a small café table. "I have some pretty good connections."

Very good ones. Though she was glad he'd found her, Jen

went to a lot of trouble to keep her private information *private*. There were a lot of wackos out there. Some who wanted to scream at her, some who threatened to hurt her. Some who offered to change her mind about men by treating her the way a woman *should* be treated. Like an unpaid servant and sex slave, per one guy.

Whatever they wanted, *she* didn't want any of them to show up at her door one night with a copy of her book in one hand and a baseball bat in the other. "I don't mean to sound paranoid, but I do try to remain hard to find. There are some really twisted people out there. I'm sure you understand."

A thunderous expression she hadn't before seen on his face made him go from an easygoing hot guy to a dark-and-dangerous one so fast it nearly took her breath away. And had her shaking a little bit in her seat.

"Has anything else happened?"

Wary, she asked, "Else?"

"Grandpa said you were getting threatening calls and letters. Have there been more since you got back?"

Someone had a big, fat mouth. Two someones—both of whose names started with the letter *I* and both of whom had crushes on Mike's grandfather. "It's no big deal. And I wasn't stupid enough to think I wouldn't be facing that kind of stuff. Publishing contract, smart-ass books, stupid men with inferiority complexes, all mixed together. Bad combination."

His shoulders didn't ease, they remained rock-solid, as did his hands, which were fisted on the table. "Tell me everything."

"That's all there is. Threats. Nobody's touched me, nobody's turned up at my door." She purposely didn't mention the recent hateful calls or the vague feeling she'd had about somebody being in her apartment. The last thing she needed to do was refuel his curiosity about whether she was nutty. "I bet Katie Couric gets a thousand times more icky mail than I do. It's part of the package of being a celebrity, even if a very minor one."

That unflinching stare of his almost made her keep on babbling like an idiot. The man was good at that, silent-but-intense, the kind of guy who'd make a robber spill the location of his stash with a simple glare. But he finally eased up. The jaw unclenched; the fingers relaxed; he even leaned back a little bit in his chair. "You'll tell me if anything else happens?"

Not that he could do anything, but frankly, it was nice to think somebody was looking out for her. Somebody other than her girlfriends and an agent whose paychecks depended on her royalties. "Yes. Now, be honest, how did you find me?"

Lifting his coffee to his mouth, he said, "I'm a cop."

She almost fell out of her seat. Even though not thirty seconds ago she'd been thinking of what a good interrogator he'd be, she honestly hadn't seen that answer coming. "A *what?*"

"I'm a detective. I've been with the NYPD for six years, ever since I got out of college."

She did some quick mental math, surprised to realize she might actually be a year or two older than Mike. He certainly didn't act like any twenty-somethings she knew. He was much more focused, which could have been a product of his upbringing, or merely a facet of his personality. Either way, it probably served him well in his profession.

His profession. As in police officer. "Oh, hell."

Just how often had she threatened to kill her aunts in front of this man? Countless times, obviously. She was lucky he hadn't hauled her in, locked her up and thrown away the key.

No wonder he'd thought her a little dangerous at first—as a cop he was probably used to people carrying through when they made as many threats as she had.

His disgustingly thick lashes lowered over his eyes, and if she wasn't mistaken his lips quirked a bit at the corners. He was obviously aware of what she was thinking.

"You know, I would never really kill anyone."

"I know."

That was it. No apology for not having told her sooner what he did for a living. Then again, she hadn't been quick to tell him about her writing, either. His grandfather had done that.

"I don't work current murder cases, anyway," he admitted. "I just transferred to headquarters and sit at a desk most of the time. Quite a change coming off three years in Vice, busting pimps, hookers and dealers."

Quite a change, indeed. But somehow, she could see Mike doing it. He was strong; he was tough. He could hold his own against any thug who happened to cross his path.

"By the way, to answer your question, no, it would not be easy for someone to track you down, and I had to pull a string or two to do it."

That both pleased and worried her, since she'd been getting those annoying, heavy-breathing calls again ever since she'd returned from Trouble. She'd hoped the guy would get tired of his game while she'd been out of town and *hated* that her creepy caller was able to track her down as easily as a detective could.

A detective. Wow. She thought for a second about asking him if he dealt with harassing phone callers. He'd almost certainly take them more seriously than the officer she'd talked to a month ago had. He'd told her to change her number and then had basically ushered her out the door.

But she said nothing, not wanting Mike to get all protective and cop-like. She enjoyed spending time around the relaxed guy with the tousled hair and those dreamy brown eyes.

"To think I wondered if you were an artist."

His head jerked back and he looked at her in astonishment. He also looked a little insulted.

"Sorry. Not that you look all lean and pale and artistic," she quickly explained. "You just have a deep and intense streak that suited a moody artist type."

"I'm not moody."

Snorting at that whopper, she replied, "Buddy, sometimes you make a twelve-year-old girl look stable."

"Well sometimes you make your aunts look stable."

Her jaw dropping, she considered flinging her coffee at him for that one, which was a majorly low blow. Not that she'd really have done it, not only because she didn't want to hurt him but also because she didn't want to waste the fabulous coffee, which was already easing her headache. And there was the whole "assaulting a police officer" issue. Before she could come up with an alternate plan, she saw the lips twitch and out came that fabulous smile.

"Lord have *mercy*," she muttered. Two young women walking by their table on the sidewalk immediately swung their heads to stare. So did a prissy guy emerging from the bodega with his own coffee. "I can't believe you hide that thing."

His brow went up. "That…thing?"

"The smile. Those dimples."

"You're exaggerating."

Maybe he wanted to think so. Jen knew better. Mike Taylor was the kind of guy who could stop traffic at Times Square—

if he was on one of those huge underwear billboards, the city would come to a standstill.

Umm. Mike Taylor in underwear. *Someday.*

Obviously uncomfortable and wanting to change the subject, he said, "I read more of your book last night. It's very clever. Where'd you get the stories?"

"Readers. Friends."

"Your aunts?"

Jen immediately stiffened, slowly lowering her coffee to the table. She managed to keep her smile on her face, but it grew tighter. *How? How could he know that?* She'd used no names. Besides, it had been *ages* ago. "What do you mean?"

Mike's expression never changed. She wondered if that was what people called a cop face, because his eyes remained locked on hers, penetrating, unblinking. He didn't frown, though of course, he didn't smile either. He simply looked interested—and determined to get answers to his questions.

Not that she had any. Not real ones, anyway.

"I remember that other lady who was at dinner the other night, Emily Baker, mentioning something about your aunt Ivy being widowed at a young age. She'd been married to a wealthy early rock-and-roll producer back in the sixties?"

She should have known rumors like that would still be flying around Trouble. The town hadn't had anything new happen since the invention of the microwave oven. Well, that and Mortimer Potts. And he couldn't very well be gossiped about to his own grandson. "Yes, she was."

"In the book, the record producer was murdered and his home set on fire to cover it up…. Was it your aunt's husband?"

Damn. A direct question. One she couldn't hem and haw over. "More like *based* on him," she admitted, opening another pack of sugar and dumping it into her half-empty cup of coffee, "I, of course, use some creative license in my books and emphasize what I want to in order to make a point."

"Oh?"

"I'm not writing rocket science. Or even real self-help books. There's no *M.D.* after my name or *expert* before it. Readers know I'm a humorist." If only more *men* did. Yeesh. You did some fantasizing in print about murdering a few cheating bastards and suddenly you were public enemy number one of men worldwide.

"How'd you find out about your late uncle?"

"Aunt Ivy talks to herself a lot." Aunt Ida Mae had talked, too. And the townspeople. And Jen's own father, who'd told Jen's mom about his sister's husband and his unsolved murder. Never knowing that a twelve-year-old Jen had been hiding under the stairs.

"Did she share the whole story?"

"Not a lot. I just know the basics," she admitted. "But, to answer you, yes, Aunt Ivy was married to a producer named Leo Cantone, and he died tragically forty years ago."

"It's funny, when I Googled the names, I saw there was a special on VH1 not one month ago about rock scandals and mysteries. Cantone's story was in it, along with mentions of the musicians he swindled, some of whom have disappeared, too."

Googled? He was Googling things she didn't even want him *thinking* about? This was not good. "Why would you do that?"

"Just curious," he admitted. "It's an interesting story and Miss Baker's comment made me realize it had happened *here*. When I looked online, your aunt turned up, too. Did you know there's a rumor that she inspired the Coasters song 'Poison Ivy'?"

Jen couldn't contain a grin of amusement. Because it made such perfect sense. "She knew everybody in those days."

Mike swirled his coffee cup, gazing at the scant inch of brown liquid left in the bottom of it. As casually as he would ask how she liked the weather, he said, "Do you think she had something to do with Cantone's murder?"

Jen froze in shock. Not just because of how ridiculous the idea was, but because of how quickly Mike had come up with it. After all, it had taken a few years of eavesdropping for Jen to come to the conclusion that Aunt Ivy knew more about her husband's death than she'd ever told. Not to mention how long it had taken Jen to realize the woman probably *was* capable of murder. So how had Mike stumbled upon the possibility so soon, especially when any articles on the case should have mentioned the fact that Leo Cantone's wife had been *cleared?*

"Are you asking as a cop?"

He shook his head but still stared into his coffee. "I told you, I'm curious. Honestly, I'm more interested in knowing if that old story helped you come up with the theme for your book. Isn't it about why murder is better than divorce?"

"Only in the most general terms," Jen insisted. "It's *really* about the stupid things men do that drive women crazy. There are dozens of books on the subject coming at it from the male perspective, that bestseller from a couple of years ago about guys not being 'into you' among them."

He nodded in concession of the point. "True."

"Ivy has lived under suspicion for years," Jen said firmly, "but she had an ironclad alibi. She was at a dinner party with a group of ten people, including a few celebrities, when neighbors heard Leo fighting with someone in their house."

He nodded again.

"Besides, she was *tiny* and couldn't even have lifted the statue he was killed with, much less whacked him in the head with it."

Jen lifted her coffee cup, not meeting Mike's eyes. This was the stickiest part—the part where the reported story and the one Jen had put together with her research and her memories went their separate ways. "The firefighters were even on the scene when she got back to the house."

"I know," he said simply. "The articles made that clear."

Jen regretted letting herself get on the defensive, relaxing at his laid-back tone. "So why did you ask if she killed him?"

"I am a cop. Suspicious by nature."

"But you know she didn't, right?"

Laughing at her persistence, he held his hands up, palms out. "I got it, I know."

"Good, just so we're on the same page."

"Same page, same playbook."

"And also so we're clear on something else. The stories I use in the books are meant to be humorous moral advisory tales, not deep evaluations of *real* old murders."

"It worked. That's a pretty strong cautionary tale…. A record-producer husband who cheats on his wife, steals from his clients and ends up bludgeoned to death on the living-room floor before his house is burned down around him."

Jen didn't remember putting that much detail in her book. He must have done more research than he'd let on. But she didn't panic. Because she knew Ivy hadn't killed Leo; the woman *had* been exonerated by the police. So it didn't matter what a present-day cop thought, *if* he was investigating the case, which Mike insisted he wasn't. After all, why would he? It had nothing to do with his former assignment catching dealers and pimps, or his new one, which he'd admitted was a desk job at police headquarters.

Finally, no matter how good Mike might be at his job, he didn't chase after killers, and he was not a mind reader. He couldn't possibly know the *whole* story. How could anyone who didn't know Aunt Ivy know the truth? Only someone who'd been around the family for years could come to the same conclusion Jen had: that Ivy had been cheating, too, with one of her husband's clients—a young, unknown singer-songwriter named Eddie James.

And that her husband had likely been murdered by her lover.

"Frankly, a man like Leo Cantone would drive any woman to murder," she mused. "Which is the only reason I included the story in my book, even though I am *certain* Ivy had nothing to do with his death."

She was. Pretty certain, anyway.

Jen did, however, wonder if her aunt had helped her lover escape and was, therefore, an accessory after the fact. The police had certainly suspected James—she knew that from the research she'd done on the case. But they'd suspected him as being one of Cantone's bilked clients, *not* Ivy's lover.

Jen knew better. She'd grown up hearing Ivy talk to her one true love, the only person her aunt had *ever* seemed to care about, besides her parents and Jen's own father. Ivy used to reminisce with Eddie, tittering and flirting, reliving old conversations and sharing secret plans to run away from her husband. Then there would come the mumbles—the cries of fear, the moans of anguish, the terror of the flames—and the confessions.

Jen's suspicions had been confirmed when she'd gone through the contents of Ivy's precious knitting box. The passionate love letters, photographs, hotel receipts and journals had made the affair indisputable.

Ivy's affair with Eddie, Jen believed, had been discovered by her husband. Leo had been killed in an ensuing fight between the men, while Ivy had been out of the house. When she'd returned home and seen what had happened, she'd helped Eddie escape. It was even possible, though Jen was only speculating, that Ivy, herself, had set her house on fire to hide the evidence in order to protect Eddie. Since Ivy had been a very wealthy woman at the time, she could even have taken care of her lover financially, letting him get away and make a new start somewhere else.

At least, that was what Jen *thought* had happened. She doubted anyone would ever know the truth. Even if Ivy admitted it, she couldn't be counted on to remember the details. And her aunt's journals ended abruptly a few days before Leo Cantone's murder.

One thing was clear—the woman had never gotten over the tragedy. One man dead. Another on the run. Her home destroyed.

All for the love of her.

It was the one reason Jen could never quite maintain her anger at her aunt. Ivy had gone through so much trauma in her life and it had left her more than a bit fragile.

None of which Jen was prepared to share with Mike. She'd alluded to the unsolved case in only the roughest of terms in her book. The only reason he'd put it together was that he'd happened to attend a party with both Ivy and with someone who knew about her past, Emily Baker. And he was a cop— with a suspicious nature. One who *Googled*.

It had been bad luck all the way around. But now that it was over, she didn't intend to talk to him about it anymore.

"You know, I'm feeling better now. The coffee did the trick. I should probably go home," she said, suddenly rising from her chair. She didn't truly want to leave. What she wanted more than anything was to stay and get back to their earlier conversation. The one where Mike had admitted just how crazy he'd been going whenever he'd pictured what he should have been doing Monday morning at that roadside hotel. But she didn't feel up to continuing to fend off his questions or turn aside his suspicions about her aunt.

He rose, too. "I'd like to know more about this."

"No." Her voice was firm, betraying none of the nervousness Jen was really feeling about the whole subject. "It's in the past, I don't know much of the story and if I thought you'd come over only to pump me for information about something that happened forty years ago, I'd be pretty annoyed." And her ego would be seriously bruised. Not to mention her libido, which would scream and take hostages at the injustice.

"Of course I didn't. I wanted…" he began to say, then he looked past her, over her shoulder at the street. Muttering, "What the hell," his eyes grew wide and his jaw dropped.

Jen began to swing around to see what had caught his attention, but before she could do it, he barked, "Get down!"

Not waiting for her to obey, he grabbed her by the shoulders and launched both of them to the left. They flew through the air, landing against the outside wall of the bodega. He obviously tried to protect her with his own body, tucking in behind her as they hit the bricks with a bone-crunching thud that hurt like hell and immediately brought tears of agony to Jen's eyes.

It probably, however, didn't hurt as much as it would have

if they'd remained where they were. Because before she had even caught her breath between what felt like broken ribs, Jen saw a black van careen out of control and crash up onto the sidewalk. It smashed the table and chairs where their coffee cups had been sitting.

And wiped out the whole area where they'd been talking just a few heartbeats ago.

CHAPTER TEN

I once read a survey in a men's magazine where they asked men and women to name the top five things they look for in a member of the opposite sex. Women said things like nice eyes, great smile, easy to talk to, muscular, good with kids. Men's lists usually read: big tits, big tits, big tits, good cook, big tits. And they wonder why we sometimes want to kill them?

—*I Love You, I Want You, Get Out* by Jennifer Feeney

"I'M GOING TO KILL THAT SON of a bitch."

Mike's hands clenched and unclenched, fisting by themselves as they had for two days, ever since he and Jen had nearly been pureed by a mysterious black van. His body was sore, as he imagined hers must be, but he'd been too furious and wired since Saturday to let that deter him. Ever since dropping her off at her place a few hours after the incident outside the bodega, he'd been focused on one thing: finding out who'd tried to kill them. Even if he had to step outside his job to do it.

"You know, considering eighty percent of the people here are on the job, this probably isn't the best place to make death threats."

Mike glared at his buddy Tom Finnegan, his former partner

in vice. Though they hadn't worked together since Mike's transfer, they remained close friends, often getting together for a beer at the cop bar on Thirty-eighth Street. Tonight's meeting was also about business, however. Mike wanted his friend to find out whatever he could about Saturday's incident. Since he still worked vice on the Upper East Side, Tom knew all the shit going on in that underground world, including rumors on the street regarding one rich thug named Ricky Stahl.

"You mean you wouldn't be ready to kill someone who'd put a hit out on you?"

Tommy shook his head. "You can't be sure of that. Maybe some drunk went on an all-nighter and was heading home early Saturday morning when he nearly took you out."

"Yeah, right," Mike insisted. "Come on, Stahl loses in court because of my testimony last week. And a day later a black van with tinted windows and no tag almost runs me down in broad daylight, then disappears into thin air?"

"I ain't saying you're wrong. Just that you need to keep cool, keep your head down. Don't be drawing attention to yourself." Tommy looked around, side to side, his normally smiling face appearing tense. He leaned across the table. "Everybody knows Stahl has people inside the blue line. Some say that's why you got shit-canned down to 1PP."

Mike shook his head, still not wanting to believe someone like Stahl could have cops on the take, though he knew it was true. Rumors had been thick about Stahl's arm of influence worming into the NYPD. His one regret at being forced to move on Stahl to prevent a murder was that he hadn't caught the rats.

"I still say you should have fought it."

"Miss my cheerful presence, huh?"

His friend grinned, that easygoing Irish demeanor never revealing that Tommy could kick a perp's ass through his nostrils in under a minute if he had to. "Gotta tell you, that new kid they stuck with me smiles so much I just want to shoot him. I miss your glares."

"I don't glare."

"Okay, if you say so. But I definitely miss your silence."

"The silence you filled with nonstop bullshit."

"Exactly," Tommy said, sounding mournful. "My new partner never shuts up. I can't get a word in."

Mike lifted his beer, missing his days with Tommy more than he'd thought. It wasn't that he didn't like what he was doing on a daily basis—digging through old cases to try to find answers other cops had given up on years ago. Solving those cases when others had not gave him a real charge, a sense of satisfaction he hadn't found when working Vice. But he did miss the action of being on the streets, making a real difference *now,* today.

Then he thought of the parents of those teenagers whose murder he'd been investigating, and knew giving them peace would be more fulfilling than anything he'd ever done before.

"Your family's been here for a few generations, running the store in the village, haven't they?" Mike asked, thinking of one case that had caught his attention recently. Ivy Feeney's. "You know anything about the rock scene from the sixties?"

"You planning to become an Elvis impersonator?"

"Funny. So funny," he said with a grunt. "I'm interested in an old case. I heard about it from a friend…."

"You don't have friends."

Mike ignored him. "And did a little digging until I found the file. A record producer was murdered in his home in the East Village back in sixty-six."

"Doesn't sound familiar. That's a pretty ancient one. As-signment? Or something you're playing around with?"

Tommy knew the way it worked. Some files were handed to the cold-case team—some came up as new evidence was developed, often during the investigation of another crime. Sometimes it was an investigator who dug the file out simply because it sounded interesting. This was a case like that.

"Playing with it, that's all," he replied.

"I'll ask the old man," Tommy said as he finished his beer. "My grandfather has a herd of elephants living in his head, every one of them full of memories he can pull out on a dime."

Nodding his thanks, Mike wondered if he'd done the right thing in looking into this case. There was no reason for him to have gone hunting for Leo Cantone's file at work today—he'd done it because he'd been interested by the story in Jen's book and by their conversation Saturday. And he hadn't for-gotten his grandfather's kidnapping.

The file had made for some interesting reading today. Though Jen didn't seem to want to talk about it, he figured she had to be interested in the whole thing since she'd included it in her book. She might like to know what her crazy old aunt had been like in those days, what the report said about her. He wanted to tell her what he'd learned. And he wanted to see if she could offer more information. Not to mention he just wanted to *see* her again.

Soon. Like, maybe, tonight.

He hadn't seen her since Saturday when they'd both nearly been pancaked by that black van. Frankly, Mike had felt guilty as hell for bringing that kind of darkness around her and putting her in such danger. So guilty in fact, that he hadn't even tried to contact her since.

Time to end that, however. He just needed to be more careful, alert. The incident Saturday morning may have been an attempt on his life, but it was at least *possible* it had been a freak accident involving a stupid driver too scared to stick around afterward. He wasn't laying any money on that possibility, but it was at least an option.

Whatever the case, he was on guard, and it was time to move forward, starting with an apology to Jen. Then, perhaps, seeing if they were finally ready to pick up where they'd left off at his grandfather's house.

"Thanks for meeting me," he told Tommy as he paid the tab. "I have to get going."

His ex-partner nodded. "Watch your back."

He would. He definitely would. He'd watch Jen's, too, if she allowed him to get close enough to do it. Unfortunately, he wasn't sure she'd let him. After Saturday morning, when he'd practically shoved her into her apartment in his hurry to get her out of danger by distancing himself from her, she'd seemed pretty pissed off. She might not be speaking to him. Or she might thank him for saving her life. She might even be armed and ranting as she'd been the first time he'd met her. Or she might throw her arms around him and kiss him in pure gratitude.

Well, that last one was a stretch. But one thing was sure— he could hardly wait to see her and find out.

EMILY HAD A DATE.

She'd never had one before, well, not a real one. A friend of the family had taken her to a high-school dance once at her father's request about sixty years ago. Since then, however, she'd only had lunch dates with girlfriends or bridge dates with the local club. Never a man-woman date.

But she did now. Tomorrow night. With Mr. Roderick Ward.

"I can't do this," she whispered as she looked at the five outfits she'd strewn across her sofa, trying to decide between them. How foolish. She owned absolutely nothing that made her feel as if she actually belonged with a man like him.

Some might look at him and see a butler to a rich man. A servant. But Emily knew he was much more than that. He was a servant to Mr. Potts in name only. In truth, they were friends. Contemporaries. Equals.

His pride insisted he still be called an employee. That was the only way Roderick would continue to live in Mr. Potts's house. From what he'd said last Sunday night at the dinner party, he had his own home, in England, and could probably live there very comfortably for the rest of his life without working another day.

But he'd miss his friend. He and Mortimer were like an old married couple who'd been together their whole lives. Or like two soldiers who'd survived a war.

Well, wasn't that exactly what they were?

"Miss Baker?" a man's voice said. It was accompanied by a knock on her door.

"Come in, Damon," she said, recognizing the voice.

Damon Cole, Allie's handsome young man, walked in, greeting her with a smile. She'd grown more attached to the boy every day. What a charmer, what a delight. And how deeply in love he was with Allie and her baby boy. It made even an expert at love like Emily realize she didn't know everything there was to know about the most tender of emotions. Damon had given up his former life to come here and be with the woman he loved, including starting up a counseling center right here in Trouble. Emily didn't know how much this would resemble his work as a child welfare worker in Florida, but considering the number of nutty people right here in Trouble, he'd sure be busy.

"I got home early but Allie and Hank aren't there."

"She ran out to the grocery store," she said. Seeing Damon's disappointment, she added, "But I'm sure they'll be back any moment. Why don't you sit down and wait?"

He glanced around the room at the dresses covering every surface. Blushing, Emily quickly grabbed them up, feeling foolish. "Sorry. I was just…doing a bit of spring cleaning."

"In August?" The twinkle in his eye said he was teasing. "Don't tell me you're going to break the hearts of all the single men in Trouble by going out on a date."

"You tease," she said, blushing to the roots of her hair. She was too old for such nonsense—dates and blushing and worrying over what to wear.

Somehow, though, she didn't feel old. She felt young and carefree. As she hadn't since she'd been a teenage girl, shortly before both of her parents had gotten sick and her quiet, lonely life of nursing them had become the only road she could travel.

It seemed like forever since she'd allowed herself to have romantic dreams about *herself*. Decades. Yes, her brother had given her a glimpse of a normal life once, thirty years or so ago. When he'd been financially able to, he'd offered to hire someone to take care of their parents so Emily could try to have some kind of life of her own. But by then, her father had been confined to a wheelchair and her mother had refused to let a stranger take care of him.

So she'd stayed. She'd always stayed.

"Is it Mr. Ward?"

That jerked Emily out of her thoughts and made her go as

stiff as a ladder. "Please tell me Allie told you that because if I thought I made a fool of myself over him at dinner last week, I'd never be able to face any of those people again." Particularly Ida Mae and Ivy Feeney.

"She hinted at it," Damon explained. "Where are you going?"

"To dinner and a movie."

Damon frowned. "Please tell me he's taking you out of Trouble. I've only lived here a few weeks and I already know the only two restaurants are fit primarily for the cockroaches that live inside their walls. And I don't think the Movie Palace renovation is finished yet, is it?"

Emily bit the inside of her cheek. Damon had the right of it when it came to local restaurants. "We're going to a place up in Weldon then to a documentary up at the college there."

"A documentary, huh? Not exactly typical first-date stuff."

That it was her first date in reality was something she did not want to admit, not even to as nice a young man as this one. "I'm sure it will be quite informative."

"Informative? Boo. You want hot and sexy," another voice said. Allie, carrying Hank on her hip and a grocery bag slung over her arm, entered the living room. Dropping the bag, she bent to give Damon a kiss, immediately releasing Hank to his waiting arms. Damon held him like an absolute natural.

Emily gave them a moment to say hello before responding to Allie's ridiculous suggestion. "I'm afraid *hot* and *sexy* are two words that are not in my vocabulary."

"Why not?" Unperturbed, Allie began tossing through the dresses. "Nope. Nope. Maybe for a funeral…like your own."

Damon cleared his throat. "You sure haven't mastered that whole tact thing, babe."

Tossing her head in a cute move that sent her brown curls

bouncing, Allie gave Emily a brilliant smile. "Who can be tactful when there's romance in the air?" Then she pointed to a dress Emily had pulled out only as a last resort—a dark pink one that was a bit too flashy, in her opinion. But it did make her eyes sparkle, so she'd included it. "Wear that one. Let him know you're interested."

"Didn't saying *yes* let him know I was interested?"

"You're hopeless."

"I'm not very experienced at this kind of thing."

Allie must have heard the uncertainty in Emily's voice because she let off the teasing. Dropping the dresses into a heap, she reached out and put a gentle hand on Emily's shoulder. At that moment, it was as if she knew Emily's darkest secret—that she didn't have just a *small* amount of experience, she had absolutely none. None with dating. None with love.

None with sex.

None.

"I can't do this," she whispered, knowing she'd been foolish to even consider going on a date at her age. "I'm going to have to call and decline."

Allie's tender touch turned into a big hug. The girl was tiny, but she had strong arms and a fierce heart. "No, you're not," she whispered. "I'll tell you whatever you need to know."

At that moment, Emily realized her secret wasn't her own at all. Allie had pegged her rightly as a spinster virgin. She pulled away, looking for pity or amusement in the feisty young woman's face. Of course, she saw neither. Allie's bright brown eyes reflected the kindness of her nature. The same sweet, cocky attitude she'd had since the day Emily had met her on a bus bound for Trouble. Even pregnant, nearly broke and carrying a yappy dog, the girl had been irresistible. The kind of daughter Emily would have loved to have, if she'd ever had that chance.

"You're doing this," Allie said. Then she pointed to the pink dress. "And you're wearing *that.*"

There was one more thing to be said for Allie Cavanaugh: she was determined. So though Emily put up a few more minutes of feeble argument, in the end, she agreed to do exactly what her young friend advised.

Picturing the next evening, she honestly couldn't say which situation worried her more—that Mr. Ward would see her in that dress with her new hairdo and get the wrong impression.

Or that he'd get the *right* one.

WHEN MIKE KNOCKED on Jen's door an hour after leaving the bar, he immediately summed up her mood. She was mad. He obviously had *not* been worrying for nothing.

"Come to protect me again?" she asked when she opened the door of her apartment. Her tone dripped sarcasm and her expression was anything but friendly.

Not that Mike noticed. He could pay attention to nothing except the huge bruise on her right shoulder, revealed by the tight, sleeveless tank top she wore. A matching one was visible farther down her arm, and a bandage on her elbow said she'd been wounded there, as well. "Damn it. Did I do that?"

She nodded toward her shoulder. "This one's such an interesting shade of purple, don't you think? Much more attractive than the black-and-yellow ones on my hip and back."

He stiffened, feeling like an abuser for having hurt her.

Apparently noticing, she grudgingly stepped back and opened the door wider to usher him in. "Not that I'm complaining." Even though she was. "You may well have saved my life."

He entered the apartment, immediately glancing around for any evidence of another man-hater party. He saw nothing out of the ordinary—no glaring friends, no wine, no ice cream or porn.

All of that was a good thing, except, maybe, the porn. He'd love to see Jen's face flushed and moist with excitement as suggestive images made her own imagination run rampant in her mind. Watching other people have sex didn't interest him in the least, but watching Jen be *affected* by it most definitely did.

Considering she was barely speaking to him, however, he didn't figure it would be a good time to mention that. Or to ask her if she was ready to pick up where they'd left off last weekend by making their way to the nearest hotel. Or her room.

For the first time in forever, he wished he'd picked up a few points on getting into a woman's good graces from Max. He was the lover of the family; Mike the fighter. Max would know how to seduce Jen out of her bad mood and into bed. Mike's instinctive response was to shove her back against the wall, slide his hands into her hair, tug her mouth to his and not stop kissing her until the frown left her face.

Then drag her to the nearest bed.

Not that he'd ever try to manhandle her—he knew Jen well enough to know that was the wrong way to proceed. Besides, she was too bruised and banged up for that. Her movements were slow and careful, shadows of painful weariness visible beneath her eyes. Which just made him tense all over again with the need to hurt whoever had nearly crashed into them both, necessitating his rough rescue.

"Anyway, um…thanks," she finally said after she'd closed the door behind him, remaining close to it in the narrow front hall of her apartment.

"Well *that* sounded sincere."

"Thank you for tossing my ass out of the path of an oncoming van," she clarified. "And saving me from being squashed by it. I know I could have been killed."

"Getting better." He was about to open his mouth again, to try to somehow apologize for throwing her against the side of a building and leaving her covered with more bruises than a teenager after a game of paintball. But she wasn't finished.

"I am *not,* however, very happy that you followed up by dumping me on my doorstep with an order to stay home."

Yeah, he guessed he had done that. Getting Jen home safely and finding out who'd targeted him had been all he could think about once he'd made sure they were both okay. He'd hustled her here after they'd made their statements to the responding officer and dropped her off as if he couldn't wait to get rid of her. When, in truth, all he'd wanted was to stay with her and make sure nobody had followed them to her place.

"I've lived here for seven years. I'm not some fresh-from-the-farm kid who doesn't understand the big city."

"But have you ever had to deal with a psycho who could hurt you?" he asked in his own defense.

She crossed her arms and cocked a brow. "Are you forgetting who my relatives are?"

Point taken.

"You acted like I'm a poor, helpless woman who doesn't know how to put on her shoes unless her big strong man draws her a diagram. And frankly, I didn't like it."

Mike simply stared, somehow knowing there was more.

She finally lowered her arms, her lashes dropping slightly as she looked toward the floor. "As for not calling me for two days afterward…"

Now they were getting to it. He hadn't called. That was twice in the past week when she'd felt stood up, which suddenly made her prickliness a little more understandable.

"I'm sorry I didn't call," he murmured, unable to keep his hands to himself anymore. He reached up and brushed the tip of his finger over that dark bruise on her shoulder, flinching when she winced beneath his touch. The raw, angry-looking thing was the size of his palm, covering most of her shoulder and disappearing beneath the fabric of her shirt. "So damn sorry," he mumbled through a throat tight with regret. "I got caught up in investigating what happened."

"Do you think it was more than a random accident?"

He didn't want to go into the whole Ricky Stahl story. He somehow felt that voicing his name would bring the filth into their lives—into *her* life—and Mike couldn't stand the thought of it. He didn't even want her to know someone like that existed, much less that he'd nearly killed her, all because she'd gone out for a cup of coffee with Mike.

So he skipped the details, instead merely telling her, "I think it could be connected to a drug case I testified about last week, but that's only my gut talking."

"Listen to it," she murmured, sounding concerned, but also a bit distracted. As if she was much more aware of his touch on her shoulder than she'd like to admit. "To be honest," she added, "that whole thing didn't seem accidental to me."

He'd read her statement to the officer at the scene, the one who'd arrived immediately after the van had taken off, so he knew she meant it. Mike was glad to know she had strong instincts—and that she trusted them. "I know. That's why I wanted to get you home safely."

She shifted closer, the tension slowly easing out of her as he continued to stroke the edges of her shoulder. Using his fingertips, he traced the outline of her bruise, carefully. Tenderly. Apologetically. "I can't stand the thought of putting you in any danger."

Suddenly the muscles in her shoulder tensed and out came that determined jaw. "I hate that protector crap."

He'd have expected nothing else.

"I don't need anyone protecting me, Mike."

The letters and threatening phone calls she'd received after her last book disputed that statement. But he didn't press her because Jen hadn't opened up about it. Most of what he'd learned had come from his grandfather, by way of her aunts.

He wished she'd confide in him. Tell him everything that was happening and admit she was vulnerable enough to need someone once in a while. And that maybe that someone could be him.

His desire for her to do that was almost strange, since he liked her toughness. A lot. He didn't want her to change. So maybe it was that innate protector instinct his brothers swore he possessed rearing up again. Or just the need to plant himself between Jen and anyone who might dare try to hurt her.

Which was pretty ironic considering she was bruised up because of *him*. That made him feel like a first-class shit.

"You might not need a protector," he finally admitted, continuing to caress her shoulder, trying to ease the tension away again. "But you could use someone to take care of you once in a while." Unable to resist the softness of her skin any longer, he moved closer, stepping in as she retreated back against the wall. She didn't seem anxious to escape him. Instead, she almost began to sway, appearing weak on her feet and needing the wall for support. As if his touch had *made* her wobbly.

Well, that would make sense. He was having a hard time focusing on anything else—including standing—because of the way her silky body felt beneath his fingers.

"Maybe you need someone to make you feel better," he whispered, as he moved closer to her shoulder. Using his mouth, he traced the path his fingers had taken, gently kissing the bruised skin, hearing her soft sigh of acceptance in his ear.

"Kisses to make it feel better?" she said, her defenses audibly dropping away with every word.

"Uh-huh. I'm sorry I hurt you, Jennifer," he murmured as he continued to kiss her, so carefully, so tenderly, not wanting to cause her one more moment of pain. With every brush of his lips, he heard her sigh, felt her quiver. He inhaled her scent…and her acceptance. "So sorry."

She moaned, lifting her hands in the air, almost putting them on his shoulders, but not quite touching him. As if knowing *he* wanted to do the touching, to soothe away every memory of pain and do penance for having caused it.

Her hands slowly fell. Her head tilted back against the wall. Her eyes drifted closed. And Mike continued to taste her warm skin, to silently apologize and kiss away her hurt.

That was his only intention, to make it up to her, give her pleasure instead of pain. But of course, as soon as he began, he knew, very soon, he was going to be in a whole lot of pain, himself. Because the need to have her, to finally finish what they'd started back in Trouble, was about to crush him.

It had already made his pants damn near unwearable.

Bringing his hands to her waist, he carefully encircled it, re-membering what she'd said about her hip. A tiny hiss told him it was her right one, and Mike moved his hand down, gently stroking her through the thin fabric of her summery skirt.

He hadn't been paying attention to it when he'd first arrived, but he did now. Noticing the flimsiness of the thing, which fell in wisps of sheer, flowering material, he swallowed hard. The skirt didn't clothe her, per se, it merely floated around her hips and over the tops of her legs. Seemingly made of shadow and light, it hinted at the lush curves it was supposed to conceal. It was a simple thing, soft and shapeless on its own, but the way it rode over her body turned it into a garment of pure, soft invitation.

When she lifted her leg a tiny bit, to slide it against the outside of his, the fabric slid higher, revealing a heart-stopping length of that smooth, creamy thigh. The soft folds of cloth slid against her, outlining the V of her thighs. More shadow. More light. More need.

Mike's heart rate kicked up a notch and the air he was hauling into his lungs grew thicker. Only a real bastard would take advantage of her now, when she was so obviously in pain. He couldn't very well make love to the woman when he couldn't be sure whether her moans were of pleasure or discomfort.

He could, however, continue to touch her. To ease the ache. To apologize in the only way he could. Slipping his fingers beneath the elastic waistband of her skirt, he moved carefully—so carefully—until he could feel the curve of her hip bone. "Does it hurt here?" he asked, his voice husky with want.

She nodded, sighing a little. Pleading a little.

He cupped her there, gently kneading the spot, then moved his hand farther. All the while, he kept his face close to her neck, gauging her response by the deepness of her inhalations and the tiny sounds of pleasure emerging from her throat.

Watchful for any sign of discomfort, ready to pull away the moment he sensed she was no longer enjoying his touch.

"What about here?" he asked when he felt her grow tense as his fingertips brushed the curve of her bottom.

"Mmm, hmm," she said on a sigh, her eyes drifting closed. Though the spot might have pained her, she still arched back, into his hand, silently demanding the same touches he'd offered her elsewhere.

As if he could resist.

Thinking of his own pleasure now as much as hers, he cupped her warm, curvy cheek in his hand, stroking the soft spot where it touched the back of her thigh. Her sighs turned to gasps as his attention turned much more erotic than tender.

It was then he realized what he *should* have noticed right away. "Did you forget something when you got dressed this morning?" he asked, half choking, though whether on laughter or on lust, he couldn't say.

Because she wasn't wearing anything underneath that flimsy bit of material pretending to be a skirt.

Jen lifted her head and opened her eyes, staring at him. Those incredible eyes had gone dreamy-blue now, no trace of stormy-gray or icy-silver. "I didn't forget."

"I hope you stayed home today," he muttered as he cupped that sweet bare ass, running the tip of his finger along the seam of her cheeks.

She hissed in response and arched harder, as if inviting him to dip his fingers and find the hot, wet center of her. "The elastic from my panties hurt me," she admitted in a whimper.

His hand stilled. "I hate that I hurt you."

"But you're making it better," she whispered.

Not saying another word, he slowly moved, kissing his way

down her arm, tasting the skin on the inside of her elbow, brushing his lips across the bruise on her forearm. He continued to drop, until he was on his knees in front of her, breathing hotly through her shirt and the filmy skirt.

"Mike…"

"I'm making it better, Jen. That's all."

He cast a quick glance up, to ensure she was still okay with his version of comforting. Judging by the way her head had gone back and her eyes had closed again, he figured she was. Especially considering her pulse was pounding visibly in her throat, and her lips were parted and wet—her breaths audibly spilling across them in short, needy gasps.

That was answer enough.

Pressing his mouth to her belly, he breathed through the fabric, inhaling an intoxicating cacophony of scents. The detergent on her clothes. Whatever lotion she'd smoothed into those incredible thighs. Her light perfume. Not to mention the musky fragrance of her aroused body.

He wanted to devour her. He settled for sampling her.

Tugging at her elastic waistband, he slipped his tongue past the material and scraped it across her soft, milky skin.

"Oh, God," she groaned, finally dropping her hands onto his shoulders, as if needing the support.

Not knowing which he wanted more—to take away her pain or to give her ultimate pleasure, Mike slowly began to pull the skirt down. He moved carefully, tugging the elastic out so it didn't scrape her in a sensitive spot, letting it gather tightly again just below her hip bone.

That kept her covered where he most wanted to get to know her. But the sight of her hip bone drove the thought away. He had to close his eyes for a second, shocked by the ugliness of the bruise and scrapes directly over the bone. "Jesus…"

"It doesn't hurt as much today," she said, twining one hand in his hair.

"I can't believe you didn't slam the door in my face," he muttered as he moved his mouth to her poor, damaged skin.

"I'm starting to be glad I didn't."

"Me, too."

Then he stopped talking, focused only on tasting her, stroking her until she began to shake. He held her outer thighs, hoping he'd found an uninjured area to grip her. When he kissed his way to her side and saw the way the bruise edged all the way onto her lower back, he gave thanks that he hadn't gripped her glorious bottom any harder.

It was a wonder she hadn't broken her hip. It was a further wonder she was up walking around when she should be lying down with an ice pack or a heating pad, and a prescription painkiller. "You should be in bed."

"I want to be," she murmured dreamily.

"Or in a hot bath."

"Mmm. That sounds even better."

He began to pull away. "Why don't you go take one?"

She dropped her hands on his shoulders, squeezing them. "Will you take one with me?"

God the idea was tempting. So incredibly tempting. He was hot and ready, as hard as a rock, every molecule in his body demanding that he sample every inch of her. And she was every bit as aroused; he knew it by her whimpers, by her tiny goose bumps of awareness, by the weakness of her thighs and that hot scent pouring out of her.

But she looked much more in need of a doctor than a

lover—he'd seen guys less banged up after a bar fight. Judging by the exterior injuries, he'd bet her hip bone itself had been badly bruised against the brick wall of the bodega. Making love to her in just about any position would bring those parts of his anatomy in close contact with those parts of hers.

Which would hurt her. And he would *not* hurt her.

So while they both wanted it—badly—he wasn't enough of an asshole to take whatever she'd give him.

"Not tonight. You need to get better." He couldn't believe he was saying it, given the dreamy look on her face and the way her whole body was responding. Her skin was flushed, her beautiful nipples puckered in invitation against her shirt.

Man, this noble stuff was going to get old really fast. But only a real ass would make love to a woman who was genuinely in pain, as Jen had been Saturday morning and was again now.

She groaned softly, but didn't argue, which convinced him, more than anything, that he'd done the right thing. That didn't make it any less frustrating, unfortunately. It also didn't make his pants fit any better.

"I want you so much," she admitted, "but it hurts when I move. And the last thing I want is for you to think I'm a block of ice in bed."

As if this hot, passionate woman could *ever* be cold. "That's nuts," he said as he glanced up at her.

"Or that I don't want you," she continued, as if she hadn't heard him.

"I definitely don't think that." Definitely not. He moved to her belly again, breathing her in, letting his hot, moist breath press the fabric of her skirt against her sex. It had to feel good. He knew it did. Her shattered sighs told him so.

"I need this so much it's killing me."

She sounded tortured, almost desperate. He understood the feeling. After all, he'd been the same way for days, ever since they'd both built up the anticipation of the incredible sex they knew they'd have…but hadn't ever had the chance to act on it.

Just as tonight, once again, they couldn't act on it. Not without causing her some real discomfort…and possible embarrassment. "It'll be worth waiting for," he told her, trying to convince himself.

"I hate waiting." She sounded like a severely frustrated kid. Or a sexually frustrated woman.

He suddenly realized he could help her take the edge off at least a bit. Maybe not satisfy them both completely, the way they needed to be. But it wouldn't take much movement for him to give Jen a little of what she so desperately needed.

"You smell amazing," he said. "I like the way this skirt feels against my face." The filmy layer on the outside of the clothing was whisper soft and delicate. The layer underneath, though, was heavier, silky and slick. He'd wager it would feel incredible when pressed to just the right spot.

Like there. And *there.*

"Oh, my," she said with a groan when he kissed her in the delicate hollow between her belly and her pelvic bone. His lips remained separated from her skin by that sensuous fabric.

"Shh," he insisted, moving his mouth down until he reached the V of her thighs. Without asking, he tugged her legs apart a tiny bit, sensing the slightest hesitation before she gave him what he wanted. Access.

When he opened his mouth on her, Mike got a double rush of pleasure. The sound of her helpless groan of delight and the taste of her warm, womanly body in his mouth. She was incredibly wet, and he made her wetter with his tongue as he licked her through the cloth.

"Mike…"

Feeling her legs shake, he held them tighter in his hands, keeping her where he wanted her. "Let me," he ordered, nuzzling into her again, focused on giving her pleasure, while enjoying every second of the experience himself.

The urge to lift her nothing skirt and devour her with no impediment nearly overwhelmed him, but he resisted it. If he *saw* her, he'd have to be in her.

Nor could he allow himself to move his hands higher on her thighs and allow his fingers to slide into that wet crevice. If he *felt* her, he'd have to be in her.

This was all they could have. For now. And while it might not be enough to last him for long, he was going to make damn sure it was something Jen never forgot.

"I can't wait to see you, but I know I'll lose control if I do," he murmured as he nipped at her, sliding his tongue—and her skirt—deeper into the slit between her legs. There was no resistance, all was utterly smooth, and he suddenly suspected the plump lips of her sex were entirely bare. The realization sent every ounce of excess blood in his body racing to his cock until it buttered against his zipper.

This had become pure torture, but he knew by her cries that she was enjoying every bit of what he was doing to her. So he kept tasting her, swirling his tongue over the sensitive nub of flesh he could feel against the material, scraping it across her drenched opening. Until finally, her legs shook so much she had to put her hands on his shoulders for support.

"I'm…"

"I know," he said, hearing the satisfaction in his voice as

he took her farther, knowing by the cries and the sudden flexing of every one of her muscles that she'd come.

While she was still panting from the pleasure of it—all flushed and heated and wild-eyed, he rose and caught her mouth with his, plunging his tongue deep, the way he wanted to plunge his fingers and his cock into her. Over. And over. And over.

He allowed himself a few seconds of her kiss, her taste, then drew away and stepped back. "Go take a hot bath," he said, pulling the words out of his gut when he wanted to shut up and carry her to her bedroom. His tone rough with hungry impatience, he growled, "I'll give you forty-eight hours to get better. Then I'm going to take you so many times you won't remember what it feels like to *not* be having an orgasm."

Without waiting for her to say a single word, he walked out the door, knowing he needed to drive fast in order to get home to the longest cold shower he'd ever taken.

Or, maybe, a hot one…during which he'd fantasize about her and give himself the same small amount of temporary relief he'd just given her.

CHAPTER ELEVEN

What any cheating husband needs to realize is that sometimes women really do take little oaths like "fidelity" and "forsaking all others" seriously. If he did, he might *not* have to learn firsthand that his wife also takes the whole "till death do us part" thing seriously...by waking up with an ax in his face.
—*Why Arsenic Is Better Than Divorce* by Jennifer Feeney

THOUGH SHE KNEW SHE SHOULD probably be embarrassed about what had happened between her and Mike Monday evening, Jen couldn't muster up that particular emotion. She still felt so good after the most powerful orgasm she'd had in ages that she wasn't complaining about anything. The heat didn't bother her. The leaky pipes didn't bother her. The noisy old Mr. Jones next door didn't bother her. Frank—the leering, butt-crack baring super—didn't bother her. Nothing did.

Maybe it was because last night, for the first time in *ages,* she'd had an orgasm that actually involved another person. But even if that weren't the case, she suspected the incredible pleasure Mike Taylor had given her would be impossible to top.

Funny. She was probably supposed to blush with mortification when she thought of that big, hot man on his knees in front of her, pleasuring her through her clothes without so much as kissing her lips first. Or even buying her a drink.

The only heat she felt, however, was between her legs, not in her face. She got hot and wet just thinking about it throughout the next day.

As she swallowed vitamins and aspirin and prayed to the gods of fools and clumsy people to grant her supersonic healing powers, she counted down the hours. Forty-eight, he'd said. Well, it had only been twenty-four and she was already going out of her mind, dying to see him, to talk to him, to make a firm date for tomorrow night.

She could call, she supposed, even if her shoulder did still hurt a bit when picking up something as light as the telephone receiver. She'd had to get an ice pack for it after a phone conversation with Ida Mae and Ivy, who hadn't shut up for a solid forty-five minutes.

Damn. She hated to think about what they'd told her—that some man had been phoning Ivy's house looking for Jen. Why? If her harasser had wanted to talk to her, why didn't he *say* something when he called her apartment, rather than whispering foul words or breathing heavily? And how on earth had he tracked her to Ivy's house?

She'd assured them it must be a reporter, then she'd tried to convince herself of the same thing. None of them had really believed it. All their anger at her from the previous week—and hers at them for not giving her Mike's messages—had dissipated as they'd made each other promise to be careful.

Their concern had warmed her. Sometimes, from a distance, she really thought the old women cared about her.

That'd last until the next time Ivy called to threaten her with death, accusing Jen of having stolen her favorite scarf or bottle of pills. It always turned out that Ivy, herself, had hidden whatever she was missing, fearing burglars, then forgotten where she'd hidden it.

"Thank you God, for letting me be adopted," she whispered. Then, glancing at the phone, she added, "Come on, Mike, call me first before I give in and call you."

But, honestly, she wasn't sure what to say. "Hi there, it's me, the woman you licked into ecstasy last night. Just wanted to remind you that you promised to bang my brains out tomorrow and I thought we should name the place. And, oh, your condom or mine?"

Uh…no. Not good. A little indelicate, and a lot pathetic.

She nearly called him anyway. Just to chat. And to let him know she could now lift her arm over her head—and her legs over his shoulders—without wanting to cry. But her kitchen phone rang before she could pick up the receiver. "Hello?"

A long moment of silence followed. She started to smile. "Hmm…cat got your tongue?" she asked, knowing she sounded mischievous. The comment might also be considered a bit suggestive, considering where his tongue had been last night.

No answer. Mike was probably equally as unsure about what to say. They'd sort of skipped a few steps in the dating process. Not that they were dating, precisely. She didn't quite know what to call what they were doing, beyond *good. Right. Amazing.*

Yes. All those things.

Where it was going she couldn't say; she just knew it would also be good. Right. Amazing. "Are you going to say anything?"

The silence thickened. After a long moment, it was broken by a deep, rasping breath. Another followed it, thick and reedy.

"Please tell me this is *you* and not some random heavy

breather," she said, stiffening. God, she hoped her psycho caller wasn't starting in on her again. She'd had a couple of calls already since she'd been home. "Talk to me or I'm hanging up."

But she didn't have to. A click from the other end signaled the end of the call.

Jen glanced at the receiver in her hand, slowly lowering it into its cradle. If that had been Mike, he'd developed a bad cold in the last day, judging by that wheeze. If it hadn't, and the relentless prank calls that had tormented her into visiting her aunts in Trouble were gearing up again, she was going to shoot herself.

Her fingers had barely left the phone when it rang again. This time, she paused to look at the caller ID, not recognizing the New York number.

Could be Mike. She hadn't memorized his number.

Could also be her heavy breather.

They could even be one and the same.

"Hello?"

More heavy breathing. And she knew, deep down in her soul, this was not Mike playing some kind of sexy phone game with her. The sound was more ominous than that—deliberate and harsh, not breathy and seductive.

Oh, how she hated this nonsense. Men could be such assholes.

"You'd better say something this time or I swear I'll deafen you." She looked around the kitchen for the small canned air horn she'd bought after the last round of prank calls, but didn't spot it. Figured. "You have one second to convince me you're not a stalking psycho."

He talked. He said exactly one word, which wasn't what she'd call convincing. "Bitch." Then the phone clicked again.

She called him a few choice names in return, somehow feeling better, even though the line had already gone dead.

Hard to believe that a month and a half ago, she'd been excited to be asked to appear on that nationally televised morning show to promote her latest book. Looking back, it was one of the worst things she'd ever done. Before that morning, she'd gotten the occasional scathing letter or book-signing rant. But since then, and since an article about her had come out in the *Times* book section, the threats had gotten nasty and personal, the phone calls deliberate and hateful. She'd had her number changed twice. Seemed as though it was time to do so again.

It wouldn't be in time to stop this next call, however, because the phone rang again before she even had time to hunt around the kitchen for the noisemaker. Again she checked the ID. It was a different number, which could merely mean the perv was using his mother's phone this time, rather than his own.

"Aha!" she exclaimed when she found the small can she'd picked up at a local sports shop. The things were popular with crowds heading to the Garden. They emitted huge, hornlike squeals—annoying in a stadium. Hopefully deafening through a phone line. She intended to beat the guy to the punch this time.

"Say hello to this, you prick," she snarled into the receiver. She put the horn right up to the mouthpiece and blasted the heck out of it. She probably damaged her own hearing in the process, but it was worth it. She only wished she could see the guy's face.

"Call me again and I'll have my big, tough cop boyfriend answer the phone," she yelled into the receiver as she prepared to slam it down.

Then she heard a voice yelling. Loudly. And it was a voice she recognized. "Jen, what the hell is going on?"

Scrunching her eyes shut and nibbling her lip, she put the can down and lifted the receiver back up. "Uh…Mike?"

"Yeah. At least, I hope so. I'm not quite sure because I can't *think* with the air-raid siren echoing in my head."

Whoops. So much for being proactive. "Sorry. I don't suppose you'd called me right before that, huh?"

He immediately got serious. "Who called you?"

Apparently not him.

"Was someone harassing you?"

Rubbing at the corners of her eyes with her fingers, she pulled out a chair and sat at her tiny kitchen table.

"Just someone playing a game of 'Have you checked the children?'" she said, quoting one of her favorite scary movies.

"Call 9-1-1."

"It was a couple of heavy-breathing phone calls," she said, somehow feeling warmed by his caveman reaction, rather than annoyed, as she'd expected.

"Any idea who?"

"No, but I imagine I'll be able to find him with the numbers on my caller ID."

"Give them to me," he said.

She did, without thinking twice. Knowing a police officer might prove very beneficial indeed, even if he had been annoyingly noble about staying away from her for forty-eight hours. She'd been ready for him to come back after hour two.

"I'll check them out," he said. He cleared his throat, as if to keep one of those rare laughs from escaping. "Unless you'd rather have your big, tough cop boyfriend do it."

Lovely. Floor meet face. Jen really felt like falling onto it in abject humiliation. "Wish I knew one."

A grunt was his only answer.

"I wasn't thinking too clearly," she admitted.

He took pity and didn't humiliate her anymore. "He really got to you, huh?"

She could have lied but didn't. "Yeah. I guess he did."

"Nothing's going to happen to you. Cowards like this one hide behind phone lines, they almost never crawl out of their holes." His tone grew serious. "You'll be *fine,* Jen."

Though he was obviously trying to be calm about things, Jen heard the tension in Mike's voice. He was concerned about her—truly, genuinely worried. How long had it been since anyone had worried about her like that? She honestly couldn't remember.

Her parents certainly had worried when she'd moved to the Big Apple, but with her father's health, they'd had other things to fear in recent months. Her friends took the harassment she received in stride as being a consequence of the books she wrote. Meanwhile, they continued to rah-rah her on all the way. So did her publisher. And while her agent might have forced her to arm herself, he also obviously took the threats as just another part of being famous. Well, semi-famous.

Well, semi-infamous.

"Listen, if you're spooked, why don't I come pick you up and take you out to dinner somewhere."

Hmm. Pick her up. As in come to her apartment. Tonight, rather than another twenty-four hours from now. She liked this idea. "That might be good."

"I'll meet you at the door to your building in an hour." His voice lowered. "I don't think I should come up. I haven't forgotten our agreement."

Mind reader.

"We had an agreement? I thought that was more along the lines of an order. You know, your manliness laying down the law." Jen didn't know where the snarkiness had come from because he honestly didn't deserve it. She supposed it was her libido talking. The one Mike had brought out of a long, dormant hibernation, then left howling in the wind like a bear awakened in February.

"My manliness?" He choked out a hoarse laugh. "I'd change our terms in a heartbeat if I thought you were up to it."

"I'm up to it. Could you be *up* to it?"

"Stop trying to seduce me."

"Is it working?"

"No."

"Would begging work?" She'd just about reached that level.

"How bad's the pain?"

Score! "Pain makes you strong. I think that was Nietzsche."

"You scare me, you know that?" He sounded both frustrated and amused. "But I'm serious. How bad is it? Are you still black and blue?"

She glanced at her shoulder and arm, then tugged her waistband away to study her hip. "Well, I'm no longer the color of a Van Gogh painting." He said nothing. Which made her sigh. "Though I suppose I'm lumpy and bent enough that I could be considered a Lipschitz."

"Sorry, not up on lumpy, bent artists. Never heard of him."

"Cretin. I thought you were raised around the world."

"I lived around the world, but I've always been a red-blooded American at heart."

She liked that about him. That he could be so down to earth when his upbringing had been anything but conventional.

Hell, she liked *everything* about him. And she suddenly couldn't stand the thought of waiting another whole day before seeing him again, even if tonight meant only decent Thai food around the corner, and not fabulous sex.

"Jennifer, I won't be the cause of your pain again," he insisted, that serious, strong man firmly back in control. Then he stunned her by admitting something so sweet, so romantic, she nearly melted onto the floor. "I've waited for twenty-seven years for you. I can wait one more night."

To her own shock, tears rose to her eyes and she blinked rapidly to contain them. Tears. Because a strong, sexy man had said something so very lovely and unexpected.

Oh, he was dangerous. Not physically—she knew he'd do just about anything not to hurt her again. But emotionally? Well, she already sensed that he could break her heart. She was falling for him—madly, passionately, crazily—falling. In a way she'd never fallen in her whole life.

She. The accused standard-bearer for man-haters everywhere. How crazy was that?

Good crazy. Wonderful crazy. Delightful crazy. "Okay," she murmured. "But I am quite sure I'll be fine tomorrow."

She'd make damn sure of it. Jen intended to spend the bulk of it primping, plucking, shaving, bathing and covering any remaining bruises with the best concealer Sephora sold.

"So," she added, "dinner it is. Downstairs. One hour."

"Great."

The moment he hung up, Jen moved as quickly as her bruised body would let her getting ready for their date, smiling as she did so. Because she, the former Single in the City girl, had a regular date. None of her readers would believe how excited she was over doing something as normal as going out for dinner with a sexy man. But it was very unusual for her, first since she now knew for sure that he was a younger man—even if only by two years. And second because her last date had been P.I.—Pre-Infamy.

Didn't matter. Mike knew what she did; he'd read some of her book and he didn't give a damn.

He'd read some of her book. Including some of the stuff he'd tried to question her about Saturday morning. Which she still did *not* want to discuss.

But she put that out of her mind. They had plenty of other things to talk about. She could certainly maneuver the conversation away from dangerous territory, and toward more pleasant subjects. Like tomorrow night. Or, more precisely, twenty-three and one half hours from now.

When, even if she fell down the stairs and cracked her head open, they would most definitely be dining *in*.

MIKE ARRIVED AT JEN'S BUILDING a little less than an hour after he'd called her. But he didn't go up right away. Instead, he stayed outside.

He looked around the neighborhood, studying everything, for two reasons. First, he wanted to make sure nobody had followed him. And within a few minutes he felt satisfied they had not. So onto the second matter: he began to assess Jen's home through professional eyes.

While still convinced he and Jen had been targeted by one of Ricky Stahl's goons, it was at least possible that *Jen*—not he—had been the real intended target. Someone had been harassing her, threatening her. It was rare for a random, letter-writing, heavy-breathing pig to take his threats to the next level. But God knew it wasn't impossible. It *did* happen.

If some creep stalker had tracked down her unlisted number, they could probably have learned Jen's address. And no matter how much Mike had insisted she didn't have anything to worry about—he, himself, was *very* worried. Especially because he'd tracked down those numbers from her caller ID in about five minutes and had discovered they were both from pay phones within blocks of here.

He knew Jen wasn't the type who wanted anyone to take care of her, however. So he'd just keep his worries to himself. For now.

The building was typical of all the others on the block, with no obvious signs of easy entry. The fire escapes on the side didn't make him feel any better, but he knew Jen had a lot of common sense and she'd keep her windows locked.

The main entrance could be opened remotely by the residents, but he already knew those residents weren't too careful about that door. When he'd shown up Saturday morning, he'd followed someone else right on in. The guy had even chatted about the previous night's ball game.

All in all, he summed up the place as risky. Which he didn't like one bit.

Knowing she was waiting, he pushed the buzzer for Jen's apartment, and got a muffled, "Be right there."

The second she arrived and opened the door, he snapped, "How did you know it was me? It could have been some creep."

The *you're a moron* look she gave him preceded her answer. "Maybe because I've been watching you scope out my building for the last five minutes from my front window?"

Mike looked up, realizing her apartment did face the street. "It still could have been somebody else. Next time ask."

"God, you're bossy. I hate bossy men."

"I'm not too fond of ballsy women, either."

"So why are we doing this again?"

"I think you like my dimples."

"I think you like my ass."

"That's a given."

She grunted. "Besides, I think I *imagined* those dimples."

"I *know* I didn't imagine that ass."

She was barely listening. "You barely even smile."

"Even so, I can think of one or two more reasons."

"Yeah, yeah, you're totally hot and you arouse me out of my mind," she admitted, sounding entirely disgruntled. "But you also drive me crazy with your macho bs and your super-sleuthing outside my building."

"I'm sorry I stayed out here spying on you," he admitted, meaning it. "I was getting the lay of the land."

Her hand flew up, palm out, and she put it over his mouth. He wanted to bite her fingers. Followed by the rest of her.

"Hey, hey, no talking of anything getting laid around here tonight. If I'm not, nothing is."

Mike just shook his head, realizing how much he'd grown to like her sarcastic sense of humor. Even when she was making him horny she amused him. He didn't think he'd ever been involved with a woman who really knew how to laugh—at herself, at life in general. Despite his protestations to her—and to himself—that she was not his type and he didn't like prickly women who charged ahead with no fear of consequences, he was dying for her. And she knew it.

"Stop trying to score. You admitted you're still lumpy."

She rolled her eyes. "You aren't like one of those hybrid cars that only needs to get charged up once a month or something, are you? You can run for weeks on one orgasm?"

If the woman only knew how much she charged him up. He'd very much like to tell her. Or *show* her. But at that moment, a hunched, elderly man walked up the steps behind her. "Shut up, Jen," Mike muttered.

She glanced around, saw the old guy and her face pinkened. "Hello, Mr. Jones."

Mike's hope their conversation hadn't been overheard was for nothing. The old guy gave Mike a lascivious wag of his eyebrows and a thumbs-up as he went inside. "The textbook dirty old man?"

"He's my new neighbor. He's all right, except for his music. The teenagers upstairs don't play their stereos as loud." Then she went right back to where they'd been. "By the way, scarier men than you have told me to shut up, Mr. Hybrid." Her words held absolutely no heat, and a strong sense of mischief. That tone brought the same unaccustomed grin to his face that he'd been wearing around her for days.

"You ever get in trouble with that mouth of yours?" he asked as they walked down the front steps onto the sidewalk. Though it was after eight and almost dark, lots of people were out enjoying the clear weather. The misty rain that had doused the area for days had finally let up and the streets felt freshly steamed with energy. New Yorkers really liked coming out after a rain, particularly at sunset.

"I think Aunt Ida Mae used to threaten to wash it out with soap regularly when I was a kid."

"Did she ever follow through?"

Jen smirked. "Not a chance. My father might be a teddy bear but he'd never let those two touch a hair on my head."

The tenderness in her tone told him just about everything he needed to know about her family. Except where they were now. When he asked her, she seemed to delight in talking about them, though, whether that delight came from the fact that they lived several states away, or in spite of it, he couldn't say. Either way, Jen obviously loved her parents and it sounded as if she visited them frequently.

Falling into step together, it seemed only natural for them to drift close. For her hip to brush his, their thighs to nearly touch in matched gaits. It seemed just as natural for him to drop an arm across her shoulders—after he'd made sure he wasn't pressing on the bruised one. She tucked up against him, her hair wisping against his neck and cheek, the scent of it chasing away any lingering smells of the city.

They didn't speak; they didn't need to. Somehow, they'd reached that point in a relationship when silence was okay. More than okay, it was actually good. Each step they took brought the sensations of Jen's body tucked against his a bit higher. He could hear her breathing, feel the pulse in her neck, was tuned in to everything going on between them.

A lot was going on between them. And it had been since the moment he'd seen her trudging up that road toward Trouble. The memory made him chuckle softly.

"What?"

"Nothing."

She poked his ribs. "Spill."

"The first time I saw you, you were standing just beyond a sign that said Trouble Ahead."

"Do you ever think you should have kept driving?"

"Yep."

She stopped and scowled up at him. "Liar."

He lifted his hand to her hair and twined his fingers in it, gently rubbing the back of her head. "You're right," he said softly. "I'm a liar."

Jen turned her head into his hand, shifting closer. Tilting her body against his, she lifted her gaze, her lips moist, her eyes wide. The last remaining bit of sunlight put a glint in those depths that made him immediately think of the sun sparkling on the Mediterranean. Then it suddenly set, the sun winking away in the length of time it took to draw a single breath, and Jen's eyes turned the dark blue of a starlit night.

She stopped his heart. And though he'd sooner be shot than considered poetic, he couldn't help saying, "You have the most amazing eyes I've ever seen."

The soft smile told him she appreciated the compliment. The flick of her tongue across her parted lips told him she wanted more than that. He bent down and she leaned up and their mouths met in a soft, effortless hello. Maybe more than a hello…an acknowledgment. From both of them.

Oblivious to anyone around them, they came together, her softness accommodating him where he was hard, her curves melding into his angles. Their mouths drifted close, shared a breath, then touched. Slowly, sweetly. Sharing both want and promise.

The taste of her tempted him to dive in for a full banquet, but he didn't do it. Because, somehow, right now, tasting was enough. It was, in fact, just right.

Not frenzied and frantic, the kiss was still incredibly sensual, both of them taking the time to lazily explore each other's lips with delicate licks and nips, and stamp every sensation into memory. It was, most of all, an admission that despite their banter, they were both very serious about what they wanted. *More.*

Afterward, they resumed walking, still silent, comfortable, but definitely very aware. Their sex talk had put him on edge. The kiss had pushed him over it. If she suggested they turn around and go back to her place, he honestly didn't think he'd be able to refuse. But she didn't suggest it, remaining quiet and introspective, as if still stunned by their first kiss of pure, lazy sweetness rather than hot, raw desire.

He understood the feeling. And though he had never bought into that Tantric bullshit about self-deprivation, he had to admit, the slow buildup was driving him absolutely crazy with want. Because somehow, in that sweet, languorous kiss, his liking for Jen the person and his hungry desire for Jen the woman had melded together into a need that almost undid him.

Jen cleared her throat, as if she was still affected by their kiss. Her voice soft, she asked, "Is this okay?"

Though he wasn't from this neighborhood and had never worked it, Mike knew the best restaurants in the city, so he completely agreed with her choice of a Thai place not far from her building. "I hear their curry's great." End of conversation. Which wasn't as much of a surprise from him as it was from her. The woman rarely stopped talking.

More surprising, he *liked* that about her.

They got a table in a back corner, as private as one could get in a popular neighborhood joint like this one, and both ordered the same thing. "Are you feeling all right?" he asked once they were alone. "The walk wasn't too much for your hip?"

"I'm okay." She sipped the water the waitress had left. "Much better than I was when I woke up Sunday morning."

Glancing into the depths of his own glass, he cleared his throat. "I hate that you got hurt because of me."

"I know you do and I also know it wasn't your fault. Any luck finding out if it had anything to do with your drug case?"

"Not sure yet." He didn't continue. Mike didn't want to talk about that whole situation. Not here, not with her. It wasn't that he didn't think she was the kind of woman who'd be able to take hearing about his job as a New York City cop. He doubted there was much Jennifer Feeney couldn't handle. He just didn't want to waste any more of his personal thoughts or energy on a thug. "Let's talk about something else."

"Deal. But only if it's about nothing more serious than how much I hate the Yankees," she said.

He answered as a die-hard Yankees fan. "Ouch. I don't know if we can get over that hurdle. You've wounded me."

The waitress returned with their drinks. After sipping from her fruity cocktail—complete with tiny umbrella—Jen murmured, "Sorry. I'm not good at being a girl."

"Why don't you let me be the judge of that?" he asked, his tone deadpan, though her comment had been completely ridiculous. The woman was among the most feminine he'd ever known.

She clarified. "I don't do girlie, poofy stuff."

"You're doing a good job with that chicks-only drink."

She grinned and sipped again. "Yeah, but I can't make myself simper and pretend to know nothing about sports or that I have no opinion on anything other than shopping."

"Maybe we should skip dinner and go to Sports Authority."

"Maybe we should skip both and go to bed."

He groaned, raking a frustrated hand through his short

hair. Obviously the sweetly contemplative Jen was put away for the night. The saucy temptress was firmly back in place. "Just shoot me, woman, it'd be less painful."

She had the audacity to pull her cherry out of her cocktail and lick every drop of juice from it, her tongue moist and decadent-looking. "You into pain?"

He laughed, deep and low, watching the pleasure wash over Jen's face the way it always did when he let down his guard and just enjoyed being with her.

"You have the sexiest laugh on the planet. I want to gobble you up when you laugh."

"God, you really are killing me here," he said, leaning over the table to be closer to her. Close enough to smell the fruity drink and see the cherry juice drenching her lips.

A frown tugged at her brow. "Wait. You don't think…"

"What?"

"Well, you don't think *talking* about the incredible sex we both know we're going to have could possibly jinx us?" She sounded stunned…slightly horrified. "Make it not so good?"

He grunted. "Elmer Fudd could pull up a chair and start whispering in my ear and I'd still be dying to have you, Jen."

She appeared slightly mollified. "So it hasn't, um, diminished your interest? I mean, I've never done this before."

His jaw dropped.

"Don't get your hopes up, big guy," she said before reaching for her glass. "I'm not saying I'm a virgin. I just meant I don't usually talk—think, dream, fantasize—so much about sex without actually having it."

She'd definitely read him wrong. "Thanks for clarifying. And for the record, I was not *hoping* for that. I was terrified of it." When her expression remained puzzled, he explained in an intimate whisper, "The things I want to do with you don't involve being overly simple and basic."

Heat washed up through her face, as if she'd eaten a bite of the curry that hadn't even been brought to the table yet. Around them, other patrons continued to chatter, but they remained silent, both, he knew, lost in thought about what he'd said. Anticipating it. Wanting it. Dying for it to start. All of it.

"Simple and basic aren't even in my vocabulary."

Shaking his head, he lifted his beer and said, "Have you always been so blunt?"

"Always. I don't play games, and I don't pull any punches," she admitted. "Whether you're taking me to dinner or taking me to bed, I'm the same Jennifer Feeney who once advised a woman whose husband kept going on 'business trips' with his twenty-year-old secretary to piss in the bastard's mouthwash bottle."

He choked a little on his beer, but managed to avoid spewing it all over her. Fortunately, it was a dark beer. Not, uh, the shade of a familiar yellow mouthwash. "I hope you also told her to have room service surprise him with a big, garlicky pizza."

"A man who thinks on his feet. I like that."

"You know," he admitted, "I've never liked women who got mad and got even, but you're growing on me."

She must have heard the tiny note of seriousness in his tone because rather than leaping on the "growing on me" part, she reached across the table and twined her fingers in his. "Tell me about the woman who made you stop laughing."

Mike gaped. The subject change came out of nowhere. Jen's mercurial mood swings tonight were making him dizzy, keeping him off balance and unable to remain circumspect about things he didn't want to talk about. "It wasn't somebody I cared about."

"Sure."

"No, *really*." Well, the woman who'd shot him hadn't been somebody he'd cared about. The girlfriend who'd dumped him out of loyalty to her nutty, murderous friend? He didn't want to go there. "That's all we're going to say on the subject." He knew how to get her to drop it. "Unless *you* want to talk about more serious things? Like the stories in your book?"

She clenched her lips together in a tight line. Mike wasn't sure whether he was glad about that or not. Because he still very much wanted to talk to Jennifer about the murder of her uncle.

He hadn't told her last night that he'd pulled the file on Leo Cantone and taken a look at the case. Mainly out of curiosity—but also, he had to admit, some concern. Jen might laugh off the insanities of her elderly aunts, but if one of them really was a killer, he didn't want the woman he was crazy about anywhere near them.

Woman he was crazy about. Now, where had *that* come from?

"Okay, fair enough. Small talk only."

They stuck to their agreement, sharing light conversation, good food and sexual tension thicker than the sticky rice that came with their meal. Every time she took a bite of food, she groaned in nearly orgasmic delight. Each sip of her drink soaked her lips in sensual red. She brushed her leg against his beneath the table and reached across it to touch his arm a dozen times. He smelled her perfume, felt her warmth, was wrapped in her soft laughter. And drowned a little more in liquid want with every minute that passed.

Despite the frustration, though, Mike couldn't remember enjoying a dinner more. Dancing around off-limit topics and unsatisfied desire heightened everything he'd been feeling, thinking and sensing about Jen since the moment he'd met her.

By the time they got back to her place, Mike doubted he'd be able to hold out another whole night before having her. If she gave him the green light, his good intentions would fly out the window and he'd have her on her back with her knees behind her ears faster than she could say *Take me*.

When they reached her building, walking in complete silence for the few blocks back, he hesitated at the bottom of the outside steps. "Mike?" she asked.

He stared into her eyes, looking for pain or discomfort, seeing nothing except a warm, welcoming hunger that probably mirrored his own.

"You're staying." It wasn't a question.

"You want me to stay." That wasn't a question, either.

She nodded. "Come up."

He didn't answer. He simply opened the door for her and held it while she entered, then followed her up the stairs to her apartment. With every odd step he called himself a weakling for not sticking to his decision to wait until tomorrow night. With every even one, he mentally swore he'd be gentle. Tender. Careful not to hurt her.

Well, as tender as a man could be when he wanted to bury himself inside a woman's body and never find his way out again.

Jen's hand was shaking as she lifted it to the lock, so Mike took her key away to open the door to her apartment himself. He just hoped she didn't notice his was shaking, too.

Shaking. Out of pure need that had been denied for too long. Had he ever wanted someone like this? Ever built something up to such a high tension that it was now a matter of fuck her or die?

No. That wasn't the right term for it. It might have been what he'd wanted to do when she'd been a stranger walking along a dusty road. Now he wanted to make love to her.

Don't be stupid, don't think that way, a voice in his head said. But it was too late. He was falling for her in a big way. And he was finally going to touch her, hold her, stroke her, explode in her the way he'd wanted to for days.

Then he noticed something and all other thought disappeared. "Did you forget to lock your door?" he asked as the key spun around uselessly in the lock.

"I can't believe I'd be so careless, but I was a little distracted when you got here, so it's possible," she admitted.

Yeah. Possible. But Mike was a cop—he didn't take chances like that. Gently pushing her to the side, against the hallway wall, he reached for his concealed weapon. He entered the apartment carefully, his senses on high alert, knowing something was wrong. When he flipped on the light, he knew why.

Her place had been trashed. Furniture was overturned, papers strewn across the floor, a glass cabinet broken. Though they'd only been gone two hours, the place looked as if it had been used for an *Animal House*-type frat party.

"Stay there," he ordered as he moved into the small apartment. The silence said whoever had been in here was gone. A quick perimeter check confirmed it. After making the brief circuit of her tiny bedroom, bath, kitchen and small living area to confirm no one was there, he came back to the entrance.

Jen stood in the doorway. Her mouth hanging open and her eyes wide, she took it all in, just shaking her head in silence.

Mike reached for her, taking her silence for shock. When he felt the tremors racking her body, he hugged her close and said, "Don't be afraid. We'll get this guy, Jen."

Shaking her head, she pulled back so she could look up at him. "You're going to have to call in police and we're going to have to sit here dealing with this for a few *hours*, aren't we?"

Unsure where she was going, he nodded. "Yes."

"Hours," she mumbled, looking as if she was about to cry. Well, who wouldn't when they'd been so violently invaded like this—had their belongings torn through and broken? It was a wonder Jen hadn't started wailing.

"It'll be all right," he murmured, gently rubbing his hands up and down her arms. When she shook her head in wordless denial, he insisted, "It *will* be, I promise. Don't worry."

"I should be worried, shouldn't I?" she asked, her tone wondering, still dazed. "But I'm not. *Hours…*"

"Let me call it in, then I'll get you something to drink. I think you're in shock."

Jen's brow shot up and her mouth opened. She snapped it closed again, shaking her head in disbelief. "Shock? I'm not in shock, I'm mad as hell."

That was the Jen he knew.

"And if I get my hands on the son of a bitch before you do, I'm going to kill him."

On came the death threats. He felt so relieved, he wanted to send up a prayer of thanks.

"Do you realize what this means?"

"Yes," he said, his amusement disappearing as quickly as it had returned. Deep-seated rage replaced it. "It means someone's targeting you." He'd evaluate that later, once he knew she was okay. The person who'd broken in was probably the same one who'd been harassing her. When Mike found him, the bastard was going to be *wishing* somebody else had killed him first.

She barely seemed to hear him, instead fisting her hands and putting them on her hips. "It means *hours.*"

As he tried to figure out what she was getting at and why

she kept saying that, Jen threw her head back and looked up at the ceiling as if shouting the injustice at the heavens. "Argh. I can't *take* this anymore."

"What is it?" he asked, wondering why she wasn't ranting or racing through the apartment to make sure her jewelry and electronics were safe, like any typical robbery victim.

Then again, Jennifer was in no way typical.

Grabbing the front of his shirt, she yanked him close, until their bodies touched, chest to chest. Her pebbled nipples scraped against him, and her heat washed over him, reminding him of exactly what they'd been thinking as they walked up the stairs to her apartment.

And suddenly, he got it. *Hours.* God help him.

"Listen to me, Mike Taylor. The next time a desperate woman throws herself at you in a lake you say *yes*. Got it? *Yes*."

Then she pressed a hard, angry kiss on his mouth, spun away and muttered, "Now, call in the damn reinforcements."

CHAPTER TWELVE

Until the moment a guy gets in a woman's pants, he's Prince Charming. Afterward, he's about as loving and romantic as Captain Caveman.
—*I Love You, I Want You, Get Out*, by Jennifer Feeney

EMILY HAD A VERY NICE EVENING. Her date with Mr. Ward—Roderick, as he'd insisted she call him—had at first seemed like something she'd dreamed about. She'd been playing the part of the poor, inexperienced secretary and he'd been every movie variation of a wealthy, dashing Cary Grant. He'd been charming, opening doors, ordering her dinner for her—but only after questioning her about her tastes. Her first date had gone exactly the way it was supposed to from the movies she'd watched over the years.

Except...something was *missing*. Roderick had been proper and cordial; they certainly hadn't lacked for conversation. He'd seemed to especially enjoy talking about things like the weather and the quality of the produce at the local market. They hadn't exactly chatted, but there had certainly been no long, uncomfortable silences.

She hadn't quite been able to put her finger on what was wrong until now, as they pulled up in front of her house. Their evening had been lovely, but it had not been terribly romantic. Not *intimate*.

He hadn't touched her once. He'd certainly never flirted, well, she didn't *think* he had. Since she'd never been flirted with before, she couldn't be one-hundred-percent sure. There had been that one moment when they'd been talking about the global-warming documentary on the way home and he'd made a comment about wearing lighter clothing. Was that flirting? An expression of interest in her?

She had no idea. But even if it had been, it certainly hadn't been emotional. Nor even, as strange as it sounded, terribly personal.

It wasn't entirely his fault. She hadn't exactly behaved like herself tonight, feeling out of her element. Not only because Mr. Ward was someone so different from the people she knew here in Trouble, but also because it was her first date.

Should she be Grace Kelly from *The Philadelphia Story*…always elegant and proper? Or Audrey Hepburn in *Sabrina*, sweet and charming?

Whatever the case, she knew whom she could not be— boring, silly Emily Baker from Trouble, Pennsylvania.

I can't do this, she thought. Her seventy-four-year-old brain wasn't up to working out these intricate mating puzzles at this point in her life, despite how much she longed to solve them. A part of her wanted to ignore the romantic movie advice that had the heroine waiting to be swept off her feet and *ask* Roderick if he planned to kiss her. That way, at least, she could be prepared for it and not do something foolish like immediately worry over her crowns.

"I had a lovely time," she murmured as he walked her to her front door Tuesday night. Though nearly 11:00 p.m., it was still quite hot, and Emily had kept her shawl draped over her arm. *Just* because it was hot, she told herself. Not because she'd taken Allie's advice and worn the bright pink dress.

Not that it seemed to have done any good. Mr. Ward had barely looked at her face all evening, and he most certainly had not looked below her chin. All her life she'd been hearing that men liked cleavage such as hers, but now, the first time she'd put it to a test, that had proven wrong.

She supposed she should have tried a bit sooner. Like a few decades ago when she'd been in her forties.

"Yes, quite enjoyable," Roderick said. He cleared his throat. "Though the meal couldn't compare with something out of my own kitchen, it was, indeed, palatable."

Allie had mentioned that he was a good cook. Before she could stop her foolish tongue, Emily replied, "Maybe you could cook for me sometime."

He didn't say anything, merely maintaining that stiff posture and tight smile.

"Well...here we are." In the movies the woman often asked the man in for a drink. But Emily didn't drink, not much anyway, and all she had in the house was a bottle of wine a neighbor had given her last Christmas. Not what one would offer a worldly gentleman, she supposed.

"Thank you again, Emily, for agreeing to accompany me this evening. Much more pleasant to attend these informative programs with someone else, with whom you can discuss them." He tsked. "Mortimer can't be bothered to sit still for so long. Nor does he much care if the average water temperature has risen in the past century. In his opinion, the earth will shrug us off like fleas when it's done with us and move on to something else."

Mr. Potts did have a point, in Emily's opinion, but she didn't say that.

Roderick had talked about his friend a few times this evening, his tone holding only respect and fondness. A very admirable trait, one she liked about him. In fact, she liked many things about Roderick…which would make him nice to have as a friend, herself, if only she weren't so curious about what it would be like to kiss him.

"Thank you," she said as she removed her key from her bag and unlocked the front door.

"You are most welcome," he replied as he watched her step inside, bowing slightly.

He reached out his hand. Wondering if he was about to kiss hers in a courtly manner, Emily extended hers, as well, her breath catching in her lungs. But Roderick merely shook it. Cordial. Proper.

Impersonal.

"Good night," he said, then he turned and walked to his car, driving off into the night.

Which meant that for the seventy-fourth year, sixth month and eleventh day, she would be going to her bed never having been held passionately in a man's arms.

WHEN THE LONG RUN OF BAD weather departed New York City, it departed with a vengeance. By Wednesday afternoon, the temperature had risen to a pleasant eighty-five and it stopped right there. The sky had turned a shade of blue usually reserved only for summertime portraits drawn by kindergartners. It was complemented by brilliant yellow sunshine and a few cotton-ball puffy clouds. The crystal-clear day was such a stark change from the unrelenting storm clouds of recent weeks that the entire city seemed to suddenly come alive and start dancing for joy.

Throughout most of the day, Jen had watched it from above, in a luxury penthouse like the kind she'd only seen in movies.

"Mr. Potts, you obviously *do* have the Midas touch," she mused late Wednesday afternoon as she finished toweling her hair dry. Slipping a thick, white terry robe over her naked shoulders, she glanced at her reflection before tying the sash.

"The bruises aren't so bad," she murmured with relief. Hopefully Mike would soon have the chance to see that for himself.

When they had returned to her place last night and found it had been broken into, she honestly hadn't thought about where she'd be spending the night. Knowing it was *not* going to be in her bed with Mike had been enough for her to zone out. But later, when the responding officers—who'd both known Mike—had left, she'd looked around and the reality had begun to set in.

They were finally alone. But she couldn't stand to stay.

Her desire for him could not overcome the ugliness of what had happened. Enraged helplessness had washed over her, making her body clench and her eyes sting with hot, unshed tears.

Someone had entered her home. Had gone through her things. Had touched this table and that chair, had opened desk drawers and put filthy hands on her kitchen towels. He'd rifled through her clothing, left his aura in her bedroom. He'd torn every piece of paper out of her filing cabinet and strewn them all over the apartment. And when he'd gone, he'd taken with him every ounce of security she'd ever felt in her own home.

Mike had seemed to know exactly how she felt and had

made a suggestion. *Come home with me.* That was all he'd said. That was all he'd *had* to say. Because without thinking, she'd picked her purse back up, grabbed her laptop—which the thief hadn't bothered to steal—and gone with him. She hadn't taken another single thing—not her clothes, her toothbrush. Not a nightie or a change of panties. Nothing that could have been touched by someone who'd assaulted her sense of privacy.

She'd heard that being robbed was something like being raped, but she'd never understood it before. No, the level of violence wasn't comparable, but the rage at the personal invasion had to be at least a little similar. Though, it appeared she *hadn't* been robbed. Because Jen hadn't been able to find a single thing missing. Everything had just been trashed and gone through.

To her surprise, instead of driving her to his house in Queens, Mike had headed uptown, toward Central Park West. Definitely not a cop's address. They'd arrived at his grand-father's vacant penthouse at around 3:00 a.m., Mike explain-ing that he wanted her someplace where neither of them could be easily traced.

Which *might* have been fine. This apartment was, after all, more exclusive than any five-star hotel she'd ever seen. It was a fairy-tale setting for a seduction. Or even an I'm-tired-but-we've-been-waiting-forever-so-let's-just-do-it-once-then-go-to-sleep-and-have-morning-sex kind of thing.

Only…she was alone. She had been for hours. Mike had deposited her here, said he was going home for his dog, ordered her not to leave, then taken off. She'd found a message from him on her cell phone this morning saying he'd gone right to work.

He'd dumped her in this magnificent, decadent playground,

leaving her feeling like the dirty mistress of a Greek tycoon in one of those romance novels. And she'd been fuming ever since. When she wasn't sleeping. Or ignoring his orders and going out to buy a few necessities. Or enjoying the fabulous view of the city and the park below. Or nibbling on some of the gourmet foods stashed in the kitchen cabinets. Or indulging in the most incredible bath to be found this side of a pricey spa.

"Not a bad way to fume," she acknowledged as she strolled barefoot across the lushly carpeted bedroom. She might have been walking on a blanket of thick, soft grass. Her feet could get used to the whole opulence thing. As could the rest of her.

The guest suite in the penthouse was obviously equipped for visitors, with every possible toiletry stocked neatly in the bathroom. From new toothbrushes and bath oils to a variety of robes and wraps, there wasn't much she couldn't live without for a few hours in the way of personal care. But there was nothing for her to wear, beyond the robes. So this morning, she'd left briefly, against strict orders.

"Orders," she said as she began combing her wet hair. "Ha."

Mike should know by now she didn't take orders, even if they were well intended. Jen wasn't an idiot, so she hadn't gone anywhere near her own neighborhood and she was gone less than an hour. A quick cab ride had given her the chance to at least grab some new panties and a little makeup. Not the Sephora concealer she'd planned on, but it'd do.

When she'd returned and found the penthouse still empty, she hadn't known whether to be relieved or annoyed. Part of her was glad he hadn't been there to gripe at her for having left. Another part just wanted him *back*.

With nothing else to do this afternoon, she'd taken a hot

bubble bath. A long soak in the huge jetted tub had seemed the perfect way to soothe away any lingering aches from Saturday's accident. She'd soothed so long, she'd nearly fallen asleep.

That probably wasn't too surprising since she'd only slept for a few hours in the luxurious bed with the feather duvet the night before. If Mike ever did come back, he'd undoubtedly collapse in the thing and remain unconscious for hours.

"I don't *think* so," she said as she opened a bottle of expensive wine and poured herself a glass. "Either we fight or we have sex, those are your only two options, Mike Taylor."

She was mad enough at him for dumping her like some helpless kid that she was ready to fight. She was also hungry enough to jump on him the moment he walked through the door.

Whatever she did would probably be entirely determined by his attitude whenever he got back here.

Mr. Potts's penthouse had a patio, where she'd sat this morning sipping coffee—black since there were no fresh supplies in the kitchen. The patio was a veritable jungle in the city, lush and green with rich vegetation. Nearly enclosed by potted palms, banana plants, ferns and some type of unusual flowered vine growing on the railing, the spot had afforded not only an amazing view, but also an incredible amount of privacy. She suspected Mr. Potts liked it that way—being able to see but not be seen unless he chose it.

Glancing at the clock and seeing it was after five, she carried her drink and a year-old edition of a news magazine outside to enjoy the remains of the day. The sound of traffic wasn't too bad because of the height. For a while, as she sipped and read, she almost forgot she was in the middle of a bulging city, not in a secluded jungle grove. Reclining in a comfortable lounge chair, she could almost have fallen asleep, lulled by the hum of the ceiling fan above her, each breath sweetened by the perfume rising off the flowery vines.

"Hey," a voice said from behind her.

Dropping the magazine, she jerked her head up and saw Mike standing in the doorway. "He returns," she mumbled.

Stepping outside, Mike tugged his jacket off and tossed it into an empty chair. When he reached up to unbutton his dress shirt, Jen held her breath, wondering if this striptease was going somewhere or if he was merely unwinding after a long day.

He stopped at the second button. Bummer.

"How was your day, dear?" Sarcasm fell off each word.

"Long." He twisted the top off a bottle of beer, which she hadn't even seen him bring out. He'd apparently stopped at the store on the way home. If he'd brought some French vanilla–flavored coffee creamer, she might just forgive him five minutes sooner than she had originally intended to.

"You left," he said.

Uh-oh.

He didn't even glance in her direction, merely staring out at the panorama spread below them, half-hidden from her by the sprawling leaves of a large palm. But the clench of his jaw and the harshness of his handsome profile told her he was angry. "There's a department-store bag in the trash can."

Busted. His cop powers must be in top form for him to have found the thing so fast. Too bad she hadn't stuck it in a drawer.

Jen immediately shrugged the thought off—she was no ten-year-old who had to obey orders. "I needed a few things."

Mike swung around, his dark eyes snapping, tension rolling off him. His body was stiff, and his mouth opened as if he was about to snap a retort. The man was all controlled energy and simmering anger, disguised in his dress shirt as an everyday modern guy, but just as dangerous as an old-fashioned warrior. Though she didn't fear him, for the first time she realized Mike could be dangerous if crossed.

She shivered a little. Then Jen reminded herself that she'd always enjoyed crossing people.

Lifting his bottle, he sipped from it in a visible stall for time. When he lowered it, he took a deep breath, as if trying to remain calm and reasonable. "I *told* you to stay here."

So much for reasonable. "I told you to kiss my butt."

"What?"

"I said it to the door after you left," she grudgingly admitted, "but the sentiment's the same. You can't dump me in a strange place, order me to stay and expect me to sit here like Suzy from the Sixties waiting for the powerful man to get back."

He slammed the bottle down on the table so hard she thought it would break. "Damn it, Jen, someone's stalking you."

The truth sounded so raw and ugly thrown out there like that. Ugly…and inescapable.

For weeks she'd been fooling herself that the letters were annoying, the phone calls a nuisance. But after last night, when Mike and the other cops had acknowledged she hadn't been robbed but rather…personally *invaded,* she couldn't brush it off anymore. "I know," she murmured.

He barreled on as if she hadn't spoken. "You've got no business being out on the street where this sicko can take things up a notch. First letters, then phone calls, then breaking and entering." He flattened both hands on the small wrought-iron table right beside her, leaning over it so she could look up at his impossibly broad chest and the tanned bare skin of his neck.

Heat that had absolutely nothing to do with the sunny day slid through her. Her mouth dry, she kept staring at the hollow of his throat, at the tiny bit of dark hair curling above the V of his shirt. She'd been dying to rake her fingers through it since she'd first seen him shirtless that day at the lake.

"He's been raising the stakes and the next step probably involves personal contact."

Umm. Personal contact.

She shivered, not because he'd scared her—the evidence of her trashed apartment had already done that, thanks very much—but because he was so incredibly *hot*. Strength and power radiated off him. She could inhale and be overwhelmed by the testosterone filling the patio. Demons were chased away, fear and annoyance tripping along behind them as awareness flooded through her.

Fighting could be fun. It was also *not* what she wanted to do right now. Trying to sound contrite, she explained, "I didn't go anywhere near my apartment, or my agent's office, or my publisher's, or any of my friends."

His fingers relaxed the tiniest bit at her subdued tone.

"I promise, I'm not a heroine in a movie of the week who gets all stupid and puts herself in harm's way right after the hero warns her not to, okay?"

He raised a brow in blatant skepticism. "Oh?"

Being contrite and conciliatory required a lot of work. Too much of it, in fact. And the thought of going through all these *words* to get to the making up part at the end of their fight seemed wasteful and stupid.

She'd waited long enough. They could fight later. So she ended their dispute without saying a single thing.

Rising from the chair, she arched sensuously, tossing her nearly dry hair back and running her fingers through it. It was silky against her hand, the robe was soft against her skin, and Mike's stare was incendiary against every part of her. She felt the burn from a few feet away.

"We're not finished talking," he muttered, though he didn't sound interested in talking anymore. Oh, no, he did not.

"Yeah, Mike. We are."

Reaching for the loosely belted tie around her waist, Jen slowly slid it apart. He continued to watch, his eyes remaining dark, his hard, magnificent body perfectly still.

Dropping the sides of the belt, she let the soft terry-cloth robe drift open. Though she made no effort to remove it entirely, without the fastening the thing parted in the center, falling open to reveal a narrow strip of her naked form to his hot gaze.

Jen cast a slow, unconcerned look over the patio railing, knowing it was at least possible someone in a nearby building could have binoculars at the ready for just this kind of thing. But the shadowy recesses of the plant-filled patio would prevent anyone from seeing details…and frankly, she didn't much care. Still, she turned a little bit, presenting her back to the world. And her front only to *him*.

"Jen…"

"Aren't you finished talking yet?" she purred as she stretched slightly, her body warm and pliant. Her exceedingly slow movements were mirrored by the movements of the robe, which drifted apart *here* and then settled back *there*.

He devoured each glimpse she provided as if they were morsels of succulent meat dripped into the mouth of a starving man. "We're not finished," he growled. "Not nearly finished."

"You really want to fight with me some more?" she asked, knowing full well what he meant but liking this crazy-hot taunting. Especially liking his reaction to it.

The man looked like a predator, a deceptive stillness keeping him rooted in place. Yet a muscle in his cheek betrayed the tightness of his jaw. "Were we fighting?"

She nodded.

"I thought we were just talking."

"Okay, then, are we done talking now?" she asked. Running her hand through her hair again, she fingered the last few damp strands, letting them absorb the sun's rays.

The movement was dual purposed, of course. Both to finish drying her hair and to drive Mike toward that precipice he was getting closer to by the second.

As she reached her arm farther to lift the hair spilling past her shoulders, the robe rose and drew back with it. The fabric scraped across one breast with agonizing sensitivity, grazing her nipple, then baring it completely. It pebbled in reaction, silently inviting him to touch, to taste.

Mike muttered something under his breath. Something that sounded helpless. Something that sounded desperate.

Something that sounded about at the edge of human control.

Lowering her arm, Jen intentionally slid the palm of her hand against her breast, sucking in a quick gasp at the sensation. The pleasure rocketed from her puckered nipple down through her body until it pulsed between her legs, where warm, liquid readiness had already pooled.

Mike let out one small, nearly inaudible groan.

Dropping her arms to her sides, Jen smiled at him, a Cheshire-cat smile full of self-satisfaction. The robe fell back into place—but didn't close *quite* as much as it had been before. More of her body was revealed—a few inches of it. More of his hunger was revealed, too. Miles of it.

Inhaling the heady scent of the huge tropical-looking flowers, she whispered, "I like it out here."

"I thought you might."

"It's sensuous."

He nodded in agreement. "Very."

Lifting her fingers to her shoulders, she slid the material farther away from her neck, letting her own fingernails scrape across her nape. The gap down the front grew wider, until Jen could feel the warm summer air brush against her collarbone and the crevice between her breasts. Trickles of air danced farther down, skittering over her midriff and her belly. And lower—into the tiny tuft of curls above her smooth, bare sex.

With every movement, every centimeter revealed, Mike's hungry stare betrayed him. He raked a thorough gaze from the hollow of her throat, going straight down, taking his sweet time about it, too. Wherever he looked, she burned. So she was soon burning everywhere. Burning and shaking, living and dying.

He wanted. She wanted. And there was nothing stopping them now. Absolutely nothing.

"I'm not sure what I most want to do with you right now."

"What are my choices?" she purred.

He finally moved, stepping around the chair, stalking her. His steps were slow, deliberate, and as he moved he reached up and undid more of the buttons on his shirt.

"You seem to like being on display," he said, his tone not revealing whether he thought that was a good thing or a bad one.

Uncertainty crept into her. She wrapped her fingers in the terry cloth, not knowing whether to pull the sleeves back up, or let the robe fall entirely to the cement patio floor.

"You want your body to be looked at."

By him? Oh, yes, she most certainly did. But had her complete lack of inhibition turned him off? Maybe he thought she was an exhibitionist. Maybe he thought she wanted to drop her robe, rip off his clothes and have wild, hot, hungry sex right here outside in this lush city jungle.

Well, she did. She had to admit that, if only to herself.

But it wasn't as if she wanted to drop everything, then turn around and lean over the railing, tilting her bottom in welcome. Have him curve in behind her and press close, his chest to her back, his groin pressing for entrance, his sex sliding between her cheeks. Let him bend her over, wrap his strong arms around her waist and drive into her while they both looked out over the city and cried to the blazing sky in pure satisfaction.

Oh, God, she *was* an exhibitionist.

A smile of such pure, visible satisfaction curved that amazing mouth up and his dreamy brown eyes glittered. "I know what you're thinking."

He did. She knew it. And the wicked smile on his face told her she hadn't shocked him at all.

"Drop the robe."

He was completely dressed. Beneath her robe, she was naked.

She dropped it anyway.

"God in heaven," he murmured, sounding stunned.

Jen had a decent body, and she worked to keep it that way by limiting the wine-and-ice-cream nights to only the direst emergencies. Decent. Maybe verging on good, though not centerfold quality, by any stretch of the imagination.

But she honestly didn't think she'd ever seen a man look at her with such vivid, raw hunger. As if he could die at that moment with a smile on his face, having seen his perfect image of woman in his final moments.

It was heady, being that wanted. Maybe she'd have savored it more if she hadn't been so insane with desire, too.

"You exceed my imagination," he said, keeping his voice low and even, though she knew—could tell by his expression—that he was hanging on to his control by a thin thread. The tension in his body indicated it, the intensity of his stare screamed it.

"I'm a little exposed here," she murmured, half wanting to do an ancient woman's one-arm-over-the-breasts-one-over-the-goods pose. The other half of her wanted to extend her arms straight out, toss her head back to cry out in decadent relief.

She settled for running the tips of her fingers in a long, slow caress over her own body. Starting at the spot below her ear, traveling down over her collarbone, then delicately over the tip of her breast. Her nipple swelled in reaction. So did Mike.

She continued to touch herself as he watched, tracing an invisible line she wanted him to follow with his hands and his mouth. When she reached her belly, she hesitated for a second.

"Don't stop."

"You know how I respond to orders."

"*Please* don't stop."

Better. She did as he'd asked, stroking the soft, vulnerable skin just above her pubic bone, then dipping a bit lower to tangle in her little patch of brown curls. The recent wax job she'd had left her exposed and vulnerable, and he took advantage, watching every move she made. As her finger slipped a tiny bit lower, there was no way Mike could have not seen the way it brushed across her throbbing clit.

"Mmm," she moaned. "Please tell me I'm not going to have to do this all by myself."

"No. Not by yourself." He unbuttoned the rest of his shirt, revealing his body to her the same way Jen had moments ago. Jen stopped what she was doing to watch him, enjoying the sight every bit as much as he'd enjoyed watching her.

When his shirt fell away, Jen held her breath, then let it out on a long, shaky sigh. Oh, the man was amazing, broad in the chest, lean in the hips. All long planes of muscle and smooth, tanned skin. The triangle of dark hair on his chest was sparse and taut, narrowing into a thin line that ran over his belly, disappearing into his waistband. Hard and beautiful and perfect.

She had a feeling he was perfect all the way to the floor, judging by the massive bulge in his trousers.

"By the way," he said as his hand moved to his belt. His thick arms flexed and rippled as he unfastened it, then unbuttoned his pants. "We're simply taking a break in our conversation. I'm still not happy about you leaving."

"Well, I *live* to make you happy," she said, reaching out to help him pull the belt free, loop by loop. It cracked as she whipped it out of the last hole, a sizzling note of wickedness in the otherwise still air of the garden patio.

"Uh-huh. I can tell." The zipper came down. Slowly. So slowly she was surely going to die.

She said nothing, waiting for him to finish the slow opening of the zipper, gazing in avarice at the bulge barely contained behind it. When he finally finished, and the pants dropped low on his lean hips, he grabbed a condom out of his pocket. Kicking off his shoes and socks, he let the trousers fall away, revealing his powerful legs, until he wore only a pair of bulging, tight cotton boxers. Very bulging. Which might explain the stubbornness of the strained zipper.

"I think you're still one up on me," she managed to say.

He didn't take off the briefs, merely stepped closer, until she was enveloped in his warmth and his hot, musky smell. Before she could even mentally prepare for it, his hands were on her hips, his rough skin easing over hers as he tugged her close, until their bodies brushed ever so lightly. Having his hands on her naked body was such a relief, she sighed at the pleasure. She rose to meet his mouth, her lips parted, waiting for his kiss.

When it didn't come, she whispered, "Please…"

"Tell me you'll do what I say and stay in the next time," he whispered as he leaned to her neck, kissing her there. His sweet mouth tasted her nape, his tongue scraping a path up to the sensitive spot just below her ear. "Promise."

Torture. He was coercing an agreement out of her. "This would never stand up in a court of law," she said with a whimper that was half laugh, half desperate plea.

He nipped her jaw. "Promise."

"Damn it, I promise." Twining her hands in his hair, she tugged him up, seeing a smile of triumph on those lips, but so needing to taste him she didn't care. He finally gave her what she wanted, covering her mouth with his, licking at her tongue in a deep kiss that stole her very last coherent thought.

As if he couldn't get enough of her, Mike ran his strong hands up and down her body. Each stroke and slide of his fingers both aroused and shattered her. Driving want gave over to pure sensation as he caressed her skin, their joint groans of pleasure mating between their lips.

Her breasts screamed for more than those light, passing

touches, especially when he trailed the tips of his fingers along the outside curves of them. With their bodies remaining a breath apart, her nipples were already throbbing because of the brush of his chest hair, and if she didn't get more, *soon*, she might jump off the balcony.

When she thought she'd die from waiting, his hands covered her breasts, plumping and stroking her into a frenzy. "Yes," she groaned against his mouth, shuddering when he caught her nipples between his fingers. Her groan turned into a whimper as Mike tweaked and plucked them into two points of pure sensation.

As if he knew exactly how long he could torment her before she'd lose her mind, he ended their long, drugging kiss and arched her back to gain access to the front of her body. With his strong arm supporting her around the waist, she let herself go, trusting him not to let her fall.

"Oh, yes," she groaned when he covered her breast with his mouth. He lathed the sensitive tip with his tongue, slowly, then tormented her with a quick, hard suck that sent frantic lust through her.

Her legs were growing weak, and he seemed to know it because he drew her over to the lounge chair she'd vacated.

"Wait," she said, not letting him draw her down onto it yet. She pointed to his briefs, now darkened with his own moisture. "Those. Off." But she didn't wait for him to obey. Instead, she slid her hands into the waistband, tugging the elastic out and over his erection, then pushed them down.

"Oh, my goodness," she mumbled as she stared at him. He was engorged—huge and powerful, his smooth, pulsing cock just as perfect as the rest of him. Her legs clenched reflexively, as did her sex as she realized she was going to *have* that. Soon.

No, not soon. *"Now,"* she demanded. "I want everything else but right now I have to have you inside me, Mike."

She betrayed her insane need with her words, her voice and her stare. But she saw the same need in him. His dark brown eyes flared, then narrowed as he slowly lowered himself onto the chair. He studied every inch of her on the way down, pausing only to scrape his lips across her belly, then blow a warm, slow breath into her few remaining curls.

"Right now?" he asked, staying close—so close—she could almost feel his lips. "You sure about that?"

Closing her eyes, she dropped her head back. "Well… maybe I could wait a *moment* longer."

"Good," he whispered right before he slid his tongue out and swirled it against her clit. Her legs buckled, but he held her hips, careful to avoid her fading bruises. He kept her still so he could slide his tongue deeper, between her drenched lips, drinking her body's juices. And after a few more flicks of his tongue, she came in an orgasm that put the one he'd given her the other night to shame.

"You taste so good," he muttered as he watched her ride out the hot waves of pleasure. "I've been wanting to taste you again for days. Without the cloth."

She shared the want, suddenly hungry to perform the same intimate pleasure on him. But not now—now she'd reached the end of her endurance and needed to be filled by him.

Apparently knowing—and sharing her desperation—Mike let go and pulled away long enough to tear open the condom and sheathe himself with it. Then he slid his hands around her waist again, tugging her down, onto him, around him.

As the tip of his hot member slid into her, she gasped, and kept on gasping as she rode down it, taking him deeper and deeper until he'd completely impaled her. Gasping, she closed her eyes and savored the invasion, wondering how she'd ever go back to the emptiness of not having him inside her.

"Ride me," he ordered as he sank his hands in her hair and tugged her mouth to his for a deep kiss.

She did as he wanted, slowly beginning a sweet, sensuous ride. With her feet on the patio, on either side of the chair, she had ultimate control and used it to take exactly what she needed—and what would give them both the most intense pleasure.

Mike lay all the way back on the lounger, watching her with blazing eyes. Not taking over, he still remained very involved, reaching up to caress her bare breasts or tangle his fingers in her long hair. He kept murmuring sweet, sexy things that she could barely comprehend but that rolled like sweet background music into her ears.

"Mike…" she said hoarsely as the intensity built.

"You're beautiful." He drew her down for a deep kiss.

Jen curled her fingers in the hair on his chest and continued taking him with long, teasing strokes and hard, fast ones. He seemed to like those because he shuddered with every one. Until finally, as if he couldn't take it anymore, he grabbed her hips and set the pace. Rocking up, thrusting hard. Bursting into her as if he just couldn't get deep enough.

"Come with me," he ordered.

Some orders she didn't mind so much.

She could do as he said, she was already so close. When he moved one hand and worked her swollen clit, she cried out. "Yes."

The familiar spasms rolled through her, pulsating from her center and radiating outward until she felt as though electricity was pouring out of even her fingertips. Clenching him tightly in reaction, she milked him and heard his guttural groan as he joined her in climax.

She stayed on top of him, breathing deep, ragged breaths, trying to regain control of her raging heart. Her legs ached, her whole body felt wonderfully exhausted. Not even opening his eyes, Mike tugged her down to lie on top of him. Jen curled onto his chest, feeling his raging pulse beneath her fingertips, and the two of them gradually began to float back to earth.

When she felt capable of speech, Jen whispered, "I don't think us talking about sex so much before this was a problem."

Feeling his chest rumble as he laughed, she tilted her head back, wanting to see that smile, to savor those dimples. She got what she wished for, their eyes meeting, both wearing matching expressions of utter satisfaction. And simple, basic happiness.

"No, Jen," he finally said as he kissed her forehead, "I definitely don't think talking about it was a problem."

CHAPTER THIRTEEN

They say some things improve with age: cigars, classical novels, wine. And men. That, supposedly, is why old married guys cheat with twenty-year-old bimbos because their wives haven't "improved" the way they have. Personally, I think the only thing that improves with age on a man is his bank balance.

—*I Love You, I Want You, Get Out*, by Jennifer Feeney

STROLLING DOWN TROUBLE'S main street Saturday afternoon, Mortimer nearly rubbed his hands together in delight. Signs of new life were springing up everywhere, and he mentally patted himself on the back.

His projects—all of them—seemed to be going along just swimmingly. The town was crawling out from under its cloak of depression. His grandson Maxwell was living in marital bliss in California. His friend Roderick was out again today, for the third time this week, with Miss Baker. And, judging by the tone in Michael's voice when he'd called to check in a few days ago, things were heating up between him and Jennifer Feeney.

Heating up? Ha. Considering Michael had been calling to

let him know that Miss Feeney was staying at Mortimer's place in the city, he'd say they were on fire.

"Soon now," he mumbled as he paused to glance in the window of a small antique shop/tearoom, its front window crowded with cuckoo clocks. They'd once hung in Mortimer's own house, which had been built by a clock manufacturer. "I'll have great-grandchildren sometime soon."

"Mortimer!" a voice said.

Startled, he saw Roderick and Miss Emily, apparently having just left the new bookshop that had opened up a few months ago. Another sign of prosperity: there were enough people around here to keep a bookstore going. Of course, Roderick probably spent enough each month to cover the store's rent.

"Well, hello. Didn't suppose you two would be sticking around here today." He'd half expected his old friend to have whisked Miss Baker off for a romantic picnic. Roderick did make a fine chicken salad and had impeccable taste in wine. Though, of course, he couldn't abide bugs. His friend had gotten a little persnickety in his old age, considering he'd once as easily smashed a desert scorpion as flicking off a flea.

Roderick forced one of those small, impassive smiles, which told Mortimer he was uncomfortable. On guard. "I invited Miss Baker to help me choose a birthday gift for my sister."

Books. Bah. Only thing one could gain from books was the inspiration to go on a journey to a new place described within its pages. "Why not go on an adventure?" he asked. "Do something spontaneous. Anything but lock yourself up in a musty bookstore."

"We're going into the tearoom for an afternoon respite."

"Taproom?" Mortimer asked, immediately perking up at the

thought, though he suspected he knew what Roddy had really said. Sometimes he quite enjoyed playing hard of hearing.

"*No.* A tearoom has opened up in the back of the antique shop and they serve somewhat palatable cucumber sandwiches."

Tea and cucumber sandwiches. Egads. Roderick had not merely grown persnickety, he'd gotten boring. "Why not order the sandwiches to go and take the lady for a picnic in the country?"

He saw Miss Baker's eyes flare, reacting with unmistakable excitement at the prospect, as would any lady with a romantic sensibility. But as she quickly cast a sideways glance at her escort, the excitement quickly faded. Roderick's spine had grown even stiffer. "Of course not. Picnicking is for youngsters."

Mortimer liked a nice picnic now and again. Especially when he was accompanied by an attractive lady who wanted to pop grapes or juicy berries into his mouth. If he'd been courting Miss Emily, an outdoor adventure is exactly what he would have proposed—she certainly looked game for one. Well, she *had.* Now she simply looked resigned to tea and cucumber sandwiches in a stuffy room crowded with moldering antiques and cuckoo clocks.

Roddy had never been the ladies' man in their partnership, but he'd still been very successful at romance. He seemed, however, to have lost his touch, along with his sense of adventure. And sense of humor. Because his date, who had been looking at the man with stars in her eyes a week ago, now appeared almost bored after only their third date.

Something had to be done. Had. To. Be. Done.

And he knew just what.

Leaning over, he took Miss Emily's hand and brought it

up to his mouth, pressing a kiss on her knuckles. "I would take you on a picnic by a tranquil lake, my dear lady."

The lady in question blushed and stammered something, immediately glancing at her date. Mortimer had no doubt about where her true affections lay, so he didn't worry about his flirtations stealing the woman away. But if a little competition would give his majordomo a kick in the pants, Mortimer was game.

Roderick glared, but also stepped closer to Emily, eliminating some of the space he'd so carefully maintained between them. The man had better watch out or he might actually touch his date sometime this year. "Emily and I are much too old for such foolishness," he snapped.

Mortimer looked skyward, not wanting to see the lady's response to that remark. Sometimes Roddy could be so unbelievably dense.

"I mean," his friend stammered, obviously having realized how his words had sounded, "our friendship is not based on silly romantic notions but rather on common intellectual pursuits."

Zounds, he was digging himself in deeper. Even Miss Emily was watching him wide-eyed, obviously not sure whether to be honored that he liked her brain or offended that he considered her old and unattractive. He wondered if she'd realized before now that Roderick considered their "dates" mere intellectual excursions. Judging by her visible hurt, he doubted it.

Turning red in the face, his friend continued. "Our enlightened conversations need no such fripperies as baskets and buttercups, which would only aggravate my lumbago and threaten both of us with broken limbs. Now, if you will excuse us, Mortimer, we'll be going to our tea." Shaking his head, he muttered, "Picnic, indeed."

Another voice suddenly piped in from behind them, an excited, familiar one. "A picnic? You're going on a picnic?"

Ivy Feeney joined them on the sidewalk, dressed, as usual, in a summery dress that floated around her in soft waves. She wore another one of her interesting hats—which were often embellished with feathers or beads that might put one's eye out if one got too close. This one wasn't half-bad, looking like a flower-studded pith helmet that hugged her head and brought out the fine structure of her cheekbones.

An attractive woman, Miss Feeney. Mad as a hatter, without a doubt, but still a looker. Mortimer quite enjoyed her company, as one also occasionally accused of being off his rocker.

Not that he'd trust her ever again. He might have enjoyed himself when she and her sister had slipped him a Mickey Finn so they could have their way with him, but that didn't mean he'd ever let them get their hooks into him again.

Still, she was pleasant company. Especially when flushed with excitement as she was now. She clapped her hands together, nearly bouncing on her toes, which reminded him of her very nice legs. "A picnic. How delightful. I'd love to come."

Roderick harrumphed. Emily's lips tightened. The two ladies were as similar to one another as motor oil and apple butter, but Ivy appeared ready to let that go at the prospect of a picnic.

"We were heading toward the tearoom," Roderick said, his chin still jutting out in irritation at Mortimer.

Ivy's face fell into a childish pout. "Oh, dear. And I so wanted to go on a picnic. It's just what I need to distract me."

"From what?" Mortimer asked.

Ivy's face flushed and she fluttered her thickly made-up lashes. "Nothing. Nothing. Just that man…"

Intriguing. Usually Ivy liked men too much to want to be distracted from them. "Who?"

"A nasty, aggravating man," she said, her brow pulling into a tight frown. "He calls every day, asking questions about Jennifer."

Mortimer wondered if Ivy was aware her niece was currently staying in his home in Manhattan. Before he could ask, the woman continued, "He says he's a reporter, wanting to talk to her about her book. Wanting to talk to *me* about her book." Lowering her voice, she added, "Told that girl no good would come of it."

"Are you mentioned in your niece's book?" Emily asked.

"No, Miss Hedda Harper, I am not."

Meow. Ladies and their claws. For her part, Emily barely acknowledged the slight, she simply rolled her eyes. This one had spirit. Mortimer knew it was there, though she'd been hiding it from Rod. He wondered why she felt the need.

"If I *were* in that book," Ivy continued with a lift of her chin—not a good pose since it brought the sunlight directly to bear on the creases in her makeup—"I wouldn't talk to some reporter who sounds like a ghost about it. My secrets are *mine*."

Secrets, ghosts, reporters. He wondered if Ivy had been tippling a little daisy wine.

"Have you tried telling him to stop calling?" Roderick asked, reluctantly drawn into the conversation, knowing he couldn't escape to the tearoom yet.

Ivy nodded, then clenched her fists. "He kept on. Even when he doesn't talk, I know it's him." Her voice shook and a shadow crossed her face. "I recognize his breathing. I recognized it the first time I heard it."

Stranger by the minute.

"But he can't call me if I'm not there." Her brilliant smile returned. "Or if I can't hear the phone because I ripped the cord out of the wall and threw it down the coal chute."

Mortimer guffawed, charmed almost against his will by the effervescent woman. A contrast to her dour sister…but then, Ida Mae had a stark charm of her own.

It really was too bad they were lunatics.

"Well, what say you, Rod, shall we escort these ladies on a picnic?" He fixed a flinty stare on his friend, sending him a silent message that he was losing his romantic battle for Miss Emily. "I'm sure your tea and sandwiches will still be there on a rainy day. Why waste this one?"

Emily's lips disappeared into her mouth as she waited, and Ivy continued to bounce girlishly on her toes. Finally, realizing he was outnumbered and outplayed, Rod sighed heavily. "Oh, very well. A picnic it is."

GOOD—MAKE THAT AMAZING—SEX HAD a way of making time fly.

Jen hadn't known it was possible to feel such intense pleasure for such an extended amount of time. Since Wednesday evening, when she'd seduced Mike on the patio, they'd indulged in every fantasy and each desire they could think of. Including spending the entire day either in bed or in the bathtub on Thursday after he'd taken the day off work.

By late Friday afternoon, however, when he was back at work and she'd actually begun to think of something other than how much she loved having his hands on her, she realized she was bored. And suffering from cabin fever.

Opulence was all well and good if it was part of a regular life. But to just stay in someone else's beautiful home, waiting for her lover to get back so they could have fantasy sex, felt like being a mistress.

She'd promised Mike she wouldn't go back to her place and he'd acknowledged that there was no way she could sit here all day with nothing to do. So they'd agreed that she'd stay in this part of town and let him know where she was going, and he'd stop being a pain in the ass about protecting her.

It wasn't as if she wanted to go back to her apartment now, anyway. The wounds and emotional pain were still too raw to walk in there and think of the way all her things had been violated. Her friend Ashley had gone downstairs and straightened up for her the other day, let in by the slimy super, so Jen supposed she could walk in and not burst into tears. But even her best friend could not remove the ugliness from the very air in Jen's apartment. The sense of invasion. Of loss.

"Only four," she muttered, glancing at her watch. A shopping trip for necessities had filled her morning, but now, she was once again bored stiff.

Realizing she needed to get back to real life mentally, if not physically, she decided to get some work done. The new book, which she hadn't yet come up with a title for, wasn't writing itself. Especially since she'd met and fallen head-over-heels for Mike Taylor. Right now, she wasn't sure she could come up with another eight chapters about how women should just take over the world and lock men in the basements.

"But I'll give it a shot," she mumbled to Mutt, Mike's dog, whom he'd brought over to stay with them.

The dog hopped up next to her. He scooted so close she had to plaster herself against the arm of the couch. She should probably push him off, but the scruffy mongrel had grown on her. He had such adorable big brown eyes. Like his owner.

Flipping on her laptop, she opened her word-processing program. She did a few deep breathing exercises, determined to get back into the rhythm of writing, despite the cacophony of thoughts going through her head.

Within a half hour, however, she knew it was no use. She couldn't work—this place was too unfamiliar and her mind too jumbled. At least in her apartment, she'd have had plenty of other distractions to get around the mental block. She had a stack of letters to answer…nice ones, from her fans. The crappy ones had been file thirteened right after she'd gotten back from Trouble.

There was a mountain of laundry in her closet, food probably going bad in her refrigerator and a number of other reasons for her to go home, like her need to reclaim the place as hers. But there was also one big reason to stay away.

Mike. She'd promised. So, bored or not, she was staying put.

Trying to console herself, she admitted there was probably nothing dire that she had to take care of. Heck, she could have left her door unlocked and not worried—judging by her first big-city robbery, she had nothing a thief would want. The most important thing she had was sitting on the table across from her, taunting her with its empty screen. If someone had swiped her computer and she'd lost the pages she'd done so far on the new book, she'd have been in major shit.

Suddenly, however, she remembered something else of great value that was in her apartment. "Oh, God, the knitting box!"

Aunt Ivy's precious box, the one she called every single week to check up on. Jen had left the other night, not even checking to see if it was still safely hidden away.

Not that a thief would likely be interested in an ancient old box, even if he *had* been able to find it. Paranoid about losing it and facing Ivy's wrath, Jen always kept the thing concealed in a tiny crawl space inside her bedroom closet.

It seemed impossible for anything to have happened to it in the brief time Jennifer had been out with Mike. What thief would find the crawl space, see an old, frayed, worn knitting box, open it, pull out the yarn, discover the stacks of papers, photos and journals beneath it and decide they looked interesting enough to swipe, when Jen's jewelry had not?

"It's fine," she told herself.

But she had to be sure. Ivy might very well lose her mind if she lost the box. So, reaching for the phone, Jen called Ashley.

And one hour later, she breathed a huge sigh of relief. Her friend was at the door to the penthouse, knitting box under one arm and a bottle of wine under the other. "Whew," Ashley said with a whistle as she sauntered inside, handing Jen the bottle. "Why do I feel like I've stumbled onto an episode of *Lifestyles of the Rich and Shameless?*"

"You found it!" Jen said, grabbing the case.

"Right where you said it was, in the crawl space."

Ashley walked around the penthouse, studying every piece of artwork, checking out the furniture, then cooing over the view. "You're telling me Mr. Stud-Who-Didn't-Stand-You-Up-After-All lives here? Is he a drug dealer or a prince?"

"He's a police officer," Jen mumbled, running her hands over the precious case, dying to open it up and dig through it to make sure everything remained undisturbed. Silly, but she just had a feeling. And not only because the kid inside her was still terrified of crazy old Aunt Ivy.

Ashley looked surprised, but took the news in stride, as she did nearly everything else. "Great view off this patio. And it's so private, you could do just about *anything* out here."

Jen hadn't blushed since she was ten. If then. But she suddenly felt warmth rise into her cheeks and she shifted her gaze away, not meeting Ashley's eyes.

Her friend, however, wasn't stupid. "Woo-hoo! You *have* done just about anything out here." Pasting a look of feigned shock on her face, Ashley added, "Oh, my goodness, was that your naked butt I saw on that undercover sex video on the Internet?"

Jen groaned. "Oh, God."

"Kidding. Are you going to open that wine?"

Nodding, Jen headed to the open kitchen, which adjoined the huge, step-down living area. She called over her shoulder, "Did Frank give you any trouble about getting into my place?"

Ashley plopped down on the sofa. Lifting her long, ex-model's legs, she crossed them and put her feet up on the table. "No, he was much too busy ogling your stuff."

Jen stiffened, staring at her friend across the expansive counter. Bad enough that the creepy super was in her apartment; had he really gone through her things? *"What?"*

"Don't worry. He insisted on coming into your room with me, for 'security' and he couldn't stop staring at your bed. But he didn't actually touch anything."

Wow. Alone in a bedroom with Mr. Icky and Brainless. Ashley was a very good friend, indeed. "Thanks so much," Jen said as she returned to her task. Grabbing two glasses, she filled them and carried them out. "I'm sorry you had to be in there alone with him—he didn't try anything, did he?"

"Nope, he didn't get the chance. I made sure we left the apartment door open and beelined for it the minute I had the box. I think Mr. Jones and that lawyer from 3B got a little freaked out about the door standing open. They were hanging out in the hallway to make sure you weren't being robbed again."

"Lucky for you—they'd have been nearby in case freaky Frank tried anything. Not that Frank couldn't blow Mr. Jones down with a warm breath or scare that lawyer with threats of leaky pipes."

Ashley sipped her wine, then studied Jen over the rim of the crystal glass. "Enough chitchat. Spill. Tell me all."

She should have known an interrogation was coming. No way would Ashley come all the way uptown without wanting to know details. Jen had disappeared for the past few days with the guy she'd labeled as scum a week ago. Her friend deserved to know the truth.

So Jen gave it to her. As carefully as she could, she explained how she and Mike had met, some of the things that had happened, and how…*well*…they were getting along now.

She also, however, voiced aloud the words that had been whispering in her mind for the past few days, ever since she and Mike had settled into this opulent love nest together. "It's not going to go anywhere. We're totally wrong for each other."

Ashley grunted. "Girl, you are so far gone around the bend, you can't even see the exit signs behind you. The time to jump off this highway was before you moved in here with him. Now you're good and stuck."

"Stuck?"

"Yeah. Emotionally stuck. You're in love with him."

Jen began to shake her head. She put her glass on the table, noticing some wine had sloshed out because her hand was shaking.

Shaking because of how ridiculous Ashley's claim was. Not because she was right. *Oh, God, please let her not be right.*

"We are totally wrong for each other."

"Doesn't sound like you're wrong for each other in bed."

"True. We're absolutely right there," she conceded grudgingly. "Jeez, I didn't know it was physically possible to have so many orgasms in a thirty-six-hour period."

Ashley glared. "Screw you. Considering I haven't had a date in eight months, I don't want to hear it." Then she shrugged. "Though, if you must share details…is he *big?*"

Oh, yeah. Not that Jen was going to share that tidbit. She ignored the question. "I can't be in love with him. He's bossy and pushy and has almost no sense of humor."

"Then how could he possibly like you?"

Good question. How could he?

"I saw the laughter on his face when I let him in last Saturday. Boyfriend obviously knows how to smile and he's about the hottest thing I've ever seen." As if giving her permission for Jen to have feelings for Mike, Ashley added, "Any woman would fall for him."

"I'm not any woman," she insisted. "I'm the ex–Single in the City girl who's been holding the Down with Men banner for every unhappy woman in the country for the past two years."

"That's not *you*, Jen. That's a role you play, like when I was a lingerie angel. It was never me, it was a character on a page of a catalog."

She hadn't thought of it like that. For so long, her work had been such a huge force in her life that she'd almost come to identify it as a defining part of herself. It wasn't until recently, when she'd let down her guard with Mike, that she'd remembered how much more there was to her, Jen, the person, than the snarky persona she presented on the page.

She was greater than the sum of her work, wasn't she?

But she still couldn't entirely convince herself this could turn into something real. "It won't work. He's so damn bossy and I'm so independent. How could I ever deal with his need to protect and order me around...and how could he ever get used to being with a woman he sometimes thinks is certifiable?"

"Sounds like a match made in heaven," a male voice said.

Jen leaped out of her chair and swung around, seeing a good-looking blond guy a few feet away. Behind him, looking over his left shoulder, was Mike. A grinning, twinkling-eyed Mike.

This stupid penthouse was soundproof. That had to be how Mike kept sneaking in on her.

Then she thought about exactly what she had been saying—which they'd obviously overheard—and wondered if it was soundproof enough to hide a scream of absolute mortification.

EMILY DIDN'T WANT TO THINK of herself as disloyal, but secretly, she had to admit, she had loved Friday's picnic. It had been the highlight of her summer so far, surpassing even her private dates with Mr. Ward. Not that *date* was the word she'd use for them. Meetings, appointments—that was more accurate.

Nice meetings. Cordial appointments. That was about all. *She'd* been meek and quiet. *He'd* been cool and impersonal. *They'd* been utterly and completely boring.

But the picnic had been different. Mainly because Rod had been different. Teased out of his ill humor by an unrelentingly jolly Mortimer Potts, Rod had finally become the man Emily had imagined him to be. Less proper, more adventurous, joining with Mr. Potts in telling outrageous stories of adventure and excitement. Actually laughing deep belly laughs the likes of which she hadn't heard come out of his mouth before.

His fine gray eyes had sparkled; the lines beside his mouth had eased and when he smiled, he looked almost youthful. When he was relaxed, ten years fell off the man's face.

He'd even—she believed—flirted with her. At least, she thought he'd been flirting when he'd smiled as he'd informed her that her lips were shiny from the fried chicken she'd been eating. Roderick had also touched her more than he had previously, taking her arm when they'd walked over uneven ground, holding her hand for a moment longer than he'd had to when he'd helped her out of the car. And for at least a short time, Emily had forgotten how romance heroines were supposed to behave and she'd simply let herself laugh and have a fine time.

"A lovely time," she murmured as she prepared herself a cup of tea that evening. "What a perfect day." She did a little spin around the kitchen as she went to the refrigerator for milk, smiling at her own foolishness but unable to help it.

It hadn't merely been Roderick's mood that had made the afternoon delightful, it had been the whole experience. Emily hadn't gone on a picnic in years—decades even. And though they hadn't had an official picnic hamper, their brown-bag carryout meal from Tootie's Tavern had been fine. Even spiteful old Ivy Feeney had been charming…. Vivacious and happy, she'd almost seemed like the girl Emily remembered from school. Not the harpy who'd returned to Trouble after being widowed.

They'd gone to a woodsy park outside of town, cleaning off a dusty old picnic table and spreading their lunch on it. Glancing around, Emily had wondered at the complete air of abandon in the place, judging that, like her, everyone else in Trouble had simply forgotten it was here.

Emily had gone by the overgrown entrance to the wooded place hundreds of times over the years, but somehow, it had never registered. She'd never taken note of the shady gravel road or the nearly unreadable sign hanging by one corner. The park had slipped out of her memories, even though her father used to bring her here with the other kids to swim in the pretty green lake.

Funny how decades of living in a place made it so entirely familiar that you no longer even saw parts of it. Like rereading a much loved book, when the eyes skimmed over familiar lines, no longer even recognizing individual words.

Emily loved to read—mostly romance stories, but any good novel would do. That was another thing she and Roderick had in common, along with their delight in history and appreciation of good art. Of course, Roderick actually knew something about art—Emily only knew what she liked and what she didn't. But somehow, their tastes meshed.

They were, in fact, very well matched, as comfortable together now, after their three or four get-togethers this week, as a pair of old friends.

Friends. That was the part that bothered her. Because today was the first time he'd acted the way she thought a man would act if he were interested in more than friendship. And it was the first time she had ever relaxed enough around him to be herself, rather than her idea of what a woman in a romance should be.

That had delighted her. But it had also terrified her. Because as he had escorted her home, he'd begun to retreat again. His smile had faded, his back had stiffened. By the time they'd reached her door, he'd become the same nice-but-aloof man she'd spent so much time with in recent days.

She liked that man. Quite a lot, in fact.

But it was the charming, laughing one at this afternoon's picnic whom she knew she would dream of tonight.

"What are you doing?"

As usual, when Allie popped downstairs into the kitchen, she took Emily by surprise. On evenings like this one, she half wished she hadn't told the girl to feel free to come and go down the back stairs of the house, which connected Emily's area to Allie and Hank's apartment. If Allie had come down a few minutes sooner, she would have seen her landlady twirling around the kitchen in her bathrobe like a witless teenager.

"Nothing at all, dear, would you like some tea?" she asked, managing to keep her voice noncommittal.

Allie hopped up onto the kitchen counter, swinging her legs so her heels touched the cabinet doors. She looked like a little girl ready to exchange secrets, except the secrets Allie wanted to hear about involved very adult activities.

Or…so Allie thought.

Unfortunately, they did *not*. Because her dates with Mr. Ward had included no adult activities. Not even a kiss. Still.

"Tell me about the picnic."

"How do you know about that?"

Allie rolled her eyes. "Duh. I work for Mortimer. They came back to the house talking about nothing else today."

Of course.

"Did Roddy finally loosen up?"

Emily thought about it, then nodded. "I'd have to say he did." A smile widened her lips. "He was delightful."

Allie's eyebrows waggled up and down. "So…how far'd you go? I mean, it's not like you guys haven't gone out before, so I sure hope you didn't stop at first."

"First?"

"Base." Allie reached for Emily's cookie jar, helping herself to a freshly baked oatmeal cookie. As she nibbled, a look of pure bliss appeared on her face.

It was nice to have someone to bake for again!

"What's that?" Emily asked, though she had a vague idea.

Allie gaped. Young people these days—they simply had no idea how different their world was to the one in which Emily had grown up. She hadn't even been allowed by her parents to wear ladies trousers until she'd been over twenty-one years old.

Allie quickly explained what she'd meant about the bases, running down the latest rules about how quickly a woman was supposed to let a man make it all the way around.

Ha. So far Roderick hadn't even picked up the bat.

Some of that disgruntlement must have shown on her face because Allie hopped off the counter to approach her. Her cheerful face appearing much more serious than usual, she said, "What's the matter? Is there anything *else* you need to know about?"

The girl probably wondered if Emily needed to talk about sexual positions or something equally as outrageous. So she was probably very surprised when Emily replied, "Yes. How on earth do you get a man to kiss you?"

For once, Allie appeared shocked into silence. She opened her mouth, then closed it again, obviously not knowing what to say. Emily understood the feeling.

"You're as flummoxed as I am," Emily murmured, almost laughing at the young woman's consternation.

"Roderick hasn't…?"

"No."

"Then I guess that means he also hasn't…"

"No!"

"I'm sorry." Allie scrunched her face in concentration. "Have you made it clear you want him to kiss you?"

Not being sure what that entailed, she answered truthfully. "I thought that was a natural progression when two people have been seeing so much of one another. In the movies…"

"Forget the movies. You watch too many movies."

She supposed she did.

"Guys in old-time movies always seemed to have some romance handbook, but real men don't, Emily. I think it's time you came right out and let Roderick know you're interested in more than he's been offering you."

Emily was shaking her head before Allie had even finished her thought. "I couldn't."

"You could. You have to. If you were dealing with Mortimer, you'd already be playing chase-around-the-desk, but Roddy's a tougher nut. I should have realized it—he's decided he's past his prime and too old for romance. He's not going to go down that road unless he is quite sure it is what you want." Staring into Emily's face intently, she asked, "So, is it? Or is a nice, quiet friendship enough for you at this point?"

She thought about it. The answer should have been easy because she'd been telling herself for ages she wanted a little romance in her life. Now that she had a male friend, however, she'd found she liked it. And she did not want to upset that by doing something to drive Roderick away completely. Finally, though, she had to admit at least one thing to herself: she'd like to be kissed. If nothing else…she wanted a kiss.

"No, Allie, I really don't think it is enough anymore," she finally admitted, the words rushing out in one exhaled breath. "Tell me what to do."

Reaching for another cookie, Allie nodded her head, then sat at the kitchen table. Talking a mile a minute, she was like a general in a battlefield, etching out her attack plan with her fingertip on the table's wooden surface.

By the time she was done, Emily was shaking her head. She couldn't do that. She just couldn't.

"Yes, you can," Allie said, as if reading her thoughts.

"I'm not making any promises."

Allie stood, walked around to Emily's chair and hugged her around the shoulders, offering as much support and encouragement as her tiny frame could manage. "You don't have to. You don't have to promise *me* anything. But you need to promise *yourself* you'll at least try to do these three things."

Emily nodded, knowing what they were. Allie had gone over them once. But her young friend insisted on repeating herself.

"First, quit playing silly games and acting like a woman in a movie—be the *real* Emily we all know and love."

"Yes." She agreed with that one wholeheartedly. She was tired of pretending to be someone she wasn't—someone proper and meek, who smiled faintly and never laughed too loudly. That wasn't Emily Baker and it was about time Roderick Ward discovered it.

"Second," Allie said, "follow your heart."

She could do that, too. She feared her heart was already engaged in the matter. It had been since the picnic yesterday when she'd realized she could so easily be in love with the smiling, easygoing Roderick she'd seen at the park.

"Finally," Allie said with a huge grin, "don't wait for him. You grab him, plant one to-die-for kiss on the man's mouth, and *take* what you want."

That was the sticky one. Because Emily honestly didn't know if she had the courage to do as Allie said.

But in the end, she gave her promise.

She would at least try.

CHAPTER FOURTEEN

Have you seen the commercial that says a *real* man should have no problem spending a month's salary on an engagement ring for the woman he loves? Ha. I don't know a man who wouldn't bitch about spending a month's salary to buy a kidney to save his own life, much less a piece of rock for a woman he's already thinking might someday cost him a lot more than a month's salary in alimony.

—*I Love You, I Want You, Get Out* by Jennifer Feeney

MIKE LIKED JEN'S FRIEND ASHLEY. Tommy liked her even more.

In fact, he strongly suspected that right now, Tommy and Ashley were liking each other in the attractive blonde's bed.

He smiled, thinking what a strange coincidence it had been that he'd brought his single buddy up to meet Jen at the very same time she'd invited her single friend over, too. Tommy had been nattering on all night about it being fate. Mike considered it serendipity.

Like the way he'd happened to come driving into Trouble at the very moment a barefoot, tire-iron-swinging Jen had been trudging down the same road.

"What's that smile for?" she asked as she returned to the living room, carrying two small glasses of brandy.

"Nothing. Just enjoying the view," he replied as he watched her walk over, her curvy hips swaying gently, her thick hair bouncing on her shoulders.

God, she was beautiful.

"Tonight was fun," she said as she sat beside him on the couch. Mike immediately stretched his arm across her shoulders, tugging her against him. She curved into him, fitting as perfectly as a glove on a hand.

"Yeah, it was."

The four of them had spent the evening together in an impromptu double date. They'd gone out to dinner, his ex-partner never shutting up. He'd told story after story, at ease with everyone, as always. Charming and full of laughs, he'd obviously gotten Ashley's attention right away.

Jen had liked him, too. But the intimate smiles and fleeting touches she'd given Mike all night had let him know where her only interest lay. Not that he needed the reassurance—he knew Jen could barely keep her hands off him. It was mutual. But it was cute to think she needed to make sure he didn't get jealous.

Mike never got jealous. Ever.

Though, he had to admit, if Tommy had made a move on Jen, he probably would have broken his best friend's legs.

"Think they'll ever see each other again after tonight?"

He had a feeling they were seeing a lot of each other right about now. "I don't know. Tommy's a player."

"So's Ash."

He lifted his glass. "A perfect match."

Hell, maybe they were. Maybe a strong, single-minded woman would turn Tommy inside out, much the way Jen had him. There was no doubt why Ashley was Jen's best friend—the two of them were a whole lot alike.

"So, tell me about you getting shot."

Mike tensed, cursing his buddy's big mouth. Because he'd danced around that story all night, playing coy whenever Jen had asked for details. He should have known the relentless woman would be at him for it as soon as they were alone.

"It was a long time ago."

She nestled closer, until her sweet hair brushed his face and neck. Lifting one hand, she placed it on his chest, zoning in on the small scar. She traced it through his shirt, lightly, delicately, as if trying to take away any residual pain that had long since ceased to exist. "I wondered about this scar," she murmured. "Was it…"

"Yeah." He sipped his drink, stretching uncomfortably. She felt so incredibly good beside him, he didn't know if he'd be able to refuse any request she made.

Jen turned a little, lifting one slender leg across his thighs. "Tell me," she said softly. "It wasn't a regular cop story, I know that much. Otherwise your big-mouthed friend would have spilled it." She hesitated. He could feel her swallow, then she whispered, "Why do I have the feeling it…involved a woman?"

"Maybe because my ex-partner and *former* best friend dropped that tidbit when I was out of earshot?" he replied dryly.

Jen sat up, meeting his stare, looking disgruntled at having been caught. "How'd you know?"

"Because I know Tommy. And I know you. And I knew the minute I got up to take that call during dinner that you were going to harass him for more details and he was going to give you a few."

Her bottom lip went out as she frowned. "Well then why don't you just tell me everything I want to know?"

"Why don't we go to bed and I'll *do* everything you want to have *done?*"

Her eyes flared, excitement shining in them as it always did when they got physical. Damn, the woman was insatiable. In that they were well matched—he couldn't get enough of her. Every time he came inside her, he immediately began thinking about having her all over again.

"Tell you what. You tell me your story. And I'll tell you some things I've never told you."

Cautiously interested, he raised a brow. "Like what?"

A sultry smile widened that sexy mouth. "Like exactly what I want you to do to me that you haven't already."

He had to shift again, this time because his pants had pulled tight across his crotch. She got him hard with a smile and a whisper. "*Is* there anything we haven't done?"

She nodded, licking her lips. "I can think of a few things."

Erotic things. Wild things. Yeah. He could think of them, too. He just hadn't been sure she'd want to *do* them.

"I've been eyeing those handcuffs of yours…."

He put his head back and groaned, sure he was going to burst out of his pants now.

"I'd love to have you at my mercy," she added.

Mike's head shot back up. "*You* want to use them on *me?*"

Out came that pink tongue again, gliding across those full red lips. "Eventually."

Hell, he was in trouble. A complete goner. He was ready to blab anything she wanted to know, his own personal secrets included. So, after draining his glass, he spilled his guts. As briefly and concisely as possible, he told her what had happened—his ex-girlfriend, her psycho friend. The shooting. The subsequent breakup and the reasons behind it. All of it.

By the time he'd finished, Jen was sitting up on the couch a few inches away, watching with wide eyes and a slack jaw. He understood the reaction.... The story was pretty fucking bizarre.

"Wait, let me get this straight," Jen said. "Her best friend from childhood is a nut who's been in and out of treatment all her life. And the friend decides she wants you for herself. So she tries to kill your girlfriend, whose life you save by taking the intended bullet."

"Right."

"Then *you* get dumped and she stands by the insane friend who tried to kill her?"

"Pretty much."

"Are you sure they didn't meet in an asylum or something? Because I think they *both* sound whacked." Jen's face paled and her mouth opened once, then snapped closed. As if she was just now putting together a bunch of things that hadn't made sense to her before. He could almost bet he knew what they were.

"She's the reason you don't let your guard down easily, I suppose," she finally murmured.

"Maybe."

"And the reason you don't particularly trust women."

"I guess."

"The reason you were so worried that I was a nut case."

Mike couldn't prevent a grin. When she saw it, Jen smiled, too, then jabbed an index finger toward him. "And there's that. I hate her for that."

"What?"

"The bitch is the one who stole your smile, isn't she?"

She sounded violent, ready to tear someone up. On his

behalf. Which turned him on so much, he immediately stood, tugging her up to stand beside him. "Let's go to bed."

Jen nodded, her eyes glittering. "You go get the handcuffs."

Throwing his head back, Mike let out a deep laugh, his shoulders shaking, his whole body relaxing. The tension he'd felt at the very thought of telling Jen what had happened in his past had been for nothing. The woman had reacted with the same feisty certainty that had attracted him to her from the moment they'd met. Breezing past the rough stuff with righteous anger and sexy humor. The way she always did.

Her hand wrapped in his, he headed toward the bedroom. But Jen paused, tugging her hand free. "Give me a couple of minutes," she said, her voice suddenly much softer. Then, pointing toward his coat jacket, which he'd tossed across the back of a chair, she added, "I believe the cuffs are in the right pocket."

Mike did as she asked, watching her almost trip as she hurried toward the guest room where they'd been sleeping. Though the waiting nearly killed him, he gave her a full five minutes, counting down the seconds on his watch. Then, swinging the metal bracelets on the tip of his finger and smiling as he wondered if she *really* wanted to use them, he headed for the bedroom.

The moment he stepped inside, he knew he was in for a night he would never forget. "Ho-ly…"

Jen had used her five minutes well. On each of the bedside tables, several lit candles provided soft illumination in the otherwise dark room. The bed had been turned down invitingly. Satiny white sheets—which had not been on it the previous night—caught the soft candlelight and reflected it back.

Someone had been shopping today.

He caught her mood—sultry, sensuous, seductive—before he even saw her. Once he did, his heart stopped completely.

"Jen," he whispered, unable to say another thing. Because she apparently hadn't shopped just for linens.

She stood between the bed and the mirrored doors to an enormous closet that extended along almost an entire wall. So his first glimpse of her included not only her lightly veiled body, but also its erotic reflection.

He simply didn't know where to look first.

"Well?" she asked, no nervousness, no trace of hesitation to be heard. She was confident and entirely sure of herself, and of his desire for her.

"You take my breath away."

She wore white. Though, *wore* wasn't the right word—she was being caressed by white, the soft, wispy fabric floating over her body, not actually clothing it.

The top of her incredibly sexy nightgown was made of satin or silk. Its spaghetti straps strained to hold the glittering fabric crossing tightly over her gorgeous breasts. Cut low, it plumped them up, pushed them together to provide a mind-numbing amount of cleavage. Her tight brown nipples jutted against the material and his mouth flooded with moisture as he imagined sampling her through the cloth again, as he had through her skirt that night in her apartment.

Directly below her breasts, the satin was replaced by some kind of lacy sheer stuff that floated around the rest of her body in a shimmering cloud of softness and light. It dropped in filmy fragments to the floor, but none were connected. Each piece appeared independent of the others, parting and settling back with her breaths and the subtle shifts of her body.

Every movement provided him with another tantalizing

glimpse of her beautiful form—a slender calf, her creamy
stomach, the line of a hip and, in the mirror, the high round
curve of her naked backside—all being displayed and then
concealed. Samples—tastes—meant to increase his appetite.

"Are you coming?" she asked as she walked over to the bed
and slid onto it, the material of her dress immediately disappearing against the satiny sheets.

He could be coming any second, just by standing here
watching her. But Mike had more control than that. He
planned to savor every bit of her tonight, for as long as
humanly possible.

When he saw what was on her legs, however, he felt another
inch of that control fall away. Because as she leaned back
against the mountain of plumped-up pillows, bending one leg
up and letting her gown fall completely out of the way, he
realized she was wearing a pair of stockings. Delicate white
fabric covered each of her legs, from her toes up over her thighs.
At the top of each was a flirty pink bow—the only glimpse of
color, other than her rosy skin, against that sea of white.

Eventually, the gown would come off. Even if he had to rip
each layer away to get at the treasures it pretended to conceal.

But the stockings were staying on.

"Come over here," she said, extending her hand for him.

Mike did as she asked, tugging off his clothes, piece by
piece, as he approached the bed. Jen never tore her gaze away,
devouring him with those blue-gray eyes until she reached her
side. When he pushed off his briefs, allowing his raging cock
to burst free, her mouth fell open in a hungry whimper.

He had no idea what she intended to do with that mouth
until she leaned over and covered him with it.

"Jen," he groaned, helpless with pleasure as she licked the

head of his shaft, sucking gently, then sliding down to take more of him.

Unable to resist, he reached down and twined his fingers in her hair, applying no pressure, just wanting the silkiness against his skin. He closed his eyes, giving himself over to her, knowing he wouldn't be able to take this intimate attention for long but wanting to enjoy it for a few moments more.

Though the thought of letting her take him to the edge with her amazing mouth was incredibly appealing, he was selfish and wanted to do too many other things to let it end so quickly. But he was no saint. He didn't ask her to stop *too* soon.

Opening his eyes, he glanced across the bed at the mirrored closet doors. Feeling what she was doing was amazing. *Watching* her as she did it almost made his legs give out.

His heart raced as he saw the way she'd lick and nibble on him—pressing tiny kisses all the way down the back of his shaft. It nearly exploded when she'd plunge her mouth over him again, taking as much of him as she could, managing to devour maybe half of what he had to give her.

Helpless little whimpers emerged from her full mouth. She shifted restlessly on the bed, her legs falling open as her own hunger built. A wisp of fabric was draped between her thighs, cupping her sex, concealing what he so wanted to see. It immediately grew damp with her body's arousal. Then she shifted again, and it fell away, revealing her in all her full, glistening glory.

His heart nearly exploded and his taste buds tingled in his mouth. "Enough…" he muttered, needing to touch her, taste her, drive her as crazy as she was him.

She obviously disagreed. With a tiny groan of demand, she reached around his body. Stroking his hips and digging her nails into his ass, she tugged him close, then pushed him back. She set an unmistakable rhythm until he was making love to her mouth.

That took him to the line of endurance and nearly sent him spiraling over it. So, though it took just about every ounce of strength he had, he gently stroked her cheeks and pulled away.

She looked up at him with wet, swollen lips. "Why did you stop me?"

"Because the night is young and we have a long way to go."

Smiling lethargically, she slid over to make room for him, her body gliding easily across the fabric. When he joined her on the bed, he suddenly understood why women liked such silky lingerie. The sensations battering his skin were incredibly pleasurable.

But it wouldn't be as soft as Jen's body, he knew that.

"Kiss me," she pleaded, opening her arms for him.

He certainly didn't need to be asked twice. He bent to her, covering her mouth with his, their tongues immediately sliding out to tangle and mate. He tasted his own essence on her, and acknowledging just how thoroughly she'd consumed him made his cock lurch even harder against her stocking-covered thigh.

"I like this," he murmured when the kiss finally ended. Bending to her nape, he tasted his way across her shoulder until his teeth caught the strap of her gown.

"I'm glad."

"I'll like it better when it's off you."

She moaned softly. "We'll get there."

"Eventually," he agreed, suddenly in no hurry to get to the end of the race. The journey was going to be much too delightful to rush through it.

So he took his time. With tender strokes, gentle nips and hungry tastes, he explored her body. Starting at the top, he worked his way down, nudging her gown out of the way as he went. He left it over her breasts for a moment as he buried his face between them, breathing deeply into her cleavage.

"Taste me," she pleaded, arching toward his mouth, her nipple slipping free of its confinement to peek at him.

Mouth watering, he went for it, suckling her and caressing her other breast with his hand until she was shaking so hard he thought she'd come right then and there. "You have incredibly sensitive breasts, don't you?" he asked as he drew his mouth away to blow lightly on that beautifully puckered tip.

"Everything about me is sensitive when your mouth is in the vicinity."

Wanting to prove that, Mike continued his exploration. He pushed the gown down, following it with his lips, his tongue, his teeth. He nibbled her ribs, dipped his tongue into her belly button for a taste. Moving lower, he scraped his rough jaw against her pert clit until she shook. "Very sensitive," he murmured before covering it with his lips and sampling it.

Her silky, feather-soft gown was now down below her hips, its bodice caught around Jen's thighs so she couldn't move, couldn't evade, couldn't shift away. She could only lie there and give herself over to the pleasure as he focused on devouring the vulnerable flesh between her slightly parted legs. He loved the smooth feel of her, loved the intensity and the ease of access. Mostly he loved pleasuring her, taking her all the way to the top and letting her leap over it. It took almost no time at all for her to come, her helpless cries signaling her release before her hips rocked up as it overtook her. And he was back up, catching her mouth with his, before she'd even stopped moaning.

As their kiss slowly ended, he stared into her glowing eyes, which reflected the golden light of the nearest candle. "You know, I really like this," he whispered as he stroked the wet lips of her sex, readying her for his possession.

"I can tell. You spend a lot of time down there."

Mike couldn't prevent a slight laugh. "I meant I like the style. Your curls are pretty, but I admit it's nice to be able to explore the rest of you so up close and personal."

She shuddered, rocking up as if she was coming again merely with his words. And the hunger to be inside her when she did this time overcame him. Shoving the gown the rest of the way down, he watched her kick it off, then grabbed a condom from a box on the bedside table. His hands nearly shook as he put it on. Jen watched his every move, nibbling her lip, her eyes wide with anticipation and excitement.

They'd done so much in the past few days, but this was still so incredibly exciting. He imagined it would be so for the next fifty years, if they were to share them.

He didn't pause to dwell on that unbelievable thought. Longevity in a relationship wasn't something he'd let himself think about in a long time. Then again, he hadn't felt about a woman the way he felt about Jen. *Ever.* That she was all wrong for him—not his type, much too fierce, much too stubborn, and in the opinion of the whole world, a man-hater, he simply didn't care.

He was crazy about her. Head over heels.

"Take me, Mike, fill me, please," she groaned when he didn't move between her legs fast enough.

He immediately accepted the invitation—acceded to the demand—climbing over her, feeling her soft thighs slide around his hips in welcome. The silky stockings felt amazing against his naked skin, as he'd known they would. As he slid into her, sucked into her warmth and her tight heat, he groaned, all sensation focused low in his body now. She welcomed him, accommodated him, murmured sweet words in his ear.

"Nothing has ever felt this good," he admitted, knowing it was true. Physically, he'd never experienced anything that came close to the things he'd done with Jen.

Emotionally? Well…maybe that, too.

She tried to hurry him, taking what he was too slow to give, but Mike laughed softly, drawing out of her body, heightening the anticipation and the delight before plunging back to bury himself to the hilt. Over and over again. They went fast and slow, with him looking down at her, or her riding him. In silence and with sultry whispers and even sexy laughter. Until the candles began to burn down and Mike realized his body had reached the end of its endurance.

"One more for you," he muttered, knowing he couldn't wait much longer. Reaching down to stroke her, he flicked his fingers across her sensitive flesh, matching each movement with his tongue in her mouth. As she began to quiver and quake, to spasm and gasp, he thrust hard, riding her the rest of the way, so that when she cried out her ultimate release, he joined her in it, groaning and shaking as well. Until, entirely spent, he collapsed into her arms and fell into a deep, dreamless sleep.

JENNIFER AWOKE DURING the night, tumbling out of sleep just as she'd tumbled in her strange dream. She'd been falling down a flight of stairs—never-ending, narrow stairs that had led straight down into darkness.

She'd been a little girl at first, crying as she fell, begging her father to save her, to catch her. But before she'd hit the bottom, she'd realized she was an adult and the arms she'd begged to catch her belonged to Mike.

She'd awakened before she'd found out whether he'd done it.

The dream disturbed her, especially because she'd been sleeping so soundly, protectively curved in Mike's casually possessive embrace, until then. She'd felt almost cherished, wrapped in his arms as if he didn't want to let her go, not even in his sleep.

Their naked limbs remained entwined, the remnants of her gown tangled around their feet, its softness caressing their calves. Her stockings had been thrown somewhere in the dark room.... Mike had actually tugged them down with his teeth.

She got all flushed just thinking about it.

Mike stirred and Jen went still, worried she'd disturbed him with her movements. As her eyes slowly adjusted to the darkness, she watched his face. A bit of moonlight spilling in from a slight part in the drapes sent a soft glow of light across him, spotlighting his strong jaw and providing contrast to the shadows in the hollows of his cheek. His parted lips were incredibly sensual for a man, and she heard the nearly inaudible breaths passing over them in smooth, even regularity.

He was the most perfect man she'd ever seen. And he was in her arms, in her bed, in her life.

She just didn't know for how long.

"How could this happen?" she asked him, knowing she spoke only to herself. Because she could no longer deny what Ashley had pointed out earlier.

She was in love with Mike.

She still didn't think they could make things work in the long run—eventually, he'd drive her crazy with his overprotectiveness and she'd drive him insane with her casual attitude about everything, including her own safety. She'd write more books that offended men everywhere and sooner or later they'd offend him. And he'd someday perhaps show up at a crime scene and see another vulnerable woman, one who needed him. One who'd let him take care of her, as he seemed to need to do.

Though she would never say it, she had enough of a psychology background to suspect Mike's need to protect and care for others stemmed from his childhood. When he'd been unable to protect his father from a war and his mother from a hideous disease. But she wasn't the type to lie back and be protected—saved—dreams of falling down the stairs being the exception.

Yes. She didn't doubt the day would come when they'd realize all the problems they'd instantly anticipated in each other from the moment they'd met hadn't disappeared simply because they'd grown to care about one another.

"But for now…"

For now, they were good. Very good. Happy—both emotionally, and oh, most definitely physically.

Jen hadn't known it was possible to feel so utterly fulfilled and satiated for so long. Nor that even a man in his prime, like Mike, could have been able to take her all over again an hour after they'd finished the first time.

This time, they'd used the handcuffs.

She might not be able to walk tomorrow, at least not with her legs anywhere in the vicinity of one another. Honestly, though, she didn't give a damn.

Trying to go back to sleep, she steeled her mind against her dark dreams, inviting more pleasant ones to join her in slumber. But that just brought the previous one to mind. And she suddenly realized *which* staircase she'd been dreaming about. Those uneven steps and the moist walls were so familiar because they had once frightened her so much.

They were the stairs that led to Ivy's basement.

Ivy. God, she'd gotten so caught up with everything else this evening, she'd completely forgotten about the knitting box Ashley had brought over earlier. She hadn't had a chance to do much more than open the lid and peek inside to make sure the papers, photos and journals were still there, hidden beneath the yarn and supplies.

They had been. But frankly, Jen didn't think she could wait until tomorrow to examine them more carefully. Something was nagging at her, an uneasiness she couldn't explain. Maybe it had been Ivy's strange attitude during her last visit. She'd been so disinterested in the box—whispering about it not being "safe" to have it in her home. And knowing Ivy and Ida Mae were being bothered with phone calls of their own added to Jen's concern.

Jennifer suddenly wanted to look through the box again.

Moving carefully, she slipped out from under Mike's strong arm, trying not to wake him. She made her way across the darkened bedroom, grabbing the plush terry robe from the back of a chair where she'd tossed it after her shower earlier. Mutt lifted his head off the floor, growling low in his throat, but with a quiet "Shh, go back to sleep," he left her alone.

Once outside the bedroom, she carefully shut the door behind her, still making her way in darkness, so no stray glimmer of light beneath the door would wake Mike up.

Why she was being so secretive, she honestly didn't know. Or maybe she did. Maybe it was because Mike was a cop— because he'd already exhibited a casual interest in Ivy's history. The last thing Jen needed at this point was to arouse his curiosity any further. If the box did pose some sort of danger to Ivy, it could only have something to do with Ivy's husband's death, and her affair with Eddie James.

"Too many secrets," she whispered as she entered the living room, finally switching on a small table lamp. Honestly, though, she didn't think she had even touched the tip of the iceberg when it came to the secrets being kept by the Feeney women. From what her father had hinted at, the history of mysteries, scandal and secrets had run through the Feeney females for a very long time.

"Until now," she mentally insisted. This sneaky midnight excursion didn't count. She wasn't, after all, keeping her own secret. It belonged to Ivy.

Quickly retrieving the box from beneath the dining-room table where she'd stashed it earlier, she carried it into the living room, setting it on the coffee table. Sitting cross-legged on the couch, she reached for the faded, padded lid. A hand-stitched sampler saying There's No Place Like Home was set into the top, and she'd often wondered whether her unknown grandmother's hands had created it.

"Please, please don't let anything be missing," she whispered, not even wanting to think about facing Aunt Ivy if she'd lost one of her precious treasures. It wouldn't matter if it was a single receipt from a lunch she and Eddie had shared at a diner. If anything was gone, her aunt would know about it. And she'd scream bloody murder.

Having been in possession of the case for more than a

year, Jen was pretty familiar with its contents. So as she began to lift things out—one at a time—she started to breathe easier.

Here were the four small journals, one for each year—1963, 1964, 1965 and 1966. The one for 1966 ended abruptly well before the end of the year. The last entry had been written a few nights before Leo Cantone had been murdered.

She had asked Ivy once why she'd stopped writing. Her aunt had told her everything had been too crazy during those final days. And after them, she'd never had enough happiness in her day-to-day life to write about.

She'd said nothing else, though Jen had asked her a couple of times about Eddie. She'd never admitted if she knew where he'd gone, or if she'd ever heard from him. Jen hadn't ever come right out and asked Ivy if her lover had killed her husband, but she had to imagine her aunt knew Jen suspected as much.

Ivy had never denied it.

"Pictures, the pictures," she mumbled as she dug farther. They were all here—Ivy and Leo shaking hands with a young, still-hot-looking Elvis Presley. Ivy and Eddie laughing beside a Christmas tree weighed down with huge colorful lightbulbs, two tons of garland and fistfuls of thick, shiny tinsel. Ivy and Leo waltzing at a Hollywood gala. Ivy and Eddie sharing a milk shake. The way their foreheads nearly touched, and their two straws descended from their lips down into the cream, they created a heart shape that suddenly made Jen's own heart ache a little.

She didn't approve of adultery—whether it was committed by men or by women. But this had so obviously been love.

"Where did you go, Eddie?" she whispered, amazed at how he'd just vanished. And, judging by the way he was staring at her aunt, she couldn't help wondering how on earth he'd been able to stay away for forty years, never once trying to come back for her.

Though deceptively fragile, Jen knew Ivy was strong. So she had to assume that her aunt had ordered her lover to stay away, fearing he'd be charged with Leo's murder if he ever returned. There was, after all, no statute of limitations on murder.

Finally, she reached the bottom of the box. Nothing was missing. Every single scrap of paper was accounted for, to the best of her recollection. If she had overlooked something, it had to have been incredibly minor. A single postcard, a hand-written note, at the very most.

So, obviously her paranoia had been for nothing—her home invader had not gone rifling through this box, no matter how valuable and important Aunt Ivy thought it was.

"God, I am not cut out to be Nancy Drew," she mumbled, rubbing at her weary eyes. Her shoulders ached from bending over the box, and she suddenly wanted to put all this away—out of sight, out of her brain—and crawl back into bed with Mike.

Reaching for the journals, she lifted them inside the case, but as she did so, the corner of one scraped the padded side of the interior. The faded satin pulled away from the hard casing. For a second, Jen's heart stopped. She'd torn the fragile thing. Her aunt would rip her heart out if Jennifer had damaged something that had once belonged to Ivy's beloved mother.

But she soon realized the lining had not torn. Instead, a few tiny hooks—so small Jen would never have seen them if the lining had remained in position—had popped open, releasing the material. "What on earth?" she whispered. Carefully touching the lining, she slid her finger along the seam, soon discovering another one of those hooks, then another and another. They ran down one entire side of the box.

Her pulse tripped as she realized she'd just discovered a secret compartment, cleverly hidden in a place she'd looked at a hundred times over the years. Though a big part of her suspected she'd open the hooks, pull back the lining and find absolutely nothing, she couldn't resist doing it, anyway.

The hooks were old and slightly corroded, but they weren't too difficult to tug apart. And as Jennifer undid them, one by one, she began to see the cream-colored edge of something stuffed between the dark wood box and the pale pink liner.

"Paper," she whispered, growing excited for some reason.

She didn't try to remove the thick sheaf of papers until all the liner had been pulled out of the way. When she did finally reach for them, she handled them carefully, seeing how fragile they were. Brown around the edges, torn in places, with curled corners, the things had to be decades old. From about the same time period as the rest of the treasures contained in the heart of the box.

Unfolding them as delicately as she could, she held her breath, wondering if she was about to find Ivy's confession. Or Eddie's. Or even Leo's.

But it was none of those things. The top page was filled with lines and dots…staffs and treble clefs. Notes and sharps and flats.

It was sheet music. Handwritten songs. That was all.

She flipped to the next page, and the next, realizing they all contained the same thing…song after song, the notes, the scrawled words, smeared in black ink. Somebody's music.

The disappointment washing over her was almost palpable. She had found no secret involving her aunt, or even her mysterious late grandmother. No love letters, no ransom demands, no correspondence between Ivy and a missing Eddie.

"Just songs," she mumbled.

Probably not even very good ones.

Curious, she glanced at the first one, which wasn't even titled, trying to mentally "hear" the musical notes. It had been years since she'd taken piano lessons, but still, she remembered enough to get a melody going in her head. For some reason, it came easily, her brain filling in the sequence before her eyes even fully scanned down the full measure.

Odd how quickly she'd figured it out, considering how rusty she was. More odd that her mind had filled in subsequent notes before her eyes had even reached them. Maybe she shouldn't have begged her mother to let her quit piano lessons when she was twelve.

Trying to read the smeared black handwriting, which was so small as to be nearly illegible, she craned to make out the lyrics. It took a few words for her to grasp what she was seeing. When she did, she sucked in a surprised breath... because they were *familiar.*

No wonder her mind had filled in the notes—this song had been a hit a few decades ago, and still occasionally turned up on oldies stations.

She flipped to the next page, reading the notes, playing them on the piano keyboard in her head, and again trying to make out the lyrics. Somehow, she couldn't manage any surprise when she realized it was another familiar tune. Another hit.

The next sheet had no lyrics.... She recognized the sequence of notes in the very first bar, anyway. It had not only been a chart-topper in the seventies, it had recently been remade by one of those teenybopper, bubblegum blondes and had littered the airwaves for months a few years back.

By the time she'd scanned through all the pages, Jen had

to pause for a moment to take it in. She'd found some of the most popular songs of the past couple of decades.

All written by hand. With scrawling notes and scratched out words in the lyrics. As if they'd been *working* copies.

That wasn't possible, of course. Even she, a relative music illiterate, knew these songs hadn't all been written by the same person. They'd been performed in different decades, by a number of different groups. It made no sense that they'd all be here, all be connected.

Still for some reason, an explanation was forming in the back of her brain. It traipsed across her thoughts, then raced away so she couldn't grab and hold onto it.

It wasn't until she saw the small note on the last page that she was able to put it all together. And when she did, she dropped the sheets, utterly shocked. Because printed in the bottom right corner, in that same spiky scrawl, were these words: *For Ivy. The love of my life.*

"Oh, my God." Realizing she'd spoken too loudly, she cast a quick guilty glance down the hall toward the bedroom door. She did not want Mike to wake up right now and walk in here. Not until Jen figured out what all this meant.

Because it appeared as if Eddie James had written these songs. He was a musician, the handwriting had been the same in the lyrics and in the brief love note to Ivy. Eddie had most certainly been in love with Ivy, judging by the soda-fountain picture. It had to have been Eddie.

"Unless…Leo?" she said, a little dazed, a lot confused.

Leo had also once been in love with Ivy, despite being a ruthless bastard. Yes, in his later years, he'd been a music producer. But from what she'd read, he'd started out as a performer, writing and singing his own stuff. So it was possible *he'd* written these compositions. There was just no way to know.

It might not even matter, really, at this point. Except that these songs had been recorded by famous singers and groups for years and years. *After* Leo's death. *After* Eddie's disappearance.

They'd been made famous. And they'd probably made the composer rich. *But who was that composer?*

Sometime after that night in 1966 when Ivy and Leo's mansion had burned to the ground, someone who'd had copies of this music had sold the rights to other musicians, probably making themselves very wealthy in the process. The royalty on music was much like the royalty on books, she assumed. Every time one of those babies played on a radio, the person who owned the rights to it dropped a few cents in his pocket.

If Leo was the composer, how different might things have been if he'd not given up his own music to produce other people's? And how tragic that he hadn't lived to see how good his stuff really was.

Could it also mean Eddie had killed him not just over Ivy but so he could steal his work?

If Eddie had written them…had he gone on to live a fantasy life as some famous music mogul, living under an assumed name? Had he become wealthy and successful while hiding a dark secret—never able to return to his former life and the woman he loved for fear he'd be charged with murder?

"This is going to drive me crazy," she said, thrusting her hair away from her face as she stared blindly at the pages of musical history. She wouldn't rest until she knew the truth.

Who had sold the songs?

And who had really written them?

CHAPTER FIFTEEN

Most people want to look good in their caskets. So a betrayed wife with a handsome, cheating husband is really doing him a favor by bumping him off while he's still attractive and virile. Unless, of course, she uses a chain saw. Then they'll probably keep the casket closed.
—*Why Arsenic Is Better Than Divorce* by Jennifer Feeney

MIKE NOTICED RIGHT AWAY that Jen was distracted the next morning. She looked tired. That was understandable; she'd gotten no more sleep than he had, and he felt completely wrung out. But she also appeared to have something on her mind.

Since it was Saturday, they could have slept in, but his grandfather had called shortly after 8:00 a.m., saying he wanted to check in on Miss Feeney. He had pretended to be surprised that Mike had answered the phone so early.

Right. As if Mike didn't know his grandfather was just praying Jen had company here in the penthouse.

After the call, Mutt had been unrelenting in his attention, needing to go out. This penthouse living was a pain in the ass as far as having pets went—no quick back-door escape for the dog. Mike had been forced to get dressed and take the animal down thirty stories to get him outside.

When he got back, Jen had already been in the shower. A morning shower with her had sounded perfect, so he'd walked in the bathroom and knocked on the fogged-up door.

She immediately swung around, looking startled.

"Sorry, didn't mean to scare you."

"It's okay," she murmured.

He waited for her to open the door and invite him in. That was what she'd done a few mornings ago. They'd washed each other *very* thoroughly, each stroke made smoother by the warm water and the bubbly soap. Jen probably still had tile imprints on her back from when he'd lifted her up, put her legs around his waist and taken her right up against the shower wall.

"I'm done," she said, surprising him by reaching up and turning the water off. She obviously had something on her mind as she reached for a towel, quickly ran it over her body, then stepped out and slipped into her robe. "It's all yours."

All his. The big, lonely shower. Meanwhile, a woman who'd been absolutely insatiable a few hours ago now barely spared him a glance as he stripped out of his clothes and took her place beneath the pulsing hot streams of water.

Maybe it was a woman thing. He hated to play the PMS card, especially because she wasn't being bitchy at all—just aloof—but he couldn't make sense out of her mood. He didn't *think* he'd done anything to piss her off between the second time he'd made love to her last night and this morning. But with a woman who advocated killing men in print, he could never be sure.

He was smiling at that thought as he showered, wondering what his brothers would think when they met Jen. They'd love her, he knew, but he imagined they'd be surprised Mike had chosen a woman so different from anyone he'd ever dated before.

Chosen. As in, permanently.

Why that sudden realization didn't stun him, he didn't know. Because sometime during the past few days, he'd begun to acknowledge how right everything was. How good it was to sleep beside her, wake up to her tousled hair and lazy smile. To come home to her at the end of the day. He liked living with her. Despite not wanting to stay here, in his grandfather's place, he didn't want to give that up. He didn't want to give *her* up. Ever.

"I'll be damned," he mumbled, wondering why he wasn't frowning or running full speed ahead out the door at that self-realization. Instead, he wanted to stay—wanted to pull her back to bed and get them both sweaty enough to need another shower. Then make her breakfast and serve it to her on the patio.

Then take her out and buy her an engagement ring.

Imagining how she'd react if he told her what he was thinking, he turned off the water and grabbed his towel. She'd either take his hand and say sure, or push him off the balcony.

Chuckling, he began to dry off, but had barely started when he heard the familiar ring of his cell phone from the bedroom.

"Mike? I think that's for you."

"Grab it for me, would you?" he asked as he quickly ran the towel over the rest of his body. "It's in my laptop case."

She came in with the still-ringing phone a moment later, handed it to him, then hurried out. The look on her face was still in evidence—secretive and distracted—and now there was something else there, too. Her mouth had been pulled tight, a frown line visible between her eyes. When she'd gotten out of the shower, she'd been quiet. Now she seemed mad.

It almost made him ignore the ringing of the phone and let it go to voice mail, but a quick glance at the caller ID convinced him to take the call. It was a friend he used to work with on Vice, and it could be important. "Mike Taylor," he answered.

"Hey, pal, long time."

"Yeah, Reg, very long time." Mike kept the phone to his ear, but most of his attention was directed on the door between the bathroom and the bedroom. Jen had closed it completely when she'd left. Either to give him privacy…or to keep him away.

Hell, he was getting paranoid. Seeing motivations that weren't there. She was just tired, that was all.

"Figured you'd want a heads-up on this. One of the uniforms brought in a suspect on a carjacking last night."

Not his purview, but he kept listening.

"Guy wants to cut a deal. He says he knows something about the attempted murder of a New York City police officer on a street corner last weekend."

Mike immediately stiffened in response. "Who is he?"

"Perp's a low-level thug, but he says he can direct us to the stolen van, and tell us who jacked it."

"I'll be there in an hour," Mike said, wanting to be on hand for any arrest in the case. He hoped the suspect implicated Ricky Stahl, himself, because he would dearly love to get more charges piled on to the mountain he was already facing.

Disconnecting, Mike pulled on some clothes and went into the bedroom, his mouth already open as he prepared to apologize for bailing on her on his day off. But the look on Jen's face—and the small white card in her hand—stopped him cold.

She had tears in her eyes. But the tension in her shoulders and the jut of her jaw said she was furious. Remaining seated on the edge of the bed, she flipped the card at him. "It fell out of your laptop case when I grabbed for your phone."

Mike didn't pick up the small piece of cardstock lying at his feet. He'd caught a glimpse of the logo and the type. It was one of his business cards. "Okay…so what's wrong?"

Jen shot up off the bed and stalked toward him. "You work in the NYC police Cold Case and Apprehension Squad?"

Mike suddenly realized where she was going. He'd told her he was a cop…. He hadn't told her what, *exactly*, he did. "Yes."

"You *don't* work Vice catching pimps and dealers. You lied."

"I didn't lie," he said, "I told you I transferred out of Vice earlier this year after a high-profile case." He was about to continue, to add that the call he'd received might well have been about that same case—which he still thought was connected to the attack on them outside the bodega last week.

Before he could get a word in, she jabbed a finger at his chest, poking him, hard. "Cold cases—like in that TV show where they go after people for crimes that occurred decades ago?"

Oh, hell. Now he knew why she was so upset. "Jen…"

"That's why you wanted to know so much about Aunt Ivy."

He couldn't lie—the case had intrigued him and he hadn't been entirely honest about how far he'd gone in looking into it.

He knew he should have. But damn, she was already so ticked off. So he started at the important part. "Look, I don't think your aunt bludgeoned her husband."

"Of course she didn't."

"I did look into the case a little," he admitted, "but only because I was worried about *you*. She has threatened you, Jen, and if she has a history of violence, who knows whether or not she might someday act on one of her crazy threats."

Her jaw dropped open. "You reopened a murder case on

my elderly aunt to protect *me?* Good Lord, you *do* take this protector crap way too seriously, Mike."

"I didn't reopen the case," he explained, keeping calm, as he always did in a crisis. This was definitely shaping up to be a crisis, one he'd never anticipated when he'd woken up today.

Your fault, asshole, you should have told her up front.

"It was never solved, so it was never officially closed. I pulled it out and took a look at it through fresh eyes, the way I would any other cold case. Just me, nothing official, no commitment to investigate it further."

That didn't seem to help because her jaw was still working hard, as if she was biting the inside of her cheek to prevent herself from screaming. So far, she'd done a pretty good job. Though, if her eyes were laser beams, he'd be a steaming pile of protons right now.

"I screwed up by not being honest with you right up front."

"Yeah. You definitely did. And you wasted your time. Aunt Ivy is innocent, she had an alibi, you admitted it yourself."

Knowing he should keep his mouth shut, he couldn't help clarifying. Because he still was not convinced Ivy posed no danger to anyone—his grandfather…or Jen. "She had an alibi for the *bludgeoning.* A neighbor saw her leave the building, then heard Cantone fighting with someone next door an hour later, while Ivy was in public with a lot of other people. He was definitely alive when she left."

"Don't forget she could barely lift the murder weapon, much less swing it with enough force to crush his skull."

"I know." He almost continued, almost admitted the suspicion he'd had in recent days, since he'd finished reading the case file. Including the autopsy report, which had never been released in its entirety to the public. But that would add a whole new level to this conversation and he didn't have the time to deal with it right now. "Can we talk about this later?" he asked as he continued pulling on his clothes and shoes. "I have to go to the precinct. There might be a break in last Saturday's hit-and-run."

She nodded absently. He'd have thought she'd look a lot more interested. Obviously, Jen's concern about her aunt Ivy's dark and dangerous past exceeded her concerns about her own present. More reason to keep her away from the crazy woman.

Just as he was stuffing his wallet and badge in his pocket, Jen cleared her throat. "I might not be here when you get back."

"What?"

Jen's chin went up in visible determination. Any evidence of tears had dissipated during their discussion about her aunt's case. Right now, she merely looked determined. Resolute. Unreachable. "I can't stay here forever."

"You *can* stay here until I get back."

She shrugged. "What's the point?"

"How about your physical safety? We still don't know who broke into your place."

"And I'm supposed to put my life on hold, hide and play house in a rich man's apartment from now on? Forget it, Mike. Fantasy time's over. It's back to reality for me."

He suddenly had the feeling she was talking about a whole lot more than just her physical address. It was as if she was saying the past few days—here, with him—had been a fantasy from which she now wanted to escape.

His heart nearly stopped as the implication washed over him. What if she was done—finished—with *him?*

He'd worried this moment would come. That she'd realize he wasn't the right guy for her. He just wasn't ready for it to happen so soon. Especially not since *he'd* realized she *was* every bit the right woman for him.

"Wait until I get back," he insisted, wondering if she could hear the way his voice shook with emotion. Did she know his order was actually a plea? Mike had never been afraid of much in his life, not since his parents had died. But he was afraid right now. Afraid she'd walk out the door and not return. "Never mind, I'll call back and tell them I can't come in."

She waved a weary hand at him. "Go. You know you need to."

He still wasn't sure. "I don't have to."

"Yeah, you do."

She was right. He'd sleep better—be able to deal with things better—if he found out for sure who'd tried to run them down. "I'll only be gone an hour or two. By then I'll have a better idea if the guy who tried to run us down was targeting me because of the drug case and not…"

She stared at him, watching him closely as he fell into silence. He should have known better than to think she wouldn't know exactly where he'd been headed. "Not *me.* That's what you've been thinking, right? That the person who almost mowed us down was targeting me because he's the one who's been harassing me?"

He couldn't deny it. "Yeah. I've considered it."

"But you never thought to share that."

"I didn't want to worry you."

She fisted her hands and jerked them onto her hips. "Do you have any idea how much I *hate* this protective macho crap?"

The sparkle in her magnificent eyes almost brought a smile to his lips. Because oh, yeah, he knew. He *liked* that about her.

But old habits died hard. He protected the ones he cared

about. And he cared about Jennifer Feeney more than he'd ever cared about another living person in his entire life.

"You're right. I'm sorry." Swallowing as he acknowledged there was more to apologize for, he added, "Not only for keeping my suspicions about our accident from you. But for not telling you I was actively looking at your late uncle's case file."

She slowly nodded but the anger in her voice didn't fade one bit. "I know you're sorry. But you still did it. You investigated an old woman I love for *murder.* And you *lied* about it. I can't forgive you for that, Mike."

He'd gotten so used to hearing Jen bitch about her relatives he'd almost forgotten how much she loved them. He'd suspected it—he'd seen glimpses of it—but he hadn't realized until right now how deep her feelings went. "I shouldn't have—"

"You deceived me," she snapped. "You kept me in the dark about your suspicions regarding our accident."

He nodded, not even trying to get a word in this time.

"You blazed on, the big man, taking care of everything and leaving little old me in the dark out of this crazy need you have to take care of everyone whether they need it or not."

"Maybe," he said with a helpless shrug, completely unable to defend himself. "I can't change who I am overnight."

Her anger visibly faded. Now she merely appeared dejected. Almost devastated. "I know," she whispered. "I know you can't."

So, it appeared, they were at an impasse. They stared at one another for a long moment. Mike found it hard to believe it had been less than an hour since they'd climbed out of that wildly rumpled bed where they'd spent one of the most amazing nights of his life. He wished they'd never left it, that everything that had happened this morning had been a bad dream.

"I won't go to my apartment," she mumbled, as if wanting to set his mind at ease, even though she was still upset.

He breathed a sigh of relief. "Good. Wait here for me and we'll talk this out when I get back." He stepped closer, reaching out to her but not touching, somehow knowing she wouldn't want him to. "Give me a chance, Jen, this is all new to me."

Jen lifted a hand to her damp hair and swept it away from her beautiful face. "I won't be at my apartment because I'm going to go back to Trouble. I want to talk to Ivy. If a police investigation is going to come crashing into her life again, I have to prepare her and apologize for my part in it."

Mike stepped toward her, his body tense with tightly controlled anger. "You are not going near that woman."

"So much for changing your overprotective ways."

He clenched his muscles, took a cleansing breath, trying to remain calm and controlled. What he *really* wanted to do was go all caveman on her, drag her back to bed and not let her out of his sight. Everything that would be entirely *right* in the short term but so very *wrong* in the long one.

"I told you, I didn't do anything official with the file, nobody else knows I'm looking at it, the wrath of the law is not about to descend upon your crazy aunt's head."

"Don't talk about her like that," she insisted, though she'd called the woman worse since the day he'd met her.

"Jen, she's dangerous."

"Nonsense. You admitted she's not a killer."

"No, I didn't," he snapped before thinking better of it. "I admitted she didn't hit her husband with a statue. That doesn't mean she didn't set her house on fire."

Jen's eyes flared. Crossing her arms over her chest, she began shaking her head. "No. The articles all said whoever bludgeoned Leo set it to try to destroy evidence. Ivy got there after the firefighters were on the scene."

"She had left the restaurant early enough to get home a half hour before the fire was called in."

"No."

"She *could* have set it," he insisted, "then left and come back to make a big commotion once the firefighters were there."

Jen was shaking her head, her whole body tense, as taut as a wire. "Why? What possible reason would she have?" Then she turned away from him. "And what does it matter, anyway? She still didn't kill anybody. Whoever hit him killed Leo Cantone."

Mike hesitated for a second, wondering if he should reveal what he'd discovered when reviewing the Cantone case. Telling Jen the true contents of the autopsy could make her realize the seriousness of the question of who started the fire.

It could also make her more determined to defend her lunatic aunt against anyone on earth—even if she placed herself in danger. Even if she did it at Mike's expense.

Been there, done that enough in one lifetime, lady.

Unable to prevent himself, he lifted his hand and rubbed at the scar on his chest, even though a voice in his head ordered him to stop even considering *this* situation to be anything like *that* one. "You need to accept the possibility," he murmured.

She spun around to glare at him. "Why? Why does it matter?"

"It matters," he replied flatly. "Because the autopsy showed the victim had smoke in his lungs. He was hurt—not *dead*—when the blaze started. Meaning, whoever set that house on fire is the one who really killed Leo Cantone."

EMILY HADN'T DECIDED EXACTLY how to execute her "plan of attack" as Allie called it until Saturday morning when

Roderick had called to invite her to lunch. He'd asked her if she cared to go up to the next town, to a decent restaurant where they'd eaten once before, and she'd said yes.

But she had already been planning something else, instead. Because the drive to Weldon would take them right past the lovely little park where they'd had their picnic the previous day. And Emily was in the mood for another one.

Digging through the garage, she finally found her mother's old picnic hamper. Its gingham lining was a bit dusty and the wicker faded, but it cleaned up all right.

She spent the rest of the morning preparing what she considered a romantic lunch—grapes and cheese, crusty bread fresh from her bread maker. Even the bottle of wine she'd been saving since Christmas. What the heck—today she was going back to being herself. That was cause for celebration, wasn't it?

When he arrived at noon to pick her up, she put a broad-brimmed hat on her head, a pair of sunglasses on her nose, and strolled to the door. She was carrying the basket, as well as a large blanket, and wearing calf-length dungarees that reminded her of the cropped pants girls had worn back in the fifties.

Seeing her, Roderick's eyes grew wide. "Why…Emily…"

"Good afternoon," she said with a cheery smile. *Be yourself,* Allie had said. *Stop acting like a helpless romance-movie heroine and be the Emily we all know and love.*

Well, the Emily everybody seemed to know and love was the Emily who laughed and baked, smiled and enjoyed herself. Not the quiet, helpless lady with the fluttering hands and the quivering heart, the one waiting for her white knight to carry her away.

If Roderick wanted to carry her away, that would be delightful. But she was no longer going to be the meek, spineless female, waiting for him to do it.

"I don't think I care to go to that stuffy restaurant after all," she informed him as she handed him the picnic hamper. She kept the blanket in her arms, sailing out the front door. Striding toward his car, she felt stronger and younger than she had in ages. "I would like, instead, to go on another picnic." She waited by the passenger side door, and as he stepped up to open it for her, Emily peeked at him through half-lowered lashes. "Only the two of us this time."

He cleared his throat and turned a little pink, from his cheeks up to the tips of his ears. How utterly adorable! "If you desire," he murmured, that formal British voice of his sounding incongruous when accompanied with a blush.

She didn't imagine Mr. Potts had blushed in decades. But Roderick still had enough of that proper British gentleman inside him to be a bit taken aback by a forward woman.

Well, *tough,* as Allie would say. "I have been meaning to tell you," Emily said as they pulled out of her driveway, "I don't know a single thing about art. It's been bothering me that I gave you the impression I did when we visited the gallery."

Roderick glanced at her out of the corner of his eye. She'd swear a tiny smile tugged at the corner of his mouth, but it could have been a shadow cast by the car's sun visor. "I did realize you might not be familiar with the styles and movements, but you have a remarkable eye, Emily, and very good taste."

"I know a bit about Impressionism from watching *Jeopardy!*"

She waited for him to gasp in shock. But instead, he chuckled. "It's amazing what one can learn from watching television. Mortimer and I have quite expanded our vocabulary with some of these new shows." Shrugging, he added, "I, for one, never imagined that someone would accuse another person of nosiness by saying they were *all up in my bizness.*"

"Yes!" she exclaimed, immediately knowing what he meant. "Imagine, I used to think of *bling* as only the sound the gambling machines made at the casinos in Atlantic City. Now it refers to all manner of jewelry."

"Who knew *dead presidents* would someday refer to money?"

"Or that *kickin' it* would mean to relax?"

"That having *junk in the trunk* would *not* refer to winter blankets and tire-changing kits in the boot of a car."

The two of them were laughing now, the first comfortable, relaxed laughter she'd shared privately with the man.

"I'm afraid we are showing our age, my dear," Roderick finally said, his laughter dying but his smile remaining.

"Don't you dare imply that I'm old," she replied tartly. "You may think that of yourself, but I am quite as vigorous and happy as a fifty-year-old." That might be a stretch. Her knees sometimes felt more like those belonging to a hundred-and-fifty-year-old.

"Wouldn't dream of it, *old gel*," he replied with a teasing chuckle. He made sure she knew he was teasing her by reaching over and covering her hand with his to give it a squeeze.

Time stopped for Emily. She stared down at his hand, covering hers. It was the first purely affectionate touch he'd offered her, and it delighted her so much she wanted to bring his fingers up and press tiny kisses on the tips of them, the way she had with her nieces and nephews when they'd been babies.

But the tingle she felt deep inside didn't resemble her gentle feelings for babies. This was much warmer.

As if just realizing he was holding her hand, Roderick slowly pulled away, lifting it to the steering wheel. But Emily felt sure a smile remained on his mouth, and the comfortable aura in the car did not fade.

When they reached the turnoff for the park, Roderick didn't ask her if that was where she wanted to go. He obviously knew. He drove his luxurious car right through the woods, parking in the same spot they'd parked with Mr. Potts and Ivy the previous day.

"How lovely the birds sound without the cluck of Miss Feeney's conversation," Roderick said as he helped her out.

Emily snickered, though it probably wasn't very ladylike. Or particularly nice. But heaven knew she'd been at the receiving end of a lot of Ivy's spite over the years.

During yesterday's impromptu picnic, they'd had to make do on dusty, splintery picnic tables. Today, though, Emily had thought to bring a tablecloth. She spread it out as Roderick slipped off his sports coat and tossed it into his car. "Much better," she murmured. "Though don't you want to loosen up some of those buttons?" Then she noticed the glint of gold in his cuffs. "Sorry. Cuff links," she said, rolling her eyes.

"Are you making sport of me?" he asked, one brow rising high above the other.

"Oh, no, everyone knows those newfangled button cuffs are never going to stay in style. You're simply ahead of the curve."

Roderick's mouth opened and he sputtered for a moment, then a laugh emerged, "Emily Baker, you are in a wicked mood today."

Emily put down the wedge of cheese and loaf of bread she'd just unpacked. Staring at him across the table, she admitted, "I'm afraid I'm being myself today, Mr. Ward. The Emily Baker you've been getting to know hasn't exactly represented the real me. I'm much more…down to earth than you might have realized."

He had unclasped his cuff links, and rolled up his sleeves.

His forearms were still strong, lightly tanned, his hands rougher than anyone would imagine for a seventy-eight-year-old butler. Evidence of the tough, adventurous life he and Mr. Potts had lived. Oh, how she longed to hear more about it. And perhaps share in just one adventure with him.

"Come have something to eat," she said, sitting on the bench and gesturing to the other side. "Will you open that?"

He glanced at the bottle of wine, then at her. "Oh?"

"I'm sure it's not quite your usual, but we're having an elegant picnic today. Yesterday was fried chicken and nasty tea from Tootie's Tavern. Today I thought we'd be more fancy."

"I concur," he said as he opened the bottle. Fortunately, it was the kind that required a wine opener—which she'd found after doing some digging in a kitchen drawer. If it had been a screw-off type, Emily might have sunk under the table, convinced more than ever that she and Roderick had nothing in common.

But as they ate, chatting and laughing lightly, she was able to convince herself otherwise. It didn't even take *that* much convincing. Because today, under the brilliant blue sky and the canopy of trees filled with gaily chirping birds, Roderick was absolutely delightful. Charming and friendly, warm, personable. Everything she'd hoped he'd be—everything he had *not* been when she'd been trying so hard to make him see her as the perfect sedate, deserving woman of the movies.

Today she was being herself…following her heart, two of the main things Allie had insisted she'd do. And it was working.

There was, of course, still that third thing. But she honestly didn't know if she'd have the nerve to do it.

As the afternoon wore on and they finished their picnic, they strolled toward the water. Emily even kicked off her sandals, walking barefoot in the cool grass. Her corns might pay her back later, but for now, the spongy, mossy ground felt too delightful to care.

"Shall we sit and enjoy the water?" Roderick asked.

Nodding, Emily watched as he shook out the blanket he'd been carrying over his arm. He carefully spread it over the grass a few feet from the water's edge, and the two of them slowly lowered themselves onto it, helping one another down. They sat there for the longest time, chatting, staring at the ducks on the lake. Even tossing small stones into it.

Eventually, with the sun blazing in the mid-afternoon sky, it grew a bit too hot for either of them to remain outside. They cleaned up their picnic and got back into Roderick's air-conditioned car. Emily had a smile on her face during the entire trip to her house. Because surely now…certainly after this lovely day, he would not simply leave her at her door with a handshake and an impersonal smile.

But a few minutes later, when they stood on the front stoop of her house, that was exactly what he did. He nodded. He thanked her. He extended his hand and took hers in it, giving it a small squeeze. His eyes met hers for a moment, during which she held her breath, waiting for him to say something. To do something.

He didn't. Instead, with a promise to call her soon, he turned to walk away, the afternoon sun bringing an angelic sheen to the few strands of blond left in his gray hair.

Emily's mouth fell open in shock. She simply could not believe this had happened. Again. They'd been intimate in so many other ways, and now, after they'd held hands and reclined in the grass and shared a few glasses of wine, he didn't even have the courtesy to kiss her on the cheek.

"You coward," she said, not sure *who* she was speaking to.

He obviously heard. Pausing, he turned on his heel, tilted his head and glanced at her quizzically. "I beg your pardon?"

Emily felt heat rise in her cheeks. She sucked her lips into her mouth, frozen with indecision. Should she let him go, try again next time, or tell him that he'd hurt her? Or just do as Allie said and take the kiss she so desperately wanted.

One thing made up her mind: the empty driveway. Damon had taken Allie and the baby on an all-day shopping trip out of town. Emily suspected Allie had arranged it on purpose, to ensure Emily would have plenty of privacy. For… whatever.

"Did you say something, Miss Baker?" Roderick asked.

That "Miss Baker" did it. Now she began to see red. Stepping down off the stoop, she strode over to him, letting the empty picnic hamper and the blanket fall to the ground.

Roderick looked down at them, his brow shooting up in surprise, but Emily didn't give him a chance to bend over and get them. "Don't you Miss Baker me."

"Wha—?"

"I've been Emily all day. And I'll remove that Miss Baker from your mouth if it's the last thing I do."

So she did. Throwing her arms around his neck, she leaned up on tiptoe and physically hauled the tall man down toward her. His gray eyes flared in shock, which almost cost her her nerve. But somehow, Emily screwed her courage down tight, then pressed her closed lips against his.

He hesitated for a second, during which she felt sure she'd just made the biggest fool of herself the world had ever seen. Then, miracle of miracles, he embraced her in return. His strong arms circled her shoulders, his lips softened against hers. He held her tightly, kissing her on and on, right out here in broad daylight in front of God and everyone.

She, Emily Baker, seventy-four-year-old spinster, was getting her first real kiss in full view of the entire street where she'd grown up. And she didn't give a damn.

Finally, when she wondered how she was supposed to breathe when her nose was squished against his cheek and their lips were glued together, he slowly pulled away. But he didn't let her out of his arms, keeping her right where she was.

He smiled down at her. "My dear Miss...Emily."

She gulped in a deep mouthful of air, wondering how people kissed for so long without breathing. She'd have to ask Allie. Or else try it again and...experiment. Maybe that was another reason for those open-mouthed kisses she'd seen people exchange.

"You have quite taken me by surprise."

"Didn't you...like it?"

His eyes glittered and he nodded, holding on to her as though he'd never let her go. She could think of few better ways to spend her time than wrapped in the strong, steady arms of this courtly gentleman. "I most certainly did. Frankly, I've been telling myself that I could ask nothing more of you than friendship. That I'm too old to offer you anything else, and I have nothing left that you'd want."

Emily tilted her head back to stare into his eyes. "You have so much that I want, Roderick. A kind smile and a warm heart. Strength and compassion and intelligence." An impish impulse made her add, "And quite a nice kiss."

He pressed harder against her, so that she could feel just what *else* he had to offer her. It took a moment for her to understand, and when she did, Emily suddenly felt dizzy. She knew how things worked, technically, but couldn't quite grasp it. She had actually inspired a man to true passion for the first time in her life...at this late point in her life.

"Roderick, I've been alone. Always." She cleared her throat. "I mean, I've had family and friends. But there's been no...no one. No romance. No love affairs. No relationships."

He appeared puzzled, then his lips parted in a slight gasp as he caught her meaning. He immediately tried to step back, but Emily kept her arms tightly around his neck.

"My dear..."

"Please don't let me go," she whispered. "Don't stop introducing me to what I've missed."

He shook his head slowly. "I've no intention of letting you go. Only, do you suppose we could continue this inside? Away from prying eyes?" Gently kissing her temple, he whispered, "I have much more to introduce you to. Much, *much* more."

Neither of them said another word—they didn't need to. Instead, Emily turned back toward the house, waiting as he bent to pick up the basket and the blanket. Then he took her arm, led her to her porch, opened the door for her.

And then, he spent the rest of the day introducing her, for the first time, to the true meaning of romantic love.

CHAPTER SIXTEEN

Gentlemen, when your wife asks you to "be honest" about whether you're having an affair, it's not one of those "Does my butt look fat in this dress?" questions where you can be cagey and fudge a little. She *means* it. You answer yes or no. Just remember, if you answer yes, it might be the last question you'll ever be able to answer...because you might no longer have a tongue. Or a face.
—*Why Arsenic Is Better Than Divorce* by Jennifer Feeney

JEN DEPARTED FOR TROUBLE an hour after Mike left the penthouse. She'd promised him she wouldn't go back to her apartment, but no matter how much he'd tried to convince her, he'd been unable to exact her promise not to go to Pennsylvania.

He'd been angry when he'd left. *She'd* been heartbroken.

Because whether they said the words or not, they both knew they'd reached the end of their short journey together. No matter how wonderful things had been between them, those same issues lurking in the background since they'd met had never quite disappeared. And they'd popped out to derail them the moment they'd hit a bend in the road.

No matter what they felt for one another—and Jen strongly suspected Mike had feelings for her, as she did for him—they couldn't change who they were. He wasn't going to stop being an overprotective, arrogant he-man who thought he could keep things from her and order her around for her own good. And she couldn't stop being an independent woman who resented the hell out of his attitude.

Maybe… Maybe they could have gotten past it. Opposites did, after all, sometimes have successful relationships. If that were all, maybe she would have waited in the penthouse. She could have planned what to say to him when he returned, making it clear that if he didn't let up, she was going to follow her own books' advice and throw a frying pan at his head.

But that *wasn't* all. Mike had secretly investigated her aunt. He'd dug out the old case file, not even telling her the truth about what he really did for the police department. That Jennifer found *nearly* unforgivable.

If he continued, and actually got her aunt in trouble with the law after all these years, she didn't think she'd *ever* be able to forgive him.

And given his integrity and honesty—not to mention his profession—she didn't know if *he'd* ever be able to get over it if her aunt Ivy was, indeed, a murderer, and Jen stood by her.

They'd reached the impasse that was destined to destroy them from the very beginning.

But what if she really is *guilty of what he said?*

"Aunt Ivy, what did you do?" she whispered as she drove out of New York, heading for Pennsylvania. She hadn't gotten on the road as early as she'd wanted to, having to pick up a few things for the trip. Then she'd had to go across town to the garage where she stored her car.

She didn't really need a vehicle, living in the city, and she paid an amount equal to the budget of a small country to park it. But for days like today, it was a godsend. Because Trouble, Pennsylvania, wasn't exactly easy to get to. It most certainly was not on any airline's radar. She didn't even think it had a bus station.

She probably could have flown down to Pittsburgh and rented a car, as she'd done once or twice in the past, but something made her choose to make the long drive instead. The hours in silence and solitude seemed appropriate, given her mood. With every mile that passed beneath the wheels of the car, she put more distance between herself and Mike Taylor.

Making him—*them*—disappear into the past.

"Ha," she whispered over the sound of the cold air streaming into the car from the air conditioner. "He's never going to disappear." Not from her memories. Not from her heart.

"Enough of that," she reminded herself, trying to think only of what lay ahead. Her confrontation with Ivy wouldn't be easy, but it had to be done. She needed to formulate a plan on dealing with the woman now, otherwise Ivy would hide, or simply make a button motion over her lips and stay as silent as a corpse.

Like those littering her past.

If Mike had thought his revelation about Ivy possibly having set the fire had taken her by surprise, he'd been dead wrong. Jen had suspected that for years. But his claim that Leo Cantone had been alive when it had been set…well, that she'd never even dreamed possible.

It changed everything. It turned Ivy from a grief-stricken woman trying to salvage what she could out of a horrible tragedy into a cold-blooded murderer.

That was what Jen needed to know. Had her aunt seen her wounded husband lying on the floor and ignored his cries for help? Had she brutally finished the job her lover had started?

"No," Jen whispered, not wanting to believe it.

But there was no way of knowing, so as the hours went on and she got closer to Trouble, any number of scenarios filled her head. The one she most wanted to believe was that Ivy hadn't realized Leo was still alive when she'd gotten home that night. She'd burned their house down out of rage and grief and to help Eddie, never knowing she was sealing Leo's fate.

Please let that be what happened.

When she arrived at the aunts' houses, Jen did not park in the driveway. Aunt Ida Mae would hear her car in an instant, and right now, Jen didn't want to see her. She wanted to confront Ivy alone, knowing that would be the only way she'd ever get her aunt to open up. If Ida Mae was around, she'd plant herself like a solid wall between her sister and her niece. And the secrets would continue, the questions remain unanswered.

Parking down the block, she went to the trunk and removed the one item she knew Ivy would most want to have. The knitting box. Then she walked to the house, approaching on the opposite side of Ida Mae's, out of sight of the other woman's windows.

Ivy's door was not locked. Not wanting Ida Mae to hear her knocking, Jen twisted the knob and stepped inside, immediately assaulted by the aromas of dried flowers, heavy powder and musty age that permeated the place. "Aunt Ivy?" she called as she closed the door behind her. "It's Jennifer, are you here?"

She didn't get a response. But hearing a creaking coming

from the parlor down the hall, she quietly walked toward it, the old uneven floorboards squeaking beneath her weight.

"Mama?" a soft voice said from inside the shadowy, darkened room. The drapes were drawn, no lights switched on, and the parlor was cast in long, late-afternoon shadows.

"It's me, Jennifer," she said as she stepped in the room, allowing her eyes to adjust to the low light. When they had, she made out Aunt Ivy, sitting in her favorite rocker by the cold fireplace, which hadn't been fit to use in years.

"Jennifer?" Her aunt sounded confused, as if she didn't recognize the name. "I thought you were Mama come for a visit."

Crossing over to her, Jennifer knelt by the chair, finally seeing recognition wash over her aunt's weary-looking face. Knowing the one thing that would wake Ivy up from her daze, Jen said, "I've brought back your knitting box."

Ivy's eyes went wide as she sat straight up, a brilliant smile making all the confusion and unhappiness fall away. "My box! You brought my precious things?"

Jen lifted the box onto the old woman's lap, watching the way her tiny, delicately boned hands caressed it. She traced the letters across the top with the tip of a finger, then nibbled her bottom lip as she reached for the latch.

"Everything's there," Jen said, somehow knowing Ivy was afraid. "Exactly as you left it."

Ivy slowly shook her head. "You shouldn't have brought it. It's not safe here. Someone wants to know, someone's trying to figure out the secret."

Stunned, Jen merely stared at her. She couldn't believe Ivy was still clinging to that ridiculous fear even though she held her treasure right in her hands. Especially now that Jen knew exactly what the "secret" in the box really was. The songs.

"Not safe, must hide it away." Her aunt still sounded confused; she was obviously not having a lucid day. Though days like this had once been few and far between, Jen knew they were now coming more frequently as Ivy retreated into her past, eschewing real life for her happy fantasy one.

"It's all right," Jen insisted. "Nobody else is trying to find the secret." *Lie, lie;* Mike had been trying to find out. But she'd put a stop to that, at least she hoped she had. "But Aunt Ivy, I think it's time you told it to *me.*"

The woman blinked twice, staring at her, then looking away. Reaching for a lamp on the table, she flipped on the light. She was frowning, almost glaring, which was when Jen realized the present-day Ivy was definitely back in the house.

"What secret? Why would I tell you *anything* when you want to force me out of my home?" She began rocking fast, the creak of the chair the only sound in the otherwise silent room.

Jen rose from the floor. *This* Ivy she knew and could deal with. Taking a seat on a lumpy settee, she leaned forward, dropping her elbows onto her knees. "I found the hidden pocket."

Ivy's gasp was louder even than the squeak of the chair.

"I saw the music."

"Oh, Lord," Ivy whispered, growing still. "Eddie's songs."
One question answered.

"I never could read music, but he'd sometimes play them for me when we'd meet in his tiny apartment," she said, probably revealing more than she'd intended to since she didn't know Jen was aware of Ivy's affair. "Even today I close my eyes and still hear them on the wind. Isn't that odd?"

No. Not odd. They weren't on the wind; they were on the airwaves. Proof for poor Ivy that Eddie had survived and was out there somewhere, alive and well, selling the songs he'd once sung only to her.

What a stab in her heart it must have been every time one of them came on the radio. And no wonder she'd been so territorial about them, right up until the last time Jen was here. Nobody in the world was supposed to know that they'd been gifts from the man she'd loved—written to, for and about *her.*

Jen swallowed away a lump in her throat, needing to know the rest. The truth about the fire. And Ivy's part in it. "I know just about everything, and I'm going to help you. But you have to trust me. You have to tell me the truth. All of it."

The old woman waved an impatient hand. "You know nothing."

"I know you were having an affair with Eddie James."

A dreamy smile softened Ivy's sharp face. She stroked the top of the knitting box as if it had taken on the physical personification of the man she'd loved. "My Eddie. He had a beautiful, kind soul. A smile that rivaled the sun. And he loved me to distraction." Lost in her own reminiscence, she looked up at the ceiling, adding, "He was much younger than I, you know. Still, he had eyes for nobody else. None of those young girls could ever turn his head or his heart."

"Unlike Leo," Jen murmured.

The old lady's lips pursed. "Unlike Leo. His musical casting couch was legendary, before we were married, and after."

"He found out about the affair."

She nodded. "He'd hired someone to follow me and take pictures. Oh, wasn't he enraged."

Everything was falling into place exactly as Jen had suspected it would. They were finally reaching the night—that final, fiery night. "He confronted Eddie?"

Ivy nodded absently, still stroking the box. "Called him over to the house while I was out. Poor, sweet Eddie, I can't imagine how he reacted. I had warned him about Leo...what he was capable of...but in the end, I wasn't there to protect him."

"But you protected him later."

Ivy finally stopped stroking and turned her head to meet Jen's eyes.

"With the fire."

The old woman remained silent. Her gaze was watchful, secretive, revealing nothing.

"I *know* you set the fire, Aunt Ivy." Jen held her breath, almost praying she was wrong, that her aunt was innocent.

The woman hesitated for a long moment, then frowned in visible petulance. "Well, yes, I did *that*," she admitted, as if she'd merely forgotten to take out her trash.

Jen released her breath in a harsh whoosh. It was true. Everything she'd thought for years was true. Her aunt had burned down her own house with her husband lying in a pool of blood inside it. Only one question remained. *Had she known he was alive when she'd struck the match?* "You acted so quickly," Jen said. "You got home..."

"Leo *called* me home," Ivy clarified. "He called the restaurant and taunted me right there on the phone."

Taunted her about having called her lover over, obviously. "But by the time you got there, it was finished. Eddie had showed up, the two men had fought."

Ivy said nothing.

Lowering her voice to almost a whisper, she added, "Your husband was lying in a pool of blood, your lover was gone and you knew Eddie would be blamed."

Utter silence. As if this story had nothing whatsoever to do with the old woman watching her with expressionless eyes and a closed mouth.

"Knowing Leo was dead," Jen added, hearing a tiny tremor in her voice, "you tried to save Eddie by torching everything. Then you sent him away for his own protection."

Ivy's brow pulled down into a frown, her lips tightening into a tiny circle. She was finally showing some kind of reaction. But rather than agreeing with Jen's version of the story or admitting she'd intentionally finished what Eddie had started, she slowly shook her head. "You poor child, you truly have been dwelling on this, haven't you?"

No more than Ivy had, obviously.

A hoarse laugh emerged from the old woman's throat. "And yet you still have it all *so entirely wrong.*"

Jen froze, hearing the note of clarity in her aunt's voice. There was no confusion, no hesitation, just pure, solid memory.

"Leo didn't call me to say Eddie was on his way over, you silly thing. Eddie was already there."

"What?"

"My husband called to tell me to come home and find what he'd left for me on the floor."

Jen tilted her head and stared at Aunt Ivy in bemusement, not yet grasping what she meant.

"When I got home," her aunt said, her voice finally beginning to shake in weakness and in sorrow, "I found *him* lying there. His head bashed in…so much blood, a sea of it."

"Leo?"

"No, you fool!" Ivy snapped, any sign of sadness or weakness disappearing into frustration. "Don't you see? Eddie didn't kill Leo. *Leo* killed *Eddie.*"

Jen collapsed back in the settee, utterly stunned. But that

didn't come near the shock she felt when Ivy continued in a prim, matter-of-fact voice.

"And later that night, I killed Leo."

MIKE HADN'T BEEN EXPECTING JEN to be waiting at the condo when he arrived back there late Saturday morning. Still, walking in and being greeted only by the dog—and otherwise silence—had nearly crushed him.

"She made her choice," he'd told himself, wondering if it was for the best. They had already admitted they drove each other crazy. Now, with her determination to stand beside her aunt who might someday kill somebody, he should just cut his losses.

But he'd known from the minute he'd left that morning that he couldn't. He was in love with her. For better and, especially on days like today, for worse. So, gathering up the dog and shoving some of his things into a duffel bag, he took off after her. He had to talk to her—not just about them, but about what he'd discovered today at his old precinct.

"Could have used the phone," he reminded himself as he drove toward Pennsylvania, probably a couple of hours behind Jennifer since he'd bet she'd left the penthouse two minutes after he had.

Some messages, though, couldn't be delivered by phone. Messages like *I love you. I want you.*

And *They caught the guy who tried to kill us.*

That, in his opinion, was the least critical of the three. But she still deserved to know that he, not she, had been last week's target.

The carjacker who'd been brought in the previous night had actually confessed to stealing the black van with the tinted windows. It had been a special-order job, and he'd delivered it to one of Ricky Stahl's known associates. They'd found what was left of the van right where the perp had said it would be, in a Jersey chop shop. And Stahl's goons' fingerprints had been all over it.

It was doubtful the guy would willingly turn on his boss, who'd obviously sent him on the job, but the D.A. was going to try to work a deal. Stahl would now face attempted murder charges. And Jennifer could breathe a little easier that the pig who'd broken into her apartment had *not* also tried to kill her.

He only hoped their relationship problems could be solved as easily as the mystery of who'd tried to run them down.

He also hoped her wacky aunt didn't get violent when Jen asked her if she'd burned down her own house in 1966. Jen was a strong woman, and Ivy an old frail one. But, despite all her bluster and threats, he didn't think Jen would lay a hand on her elderly aunt, not even in her own defense.

That worried him more than anything. And so, while he was still a few hours outside of Trouble, he'd called his grand-father. Mortimer had been excited to hear Mike was coming for another visit so soon. And half out of his mind with delight when he'd learned he was chasing after Jen.

Mike hadn't wanted to reveal too much, especially not his suspicions about a woman his grandfather had once been… intimate with. But knowing Ivy and her sister were always on their best behavior around Mortimer, he figured his grandfather could be of help. So he'd asked him to swing by and check on things, to make sure Jen didn't get in over her head.

That had seemed like a really good idea when he'd first thought of it, but as Mike got closer and closer to town, he began to worry as much about his grandfather as he was worrying about Jen. If Ivy went off the deep end, his grand-father could be in danger.

"Stupid ass," he muttered, shaking his head as he realized he still had a half-hour drive ahead of him. Mutt lifted his head off the back seat and groaned a little. "Not you. The stupidity was all mine." In so many ways lately.

Unable to stand it, he dialed Mortimer's house again, but got no answer. Though he wasn't sure his grandfather knew how to use it, Mike knew he had a cell phone. Morgan had bought him one for Christmas last year. Punching in the preprogrammed number, Mike almost held his breath until the old man answered.

"Is this thing on?" the querulous voice said. "Is someone there? Blasted buttons are too small to make out. Hello?"

Relieved, Mike leaned back in the driver's seat. "It's me, Grandpa. Just checking in."

"Michael! Yes, yes, good. No news yet, I'm afraid."

That surprised him. He'd have figured his grandfather would have gone over to check on Jen five minutes after Mike's previous call.

"I haven't been able to find Roderick to ask him to take me today," Mortimer admitted. "He's disappeared off the face of the earth." With a lascivious laugh, he added, "I believe he had a date with Miss Baker this afternoon. Perhaps it turned into a very *long* one."

Mike hoped Roddy's love life was progressing a little better than his own. "It's all right, Grandpa," Mike said, glad the old man hadn't yet left. "Stay home, I'm not far anyway."

"Nonsense, boy, I'm nearly there."

"What?"

"No need for Rod to get back with the car. It's just a good stretch of the legs to Miss Ivy's house."

He'd walked the mile or so to town. Mike sighed deeply, kicking himself more than ever for involving his grandfather in this. "Look, why don't you go visit your friends in the tavern. You don't have to go to see Jen, I'll be there soon."

"Pish. Dying to see her... Hmm, I wonder who that might be."

Mike waited, wondering which of his Trouble-ing friends or neighbors his grandfather had spied.

"That looks like some skulking. Bad business afoot," the old man mumbled.

Immediately pushing the gas pedal harder as his body tensed, Mike asked, "What's going on?"

"There's a stranger lurking around outside the Feeney sisters' houses. He's definitely trying not to be seen, but my eyes haven't failed me as much as other parts of m'body have."

Shit. Someone had followed Jen to Trouble. "Grandpa, get away, I'll be there soon." Then he thought about it. "Better yet, call the police, they'll be quicker. I'm afraid someone might be after Jen."

"The letter writer?" Mortimer asked, his voice losing all trace of age, sounding strong and determined. "He won't lay a hand on her, by God." He muttered something that sounded suspiciously like "Should have brought my sword."

Mike groaned. "Grandpa, I mean it. Don't do anything yourself. Call the police and wait for me."

"He's found a way in through a basement window," Mortimer said in a loud whisper, as if fearing the thug would overhear. Which meant Mortimer had moved closer, rather than farther away.

"Damn it."

"He's...oh, dear..."

And the phone went dead.

IVY HADN'T REALIZED what a great relief it would be to talk about things, to bring her memories out of the darkest corners of her mind and whisper them back into existence. So often she retreated into herself, reliving all the moments in silence, in solitude, but she hadn't spoken aloud of these things in years. Decades. And she'd never whispered a hint of them to anyone except Ida Mae, who, since she had secrets of her own to guard, would never breathe a word to anyone.

"I don't understand," Jennifer said. Poor child looked shocked and confused.

Ivy supposed that wasn't surprising. The girl wasn't the only one to have gotten the story all wrong—the police had, too. The media. Friends and family. Everyone had believed exactly what Ivy had wanted them to believe.

"By then I hated Leo, you know," she continued, slowly beginning to rock again in her chair. "Our marriage had been lovely at first, then he started to cheat and lie and steal." She lifted a hand to her cheek. "The first time he struck me, he drove every last remnant of love I'd ever felt for him right out of my heart."

Jennifer remained silent, watching with wide eyes.

"Of course, Eddie filled it right back up. I loved that man more than my own life. And coming home that night to find him dead on the floor just about killed me."

"Dead on the floor…"

Ivy ignored her, going on, the memories spilling out of her almost on top of one another now. "I fell down beside him, swimming in the ocean of his blood, begging and pleading for him not to be gone, but it was too late. No one could survive that much blood loss and I could see bits of bone sticking into my poor, sweet love's brain."

"Oh, my God," the girl whispered.

"Then the phone rang. Leo called to make sure I was home and to ask what I thought of his *present*." It still sickened her to think of his gloating voice. "He told me exactly where he was and how he planned to buy himself an alibi from some wannabe musicians who'd do anything for a break. He asked me if I'd touched the statue, if I'd kissed Eddie's corpse…if I'd left enough fingerprints so the police would have a strong case against me."

"He was setting you up to take the fall."

Ivy nodded. "The fool. He didn't know me at all, did he? As if I was *weak*. As if I, a Feeney woman, would ever *panic*." The thought infuriated her to this day.

"You acted quickly," her niece prodded.

"It wasn't thirty seconds after I hung up the phone that I went into action. I grabbed my knitting box…the only thing I cared about in that cold, lifeless house. All my other treasures—my photographs, everything else—I'd already brought to Mama for safekeeping on my last trip."

Thank goodness for that, otherwise she'd have wasted precious time tracking them down, not willing to let them burn along with the useless art and jewels Leo had showered upon her.

"I found a clean dress that resembled the bloody one I had on. Then I went to the kitchen and got the kerosene." She'd moved quickly, in a furious, enraged daze, she remembered that much. "When I was ready, I kissed Eddie's sweet, still-warm hand, then I put some of Leo's flashy jewelry on him. Even then I knew, you see, what I intended to do."

She'd planned to kill Leo from the very second she saw Eddie's lifeless form.

"You wanted everyone to think Leo was the one who'd died."

"Of course. Eddie was young and unknown, he could disappear into history, and I'd protect his memory all my days. No one would miss one more musician from the Village." She pursed her lips in disgust. "Leo was a different story. He'd definitely be missed. So I poured kerosene all over the room and on my sweet man…."

Ivy's voice finally broke, and she felt weak for the first time since she'd started speaking. Hot, angry tears blurred her vision. But she forced them away, as she'd been forcing them away for forty years. "I lit the match, and hurried out the back door. The next day, I identified the jewelry on the body as Leo's and others concurred. That was all the proof they needed. No one even *noticed* the fact that the body was taller than the much-reviled Leo Cantone, because, I think, no one cared that he was dead. He was *that* despised." With a shrug, she added, "It was, my dear, remarkably easy."

She and Jennifer looked at one another, and in those clear eyes belonging to her niece, she saw no judgment, no condemnation as she had always suspected she would. There was merely calm acceptance. And definite sadness.

"You understand?"

"Better than you know," Jennifer replied. "But Leo…"

"As I said, I knew where he was going. So later that night, when the firemen were working, I slipped away and confronted him. I used his own gun and shot him in the chest with it. Eddie's best friend helped me get the body to a construction site, and we dumped it there, knowing it would be buried forever in the new foundation." She shrugged. "Obviously, it was. Goodbye, Leo, may you still be burning in hell."

Jennifer murmured something, but Ivy couldn't quite make it out. Because she'd swear she saw a shadow moving past the doorway. She sat straighter in her chair, wondering if it was Eddie's ghost, coming to visit again. Or her father's. Or even wicked Leo's. "Who's there?" she asked.

Silly. The ghosts never answered.

But to her utter shock, this time it did. As the shadow moved closer, into the room, coming up behind Jennifer, a voice she had heard in her nightmares for decades replied, "It's just me, Ivy. Satan gave me the day off to pay a call."

CHAPTER SEVENTEEN

I have to admit it…. Not all men are going to cheat and not all women are going to kill the ones who do. That's about the only thing that gives me hope for my own romantic future.

—*Why Arsenic Is Better Than Divorce* by Jennifer Feeney

AT FIRST, JENNIFER THOUGHT her aunt Ida Mae had come over. Ivy's face had gone from sad-but-angry reminiscence to shocked confusion and even fear. Only one person had ever made Ivy fearful and that was her sister. But as Jen turned and glanced at the person who'd spoken from the darkness, she realized it was not her other aunt. "What on earth are *you* doing here?" Because, as bizarre as it seemed, she recognized the newcomer from her own building in New York. "Mr. Jones?"

Ivy confused the issue even more. "Leo," she whispered with a long, ragged breath.

That was impossible. Leo Cantone, as she'd just learned, was dead. Her aunt had confessed to murdering him not two minutes ago. "What is this all about?"

"Shut up," the old man said. It was then that she saw the

gun in his hand. "You had to open your fat mouth, didn't you?" he said to Ivy, malevolence dripping off him in waves.

"I killed you."

"Not quite."

"You've been dead for forty years."

"Again…not quite."

Jen took two seconds to make herself believe it was true. Her aunt's supposedly dead husband was here. And he'd been her neighbor for the past month and a half!

There was another book in this. If she survived, she was going to have to write this story.

Or maybe not. Reviewers would crucify her, saying it was too far-fetched.

"It would take more than a bullet to the chest to kill me, dear heart. I crawled out of that tomb you dumped me in, only to discover that in the eyes of the world I was dead."

Jen remained still, never taking her attention off the gun.

"It didn't seem a bad time for me to be dead, you know," he continued conversationally.

"Because all the people you cheated were after you," Ivy snapped, having regained her composure a lot faster than Jen would have in her position. "Not to mention the police."

"Right. Things like theft and embezzlement don't go over too well with the police. I had the money in a safe place and was able to get to it, so I knew I could start over. There was no longer my beautiful house to go home to."

Ivy smiled a little, her eyes glittering, as if that was *exactly* what she'd intended should her plan to kill Leo fail.

He shook his head, a humorless laugh emerging from that phlegmy throat. "Oh, I was tempted to throw my chance at a new life away, Ivy. I wanted you to pay. But you'd done a good job of giving yourself an alibi when your lover was killed. I knew it would be a fight to get you convicted of trying to kill *me* without getting *myself* convicted of killing Eddie."

Ivy shot to her feet, showing no sign of her advanced age. "I'll kill you again for that."

"I could have taken you any time over the past forty years, but I let you alone," Leo snarled. "You should be on your knees thanking my merciful nature."

Jen suspected the man had been much more malicious than merciful. It wouldn't have taken a stranger five minutes to realize Ivy would punish herself all the rest of her days over what had happened to Eddie.

Killing her might, in the end, have been kinder.

"Aunt Ivy, please sit down," Jen murmured, still watching that gun and the way Mr. Jones's—er, Leo's—liver-spotted hand was shaking. "What is it you want?"

"What do you think I want, stupid girl? I want the box." He cast an avaricious glance at Ivy's knitting box, which sat on the floor by her chair. "You kept copies of his music in it. I knew you had them, and there was only one place you'd consider safe enough to put them." He shook his head. "I thought that hideous thing had burned up along with the remnants of my old life."

"The music," Jen said, suddenly realizing why, after all these years, Leo Cantone had come out of hiding. "You took Eddie's songs and sold them as your own, thinking the only other copies had been destroyed in the fire. Now you have to destroy them before anyone finds out."

Leo looked at her and nodded, his saggy cheeks wobbling. "Not as stupid as you, is she, Ivy? Yes. That's exactly what I did. I was the most prolific—but reclusive—music writer in history, living quietly in California. But when I saw you on that talk show, then got your book and recognized my own murder in its pages, I began paying very careful attention to you."

Of course he had. After forty years, he must have thought he'd gotten away clean. He'd probably piled up a fortune off the money he'd embezzled, and Eddie's stolen music. Then to see the possibility of exposure—to realize there might be proof out there of all that he'd done—he must have been in a panic.

"Seeing that 'at home' interview with you in the *Times,* I realized my worst fears had been realized. Imagine my shock, looking at your picture in the paper and seeing that hateful box right there in the background."

She had totally forgotten she'd had the box out when the newspaper reporter and photographer had come over. Aunt Ivy's knitting box had been, as Leo said, right there in the open for all the world to see. And the one person with a lot to lose because of its very existence had seen it.

"Been trying to find it ever since," he admitted. "I looked here." He glanced around. "Good God, Ivy, couldn't believe it when I saw you'd become a crazy old lady living in a ruin."

"You destroyed my life," she mumbled.

He ignored her. "I couldn't find it in your place, either," he said to Jen. "I almost fell over in shock when I saw that blond bimbo friend of yours leave with it yesterday. I knew she'd brought it to you and that you'd bring it right back to Ivy, so I came here to wait."

He headed for the box. "Now, I'll have that."

Ivy grabbed his arm, digging her sharp nails into it like a cat clawing with its talons. Jen launched off the settee, not sure if she was going for the gun or the man himself. But Leo was quick for an old guy. He swung the gun right into Ivy's face a moment before Jen reached him. "Sit down," he barked, "or I'll kill you right now, as you once killed me."

Jen stared at her aunt, silently pleading with her to do as Leo had demanded. Ivy's eyes were sparking with rage, but she finally stepped back, lowering herself into her chair.

"Take it," Jen said. "Take it and go. No one will ever know. Once the originals are destroyed, there will be no proof."

She hoped he'd go for it—hoped he'd be so focused on the money he'd lose if it was proven he'd stolen someone else's songs that he wouldn't think about the people who could accuse him of so many other, more recent, crimes.

His next words dashed those hopes. "I'm afraid I can't do that. I will not be able to leave any witnesses." He cleared his throat and shrugged, not seeming terribly concerned about committing two more murders. "Goodbye again, Ivy."

He lifted the gun. Jen tensed, ready to launch at him, but before she could do it, two shapes appeared from the hallway. They flew across the room in a flash of white and a flurry of silent motion.

Jen didn't think, didn't question, she merely leaped around Leo Cantone as he was tackled to the floor, and grabbed her aunt Ivy, dragging her toward the door.

"It's all right, my dear," she heard. "He's quite subdued."

Recognizing Mr. Potts's voice, she paused and looked back to see the old man standing above Leo, gun in hand. Leo was prone on the floor, held in place not only by Mortimer's foot on his forehead, but also by her very solid aunt Ida Mae.

Who was sitting on the man's chest.

WHEN MIKE PULLED UP TO JEN'S aunts' houses and saw there were no police cars in the driveway, he felt his heart double its rhythm. It had been pounding like crazy during the final twenty minutes of the drive—now it was ready to explode.

Hopping out of the Jeep with Mutt on his heels, he raced across the yard, scanning it for his grandfather but not seeing him. He hadn't expected to. Mortimer Potts would never remain safely outside while womenfolk were being threatened.

When he reached the porch of Ivy's place, where the door stood open, he heard voices coming from inside. Hell. His grandfather was probably now being held hostage, along with Jen and Ivy.

Pulling his service weapon from the holster on his hip, Mike proceeded into the shadowy house, following the voices. Trying to formulate a plan, he realized the best option was to free Jen first because, physically, she was the best equipped to help him deal with the thug. He knew what she was like when she was angry.

Strong. Tough. Fierce. All the things he loved most about her. God, he prayed he'd have the chance to tell her that.

His grandfather might never forgive him for relying on a lady rather than him. But he'd deal with that later.

Mutt, unfortunately, hadn't been trained in police procedure. He raced down the hall, his nails slipping on the wood floor tipping off whoever was inside. Mike tore after him, erupting into the room where the voices had been coming from. What he saw stunned him.

There was no hostage situation, at least, not the one he'd expected to see. "Jen?" he asked, spotting her standing safely with her arm around her aunt Ivy.

When she saw him, she flew into his arms. "You're here! Oh, Mike, I couldn't believe it when your grandfather told me you were coming after me." She pressed kisses to his cheeks, and his mouth, and she felt so damn good he wanted to haul her against his body and never let her go.

"Are you all right?"

"We're fine, Michael, just fine," Mortimer answered.

Needing to make sure, Mike looked Jen over head to toe, confirmed she was unharmed, then did the same with his grandfather. The white-haired old gentleman looked healthy and fit as usual. The only odd thing was the gun in his hand.

It was pointing directly at an elderly man sitting in a rocking chair, his arms and legs tied to it with velvet cords from the curtains. He looked familiar somehow, though Mike couldn't place him at first.

"Put down the gun, Grandpa."

"Don't shoot me, boy, I don't intend to hurt him now that he's started to behave."

"I wasn't going to *shoot* you," he said between clenched teeth. "I want you to put it down before you hurt yourself."

"Bah. Have you forgotten who taught *you* how to shoot?"

His grandfather had him there. "Okay," Mike said, calming his tone to reason with him. "I see you caught the bad guy and he's tied up, so we can *both* put our guns down."

Before somebody got shot. On purpose, or by accident.

Mortimer finally did as Mike had asked, bringing the weapon over and placing it on the top of an old-fashioned upright piano. Mike took a moment to study the old man in the chair and suddenly recognized him from the night outside Jen's apartment. The man was her *neighbor.*

Mike could barely take it all in. "What is going *on* here?"

Mortimer, Ida Mae, Ivy and Jen all looked at one another and shared a moment of silence, as if they simply didn't know where to begin. Then they all started talking at once, saying crazy stuff about murders that weren't murders, arson, knitting boxes and stolen music. It took a good twenty minutes for him to make heads or tails out of any of it.

All he knew was that by the time their sketchy tale was done, he was looking at the man who'd been stalking Jennifer and making her life so miserable. That was enough to make him want to kill the son of a bitch, no matter how old he was.

"Hello? Miss Ivy? Mr. Potts?"

"Ahh," Mortimer said as they heard a man calling from the front of the house. "The chief has arrived at last. I called him, just as you suggested, but unfortunately, he was out at his farm dealing with the early birth of a calf."

"Why the hell do you live here again?" Mike muttered.

Mortimer shrugged. "Trouble's my home, dear boy." Offering both arms to Ida Mae and Ivy, he said, "Shall we go to the kitchen, ladies? I am feeling quite invigorated. Perhaps we could all have a spot of tea after our adventures."

"I'll make the tea," Ida Mae declared.

Ivy shot her a glare. "You'll do no such thing. It's my house." Then she turned and looked over her shoulder at the man tied up in the chair, who, if Mike was to believe their stories, was, in fact, the supposedly dead Leo Cantone. She stared fire at his head. "I'll make *you* some of my most special brew."

"Now, sister," Ida Mae scolded, "you've just been cleared of one murder, don't be so quick to commit one again." That was about as tender a tone as Mike had ever heard come out of the stern woman's mouth. The soft look the sisters exchanged convinced him that Jen was right about one thing: despite outward appearances, the old ladies did care very much about each other.

Over the next hour, Mike worked with the local police on

the case, as well as calling his lieutenant back in the city. Knowing from experience how these things worked, he suspected Leo would be sitting in Trouble's jail cell, charged with all manner of crimes against Ivy, before the paperwork arrived charging him with a forty-year-old murder in New York.

One thing was certain—the man wasn't going anywhere.

Eventually, Leo was hauled away. Mortimer left, too, having basked in the glow of being a hero most of the afternoon. Ivy and Ida Mae were upstairs, going through the things in Ivy's precious box—apparently she had some explaining to do about some of the things she'd been hiding for so long, even from Ida Mae.

And he and Jen were finally alone. With no more secrets between them. Nothing either of them could hide behind.

They had only to deal with their own feelings. "Jen…"

"Not here."

He quirked a brow.

"Come on. Let's go for a drive."

She didn't have to ask him twice. Without a word, he took her hand and walked with her out into the sunshine.

NOT EVEN KNOWING WHERE SHE wanted to go, but certain she had to get away from the suffocating aura of Ivy's tired old house, Jen led Mike to his Jeep. Mutt followed, leaping easily into the back seat as the two of them climbed into the front.

"Where are we going?" Mike asked when he was inside.

"Anywhere. I just can't do this *here*," she murmured, glancing toward the house. "I know most of Ivy's skeletons were brought out of the closet today. But it's still too sad, too haunted. And I think there are still more mysteries left to uncover." Shaking her head as she thought about everything the old woman had revealed, she murmured, "Mike, will you do something for me?"

"If I can." He sounded on guard, which she understood. She hadn't exactly been easy to deal with lately.

"If you can avoid it, please don't ever tell Ivy what you told me about the autopsy." Hot tears rose in her eyes as she thought of what Ivy had said…about the blood. And the kerosene.

And the way she'd kissed his still-warm hand.

"She loved him, you see," her voice broke at the awfulness of it. "She was sure he was dead."

Mike nodded slowly, giving her a sorrowful look out of the corner of his eye. "I won't tell her, Jen. I can't imagine how she'd ever live with that."

Neither could Jen.

"If it makes any difference to you," he added, "the coroner's report also said there was no way Leo…I mean, *Eddie*, could have survived the blow to his head, fire or no fire. He was obviously unconscious—probably even brain dead given the viciousness of the blows—when the fire started."

Thank heaven. That was small comfort, though Jen knew it would not be to Ivy. So she must never know.

"She didn't kill her lover," he continued. "And her husband is alive and well—there's no way she'd be criminally charged with shooting him after all these years."

"And Leo?"

"He'll probably be charged, but I honestly doubt he'll ever go to trial. I'm not sure if you noticed, but the man looks like he's in bad shape."

Jen had noticed that, hearing a rattle in Leo's cough and seeing an unhealthy yellow tinge to his skin. Maybe the man's crimes were finally taking their inevitable toll on him.

"Secrets, sadness, mystery... I've had enough of them all," she murmured. Turning in her seat to face him as he started the Jeep and backed out of the driveway, she studied his handsome face, letting his warm, masculine scent engulf her. "I want to move forward." *With you.*

He met her glance briefly, then focused on the road. When he turned toward the outskirts of town, Jen knew where he was taking her. "Good day for a swim."

"I don't have a suit."

"Me, either."

He smiled. A tiny bit. But it was a start—a beginning. His defenses, and the tension, were easing.

"Thank you for following me," she whispered. "I don't think I realized how much I wanted you to until I saw you burst in."

"Even though I showed up too late?"

"You came. That's all that matters."

"Why?" he asked, his jaw tightening. "This morning all you wanted was for me to *stop* trying to protect you."

Jen deserved that accusation, because he was right. She had felt that way this morning. Now, however, she better understood the true meaning of love and sacrifice. Having learned all there was to know about Ivy's tragedy and lost love, she was in no way ready to let a simple misunderstanding or minor clash of personalities come between her and Mike.

Life was simply too capricious to give up a moment with someone you truly loved.

"I don't need you to protect me," she said, trying to verbalize her feelings. "But...I'm humbled by the lengths you'll go to because I *think* it means you care about me."

They'd reached the turnoff for the old park and Mike steered the Jeep toward the parking lot. To her surprise, Jen saw remnants of a picnic—trash in a can, a forgotten empty bottle of wine on one of the tables. Apparently others had begun to rediscover this magical little place.

Too bad. She kind of liked the privacy here.

For now, at least, the park was still silent, empty.

Private.

"If I'm right, and you do feel the way I do, I can put up with a lot. I can live with your need to *physically* protect me once in a while as long as you promise to be honest with me," she said. "No more lies, no more emotional protection like keeping secrets you think I can't handle."

"I was stupid…"

"I forgive you," she whispered, wondering if he heard what else she was saying with every heartfelt word. *I love you.* "I think I'd forgive you just about anything. Except letting me get away again."

Cutting the engine, Mike got out and came around to her door. He helped her down, though she really didn't need it. Jen slid down his body, needing the connection. Needing some response to the last thing she'd said.

Had she misread him? Did he *not* feel the way she hoped he did? Staring up at him, she sought the truth in his brown eyes, not attempting to hide it in her own.

"I love you, Jen," he finally said, the words falling soft and sweet around her, like the tender leaves shaken down by the summer breeze above them. "I love you and I died a little when I thought you were in danger today."

"I love you, too. And I died a little when I left you."

He lowered his mouth to hers, kissing her so sweetly she started to cry. Their mouths silently shared many things, all of them tender, all of them emotional. Questions and answers.

Promises and oaths. Words of love that didn't need to be said to be conveyed.

But oh, it was so nice to hear them. "Tell me again," she demanded when he ended the kiss.

"I love you."

She gazed up at the sky, letting the warmth of the sun fall on her face and shouting with sheer joy. "He loves me!"

Mike whispered, "Yeah. He does."

Looking back at him—filling her senses with him—she asked, "Even though there's a bit of murder and craziness in my family?"

He reached his hand up and scratched his jaw as if thinking about it. "Well..."

"Mike Taylor!" she snapped, fisting her hands and putting them on her hips.

He slid his arms around her waist and tugged her close again. "You are exactly what I was too stubborn and stupid to realize I needed. You're *also* everything I now know will make me happy for the rest of my life."

"And you're the kind of man I always hoped existed, even when I was screaming to the world that you didn't," she admitted.

He smiled, as if pleased, then whispered, "Marry me, Jen."

The proposal came suddenly, as if out of nowhere, but she knew this man. He did nothing without thinking about it first. He wanted her—truly—for the rest of his life.

"Oh, yes, I will." Sighing, she kissed him again, deeper this time, sliding her tongue against his. Remembering all the amazing things he'd made her feel from the moment they'd met.

Especially last night.

"Remember the last time we were here?" she whispered against his mouth.

"How could I forget?"

She reached for the bottom of his shirt, tugging it from his jeans. "Think the water would feel as good now as it did then?"

A gleam in his eye as he caught her meaning, he nodded. "I imagine it will feel even better if we're wearing nothing."

That sounded good to her. In fact it sounded great to her. With laughter on her lips, she said, "Race you!" then started running down toward the water's edge. She flung her clothes off as she ran, her shirt flying right into Mike's face. But she hadn't reached the lake when Mutt leaped in front of her, excited and joining in the race. She had to jog around him, almost falling, losing a few precious seconds.

"I won," Mike called with a smug look as he raced past her into the lake, still fully dressed.

"Your had an accomplice."

He looked at Mutt. "Good boy. Go lie down." As always, the lazy thing didn't need a second invitation to take a nap. He ambled to the picnic table and crawled beneath it.

Wearing only her bra and panties, with her shirt gone and her skirt tangled at her feet, Jen glared. "You also cheated. You're still dressed."

Unrepentant, he shrugged. "Hey, I didn't say I wouldn't swim naked. I just didn't necessarily mean I'd waste time taking everything off before I got in."

He reached for his belt, slowly unbuckling it and tugging it free. Jen watched, slipping out of the last of her clothes, not sure which excited her more—the incredible body being revealed before her gaze, or the look in his eyes as he watched her walk toward him in the water.

They met in the shallows, as he was tossing his shoes and

the rest of his clothes onto the shore. His hard, powerful body gleamed in the sunlight, strong, rippled and best of all *hers.*

"You are beautiful, Jennifer Feeney. I can't wait to make babies with you."

Again he surprised her, saying something so unexpected—so sweet and tender—she gasped at the shock of it. "I hope they look like you," she replied as she slid against him, all his bare skin warm and perfect against hers.

He treated her to one of his enormous, brilliant smiles, flashing those amazing dimples that stopped her heart. "As long as they don't take after your aunts."

"Not nice," she murmured, wondering if she should go ahead and tell him she'd been adopted.

Before she could decide, he began kissing her, running the tips of his fingers up and down her sides, caressing her hip and her waist and the bottoms of her breasts. Mmm, he was glorious…hot, hard, sensual. And she wanted him desperately.

Melting into him as they moved deep in the water and continued to love one another, she decided she'd tell him later. She wanted him too much right now to waste the words.

Besides…as Jennifer Feeney well knew, it was never a bad thing to keep a man wondering.

EPILOGUE

THE BRIDE WORE BLUE. A light, icy blue just perfect for the cold December morning on which the wedding was held.

The event was small, taking place in the parlor of Mortimer Potts's house, as the engaged couple had wanted it. Witnessed only by family and a few close friends, the quiet ceremony suited the pair, who'd remained glued to each other's sides throughout the ensuing reception.

Funny, Mortimer realized as he hid behind a potted plant on his patio, sneaking a cigar—his house was becoming a regular wedding chapel. First Max's nuptials last Christmas, now these.

"And hopefully a few more soon," he mumbled.

The whole family was in attendance—Max and Sabrina home from California for the holidays. Mike and Jen, of course. Even Morgan, making a five-day stop between photographic adventures in Bali and Singapore.

Ahh, that was the life. What Mortimer wouldn't give to be going with him.

"You know, if Rod sees you smoking, his bow tie's going to pop right off his neck," an amused voice said.

Mortimer quickly glanced around and saw, thankfully, his

oldest grandson, Morgan, standing behind him on the patio. Morgan, he was well aware, knew how to keep his mouth shut.

The boy wasn't taciturn and private, like Michael had been before he'd fallen madly in love with Jen. He was just always caught up in his own thoughts. Much too focused on his own affairs to stick his nose in other people's. Max called him the Indiana Jones of the family, but rather than going on adventures to search for ancient treasure, he went to expose suffering and corruption wherever they existed.

"Max, you rascal," he said with a smile, watching through the window as his middle grandson goosed his wife right in the middle of the party.

Had Max been the one to catch Mortimer out here, smoking in the cold, he would have laughingly scolded him, then demanded a Cuban of his own as hush payment. The always protective Michael would have crushed the damn thing against the side of the house.

Morgan simply minded his business.

Mortimer puffed again, continuing to watch, Morgan right beside him. A few of the bride's closest friends were in attendance, as was the groom's sister and some friends from the old days. Did he and Rod, Mortimer wondered, look as old as they did?

"How do you like the bride?" he asked his grandson.

"I just met Emily yesterday, but Roderick seems happy."

"Yes, he is. Took him a while to loosen up, but he's landed a good one. Maxwell is very happy, too." Staring straight ahead, Mortimer didn't dare meet his brilliant grandson's eye. "Marriage does seem to agree with him. I'm sure Michael will be just as content when he and Jen marry this spring."

"Mmm, hmm."

Mortimer reminded himself to tread carefully. Morgan was the oldest and had been single and traveling the world for years. He wouldn't give that up easily. "What do you think of Jennifer?"

"She's perfect."

Yes. His oldest grandson saw exactly what Mortimer had seen the moment he'd met Miss Feeney. She was the perfect woman for Michael. *If only she had a sister.*

"The parents seem like good people," Mortimer said. He watched as Jen's mother and father—who'd come to town for the engagement party scheduled for tomorrow night—socialized with all the others. They'd taken to Mike right away, her father declaring him man enough to keep Jennifer on her toes.

That was mutual, in Mortimer's opinion.

Ida Mae and Ivy hovered over their baby brother. He, obviously, was the apple of their eye, and they'd barely looked in Mortimer's direction all day. He hadn't taken offense. After all, no one knew better than Mortimer Potts that family was more important than anything else in the world.

"The grandmother's a bit of a kook, though," Morgan said.

Following his grandson's stare, Mortimer realized with surprise that he was staring at Ida Mae. "She's not Jen's…" Then he paused, looking closer. The resemblance between Ida Mae and Ivan *was* startling. Much more obvious than any between the two sisters. The age difference made it very plausible. He suddenly realized Morgan's assumption made a great deal of sense.

"Best not tell Michael," Mortimer said. "He's happy the Feeney sisters are his wife's *adoptive* aunts. I don't think he'd like his children having one of them for a great-grandmother."

"You, on the other hand, will be the world's best great-grandfather."

The words were so unexpected coming from his oldest grandson that Mortimer turned to him and smiled. The December wind caused a bit of moisture to rise up in the corners of his eyes. Only the wind, of course. "Soon, I hope."

Morgan nodded. "Max said he and Sabrina are trying."

Wonderful. Perfect. Delightful.

Oh, how he longed to see a sweet little face wrapped in a soft blanket.

Stepping to the side, Morgan blocked the wind with his big body so it didn't touch Mortimer's skin. The gesture was silent, instinctive. Protective and loving.

How in God's name had he and Roddy ever managed to raise such good, *good* men?

Morgan remained silent, continuing to watch as Roderick—who'd been another father to him for so many years—celebrated his marriage to Emily Baker. Finally, though, he murmured, "Are you going to be all right without him?"

Mortimer snorted. "Without who? You can't imagine Roddy living in that little house of Emily's, can you? No, indeed, they rented it out to Allie and her young man. Rod and Emily will be staying right here." He crushed out his cigar, then smiled. "Maybe they'll even have the house to themselves. Might be time for me to take myself off on an adventure."

Morgan merely lifted an eyebrow.

"Need a good man along in Singapore?"

A slow, deliberate smile widened his grandson's mouth. What a handsome one he was. Just like his grandfather. "I might."

Puffing his chest out, Mortimer added, "No problem with a fellow who has a bit of experience on him, is there?"

Shaking his head, Morgan said evenly, "Experience is a definite plus."

Mortimer stared into his grandson's eyes—startlingly blue, like his own—and like his daughter Carla's.

Swallowing away a lump in his throat, he added, "I'd have to be back in time for Michael's wedding. Especially if Max has a baby on the way."

"Absolutely."

Mortimer frowned. "I won't be coddled."

"Wouldn't dream of it, old man."

They held each other's stare for a long time. Morgan, of all his grandsons, knew Mortimer the best. Perhaps because they had so much in common, always longing for a new adventure, wondering what was beyond the next horizon. Ready to take on the world—fight the corrupt, break a few hearts.

Live and live *well*.

"The others might not approve," he cautioned.

Morgan nodded, something glittering in his eyes. Acceptance. Understanding. Love. "Since when have we let that stop us?"

Laughing, Mortimer clapped his hands in delight. He should have known Morgan would understand that even more than eight decades of life weren't weight enough to keep Mortimer Potts in one spot for long. There were so many places out there waiting for him, and now he had a perfect home to come back to at the end of whatever new adventures life would grant him.

This was his home now, no doubt about it. But that didn't

mean he couldn't see a few more sights before he was finished on this earth.

After all, there would always be Trouble to come back to.

* * * * *

Want more Trouble—now?
Look for Allie and Damon's story,
Getting into Trouble
in Harlequin's Heat Wave collection,
available July 2007.
How can you resist?

REQUEST YOUR FREE BOOKS!

2 FREE NOVELS FROM THE ROMANCE/SUSPENSE COLLECTION PLUS 2 FREE GIFTS!

BOB07

HQN™

We *are* romance™

When desire leads to devastating consequences...

A sizzling new title from multi-award-winning and *USA TODAY* bestselling author

SUSAN MALLERY

For years, Dani thought she was the black sheep of the Buchanan empire. Until her grandmother lets the bomb slip: Dani was never truly a Buchanan at all. Her real father is in fact a Washington senator considering a run for president. Dani's thrilled when the senator welcomes her with open arms. But his adopted son Alex remains suspicious—it's obvious to him that Dani wants something. And he's prepared to do anything to uncover her secrets, even if it means keeping her very, very close....

Tempting

Catch the final book in the much-loved Buchanan series in stores now!

Leslie Kelly

77133	HERE COMES TROUBLE	___	$5.99 U.S.	___	$6.99 CAN.
77031	SHE DRIVES ME CRAZY	___	$6.50 U.S.	___	$7.99 CAN.

(limited quantities available)

TOTAL AMOUNT	$ _____
POSTAGE & HANDLING	$ _____
($1.00 FOR 1 BOOK, 50¢ for each additional)	
APPLICABLE TAXES*	$ _____
TOTAL PAYABLE	$ _____

(check or money order—please do not send cash)

To order, complete this form and send it, along with a check or money order for the total above, payable to HQN Books, to: **In the U.S.:** 3010 Walden Avenue, P.O. Box 9077, Buffalo, NY 14269-9077; **In Canada:** P.O. Box 636, Fort Erie, Ontario, L2A 5X3.

Name: _____
Address: _____ City: _____
State/Prov.: _____ Zip/Postal Code: _____
Account Number (if applicable): _____

075 CSAS

*New York residents remit applicable sales taxes.
*Canadian residents remit applicable GST and provincial taxes.

HQN™

We *are* romance™

www.HQNBooks.com

PHLK0707BL